CW00707084

Needless Alley

NEEDLESS ALLEY

NATALIE MARLOW

BASKERVILLE
An imprint of JOHN MURRAY

First published in Great Britain in 2023 by Baskerville
An imprint of John Murray (Publishers)
An Hachette UK company

I

Copyright © Natalie Marlow 2023

The right of Natalie Marlow to be identified as the Author
of the Work has been asserted by her in accordance with
the Copyright, Designs and Patents Act 1988.

Extract from 'Mad About the Boy' © The Estate of Noël Coward
1932, from *The Lyrics of Noël Coward*, 2002, Methuen Drama, an
imprint of Bloomsbury Publishing Plc. Used with permission.

With thanks to the Noël Coward Foundation: www.noelcoward.com.

A CIP catalogue record for this title is available from the British Library

Hardback ISBN 9781399801799
Trade Paperback ISBN 9781399801805
eBook ISBN 9781399801829

Typeset in Bembo by Hewer Text UK Ltd, Edinburgh
Printed and bound in Great Britain by Clays Ltd, Elcograf S.p.A.

John Murray policy is to use papers that are natural, renewable and
recyclable products and made from wood grown in sustainable forests.
The logging and manufacturing processes are expected to conform
to the environmental regulations of the country of origin.

Baskerville, an imprint of John Murray
Carmelite House
50 Victoria Embankment
London EC4Y 0DZ

www.johnmurraypress.co.uk

To the working-class bohemians.

But down these mean streets a man must go who is not himself mean, who is neither tarnished nor afraid ... He is the hero; he is everything. He must be a complete man and a common man and yet an unusual man. He must be, to use a rather weathered phrase, a man of honor — by instinct, by inevitability, without thought of it, and certainly without saying it.

Raymond Chandler, The Simple Art of Murder

Part One

I

Birmingham. Sunday, 4 June 1933

William's footsteps sounded heavy on the bare linoleum. The lighting in the corridor was poor; a single bulb, covered by a pink glass shade, dangled unlit from the ceiling rose. There was a faint smell of disinfectant, and a large vase of silk carnations stood dusty on a console table under a mirror advertising *Pale Ale*. The tinny buzz of a wireless, played behind closed doors, hummed in the background and pricked at William's nerves. Sweat trickled down his collar in rivulets, pooling at the base of his spine, and his camera – prized, weighty, metallic – bagged out his jacket pocket and was awkward against his hip.

Room ten was at the end of the hallway and close to the window. William looked outside. Hurst Street was Sabbath quiet. This part of the city was red with Warwickshire clay, the bricks of the buildings warm with it: drapers, bicycle shops, insurance offices: all with Victorian frontages a touch soiled with soot. An empty tram swayed past, creating clouds of hot dust in its wake, and across the road, modern signage flickered *Ansell's* in electric blue on the hard tan tile of the Cross Keys pub. William glanced at his watch and waited in silence for the minute of the o'clock. This was well-planned, all solid and tactical, but the job gave him the wind up, always. And so his stomach lurched and fell heavy into his bowels as he unlocked the door. The fob swung like a pendulum, and he watched it spin until it steadied, and then he entered the room.

Lace curtains trembled against the open casement window like a bird's wing. The couple were perfectly framed. The woman had not been given roses, but gladioli. Their long stems, pink-tipped in bud, were strewn across the counterpane. She was wide-eyed, her pretty, open mouth formed a near perfect 'O'. Lipstick smeared red across her left cheek, and, in the late afternoon light, a halo of dust motes danced above her soft pale curls. William heard nothing but the perfect click-whirr of his camera. He wound the film on. On the floor, kneeling in silk knickers, her stockings half-mast on rounded, dimpled thighs, the blonde looked towards William and let out a low, guttural moan. *Click, soft purr of a whirr.* The man stood comic. The dark stuff of his trousers pooled about his ankles. Behind him, on the nightstand, a bottle of good whisky remained half-empty next to an unopened packet of prophylactics. Thigh muscles twitching and flexing, cock softening with shock, the man reached down to stroke his lover's hair, but turned his face away from William's camera. *Click, whirr.*

William dropped the room key and closed the door behind him. The woman, Winnie – yes, Winifred – had not screamed, but William heard her heavy sobs of panic as he descended the back stairs of the hotel. William never ran – experience taught him better – but instead walked at speed through passageways, drab brown and dark cool, towards the tradesman's exit.

Outside, the day was too warm for William to gulp in air.

He tried, but the tightness in his chest became worse with each breath. He slowed his pace, loosened his tie, and immediately felt his collar lose its sweaty grip on his neck. And he took the long way home, attempting to trudge away those shameful nerves. On Cherry Street, he passed a brewer's dray whose driver tipped his cap towards the Wesleyan Chapel. The road then bent and widened and changed its name, and although William could still hear the rattle of the cart and the heavy pounding of hooves on cobblestones, he was now in a place of quiet order; of three-storey buildings; of Morris Oxfords; of sharp railings shining thick with black paint; nameplates and door furniture polished proud Black Country brass.

Then he turned again and was home. William smiled. Buried between the lawyers of Temple Row and the merchants of New Street, and always in shadow, for the street was so narrow and the buildings so tall, Needless Alley caught little passing trade. However, William did not need it. Those who required his services sought him out, and the only indication of William's business was his own piece of shining Birmingham brass, a small plaque above the narrow door to his office which read: *Mr William Garrett, Private Enquiry Agent.*

2

William unlocked the main door to the building. The army doctors had once called his nerves 'neurasthenia'. They told him what could not be cured must be endured, and that his illness was a war wound which would flare in bad weather. And so, as he climbed the flight of stairs past his office, the inevitable, anxiety-driven nausea rose and surged until he was at the top of the house and at his digs. Once in the bathroom, William lingered over the lavatory and breathed deeply, waiting for his queasiness to peter out. It didn't. He flushed the chain, then turned and filled the wash basin with cold water, splashed his face and stared at his reflection in the mirror. He inspected the incipient jowls, calculated the extent of grey in his five o'clock shadow and fingered the dark hollows under his eyes.

The small bathroom served as a makeshift darkroom. William glanced at the shelf of neatly stacked enamel basins and chemicals, his kit for developing photographs, closed his eyes and recalled Winnie Woodcock's primal, rasping sobs. His camera still hung weighty in his jacket pocket, burdened now with exposures of Winnie, all intimate and softly vulnerable. He opened his eyes once more. He would not develop the pictures today. Shifty Shirley, Mr Woodcock's solicitor, would have to sing for them.

William needed food to settle his stomach. He glanced at his watch. It was tea-time. A decent brew and a slice of toast would do the trick, and so he walked the few steps to the kitchen and filled the kettle. He left it on the gas ring to boil, watched the bread brown under the grill, sniffed at the heat-yellow butter, and calmed himself with domestic tasks and the thought of food. Suddenly, to his right, there came a theatrical cough. William turned to see Ronnie Edgerton enter the room like a film star.

'Do I smell vomit?' he asked. Handsome in a navy suit, fresh, for he was impervious to the heat, Ronnie had all of William's height but none of his bulk. 'It's sort of permeating the flat like some medieval miasma.' He leant against the door jamb and wrinkled his nose. 'Why didn't you tell me your nerves were playing you up?'

William shrugged, and then opened his kitchen window. 'It just happens every now and then. Flares up like a rheumatic leg, or something. Do you want a cup of tea?'

Ronnie shrugged. 'Did you know there's a monster in Scotland, in a lake?'

'It's called a loch,' said William.

'It's rather lovely though. A monster in the loch, in the gloaming. Did you see it in the newspapers? I read about it in the *News of the World* this morning. Absolutely fascinating, and an opportunity, I feel.'

'It's a fake, Ronnie.'

'My dear, I know that.' Ronnie lit a cigarette and blew practised smoke rings into William's cramped kitchenette. 'We could go up together. You with your expensive camera, me with my charming manners. Think of the cool Scottish breezes. We could monster-spot. Or monster-fabricate –' he grinned – 'and get some real doozies. Sell 'em to all the press. Make our fortune.' There was a pause. 'Neither of us would

7

ever have to make beastly compromises again. Don't you just hate being poor, Billy?'

'I'm not poor. Not anymore. Not really.' William had savings in the Lloyds Bank on Colmore Row, like a respectable businessman. A cushion, the manager had called it. If William fell, the money would soften his landing. But William didn't want a cushion; he wanted a mattress. 'Yes, Ronnie. I hate being poor.'

'I've been thinking.' Ronnie moved thick swathes of dark hair from his forehead. 'A man like you should be an American; a self-made man. They'd love us over there. What do you think? It's a good idea, isn't it?'

William was deadpan. 'I like Birmingham, Ronnie. I like the rain, the pubs, the pasty women, the canals.'

'Don't lie to me about the canals. You despise the canals.'

'Yes, I hate the canals. Do you want tea or not?'

'Sam Spade doesn't drink tea.' Ronnie grinned once more – beautiful, film-star chops. 'And he manages to do our line of work without being so very vulgar and ordinary.'

'He's make-believe. I bruise easily and like my tea sweet.' William added an extra spoonful to his cup and stirred. 'Real detectives aren't tough guys, you know that. We're nothing but solicitor's clerks with fallen arches.'

'Shame, I'm rather fond of tough guys.' Ronnie blew him a kiss. 'I'm terribly sorry about your feet.'

'Don't worry yourself, I've got orthopaedic shoes.' William glanced at his mug and toast. 'Do you want a cup of tea or not? I'm getting really fuckin' tired of asking you.'

Ronnie inhaled deeply and then flicked ash onto William's clean linoleum. 'Keep your wig on, Aunt Agatha. I know it's half-past four, but I'm a red-blooded male, and I think I'd prefer a whisky.'

'I've got a bottle of Glenfiddich downstairs, and your money, of course.' William wiped the beads of sweat from his upper lip and glanced at the open window. He couldn't feel a breeze. 'Christ, it'll be cooler in my office, anyway.' They walked in companionable silence down the staircase, single file, William carrying his tea and toast, Ronnie bringing up the rear. The hallway filled with the sharp lime scent of Ronnie's cologne. An expensive London brand, it was over-applied.

'I made my excuses to poor Winnie, you know. I'm not a cad.' Ronnie blurted it out, like a guilty child. 'I could tell she wanted me gone. She became terribly panicked about her little boys. Conscience-stricken, I suppose.'

Winifred Woodcock's children were lost to her the moment she and Ronnie entered the hotel bedroom. This was the plain fact of William's business. However, furnishing Ronnie with plain facts often proved counterproductive. 'It's best just to scarper,' William said. But he knew his own role in the business was one of detachment. He was a walking camera with a well-rehearsed courtroom patter, but Ronnie was intimate with the women. He knew them, biblically, and became fond of them. 'Leave them to it. Don't get involved.'

'Did I mention my charming manners?' Ronnie raised an admonitory eyebrow. 'I can't just scarper, as you call it. I have the ladies to consider. It has to feel real to them, Billy. If they're nice, I want to give them a nice time.'

William unlocked the office door, and the Sunday newspapers, which were scattered across his desk, fluttered and then lifted. It was an unaired room, close and still redolent with the morning's cigarette smoke. William put down his tea and toast and began the business of tidying. He fussed with the window, propping it open with a rolled copy of the *Birmingham Post*, and the resulting breeze was a small mercy.

William stood for a while and inhaled. 'I got some good photographs. You did a good job, Ronnie. Shifty Shirley will be pleased.' He then retrieved the bottle of Glenfiddich and a glass from his filing cabinet, waiting until Ronnie was settled into his usual chair before pouring the whisky with a trembling hand. 'But you don't have to go so far with the women, you know. All I need is semi-nudity in a hotel room.'

Ronnie feigned ignorance of William's shot nerves and placed his well-shod feet on the desk. He flicked through the *News of the World* and lit a cigarette. He was chain-smoking, but this was usual. 'Oh dear, these vicars are dirty dogs, are they not? They put you and me to shame. It's probably all that tea they drink whilst visiting aged parishioners and whatnot.' He folded the newspaper in such a way that William only saw the headline, stark with smut and outrage. 'Tea must inflame the baser instincts.' Ronnie gazed pointedly at William's teacup and toast and then became silent. Eventually he said, 'It's rather sad to have such a name, don't you think?'

'Christ, man, what on earth are you talking about?'

'Woodcock.' Ronnie sipped at his whisky and blew more smoke rings.

'Winnie Woodcock sounds alright to me. A bit common, perhaps. But who are we to talk?' It was nearly five o'clock, and William considered joining Ronnie in a whisky. But drinking with Ronnie necessitated a full commitment to pissing his money away until the early hours; scrapping with every passing fellow on Broad Street who called Ronnie a nancy-boy, and spending the entirety of the following day sweating Scotch and shaking like a mad dog. At thirty-six, William realised he was getting too old to endure those booze-saturated lost weekends of his youth.

'He can't get it up,' said Ronnie.

'Who?'

'Oh, Billy, do keep up,' Ronnie sighed. 'Mr Woodcock, that's who. Winnie's husband, it's why she strayed. She told me.'

'Oh yes, I see.' William frowned. 'Keep that bit of information to yourself. It might prejudice the case. I'll speak to Shifty about it in the morning.' Although William doubted Mr Shirley – solicitor, amoral, and Shifty to both his few friends and many enemies – would, after examining the photographic evidence, consider the Woodcock case to be anything other than a dead cert.

'I don't think you're quite understanding me, Billy. There is a certain amount of pathos in being called Woodcock, and yet being fundamentally unable to perform your conjugal duties.'

'Men like Woodcock are our bread and butter. Who's to say who he can or can't fuck? Perhaps he prefers brunettes –' this time it was William's turn for pointed speech – 'or muscle-men?' Ronnie laughed. It was a deep, charming rasp, the kind women thought full of sex appeal. 'Ours is not to reason why, old son,' William said. 'Ours is to provide photographic evidence for the divorce proceedings.'

'And yet you heave your guts up after each job.' Ronnie grinned hard and ferocious, holding William's gaze. 'I do believe you're too principled for this sordid little business of yours. As your oldest and most intimate friend, I want to rescue you from it. Hence the rather marvellous money-making schemes I've been putting your way.'

'I just keep my moral qualms where they should be, buried deep in my subconscious.' William finished his toast and smiled. 'At least until you come up with a money-making scheme that doesn't make me want to shit myself with nerves or leave the city. I'm sticking with my sordid little business. It's a good earner.'

'The way I see it, is you're either a moral man or a business-man. You can either live a quiet life of honest toil, or you can dedicate yourself to Mammon. The more money you want to make, the more immoral you must be. It's rather simple, really. Those who have money live by this code. Gangsters, pluto-crats, aristocracy, they all understand this.' Ronnie, warming to his subject, waved his arm in the manner of a firebrand politician. 'Those men don't vomit and shake after factory fires or after they break a strike; they smokescreen their immorality by endowing a library or an orphanage or some such and carry on as usual. Charitable giving is just loose change to them and worth it for the good press. They under-stand what it takes to be rich.'

'Christ, you sound like Queenie.' William spoke without thinking. Beautiful Queenie, Ronnie's little sister, was full of opinions. God, she had brains. William had once loved her.

'Well, Queenie's no fool.' Ronnie's deep voice quavered. 'Apart from for you. She was a fool for you, as the song goes.'

William blushed in the heavy silence. The subject had got out of hand. The childhood William shared with Ronnie and Queenie hung over him like a storm cloud. But gradually, and with each passing year, the sky had begun to clear. William no longer needed his oldest friends; in fact, he wanted to be free of them, and this realisation terrified him. He glanced at Ronnie. He was acting the part of Man Reading Newspaper, and doing it poorly. 'Do you want your money, or do you want to talk to me about love?' William asked.

Ronnie looked up from the sports pages. 'You mistake me. I have no interest in the state of your beastly romantic life. However, I am in rather desperate need of remuneration. The gentlemen of the turf have become impatient with me, I fear. But Billy, this was positively the last time. I find it all a bit sickening, especially when I quite like the mark.'

'Christ, Ronnie. You like everyone, that's your trouble. You have no discernment.' William counted out six fivers from a wad of bills in his locked desk drawer and handed them to his friend. Ronnie resigned after each job. Then the bookies became predatory – circled, bared their teeth and howled for their dues – and Ronnie, penniless and luckless, returned to William and to Needless Alley. 'How much do you owe?'

Ronnie pocketed the money. 'Nothing, once I back a winner.'

'It's a mug's game.' William thought bookmaking to be a good business model and therefore never gambled. 'I can help you out if you need it.' Ronnie's face was his fortune; he didn't need it mangled by a bookies' runner with a strong grievance and a knuckleduster.

Ronnie ignored him and continued to read from the *News of the World*. 'Here's a murder in Birmingham, look.' He peered at the newsprint, too vain to admit the need for spectacles. 'Another blonde, very young this time and strangled.'

'Why is it always blondes?' William preferred women with dark hair. 'It's all acid baths in London. The mental cases kill girls and dump their bodies in acid to get rid of evidence.'

'This one was thrown in the cut.' Ronnie helped himself to more Glenfiddich. 'Poor little cow.'

'Christ, I hate the canals. The Grand Union, or an acid bath, it probably amounts to the same thing.' William rose and read the grim headline over Ronnie's shoulder. The dead woman warranted two columns on page five. Her blurred photograph was nothing but a mess of grey dots: hard bobbed curls bright white, blonde; her face a distortion of newsprint.

Ronnie squinted at the page. 'Does she remind you of anyone?'

Winnie Woodcock, Jean Harlow, the girl behind the bar at the Shakespeare; William shook his head. 'No, they all look the same to me, that type.' William read further. 'Fay Francis. Don't know her. The alias of a good-time girl, no doubt.' He read on, wincing. 'Sixteen, blonde, and strangled with her own stockings. No longer virgo intacta. Christ, why write that?'

Ronnie downed his second whisky and looked up from the newspaper. 'God, Billy. Women really do have it rough, don't they?'

3

At first sight, there was something of the funeral parlour about Shifty Shirley. Grey, gaunt and with a dowager's hump, his conservative black suit was pristine, his gold watch chain was hefty but plain, his scent was carbolic, and his smile was a strange rictus. But this was a cultivated formality of dress, and one used to mitigate his natural inclination towards a speech peppered with both broad Midlands vowels and sharp con man's patter. 'Good morning to you, Billy old son. I was chipper at your news, I can tell you,' he said. 'I didn't want this Woodcock case to get untidy. When things get untidy, I get the creeps.' Shifty rose to shake William's hand. 'Did Delores offer you a cuppa?' He motioned to the door by which William had just entered. Behind it, the exceptionally dour Delores typed at speed. William knew she made tea under sufferance, and it was a bitter, stewed brew.

He shook his head and handed Shirley a large manilla envelope. 'No thank you, Mr Shirley. I've just had breakfast.' And he sat and watched as Shifty spread the compromising photographs of Winifred Woodcock across the vast desk. Polished mahogany with fixtures of filigree brass, it reminded William of a rich man's coffin. 'I think you'll be pleased with what I've got.' William glanced over the pictures and felt a strange, shameful pride. He had done well in prettifying Winnie. In life, he thought her rather tough and flashy, but his lens had tempered her into Jean Harlow, all silk drawers and soft pale skin.

'Quite nice. Oh, yes.' Shifty peered above his spectacles. He had the blue protuberant eyes of a jackdaw. 'Very nice indeed, Billy old son. Quite tasty.' Shifty's large black pupils glittered. He was now the impresario of some seedy burlesque assessing the potential of his latest girl. 'You've got quite the gift, Billy boy. You're an artist,' he simpered. 'If I want a job done with a bit of flair, I always come to you.'

Dirty photographs as evidence *prima facie* – yes, William did his job well. In a few months, the case would see court. The jury's civic duty would be the appraisal of Mrs Woodcock's moral fibre, and in the pub afterwards, the same gentlemen would share, with glee, the salacious details of Winnie – bottle blonde, town bike – *in flagrante delicto* with some pretty-boy gigolo. Proved to be a harlot in public court, Winnie was in for a rough ride.

Shifty fingered the picture of Winnie engaged in fellatio and became lyrical. 'Sweet rosebud of a mouth,' he said. 'Just like a china doll.' He offered William a seat and a fat cigar, and William accepted both. 'What else do you have on the little lady?' he asked.

'She's a fast mover. Didn't waste any time. She's living in sin with a used-car salesman out in Solihull,' said William. 'Met him in a dance hall way before we set her up with Ronnie. But she was keeping him at arm's length back then. It was quite a chaste little romance. Mr Second Best wears a wig and breathes with his mouth open, but beggars can't be choosers. And Winnie's quite the beggar, these days. It's all in my report.'

He nodded to the three sheets of foolscap on Shifty's desk and thought about the adulterous Winnie. The last time he had seen her, she was holed up in a suburban bungalow sporting nothing but department store lingerie and a purpling black eye. That day, she had played Ray Noble's dance band loud on her new gramophone, and it sounded out plaintive through the open French doors. William had watched her dance a solo waltz to 'Love is the Sweetest Thing'. Women had it rough, no doubt, but they were survivors.

'You really are the best, Billy boy.' Shifty tugged at his desk drawer and produced a large, leather-bound chequebook, and then glanced at the invoice clipped to William's report. 'I see your rates haven't changed.' William remained impassive. 'I don't like this daily-rate business, Billy. You should be under my employment. I put enough work your way. It would be easier for me to have you on my books, and you know I'll see you right.' Shifty leant forward and whispered, as if to a lover. 'I'd dearly love a more exclusive arrangement. You're valuable to me, but I feel you drag these cases out.' He paused, chomping at the Romeo y Julieta with his back teeth like a dog chewing a toffee. 'And I'd appreciate a little more loyalty. Don't take advantage of my good nature. It hurts my feelings.'

'I'm thorough in my work, that's why you like me. But thorough takes time.' William hadn't lingered over the Woodcock case for money. He simply couldn't face Shifty's chequebook until he knew that Winnie was safely away from her fist-happy husband and shacked up with her devoted used-car salesman. 'And I like my independence,' William added. 'I can take my holidays when I please, refuse any case I don't much fancy.'

Shifty wagged his finger. 'Now you're just playing hard to get, Billy. Refusing cases indeed! It's never been known.' His pen hovered over a fresh cheque. 'You're not in the first flush of youth, you know. There are always young fellows itching to take your place, and I might lose interest. Grab my offer while you can.'

William smiled and stubbed out his unsmoked cigar. 'I'm always flattered by your interest, Mr Shirley. Never stop asking.' Sensible men did not enter permanent business relationships with Shifty Shirley. If you picked Shifty up and wrung him out, you would get enough oil to grease all the foundry presses in the city. 'I'll consider a full-time arrangement, but it'll cost you.'

'I'm generous, Billy boy, but never wasteful.' Shifty grinned, and placed William's unsmoked cigar back in the silver box on his desk. He paused for a moment, and then said, 'I do have something else to put your way.'

'Divorce job?'

'No-no-no, not quite.' Shifty shook his head a little too vehemently. 'He's not a client of mine, as such. He already has solicitors. A venerable London firm in an association which spans generations, I believe.' Shifty spoke of the capital, and its lawyers, as if both were hallowed. He knew where the money was, and money, to Shifty, was sacred. 'This gentleman is an acquaintance of mine. We attend the same clubs, same charitable organisations.' Shifty smiled. 'He's very much of the right sort socially. He's a manufacturer and a politician and absolutely top-drawer. Quite the connection to cultivate, I feel.' His bird-like eyes shone once more. 'Gentry family, Billy. I do so love the gentry. I have no time for these so-called radicals and revolutionaries. Where will the likes of you and I be if there were no more rich men with secrets?'

Shifty's growing excitement made William's sensitive gut grumble. Nonetheless he asked, 'What's the job about, Mr Shirley?'

Shifty shrugged his shoulders and held out his hands, still smiling. 'I genuinely have no idea, Billy. All I know is that it's terribly sensitive. He needs a quiet man capable of a gentle touch, so he tells me. I mentioned that you were a man of discretion. He will only deal with you directly. Delicacy must be your middle name on this one, Billy old son. Make the chap feel taken care of, like a waiter in one of those old London clubs.' Shifty was prone to creative flights of fancy. 'It would be good for both of us, if this was a gentleman we could cultivate as a friend, an associate. Yes?'

'What's his name?'

'Morton. I told him you'd be available on Friday morning nine o'clock sharp at your office. Doesn't do to keep that type waiting. I gave him your card.'

'I only do divorce work, Shifty. You know that.' William glanced at the cased, leather-bound law books. 'I don't like to mess about with anything that'll cause me too much strife.'

Shifty, ignoring the informality, leant forward. 'There's a shit ton of money in it for you, lad.' He tapped his nose. 'And a shit ton of kudos for yours truly if you do a nice job.' Rumour had it that Shifty ran a circus sideshow before the war. He travelled with a tattooed girl named Kitty La Marr. She sat in a darkened tent, smoking a cheroot and wearing nothing but her ink, whilst Shifty persuaded the punters that the lovely Kitty was the eighth wonder of the world. William knew this to be a rumour Shifty himself had started. 'He's worth a fortune and is a rising man politically. They say he's in the middle of a deal with some Americans over manufacturing a new kind of artificial silk. He would need reliable men to protect his interests, I should think. Make sure he only makes the papers for subbing orphanages, that sort of thing.' Shifty hummed, ponderous and low. 'Like I said, quite a nice connection to cultivate.' Morton was a sucker. He was not to be cultivated but shilled.

Shifty was still a flimflam man, but he was honest in his vulgarity and candid in his desire for money. William admired this dogged pursuit of cash and understood it as part of his own personality. This fellow Morton probably had a mistress in need of paying off – or a wayward daughter to manage – easy work. William ignored that cramping feeling in his stomach, that heartbeat he could hear which meant his body sensed danger, and said, 'Alright, I'll see him. I'll sound him out.'

And as he said this, Shifty grinned and signed the cheque for the Woodcock case with a showman's flourish. He handed it to William, saying, 'Good man. I see great things ahead, Billy. Great things.'

William examined the cheque, making sure there were the requisite number of zeros, and that Shifty had signed it in his own name. It was best not to act like a gentleman around Shifty, but Shifty took no offence. 'It's a pleasure doing business with you, Mr Shirley.'

William rose and shook Shifty's soft, clammy hand.

4

William wiped his feet as he left Shifty's office. Outside, Birmingham smelt of piss and beer. It was a Monday morning stink; the residue of weekend revellers drinking away their pay. William checked his watch. Eleven o'clock, and so New Street was no longer home to drunks, but to typists running errands and shoppers stepping off trams outside the Queen's Hotel. Above the clatter of their chatter and the weekday traffic, William heard Winnie Woodcock's sobs for her lost children and the heavy plaintive crooning of Al Bowlly. He shook his head at the memory, like a dog batting away a fly, and placed Shifty's cheque snug in the breast pocket of his jacket.

The air was hazy, humming with petrol fumes and the threat of more heat. He was irritated, angry, and he longed for rain and wind, something to blow the stink off the town. There was a dissonance to the city – no, in himself – which made his skin itch, and instead of cashing the cheque directly, he avoided the bank and headed for the Lyons' on Galloway's Corner. The commonplace respectability of the tea rooms would offer a comforting contrast to the ponderous corruption of Shifty Shirley's office. And besides, he had lied about having breakfast. Food would mellow his mood, calm the nausea.

He sat amongst the potted palms, hulking and single at his table for two, and ordered buttered muffins and strong tea. The waitress, too harassed and sardonic to be a natural nippy, brought him a bad tepid coffee and a good toasted teacake, but he didn't complain. Instead, he smoked for a while, watching the place fill up with shoppers stopping by for elevenses. Women, mostly, in from the suburbs and the satellite towns, they were a jolly bunch, flushed with chatter and happy companionship, talking of silver gifts for godchildren, the sale on linens at Lewis's, whether the double bill at the Odeon would be any good.

William shifted in his seat, increasingly self-conscious at his own solitariness. Yet he was not the only customer who ate alone. On the opposite table, and facing him, a redheaded woman, pale, demure in a blue suit, sipped tea and ate walnut cake. She had laid a large basket of fruit – oranges, lemons, pomegranates – on the place setting nearest William, so that he had to stretch his neck and peer over the handle to get a better look at the woman. She saw him watch her, and smiled and nodded as if he were a forgotten acquaintance. William blushed and returned the nod. He was struck by her eyes – large, heavy-lidded, and green. Sad eyes, like the girls in the paintings at the city museum. The waitress passed and the redheaded woman asked for her bill. The nippy returned, hovering with polite impatience as the woman felt in her handbag for her purse.

William watched the drama ensue as if it were a play.

'It must be here somewhere.' The redheaded woman rose sharply, tipping the contents of her handbag out amidst the uncleared tea things. 'Oh, Lord. I can't see it anywhere.'

The waitress peered myopically at the mess. 'When did you last have it?' she asked.

'At the Bull Ring when I bought the fruit.' The redhead nodded at her basket.

'Well, I suppose it could've dropped out of your handbag there. Someone could've picked it up.' The waitress sounded unconvinced at her own prognostications. 'You should go back and ask the stall holder. Someone may have handed it in.'

'Yes, yes. I should do that. It has my money, my return train ticket in it, everything, really. Yes, I should leave.'

'Ooh, I don't know about that. What about the bill?' The waitress's tone was sympathetic. She looked about the room as if checking for the manageress. 'I don't think I have the authority to just let you go without paying.'

'I shall come back as soon as I have my purse. I shall leave you with my telephone number and my address. Once I have money, I shall settle the bill.'

'I'll have to ask the manageress. I can't make that sort of decision by myself. I'm just a waitress. If it were up to me, I'd let you off. I can see you're panicked.'

'I can pay.' William stood and patted his wallet. Both women stared at him, silent. William blushed, thinking now that he had interrupted a personal conversation. The waitress frowned as though she misunderstood what he was saying. 'I can pay the lady's bill,' he repeated. 'It can't be much.' He moved forward. For a moment, they became a curious theatricality, watched open-mouthed by the other customers. The waitress spoke first.

'Well, if it's alright with the lady.' She turned to the redhead. 'It wouldn't half save a lot of bother.'

The redheaded woman flushed rose pink and stood to greet William, but as she did so, she knocked the basket of fruit onto the floor. Once more, a brief hush descended upon the diners. They glanced, curious, with craned necks for a scant second, and just as quickly returned to their teas. William bent and picked up an orange, and the redhead joined him. 'Thank you, you are kind. But it wouldn't be right for you to pay; we're strangers.'

The waitress crouched with them. 'Shall I put the lady's sixpence on your bill, sir?'

'Yes.' William was decisive.

The waitress nodded towards the redheaded woman and said, 'You should pray to St Anthony of Padua. He's the patron saint of lost things. My mom swears by him.' And then she left them to their fruit.

'I shall pay you back as soon as St Anthony and I have found my purse. I would feel awful if I didn't.' A pomegranate rolled and settled beneath an empty neighbouring table. William reached for it, as did the redhead. He touched her hand. Her fingers were mucky with paint, or soil, and she had hands like a boy, nails stubby and bitten, the flesh creamy and soft. She noticed his glance and said, 'I'm an artist.'

William withdrew and they both stood. 'I've never met an artist before,' he replied. 'I like to take photographs,' he added, improbably. He smiled and felt in his pocket for a business card. 'Telephone me, or visit, when you're ready,' he said.

She took the card, read it and smiled. 'You're very good, Mr Garrett. I feel you've rather come to my rescue. It's terribly kind of you. Thank you so very much.' The redheaded woman gathered her things. 'I really must get to the Bull Ring. I shall telephone you once I have my money.'

William remained standing and watched her leave. Then he paid the bill, tipping the little nippy well, and he too left. Buoyed by the redhead's words, William felt momentarily virtuous, as if he truly were a terribly kind man.

Out on New Street, the crowd had changed. The city's clerks headed, heads down, towards pub lunches or sandwiches with sweethearts in the cathedral close. And girls, buttoned up in black shirts and heavy serge skirts, handed out furious grins and fascist leaflets to stragglers off their guard. One made a beeline for William and offered him a slip of paper printed stark in red and black. *Britain First.* William worried that he looked the type, and his good mood faltered.

5

Wilheart illiam sat at his desk and flicked through a book of
modern verse. He'd been reading it all week, killing
time until the redhead appeared with his sixpence. But by
eight-thirty on Friday morning, he knew that the woman, the
money, and having any understanding of the poetry were a
write-off.

The air in his office was heavy with heat, so William
propped the window open with a stiffly rolled newspaper.
Perspiration began to pool in the crevices of his shirt. He
wiped his forehead and looked out onto the old red brick of
Needless Alley. Printers, early shift finished, streamed out of
the back of the *Post and Mail*, taking the short cut up to the
tram stops on Colmore Row, discarding their flat caps and
jackets. A couple of shopgirls traipsed towards the milliners,
fanning themselves with copies of *Woman's Weekly*.

And then a Daimler sailed down the alleyway. The printers
and the shopgirls parted in its wake. It parked a short way
along the street, skew-whiff and odd-looking like a liner in
dock. A big man sat in the back seat, but it was a tall, slim man
in a peaked cap who did the driving. The rear door of the
Daimler opened with a smooth, wide swing and out stepped

William's client, without the aid of his chauffeur. Mr Morton, then, was both rich and eager for help, just as Shifty had described him.

And it wasn't long before William heard his client, tread weighty and breathing laboured, tap on the glass of the open door and enter. Heavy and in his late forties, well-suited, hatless, and sweating from both the short climb up the stairs and the heat of the day, Morton patted his face with a large white handkerchief. William crossed the room and offered Morton his hand. And when they shook, Morton pressed his thumb hard on William's second knuckle. William motioned for his client to take a seat opposite his desk, and Morton did so with what looked like relief.

'Mr William Garrett, I assume?'

'I am he.' William believed it best to remain formal towards a man who probably shared a tailor with the King.

'I understand from Mr Shirley that your discretion is guaranteed, Mr Garrett.'

By his own admission, Shifty Shirley was a member of many clubs and associations – the secret kind with funny handshakes, no doubt. William knew such men valued discretion only slightly more than they valued gossip.

'My business relies on it.' William settled in his chair, lit a cigarette and waited.

'My name is Morton.' The man continued to pat his great sweaty face. William thought it a gesture borne from nerves rather than heat. 'I'm in hosiery, ladies' stockings and undergarments.'

William grinned. 'Don't worry about that, Mr Morton, I've seen it all.' There was a fat pause, and William immediately regretted this lapse into frivolity.

'That's a very tired joke. I dislike low comedians.' He offered

William his card. 'I manufacture artificial silk.'

William glanced at it. 'And what do you want from me, Mr Morton?'

'I imagine you're not a romantic, Mr Garrett. In your line of work, it must be difficult to maintain a confidence in the rectitude of the fairer sex. I am a romantic. It's my chief failing. Ladies can be, should be, superior. Therefore, my current predicament is quite concerning.'

'Rectitude?' he asked.

'It means virtue.'

William knew what it meant. 'Please go on, Mr Morton.'

'My wife is a young woman, some years younger than I. She is girlish and rather naive. Not stupid intellectually, in fact she's rather bright, but socially gauche, backward even. I once thought her an innocent.' Morton paused and squinted his eyes against the hard morning sun. 'I believe she is easily led.'

'By other men?'

'I don't know. Although I should very much like to know it, to be sure. I have, quite recently, received letters.' Mr Morton pulled a bag of boiled sweets from his jacket pocket, and sucked on one, slowly, his forehead creasing. 'I have low blood sugar and am prone to fainting.' He offered the packet to William, who refused. 'Poison-pen stuff. The writer accuses my wife of enjoying sexual relations with other men. Handsome men, much younger than myself. Filthy female nonsense, probably. They say it's women who write such tripe, do they not?'

'I honestly don't know. It tends to be a plot device in cheap novels, but that's not real life. What makes you think they're written by a woman?'

'Spite. They are dripping with it.' Morton paused. 'And a certain florid tone.'

'And you've brought them with you? May I read them?'

'No. No, you may not. I destroyed them.'

'I don't think that was wise.'

'I'm not here for you to pronounce judgement on my wisdom, Mr Garrett.'

'Then what are you here for, if not my advice and expertise?'

Beads of sweat formed on Morton's forehead. 'I want you to find if there is some semblance of truth with regards to the content of the letters. In short, I would like to know if my wife is cheating on me.'

'You have spoken to your wife about your concerns? Shown her the letters and so forth?' said William.

'I've tried many times. We are not enemies. We are not estranged. I'm in an uncomfortable position. To accuse her without proof would put an unbearable strain on our marriage. May I talk frankly?'

'It would be best if you do.'

The man breathed deeply and then arranged himself, as though preparing to give a performance. 'I am a weak man, Mr Garrett.' Morton paused and lowered his eyes. 'No, there's no need to contradict me.' This was not William's intention. 'I am weak and full of pride, but I am not stupid.' Morton looked William in the eye and smiled. 'In a marriage, a man must have the upper hand. I'm not talking of cruelty but of mastery. A man must always have control of his marriage. To accuse my wife of adultery without proof would be a pointless act. She would simply deny it and maintain her innocence, regardless of the truth of the matter. She would control that truth whether she is innocent or not, don't you see? I would never know. I would be constantly on the back foot. It would give her the upper hand. And the natural order of the holy estate of matrimony, which I hold in the greatest esteem, would become unbalanced.' Sermon over, Morton preened at his own rhetoric, and was every inch the budding provincial politician.

William remembered Shifty's description of Morton: gentry, manufacturer, a rising man politically. 'Are you hoping to run for Parliament, Mr Morton?'

Morton smiled. 'You are a very astute fellow. Yes, sir. Indeed, you are.' He reached into the inside pocket of his waistcoat and pulled out a political newspaper limp with sweat. 'If there is any doubt about Mrs Morton's moral standing, it would put me in a very difficult position with the party. Yes, quite difficult. Mosley is not a backward man.' He placed the paper on William's desk and ironed out the creases with his pudgy hand. William saw the lightning strike of the BUF. *The Blackshirt. Britain First.* 'The lawful dissolution of a failed marriage is a mark of civil society. But to be a cuckold, well, it just wouldn't do.'

Fascism was a modern fad, like nudism and vegetarianism. William, old-fashioned, hated all three. 'And you've been married for how long?'

'Quite ten years, now.'

William took his notepad and pencil from the desk drawer. 'Did the letters contain names, places, dates of assignation? Anything one might call proof. Anything to spark your concern?'

'No, only vague filth. Explicit. The letter writer was no frustrated spinster, I can tell you that. Unnatural acts were mentioned.'

'Unnatural acts?'

Morton held up his hand, in the manner of a traffic policeman, gesturing that William should halt. 'Please do not press me on the subject matter, Mr Garrett.'

William stubbed out his cigarette and sighed. 'Your reticence will only hinder a quick and discreet resolution of your case. You speak of unnatural acts. It's an old-fashioned legal term for buggery, bestiality, incest.' He watched as Morton reached for another boiled sweet. 'Other offences would be rape, indecent assault, or having carnal knowledge of a girl under twelve years old. Even a married woman of some sexual experience would have little understanding of such things unless her husband was a brute. It would suggest that your letter writer, if female, was a prostitute –' William paused and smiled – 'or perhaps a lady solicitor who dealt with sexual crimes. If these acts were mentioned in the letter, I would suggest the writer were a man. A voluptuary and obsessive. It is important, therefore, that you are specific. Of what unnatural act is your wife accused?'

'Men and women together, all at once in what one might call a bacchanalia of sexual congress.' He sucked at the boiled sweet with violent force, and his small lips pursed and puckered. 'It would be personally disastrous for me if Clara were involved in such activities, yes . . .' Morton paused. 'It would be a tragic thing.'

'Has the writer threatened to go to the newspapers? Have they demanded money?'

Morton crunched at his sweet and swallowed. His jowls and Adam's apple quivered slightly. 'No, the letters are purely informative, although somewhat grotesque. However, you are missing the point. The identity of the letter writer is of secondary importance to me. I simply want to know if the content is true. I simply want you to find out if my wife is still a woman of good standing, of virtue.'

Rectitude.

William's hackles rose. Morton, the manufacturer and budding politician, had strangely skewed priorities. 'Alright.

31

Have it your way, Mr Morton. However, the letters are an obvious line of enquiry, and one I must pursue if we are to find out if Mrs Morton is still virtuous.' The word cloyed in William's mouth. 'There are other ways to investigate, but the letters are an obvious starting point.'

'Yes, I do understand.' Fat droplets of sweat gathered on Morton's upper lip. 'It is not my intention to be obtuse. It is only that, as a gentleman, I find the subject matter a little offensive.'

William smiled. 'It's fortunate for us both that I am no gentleman.'

'Sir, I meant no disrespect. I can see that you are a man of discretion and intelligence –' Morton gestured to the shabbiness of the office and wrinkled his nose – 'despite appearances.' William wondered if the man had caught a whiff of damp.

'My business relies upon both my discretion and my intelligence, Mr Morton.' William stopped taking notes and lit another cigarette. 'Let me put the case to you as I see it. Would that help?'

Morton nodded.

'You are a man of wealth and good standing in your own district and soon hope for a more national influence.' Morton nodded at William's implied question. 'Your wife is beautiful and young, and up until recently you have been quite content in your marriage.' Again, Morton nodded. 'Lately, you have been receiving obscene letters, typewritten and through the post.' Morton nodded once more. 'When did you receive the first letter?'

'The twelfth of June, and then daily ever since.'

William paused; his war-honed nerves sensed danger. Daily pornographic letter writing spoke of obsession and vendetta.

Finally, he said, 'The letters tell of unusual and adulterous, but not necessarily illegal, sexual relations between your wife and a series of men and women. You say your wife is intelligent but naive. Tell me about her friends.'

Morton frowned in concentration. 'She is a quiet woman, solitary and very much a homebody and, how can I put this?' Morton frowned further. 'Rather nervous, socially. She can be reclusive around our friends. She attends dinner dances and so forth, the more formal political and business events, but is not one of these women for lunching out. She is an amateur artist and paints watercolours. Sometimes landscapes in oil. Much of her time is spent in this hobby. Although I must be truthful, I spend little time at home nowadays. My business, my political duties . . . well, perhaps I have neglected Clara rather. She relies on me so.'

This was not the portrait of an orgy-lover. William wondered if Morton was a neurotic obsessing over being cuckolded. And then he wondered if Morton was a liar. 'It would be very out of character for a woman such as you describe to suddenly become promiscuous. Has there been any event, a shock, an argument, which may have precipitated a change in character?'

'Event? Whatever do you mean? Event?'

'Like I said, an argument, or an accident, perhaps.' William watched as Morton dabbed at his forehead. His large handkerchief had become sodden. 'Pardon my bluntness, but have you ever raised a hand to your wife in temper?'

'No, nothing of the kind.' William sensed a faux affrontery in Morton's voice. 'We are quite content with each other. I rarely raise my voice to Clara, and never my fists.'

'So, your marriage is a happy one, although you admit to being rarely home, and your wife is demure and near

33

reclusive.' It was time to end the conversation. William stubbed out his cigarette. 'My advice is to take the next letter to the police, Mr Morton. From what I can tell, someone is simply out to make mischief. I imagine you've made a few political or business enemies in your time.' Morton's jaw slackened as if he were considering, but not deciding upon, a response. 'Go home, Mr Morton,' William continued. 'Enjoy your beautiful wife. If the source of the letters is of no interest to you, and your married life is just as you have related, then you have no need of a private detective. I doubt very much that your wife is being unfaithful. I tend to choose my cases on potentiality for profit. Protracted divorce cases, mostly. Your case offers me no scope, and I am a busy man. I hope you understand.' William stood and offered Morton his hand. 'Goodbye, Mr Morton.'

However, Morton did not rise but shifted forward, his chair creaking under his weight. 'Mr Garrett, I shall have no peace of mind until I have proof of my wife's innocence. I've tried to dismiss the letters as the ravings of a crank.' William could not tell if there were tears or sweat in Morton's eyes. 'You were highly recommended by Mr Shirley. You know him well, of course.' William sat down.

'We nod to each other occasionally. I'm sure Mr Shirley has informed you of my terms of employment, costs and so forth.' William's tone was cold.

'Mr Garrett, have you never been in love?'

'I once bought a girl a zirconium-set ring and a fox fur stole, but she didn't like the suburbs.'

'I see, yes. Hardened, perhaps. I, unfortunately, am more vulnerable.' Morton glanced over at the camera sitting on top of William's filing cabinet, avoiding eye contact. 'I love my wife, Mr Garrett. She is precious to me. Very precious. My most prized girl. I have no shame in admitting it.' Morton fiddled with the buttons of his waistcoat. They were all intact, in order. 'But I am ashamed to say that the letters have upset my nerves, rather. I'm ashamed of my weakness. It has been preying on my mind. I'm not sleeping. I need to be sure that Clara is still good. My good, sweet girl.' Morton's voice cracked.

William shook his head. 'This is a vanity case, Mr Morton. No one can guarantee your peace of mind or your wife's love.'

'That is plain talking, indeed, but it does show an understanding of the situation.' Morton's waistcoat buttons were fascinating to him. 'I don't expect guarantees, but hard probabilities that Clara has remained faithful. A man like yourself could provide me with a detailed itinerary of my wife's movements. You could be a proxy. I cannot be in my wife's company, but you can, as a shadow. You can be my eyes. I would like a comprehensive daily report to show where Clara has been and who with, so that I might ask her, in the evening, if she had a good day and know her response to be truthful, for you have given me proofs of that truth for that day. I shall be paying you so that I may rest easy in my bed for that day. I should pay a great deal of money for peace of mind and to be, once more, easy in my wife's company.'

Yes, it would take a great deal of money to persuade William to act as lackey to a neurotic fascist. The magic words: *a great deal of money*. And to William, they were more powerful than *abracadabra*. 'I should want a great deal of money to take your case, Mr Morton,' he said.

Morton looked up and smiled. 'I have money, Mr Garrett, and you shall have it if I get what I want.' The man's demeanour had changed. For the first time, William believed him the powerful industrialist Shifty had described. 'And if you do a good job, you will soon learn that I value reliable men. I have no time for the stultifying snobbery and classism which has lost us our position in the world. Our once Great Britain is now nothing but a minion of the Americans and the Hebrew bankers—'

William suppressed his disgust and interrupted. 'I shall need details, Mr Morton. First, may I have your home address, of all your homes, and the addresses of your offices and factory premises. I should also like the names of your wife's friends and family.'

'I can give you my details,' he said, 'but my secretary will telephone with the names of our friends.' William gave Morton a notepad and pencil. The man began to write.

'Do you have a photograph of your wife? Something recent?' Morton looked up from his scribbling and nodded once more. Then he fumbled in the pocket of his waistcoat and produced a conventional professional portrait of a woman in evening dress, and placed it next to the copy of *The Blackshirt* on William's desk. 'I want you to understand that whatever I find, I cannot guarantee you peace of mind.' Again, Morton nodded. 'You must prepare yourself. I may find that Mrs Morton has a lover, but the likelihood is that I shall not. You, Mr Morton, must prepare yourself for innocence.' William lit another cigarette and offered one to Morton. 'The case will involve a protracted amount of legwork, following Mrs Morton for a matter of months, compiling a detailed itinerary of her movements, and so forth. I will have to refuse other cases or employ an assistant.'

'Our arrangement would be for you, and you only, to see to my needs.' Morton handed back William's notepad.

'I can guarantee that no other man will tail your wife. If you agree to my terms, I will consider your case my priority,' said William.

'And your terms?'

'Ten shillings an hour plus expenses. I will give you a fully itemised bill along with the daily report on your wife's movements. I shall wrap up one or two items of business and start on Monday morning.' Relief flashed across Morton's face. William was unsure if Morton found the rates to be low or that he was reassured of William's commitment to the case. 'My rates are fair for the service I offer. I'm not a thief.'

Mr Morton, who had refused William's cigarette, now shook his bag of boiled sweets in William's direction. 'Humbug, Mr Garrett?'

William, sweet-toothed, took one. Morton rose and shook William's hand. 'I like you. I appreciate men with candour and intelligence. Do not disappoint me.'

It was only after William watched the great black Daimler manoeuvre its way out of Needless Alley that he looked at the photograph of Mrs Morton. It was a cursory glance and provided him with scant information to the woman's character or appearance. She seemed typical in her bland prettiness. A girl in pearls, well-lit and in half-profile, with stiff-set curls of indeterminate paleness, soft rouged cheeks, lowered eyes, small receding chin; a portrait so commonplace that William worried he might fail to recognise the true Clara Morton in the flesh.

But there was something about those heavy-lidded, down-cast eyes, the thick dark lashes, the melancholy set of the chin, which forced William to look closer. The portraitist had attempted to disguise Mrs Morton's features into fashionable modernity with clever lighting and composition. This woman was the Victorian type, not a potential cover girl for *Country Life* but a muse for Rossetti or Burne-Jones. William would have photographed her surrounded by old roses or holding a pomegranate. He placed the portrait back on his desk, crunched at his boiled sweet and swallowed. William's stomach lurched in paranoia. Clara Morton was his redheaded debtor from the Lyons' Corner House.

6

It was two o'clock when William entered the public bar of the White Swan, and on a Saturday afternoon, the clientele was exclusively masculine. A few metalworkers, the grease still on them, stood about in groups of three or four, supping pints, drawing on Woodbines, circling the long shots on their folded copies of the *Sporting Chronicle*. A couple of bookies' runners lounged predatory in the corner waiting for the punters to pick a winner, or not, for the next race at Warwick.

William made his way to the door at the far end of the bar and then into the smoking room. A creature of habit and easy to find, Ronnie was there, as expected, louche on a leather bench. A frowzy blonde, shoes off and feet on the seat, leant against him. Her head was on his shoulder, and she sipped what looked like port and lemon with deliberate delicacy. She was three sheets to the wind. On his left side was a boy, dressed like the Prince of Wales on his day off, hair sharply cut, features fine, skin like porcelain, his head back against the tiled wall, fast asleep. And next to the boy lay a beautiful girl – a foreign type – hair in disarray, dark, deep-set eyes, and her blouse a little unbuttoned. Film-star allure and swilling down cheap rum in a rough pub with an out-of-work actor; she didn't know her worth. Ronnie waved and gave him a wide grin.

'Have you been to bed yet?' William was sharp, irritated, jealous.

'Darling, don't be so personal.'

'You look like shit.'

Ronnie ran his fingers through his dark hair. 'Now, you know that's not true.'

'Where have you been all night?' William knew the answer: a party with so-and-so, and then off to some place in the country, and then back to the city to breakfast on booze in a Digbeth dive.

'Was *he* at the party?' The beauty was stupid with drink. She blinked at him, tried to focus. 'He's nice-looking, isn't he?'

The boy opened his eyes, suddenly. 'What has it to do with you where we have been?' His voice was clipped and aggressive. 'You do seem unduly interested in other people's business.'

A few men, dapper in their caps and waistcoats, gold watch chains hanging heavy like anchors, glanced up from their pints, blinked at the boy, and then went back to their low, monosyllabic talk.

'I admire your friend's diction, Ronnie, and his tailor.' William had never seen a boy of that age so well dressed. 'He must be the toast of the upper sixth.'

Ronnie placed his arm around the boy's shoulders and squeezed. 'Don't worry, darling. Billy's my oldest friend, hence the appalling lack of manners.'

The boy turned to Ronnie, blinking blue eyes like willow pattern saucers. 'You're a local? I didn't know. Didn't guess.' The new boy blushed. This one wouldn't last. Ronnie's lovers came and went like spring flowers, wilting under the hot, heavy charm of his personality. 'I thought you were like us.' The boy broke off.

Ronnie laughed. 'Darling, I am like no one.'

'Ain't that the truth,' said William. 'Ronnie and I were once brothers of the sooty back streets. Before you were born.' It was a deliberate jibe. William watched as Ronnie winced. 'The war changed him, son.'

'All of those lonely subalterns at the Somme did so want to learn me to talk proper.'

The frowzy blonde guffawed. 'Ronnie can pass for posh.'

'However, the same cannot be said for dear Billy.' Ronnie waved his hand, a regal gesture, for he was king of the smoking room. 'Do sit down and have a drink, William. You're looming, and we're all feeling rather sensitive. We've had a late evening and we have not yet properly breakfasted.'

'No, I don't have time for a drink. I've got a proposition for you.'

Ronnie raised an eyebrow, and the blonde snorted in laughter.

'Ivy, do shut up, there's a dear.' The boy's hangover was probably kicking in. William knew that not everyone had Ronnie's remarkable constitution.

'Well, seeing as you are so intent on casting a pall on our little party, I shall hear your proposition.' Ronnie extracted himself from Ivy, who looked startled and wobbly without him, and crooked his finger at William. 'Come to my office.'

The ladies' lounge was empty and spotless. It was a small room with pressed glass vases of wax daffodils on copper-topped tables, and a hatch in the wall for a bar; an elaborate mirror above the tiled fireplace advertised Ansell's Pale Ale.

'Does anyone ever drink in here?' asked William.

'Every now and again a true lady crosses the threshold, so the landlord must be prepared. What do you want with me, Billy?'

'I have a new client.'

'I'm not interested. Consider our business arrangement –' Ronnie struggled for the correct word – 'annulled.' Nearly right, old son, William thought.

'No, it's not what you think. I want you to tail a fellow for a few days. Make a few discreet enquiries on my behalf. That sort of thing.'

Ronnie smiled. 'That all sounds suspiciously like sleuthing.'

'You have to take it seriously. You must lay off the booze for a few days. Keep your gob shut, too.' William gestured with his thumb to the party in the smoking room.

Ronnie shook his head. 'It's filthy work, all this sneaking about and spying and lying, no matter how you dress it up, and I'm afraid I'm rather sick of it.'

'Filthy work? Christ, Ronnie. You and I know what filthy work really is. There's no hardship in this; nothing to break your bloody back, no danger, no whizz-bangs.' William knew he'd already played it wrong, as Ronnie's instinct was to work contrary to given orders. Moreover, it was stupid to talk of quitting drink, and so William changed tack. 'It's a fella, a fella I don't much like. He's been getting these poison-pen letters saying that the missus is a bad girl, and it's given him the wind up. He wants me to follow the wife and give daily reports on her movements.' William deliberately failed to mention his growing paranoia over the meeting with Clara Morton at Lyons' Corner House.

'What's his name?' Ronnie asked.

'Morton. A bona fide fascist shitbag from out near Coventry.'

Ronnie paused, licking the residue of whisky from his lips. 'Pleasant fellow?' he asked.

'Indeed he is.' William smiled. 'And he's very big in women's knickers.'

'Darling, I've known quite a few like him.'

William fed Ronnie the line on purpose, for William was Ronnie's straight man.

'Have another whisky.' William walked over to the small opening to the main bar, turned to Ronnie and said, 'Let's take a seat. Let me talk you through it, at least.' William returned with a double Glenfiddich and began his pitch. 'He's fat and pompous. A fucking Freemason mate of Shifty Shirley, and whoever's been writing these letters has done a proper job on him.'

Ronnie raised his glass of whisky. 'Are you going to keep me company?'

William shook his head. 'I've already done a bit of research. Spent most of the day in the library. Ronnie, listen to this.' William took a few sheets of paper from his breast pocket and glanced at the notes he had made that morning. 'The fellow inherited half of the Warwickshire coalfield from his father.' Ronnie looked up from his drink and whistled through his teeth. 'But that ain't enough for him. He's invested heavily in textiles, and built factories in Coventry and its satellite towns, employing thousands of women machinists. He's in talks with the Americans over patents for a new kind of artificial silk. The business pages are calling it a Midlands boom amidst the international bust of the Depression.' William quoted from the *Birmingham Post*.

'Your eyes glitter so when you talk of money. It's rather prettifying.'

William ignored the jibe and lit a cigarette with a shaking hand. 'My nerves are playing me up. It should be an easy case. Keep an eye on the wayward wife and make sure no naughty business hits the headlines to upset the Yank investors, that sort of thing.' Ronnie was silent. William looked away from his friend and out of the window onto the scrubbed brick yard beyond. 'But there's something about it that puts me on edge. There's something deep about it that I've not quite fathomed.' William paused. 'The way he talks about his wife is, well, it's not normal. He's obsessed, I think. He uses words like *rectitude* and *virtue*. He wants me to tail her to find if she has a lover. But I don't like it. All of this letter writing, too. He's cagey about it. It feels wrong in my gut. What I need, is for you to see if my gut is right. See what this Morton is up to while I'm snooping on his wife. That way—'

'Why don't you just drop it? Drop the case.'

'All the brass and all the needful. Spondulicks, old son.' William rubbed his thumb across the tips of his fingers. 'If I stay on the case, there could be two or three hundred in it, or more. A good chunk of which will be yours. I just want to make sure Morton isn't the kind of bloke to turn lunatic if we give him news he doesn't like. Cause a scene, or send his fascist crew after me, or sue, or refuse to pay up—'

'Oh God, it's always the bloody money with you.' Ronnie slumped down on the bench seating, wiped a little spilt whisky from his dinner jacket and lit a cigarette. He offered one to William, but William shook his head. Ronnie patted the seat next to him. William sat down and wished he had a drink after all. 'Billy, darling, do you think there's such a thing as true love, fidelity, loyalty, friendship, finding one's soul mate and so on and so forth?' Ronnie considered his drink. William knew that he would soon demand a top-up.

'Christ almighty, Ronnie, what kind of question is that?'

'One that I think a best friend would answer with honesty.'

William wasn't in the mood for one of Ronnie's drunken heart-to-hearts. 'Fuck me, Ronnie. I don't know. It's a rare thing, I think.' He sighed. 'Precious when you find it, but people let it go, take it for granted. I think you must fight for it, when you have it, fight to keep it.'

'Are you talking of Queenie?' Ronnie asked.

'God, no. No, not anymore.' But perhaps William was, really. She haunted him because he loved her, had loved her, man and boy. He drew strength and comfort from her. Succour, the Bible called it. But there was no compromising with Queenie Maggs. A man might drown in the powerful swell of her personality. 'I think I shall have that drink.'

'Good man. Start the day proper. Make a weekend of it, why not? We could go on a spree. Have you any money? I'm rather short, I'm afraid. I've found some delightfully pretty girls, did you notice?'

'No.'

'Liar.'

William laughed.

'I think you're wise when you talk of love. I think one must fight for it,' Ronnie said.

'Christ, Ronnie, have you finally succumbed to hearth and home?'

'Oh, my dear, no. I always get a little melancholy after a heavy night.' He paused for a moment, eyes rheumy, and shifted closer to William. 'I've just been thinking about Alice. I don't believe I've truly loved anyone since Alice. She was so very good. I feel sort of hollowed out. I don't know if it's the war that made me incapable of the necessary –' he paused – 'tenderness.' He moved his lips away from William's ear.

This was a common refrain. Alice, dead of a broken heart, was the love of Ronnie's life. Ronnie idealised the girl, and in his wistfulness, he romanticised a relationship which was doomed to fail. William sighed. 'But you don't like women in that way anymore. I mean, I thought you preferred to –' he paused – 'to go to bed with men.'

'In all honesty, I do, mostly. But there are as many kinds of love as there are hearts, so the poets say—'

'Tolstoy said it. Russians understand complexity.'

Ronnie turned and grinned. He fluttered his long lashes. Ronnie was the only man in Birmingham who made up his eyes. 'You always were a literary bastard.' He offered William a stage wink, then shook his empty glass. 'Buy me another before you head back to the library, Professor.'

William got up and walked to the hatch in the wall and peered through to the main bar to see the publican polishing pint pots and chatting with a couple of fellows in overalls. He ordered a pint of mild. Ronnie called out for a large gin. William returned with their drinks. 'If you need money, this is the job for you.'

'Isn't money frightful? The root of all evil, so it says in the Good Book.' Ronnie knocked back his gin. 'Although perhaps money is only frightful because some of us don't have it, yet deserve it, need it, so badly.' He rose and stumbled over to the bar – ordered another drink.

William called out, 'A pound per day, Ronnie. Maybe more. We'll rent you a car, so you can follow him about like in the movies.' It was a childish gambit. 'You could use your lovely manners and pry about suburban golf clubs, or whatever. You'll come up with something. Join the Masons, God knows. It's what you're good at.' William had won. Ronnie was broke, and Ronnie was vulnerable to flattery. This is how it always went: the initial refusal, the cod philosophy, then Ronnie recalling a bank balance in the red, or worse, a bookies' bill unpaid. And Ronnie appeared more tired than usual, worn. 'Come with me, we'll have lunch at the Kardomah and talk it through. I've got a list of places he visits. His home address, businesses and so on. His wife, well, I think she's a decent sort. I have her photograph.'

'You do?'

William noticed that the grey smudges beneath Ronnie's eyes were not make-up. Ronnie was fagged out. 'Come and get a decent feed, for Christ's sake. You live off gin and Lucky Strikes.'

'No, I have ladies to entertain. They'll be getting fractious without me already, no doubt. Ivy can be rather trying.'

'The blonde?' William asked.

'Yes, if you like her, you can have her. Be my bloody guest, old boy.'

'Have some food instead. My treat.'

'No, but I will take your job. A pound per day, well, it'll go a long way. And it's better than the usual stuff you throw my way.' Ronnie stood and considered his reflection. He glanced at the photograph of Clara Morton – the generic English rose – which William had placed on the table before him. 'What's she really like, this Mrs Morton?' He touched the photograph with his fingertips. 'What can you tell me about her?'

William shrugged and stubbed his fag out on the scrubbed linoleum of the ladies' lounge. 'Like I say, she's alright, I reckon.'

7

Sunday, 25 June

Dick Powell sang a serenade. His sweet high tenor was thin and distant, for the stage was very far away. *I only have eyes for you, dear.* Behind the crooner was a painted backdrop of Elysian fields, nymphs dancing, the Muses. The song rose and fell like the lapping of waves. And she was selling oranges in the theatre. A whore in the gods, draped in red velvet and clutching a basket of fruit. When she saw William, she let go; oranges and pomegranates thudded and rolled and tumbled down towards the stalls. Dick Powell looked up.

'You're desperate for a decent fuck,' she said. William could smell citrus on her breath, bitter pith.

'No, it's only loneliness,' he said. 'I'm so lonely.'

My love must be a kind of blind love.

'But there's no need for that,' she said. And she led him down the aisle to a balcony seat.

When she straddled him, William buried his head in her breasts and cried as she rocked on his cock. And Mr Morton watched from the wings, sucking hard at his humbugs.

Women and war, it was all he ever dreamt of.

William woke in a cold sweat with sore muscles and a sick feeling. He sat on the edge of the bed, ran his fingers through his hair, blinked away the night's sleep, and listened to the clatter of the telephone for a few moments until he ran downstairs to the office and answered the call. 'Hullo.'

For a moment, there was no answer. 'Mr William Garrett?' It was a woman's voice, hesitant and low.

'Yes.'

'Mr Garrett, I'd like to return your sixpence.' It was the woman of his dreams, Clara Morton. William was not yet truly awake.

'Yes, no, there really is no need.' His own voice, muddy with sleep, sounded strange and disassociated, as if he were appearing in a play on the wireless. Outside, in the bright of morning, the bells of St Philip's and St Martin's rang out the call to Sunday service – slightly off kilter. 'I mean I would feel wrong to accept it.'

'Did I wake you? I'm terribly sorry.' Clara Morton became quiet once more. 'It's just that I'm in Birmingham today, and I thought I might repay my debt. It's been playing on my mind rather. You were so kind.' She paused again. 'A bright note in what turned out to be a rotten day.' Another pause. 'I never found my purse, you know.'

'How did you get home?'

'By taxi. There was money in the house, thank goodness.'

'There's really no need to repay the sixpence, Miss ...'

Calling her 'Miss' was an underhanded move, and William knew it.

'Morton, Clara Morton. And please, just call me Clara.' She did not lie, but she did omit. Again, she was hesitant. 'And I do want to meet, Mr Garrett.' Silence, again. William felt that she was waiting for him to talk. 'I could buy you tea at the museum,' she said, 'by way of honouring my debt. There's a good photographic exhibition on by a young artist called Bill

49

Brandt. You may enjoy it.' Another short silence. 'A fellow William. A fellow photographer.'

'What time were you thinking?' The last chime of ten o'clock sounded from the cathedral bells.

'Would eleven o'clock be too early? We could meet outside the main doors to the museum, yes?'

'Yes, Clara,' he said. 'That would be fine.'

Fine. It would be fine to see her again. He liked her voice. It was a fine voice. She liked art and had good taste in modern photography. He had nothing on this Sunday. She had good eyes. He had not properly made up his mind over taking her husband's case. Clara Morton interested him. Yes, she did. He dreamt of her. And besides, she owed him sixpence.

'Thank you, Mr Garrett. You are very kind.' William believed there to be a note of relief in her voice as she said her goodbyes.

Just before eleven o'clock, he left Needless Alley and walked the pleasant route to the museum, avoiding New Street and taking in the Georgian beauty of St Philip's and Colmore Row. The faithful streamed through the church doors; the morning service over by the time he passed. Suddenly, the congregation stopped as one, stretching their necks to look at the sky. William joined them. Above the looming baroque of the cathedral, the clouds were grey and fat like Zeppelins, and below them was a vapour trail of an aeroplane. He stood with the crowd and watched. The machine was spelling something out, looping and returning: a 'B' perhaps, and an 'I' and then an 'R'; an advertisement.

'It's for custard!' A woman was shouting and pointing. 'Yes, yes! Look! BIRDS!'

A young man, with that residual acne boys in their twenties

often had, said: 'He should spell out CUSTARD. You can't just write BIRDS in the sky. It's too odd. Confusing.'

A woman turned to William. 'Is it sinful to advertise custard on the Sabbath, do you think?'

William shrugged. 'In the grand scheme of things, I think not.'

The congregation lingered for the rest of the message, frowning. But the aeroplane had gone for good, and the small party soon scattered outward towards the trams and buses which took them back to their suburban villas. William crossed Colmore Row, dodging a tram, and made for the museum and Clara Morton.

The clock was striking eleven when he saw her. She was waiting for him at the main doors as arranged. She wore a short-sleeved cotton print dress – no pearls – and carried her white gloves, and a small leather clutch, in her right hand. Of average height and build, he thought, and too heavy about the hips for her figure to be fashionable. But William didn't like fashionable figures. Hatless, her hair was the colour of autumn leaves – hornbeams in late September – and it shone out bright under the heavy Sunday cloud. She waved and moved forward as she saw him. A familiar tightness formed in William's chest. 'Did you see the aeroplane?' he asked.

'Yes, but why write BIRDS in the sky? It seemed like a Dadaist stunt. So strange.' She replied as if they were old friends, as if their meeting were a regular date and part of their normal weekend routine.

'It was an advertisement for custard,' he said.

Clara Morton laughed. 'Advertising men are natural surrealists, perhaps?' She took another step towards him, smiled and asked, 'What first, coffee or art?'

'Art, I think.' William led the way, opening doors like a gentleman. On their way to the exhibition, Clara chatted, and he listened. He listened to her apologies about the sixpence, and the trouble she had over her lost purse, and how the desk sergeant at Steelhouse Lane thought there was little hope in recovering it, and finally, how kind William was. How very kind.

Soon, they were in a museum anteroom of the sort kept for small travelling exhibitions, somewhere on the lower floor and painted bright white rather than the usual hefty red. The pictures were hung at eye level, regimented and grey scale, stark against the brilliant wall. And he and Clara were alone, absolutely alone. 'Well, here we are,' he said.

Clara stood back and considered a photograph of a man covered in coal dust. The man was sitting down to supper. His wife, a woman worn beyond her years, looked on without food. William wondered if the miner's missus still had her teeth. 'This is what I'm attempting in my own work,' she said. So Clara Morton was not the genteel lady watercolourist her husband believed her to be. 'This realism, it speaks of my childhood.' She paused for a moment. 'The people I knew and loved and admired. The establishment think it gritty, but it's just life. We shouldn't romanticise it or allow the viewer to gawp at people as though they aren't human. This is the norm.' Clara motioned to the picture as if giving a lecture. 'The ruling classes are in the minority.'

'Your father was a miner?' William failed to keep the note of surprise from his voice.

'Yes, in the Warwickshire coalfield,' she said.

And he was a Red, William thought. Clara had used the language of union men. She was the daughter of a working-class socialist married to an industrialist and a fascist.

'We're looking at Durham.' William winced inwardly, kicking himself for his pedantry.

'Slag heaps are the same no matter what part of the country you're from.' As if illustrating her point, the next photograph featured a mountain of black spoil, threatening and precipitous, behind a narrow row of miners' cottages. Clara nodded towards it. 'Look,' she said. 'It could be anywhere around here.'

'You've lost your accent.'

Clara Morton smiled a wide, genuine smile – a good smile. 'Some of us can manage it.'

'I reckon the twang gives me character,' he said.

'I reckon you're right.'

In the next picture, three mucky children peeped out of a basement window. The lacklustre net curtain was twisted about the body of the smallest child. The eldest of the trio held an empty jug, thrusting it out towards the viewer as if asking for it to be filled. 'I find them a bit painful. These streets, this landscape, these children,' he said. 'It's like being reminded of a scar or a deformity. Something you want to forget or hide.' It was a second before William realised that he had spoken aloud. He had become comfortable with this woman. She had that gift.

Clara Morton touched him gently on the arm. 'I suppose Brandt feels he is telling the truth about the landscape and its people, that's all. I don't find his pictures difficult to look at because my childhood wasn't so bad.' She blushed pink, an English rose after all. 'Yours, well, perhaps it was different. I don't want to pry.'

They were quiet for a moment. 'You owe me coffee,' he said.

She smiled. 'For sixpence, you get both coffee and cake.'

It was a cheering thought.

A quarter to midday on a Sunday, and the museum tea rooms were near empty. The sole customer was a young woman sat in the far corner of the room. With shingled hair boyishly fashionable, and in a plain sleeveless frock, she flicked at her sketchbook with studied appraisal, licking toast crumbs and jam from her fingers as she turned each page.

William and Clara chose a table near a window with a cheerless view of the Council House. Then the day brightened, and above the municipal rooftops, William saw nothing but deep blue air. White light poured in and Clara Morton, sitting opposite and looking onto the entrance of the tea rooms, became illuminated like a burnished Madonna in an illustrated manuscript. He felt the too familiar nausea and reached for a cigarette to settle his stomach, and then offered one to Clara, which she accepted. William lit it for her and watched as her eyelids fluttered when she took her first drag. She had the longest lashes he had ever seen, and they brushed her cheeks as she blinked. 'You've ordered the walnut cake,' she said. 'It's my favourite. Is it good here?'

William laughed. 'I don't know. I've never been here before.'

'To the art gallery?'

'No, I mean to the tea rooms. But I like it. I like tea rooms when they're empty.'

Clara inhaled once more. 'Oh, me too,' she said. 'It feels like luxury, and I like the noises from the kitchen.'

The waitress brought their order. William took a sip of coffee. It was better than the stuff they served at Lyons. 'Do you want to try the walnut cake?' he asked. 'We could share.'

'Oh, I don't think I could.'

'I do.' William sliced the cake in half and pushed her portion across his plate. 'Try it.'

'Oh, you are kind.' Clara leant over and scooped up a piece of the walnut cake with her teaspoon. 'You are very kind, Mr Garrett,' she repeated.

The third finger of her left hand was naked, but William saw the strip of blanched, pinched flesh where a wedding ring should have sat. 'My name is William, and I'm not that kind, you know.' He had mustered some candour, some honesty. 'Please stop saying that.'

The clock of St Philip's struck midday, and on the final echoing chime, the two little Blackshirts, who had been handing out leaflets in the city centre all month, entered the tea rooms – all the time grinning their remorseless, cheerless smiles. Clara Morton looked briefly towards them. William felt the air sucked from the place. 'Why are the young so fanatical?' he asked.

'It's the old men who are to blame. They stir these tensions and peddle their ridiculous utopias for their own means. It's deliberate and calculated.' She stubbed her cigarette out with careful force. 'Do you really think Mosley is a true believer?'

'I wouldn't know.'

Clara glanced at the fascists and then at her watch. 'I have to be back in Coventry by one o'clock at the latest. I really must rush.' She reached for her purse and placed a shilling on the table, standing up, gathering her white gloves and leather bag, and then looking once more at the now seated Blackshirt girls.

William gazed upwards at her pale, solemn face and asked, 'Why did you want to meet me, Clara?'

She sat down. 'I wanted to see what sort of person you were.'

'Why is that important? What is it that you want from me?'

'I . . . I don't want to talk here, but I'd rather like your help, your advice. Will you come and see me tomorrow?' She smiled, but she was anxious. 'Do you like the country?'

'Yes,' William lied.

'Meet me here. It's very pretty and very quiet. Quite off the beaten track.' She opened her handbag and reached for a notepad and pencil. William watched her scribble an address down on a sheet of paper. This time, when she stood, so did he. 'I really must go.' She shook his hand. 'Thank you, William. I was thinking some time in the afternoon. Does four o'clock suit? We can have more tea. I'll buy a walnut cake.' She grinned.

Watching Clara Morton leave a tea rooms had become a regular event, like a recurrent dream. But she wasn't the woman of his dreams, and neither was she the woman of her husband's imagination. Clara Morton was absolutely herself, and she needed William's help.

8

Monday, 26 June

William drove through a warm summer rain, the kind that greyed the English countryside. He peered at the road ahead through a windscreen misted with his own hot breath. There were no directions on the scribbled note Clara Morton had given him in the tea rooms, just the name of the house and the village, and both, tellingly, were the same. A small hamlet buried deep in the remains of the Arden, Hindford was a half-hour's drive from Birmingham. It was a short journey, but one long enough for him to indulge in daydreams of Clara. A film reel of shared intimacies, brief visions of a fantasy future – conversations, laughter, kisses, small domesticities – ran through his head. He reddened at his own vulnerability. She had made a schoolboy of him.

William exhaled and rolled down his window. He slowed the Austin to a crawl. A decorative signpost stood proud on the grass verge to his right. William squinted. It was painted with a reclining white deer tethered to an oak with a golden chain. And above the deer, the name of the village solemn in Tudor red.

Hindford was a cluster of ancient cottages. A picture postcard of a place, it shimmered golden and silent in the late afternoon sun, for the rain clouds had lifted, and the sky hung low and blue. A plain church stood away from the road on higher ground, squat on a hillock so heavy with grass and wildflowers that only the tops of the modest gravestones could be seen. And William was lost. He had travelled through the village and for a mile beyond – twice – and could find no grand manor house.

So he parked the car and grabbed his map from the glove compartment. An old man had been watching him from the churchyard. He waved to William as he got out of the Austin, and then shook the sweat out of his cap with a brisk flick. William crossed the lychgate and walked up the hillock. The grass seeds clung to his turnups.

'You lost, young fella?'

The old man was nut brown with age and sun. Sinewy too, and toothless.

'I am. I'm after Hindford House?'

'You want Mr Edward?' the old man asked.

'I reckon.' William nodded.

The man had scythed swathes of grass and raked it into heaps of hay, now drying in the sunny spots of the graveyard, yet most of the meadow remained. Halfway through the job, the old man was on a break, and his tools were resting against the east wall of the church. He sat on the steps of the porch and reached for a bottle of beer, kept in the shade of the doorway. William followed.

'They're all buried here, the Mortons.'

'I don't doubt it.' William offered the old man a cigarette. And then sat, peaceable with him, in the shade of the porch. He watched their smoke trail out on the breeze, then disappear into the sky. 'What's he like, Morton?'

'He's like 'em all, ain't he, lad?'

'He often here?'

'He ain't much for the country, is Mr Edward. No money in farming. Got a big modern house out near Coventry. The manor is in a bad way although they say he's got the cash to sort it.' The old man was a talker, and William liked a talker. 'No staff left there now. Only a few women from the village to keep it clean and tidy. Keeps Home Farm nice, though. I reckon the old squire'd swivel in his grave if Mr Edward didn't look to the beasts.' The man chuckled.

'What about his wife?' William asked.

'You're more likely to find her here than him. Traipsing about the country with her easel and big hat doing paintings. She wouldn't say boo to a goose, that one.' The old man took a swig of his beer. 'Ain't proper gentry. Ain't got no prerogative.' The old man hit his heels on a slab of stone at the entrance of the porch. 'You know who's buried here, standing up, unmarked?'

'No.'

'A Morton. One of the first. He built this church and got buried upright in the doorway as a penance.'

'What did he do?' William asked.

'Murdered a priest.'

'Why?'

The old man laughed a filthy laugh. 'Caught him tuppin' his missus, so he beat him to death. Didn't even waste the good edge of a sword on the fella. That's the Mortons for you.'

'What happened to the missus?'

'She gave him six more babbies, then upped and died. Her job was done, so to speak,' the old man said.

'Is he in heaven, do you think, due to this penance?'

'Nah.' The old man spat. 'He's in hell alright. Despite his unusual burying.'

The old man and William smoked in silence. William looked out at the churchyard. The long grass changed colour with the shifting light and the breeze, the heads of straggling cornflowers and poppies fluttered filmy like the wings of butterflies, meadowsweet hugged the boundary wall and its damp corners. And then the sky suddenly darkened. Not from a cloud but a great swell of birds, ballooning and billowing in their thousands, their beating wings like the sound of distant gunfire. They danced together as the sky reddened.

'Starlings. They often do it this time of day.'

The birds flew in formation: funnelled and mushroomed and swooped low to the ground as one. William stood and stubbed out his fag on the head of the long-dead Morton. 'Wonderful.'

'Well, it was good talkin' with you, young fella. You've come past Hindford House.' The old man heaved himself upright and pointed north. 'Turn back on yourself, take the first right. Ain't no tarmac on the road. The entrance to the big house is fifty feet to your left.'

The old man continued to scythe around the dead. William could see him in the rear-view mirror as he drove away from the village.

Late afternoon and the edges of the day, blurred and gauzy, filtered through the leaves of the overhanging oaks which bordered the lane to Hindford House. He turned a sudden sharp left onto an ungated road, but as yet, he could not see – what his mother would have called – the big house.

The drive was wide and lined with limes, their slim trunks and branches silver and decorous, like a lady's gloved hand. But the pale gravel had not been weeded, so the parkland encroached, and dandelions sprang up like upstarts on its rutted surface. Sheep and a few small red cattle grazed. He saw the roof first, for the house was built in a valley, turreted in local stone the colour of raw liver in the soft light. The rest of the house revealed itself gradually in a long, coy unveiling of chimney pots and arched windows, of walls thick with ivy and great deep porches and wide stone steps, their treads worn at the middle. And standing before this ancient frontage, hulking in its modernity, was a beautiful Armstrong-Siddeley – marketed as the motor for the daughters of gentlemen. And the lady of the house was at home. Clara Morton leant against the motor car, as if waiting for his arrival.

He watched as she waved him forward with her right hand and ran her left through her already dishevelled curls. He parked the Austin next to her car and felt suddenly like a poor relation. 'Am I late?' he called out from his open window.

She wore men's slacks tucked into thick socks and walking boots, and a short-sleeved cotton print blouse. A battered leather satchel rested on her hip. 'No. A bit. Just five minutes. It's nothing.' Clara Morton's eyes were round and wide, like a child in an advertisement for soap.

William locked up the car – an urban habit – and moved towards the main doors of the house. 'I got lost,' he said. 'This place is out of the way.'

'We shan't go in the main house. It's unused and I don't have a key.' She blushed, perhaps ashamed by her lack of domestic power. 'We can have tea where I paint. Don't you think the country around here lovely?'

'Yes, very much,' he lied.

He followed her to what was left of the formal garden. Thick with neglected roses, the afternoon air was heady with their scent. And flowing deep and fast no more than thirty feet from the rose beds, was the River Avon. It ran through the land, cleaving the estate like a great scar. A stone bridge,

Romantic in style, spanned the river. Clara paused and pointed to a rough pathway ending at a small plantation of non-native trees. 'We'll walk over the bridge and then head for that copse. There's a summer house there, where I paint.'

They crossed the river and were soon amidst the thick fat trunks of the giant redwoods. The meandering woodland path was so dense with pine needles that each footstep produced a deep woody fragrance reminiscent, he thought, of Ronnie's expensive aftershave. Five more minutes of walking, and William saw the summer house. He had expected something like a gazebo at the Botanical Gardens, all rattan furniture and rubber plants labelled in Latin, but this building was miniature grandeur, turreted and impractical, a true folly. Made from the same stone as the main house, it too was covered in ivy. The door and mullioned windows were Gothic arches and seemed placed upon its façade as if by a child. It stood in a clearing shaded by a dark canopy of larch trees and seemed therefore to be an unlikely studio for an amateur artist. He was struck by an oppressive, portentous stillness, an instinct he shook off shamefully and immediately.

Clara Morton reached into her satchel and produced a large, iron key, like something from a story book. 'We're here,' she said. She unlocked the door, turned the handle and they entered the building. William waited the few seconds for his eyes to adjust to the dim interior. The folly was one large, square room. The lofty ceiling was beamed like a church, each timber meeting in the middle at a gilded boss of carved, clustered oak leaves. In between the struts, the deep blue plaster was punctuated with a canopy of gilded stars.

'It's beautiful,' he said, in truth.

Clara stood with him, gazing up at the painted ceiling, joining him in his wonder. 'Yes, it is very beautiful. It was painted by a lesser Pre-Raphaelite. One of Burne-Jones's chums, so it's not original to the building, but it suits, don't you think?'

It suited her, William thought. It suited her red hair, and her green eyes, and her pale skin, and her mystery, and her vulnerability. I should be wearing shining armour, he thought again.

Clara moved towards the mundane, a kitchen area on the far wall. Tea things lay draining near a modern Belfast sink, a kettle stood on an electric stove. 'I should put the kettle on. I expect you'll be wanting your tea.'

'Yes. Yes please.'

'Please sit down. I'll bring the tea over.' There was a Victorian day bed in the centre of the room, and on it a series of oil paintings. All of Hindford: the church; the soft rolling meadows; the tunnel-like lanes; the river; the elms and the crows: and all executed with a clarity and sensitivity William found moving.

A table was set up beneath one of the mullioned windows. And on it, his eye was first caught by a vase of pinks. The flowers were fresh, their petals spiky with life. About them were cluttered her work things: jars of brushes; a small canvas stretching on a frame; tubes of paint all squeezed out; bottles of turpentine and linseed oil; a few oranges; a bowl of pomegranates, one split open, its pale pith fractured, its seeds now bloody dark. William had a sudden vision that this was Clara Morton's home. The folly was a private space, carved out from Edward Morton's holdings in an act of self-determination. 'Should I clear your painting things?'

'Oh, yes, do.' She turned and pointed to a large double screen in the corner of the room. 'Leave the flowers and the fruit but pop my kit behind the screen.' Clara smiled. 'You must think me horribly messy, but I'm not used to visitors, not here. No one but me comes here.'

William shifted the oils and canvas as directed. The corner of the room, behind the screen, was chaotic with sketchbooks, finished pictures in oil, but also rejected canvases, scraped and ready for repainting. He flicked through a few, and was struck by a singular painting, disquieting, intimate and suffused with light, like a forgotten memory. William felt a jolt of dismay. A back kitchen on a good wash day, a woman was asleep in an armchair. She was fully clothed, but her skirts were rucked, exposing greying petticoats, fat knees and black rolled stockings. All a woman of that age would not want on show. Her head lolled to the left so that the flesh of her cheeks pouched against the greasy upholstery of the armchair. Mouth slack open, her lips and gums pink like carnations, she was blissful in sleep, catching flies. His mother resting her eyes – forty winks, a little nap. It was all so visceral. *Boo! Wake up, Mom.*

Suddenly, William sensed Clara Morton's movements as if she were very close to him. He heard her husky breath. He smelt her perfume – old roses, like Turkish Delight. William stilled himself, shutting his eyes tight as if playing a game of hide-and-seek, but opened them immediately, feeling embarrassed at his foolishness. And she was there, next to him, looking at him looking at her painting. 'Mrs Morton, you said you wanted my advice. Is this a business meeting?'

She moved away from him, leading him back to the table now set for tea. The tea things were mismatched oddments, all beautiful and very old. Scraps from the main house, he thought. They were both silent as she poured. 'I have walnut cake, see.' She smiled and offered him a slice. 'Fullers. It's very nice.' William remained quiet. He needed her to be the first to talk. 'I'm terribly sorry for what must feel to you like cloak and dagger stuff,' she said. 'It just seemed to me that when I met you in Lyons, and you were so very kind, and then you gave me your card, and I saw you were a detective, I just thought you were a blessing or a sign from God, and that I must finally act, do something, and that you could help me.' She paused and blushed. 'Of course, I've only just realised that you may charge for the initial meeting. It's just that it's all so awkward and personal and –' she took a deep breath – 'rather shameful.'

'I've been in this kind of work for ten years now, and I've learnt that what my clients consider to be personal and rather shameful problems, and perhaps unique to them, is actually, if not universal, then a distinctly average situation. And I shan't charge for my advice today. And I cannot guarantee that I will take your case.'

'You called me Mrs Morton.'

'I know that you're married,' he said.

She felt the void of faded flesh on the third finger of her left hand. 'I've been married so long that the ring, even in its absence, is forever present. Like a tattoo or a scar.'

'How long have you been married?'

'Fourteen years.'

Her husband had told William ten. 'You don't look old enough to be married that long.' It wasn't flattery, for William was now compelled to be honest with Clara Morton.

'I'm twenty-nine years old.'

'You were married before the law on the age of consent changed,' he said.

'Yes.'

'You told me that you're from a mining family, and your husband –' William indicated the whole of the Morton estate with a broad sweep of his arm – 'is from quite a different background.'

'Quite different.' She poured herself more tea. William's cup was still full. 'Did you like my painting of the sleeping woman?'

'Yes, very much. She reminded me of my mother.'

'Do you want it?' she asked.

William laughed. 'I can't just accept something like that as a gift.'

'It wouldn't be a gift. It would be a payment. A sort of deposit for your work until I can . . .' She paused for a moment. 'Organise funds.'

'I don't know what kind of job you want me to do, yet. And you don't know my terms.' But William knew that Clara Morton could set any terms she wished. For him, it had gone that far. And now, startlingly, he cared nothing for her husband's money.

'I want to divorce my husband. I would like you to find grounds for a divorce.'

'Why do you want to divorce your husband, Clara?' Not to indulge in orgiastic party-going, no, not her. 'It's a messy business, particularly for the woman, and forgive me, it seems you live a rather good life as his wife. I know couples who lead very separate lives quite successfully, particularly if there are no children.'

'We have no children.'

William had spoken to desperate women before. He had let them down with bad news over their legal position many times. 'You have no grounds for divorce, as a woman, unless we can prove both adultery and cruelty. You personally have no grounds unless we can prove he beats you –' William paused – 'or he is incestuous, or he has committed acts of sodomy with you. And we would have to prove this in a court of law. These are the facts, and I'm so terribly sorry.' William drank his tea and waited for her to speak. She did not, and so he continued. 'Does he beat you, Clara? Has he sodomised you?'

66

Outside, the early evening sky clouded, so that the light inside the folly gave all it touched a soft metallic sheen, like pewter or unpolished armour.

She shook her head. 'He's an odd man. And he's growing increasingly odder. I've hardly seen him since early June, but when he has been at home, he's behaving like a child. He's weeping a lot. He's odd. He's rather frightening and strange at times, but he's never beaten me.' Clara Morton pushed her walnut cake about her plate. It was some moments before she spoke once more. 'He bought me, you know. I am literally Edward's chattel. And I cannot remain so. It's undignified. My marriage is degrading to me. I have a right to freedom.'

'Bought?' William had heard of beautiful working-class girls cherry-picked from the crop by wealthy men. Educated as ladies – all the natural mouth and brains refined out of them – and then set up as semi-permanent mistresses. But Clara Morton had become a wife.

'He bought me from my brother in 1919, when I was thirteen years old. I – I don't blame Stanley. Our parents died from Spanish flu, and he had had a terrible time in the war. Lungs all shot, and it made mining difficult. He rather numbed himself with drink.' William knew there were two types of miners: the Methodist kind who drank up tea and self-improvement, and the other kind who simply drank. 'He made Edward swear on the Bible that he would marry me, and then Edward gave him fifty pounds. I was sent to school in Switzerland for a few years. He married me as soon as he could.' She abandoned the cake and sipped at her tea with finishing-school finesse. 'He tells his friends I'm thirty-five. He's ashamed of what he's done. He knows it wouldn't play well in the sticks. What would the people of Leamington Spa think of his child bride?'

'Is that where he's aiming to run for Parliament?'

'Yes, the old Tory incumbent is dying of cancer. They say he won't last long.' She placed her teacup in its saucer. It rattled, stark. Clara looked down at the dregs. 'How did you know that?'

'Your husband told me about his political ambitions.'

She turned; her gaze was fixed, terrified. 'You're one of his fascists. Oh, God.'

'No,' he said, quiet, clear and deliberate. 'I have no particular politics. He consulted me as a private detective last Friday.'

Clara stood, toppling her chair to the ground. She looked at it briefly, gathered herself, and then leant, bracing her weight against the tea table. She was silent, and William saw her take several deep breaths. 'Oh, Christ. Oh, my Christ. Oh, no,' she whispered. 'This has all been deliberate. This meeting. Helping me with the sixpence at Lyons. Giving me your card. How did you know I was in Birmingham? I told no one I was going, not even Edward.'

'I didn't know who you were. I met you on Monday, and I consulted with your husband on Friday. I didn't know who you were until he showed me your photograph, honestly.' William moved towards her and placed a tentative hand on her shoulder. 'Please, Clara. I don't want to hurt you. It's the last thing on my mind.'

She shook him off. 'Oh God, what are you going to tell him?'

'Nothing.'

'I feel sick.' Then she let out a small animal-like moan. It was a familiar sound to William, the sound of a cornered, terrified woman, and he felt a jolt of shame. 'Why did you do this to me?' she asked. 'Is this a scam? Oh, God. He gives me no money. I have nothing. He keeps my jewels in a safe. I have nothing.' She rushed towards the door of the folly and stepped out into the silent clearing. 'Is this Edward playing one of his rotten games?'

And William, again, followed her, but at her heels this time, calling out, 'I don't think so, no.' Grey English light flickered through the canopy of larch trees. 'I'm pretty certain he has no idea we've met. I've been thinking about it a lot, this coincidence. My meeting with your husband was organised via a solicitor called Shirley and weeks before we met. It was all a coincidence, that day in Lyons. I'm sure of it.'

Clara turned towards him. 'He'll never divorce me, Mr Garrett,' she spat. She was so close, and she was so angry. 'I have to divorce him. If you're his lackey, then surely you must know that he will never let me go.' William felt her breath on his face. 'I don't know what your game is, or what Edward's game is, but don't try to persuade me that he wants a divorce. That will never happen.'

'He has no grounds for divorce.' A crow called out a hollow warning to an unknown woodland creature. 'I'm sure of that. However, I do think he'll divorce you, if he has grounds.'

'Then what are you doing here?'

'I like you. I like you, and I don't like him. You seemed so lonely. And I'm lonely, too. I think ... I think we have things in common.' William sensed her relax a little. 'I never should've taken the job. My instinct was that your husband was trouble, not a good person. I'm even having him followed. But the money was good. I'm swayed by money.' He felt himself blush. 'My friends say I'm driven by money.'

'What was the job? Tell me now and be honest.'

In truth, William had decided to be honest with Clara Morton the minute he set foot in the folly.

'He wanted to employ me, perhaps on a near-permanent basis, to note down your every move. He says he wants peace

of mind. He doesn't want to be humiliated, cuckolded.'
William winced at the word. 'He's been getting anonymous
letters. Explicit, he says. Although I've never seen them. I
think it's obsessing him rather. They say you've been with
other men. It's got him rattled.'

Clara let out a short, brittle laugh. 'I bet it has. He would
hate the thought of having me, his little girl, soiled.' She
appeared wearied, drained. 'Oh, God. Let's go and finish that
tea. I think you're an honest man, William Garrett. Please
don't prove me wrong.'

William left Hindford House with Clara Morton's painting
in the boot of his Austin. His first thought was that he would
telephone Edward Morton's secretary in the morning claim-
ing ill-health, or a sick mother, kindly refusing the rich man's
offer of work. However, another idea was taking root in his
mind. There would be a way to rescue Clara Morton from
her husband, a way he could use his skills and experience to
help, rather than entrap, a woman. It would be a moral act,
redemptive. William's silver armour glinted.

It was only after he drove past Hindford village church
that he remembered the murdered priest. William shivered.
Someone had traipsed over his grave.

9

Tuesday afternoon and William's office hummed with heat. He propped his window open with the stiffly rolled newspaper, but breezes were scarce and as soft as whispers. He had spent most of the morning, sitting at his desk, smoking, drinking tea, fantasising about Clara Morton, and planning (what he now called) her rescue. He was cast as a shabby knight errant in Clara Morton's drama and was aware of the foolishness of this self-imposed position. But, over the course of the day, he began to believe that in freeing Clara from her marriage, he would be redeemed for his own moral failures. It would be a payment to all the Winnie Woodcocks whose privacy he had invaded, a recompense for the humiliation he had caused. Helping Clara Morton would be a kind of salvation, William told himself. It would be a balancing of God's books.

But he was heavy with poor sleep and the heat of the day; the muscles in his shoulders ached, and his heart fluttered, and his mind raced with each thought of Clara. William lit another cigarette, distracting himself with tobacco and the morning paper. Germany was re-arming; the headlines were stark with Herr Hitler's antics. Mr Churchill had expressed his concern on the matter in the House of Commons. Mr Churchill was anxious about a future war. 'You and me both, pal,' William thought. There was a ring, sudden and shrill. He picked up the telephone receiver and spoke into it sharpish. 'William Garrett.' Perhaps it was Morton or his secretary. He hoped it was Clara.

'Come away with me to America.' It was Ronnie on the line.

The initial disappointment at hearing Ronnie's voice soon became a comfort. William settled into the routine of their relationship. 'You mad, romantic, impetuous fool. Don't you know I'm not that kind of girl?'

'That's not what I've heard.'

'Don't believe anything those rough boys tell you.' William's sweat continued to pool. 'What are you after, anyway?'

'I am after nothing, my child.' Ronnie was giddy with drink. 'In fact, Uncle Ronnie has come up trumps on the Morton case and intends to favour you with the skinny.'

'Christ, that was quick work.' William stood up, receiver wedged under his chin, and took off his tie. 'Spill it.'

'He's an immoral man. Rotten and stinking like graveside flowers.' There was a pause; Ronnie sniffed. 'I often think about morality. What it means. What's good. What's bad. Do you ever worry about the state of your soul, Billy?'

Ronnie was lying; he rarely thought of morality.

'Sometimes, no, never.' William sensed that Ronnie was nearing the maudlin phase of his drunkenness. 'I lose sleep over it, Ronnie. What do you know about Morton? Tell me, before the girl at the exchange interrupts.'

'Oh, don't concern yourself with that,' he replied. 'I have plenty of pennies; otherwise, I'd have reversed the charges.' Yes, he would've done that, if he was broke. A win on the horses, that's what he'd had, and all spent on drink and never his dues. He was pissed up at two-thirty in the afternoon and not a bookies' bill paid. 'But perhaps it's best for us to talk in person. Telephone boxes lack the necessary privacy. There's a chap waiting outside with quite a desperate look on his face. I can't tell if he wants to make an urgent call or if he needs a piss.'

William suddenly, and perhaps inexplicably, became worried for his friend. 'Early supper at the Grand tonight. At the chop house. Meet at six. Let me feed you, for God's sake.'

'How lovely. I can dress up.'

'Ronnie, we can both dress up.'

Ronnie laughed, and William heard the click-buzz of a terminated call.

The Grand was Birmingham's pleasure palace, like one of those places in France; the hotels in Le Touquet where generals drank champagne. Fancy with stucco and stone, white as a wedding cake, it faced down the cathedral, bigger and brasher than the house of God. William arrived at the restaurant dead on time, and Ronnie was waiting for him outside the main door looking every inch a toff. His suit was off the peg, but you wouldn't know it. He had the figure for clothes: hips slender, shoulders broad, hairline resolute, Ronnie was a work of art. But it was a practised stylishness. William had been a key witness to Ronnie's evolution. Once a desperate boy, gawky in khaki, Ronnie was clever enough to know that he was fighting for an England that could not value him. Cannon fodder, then factory fodder; no, not for Ronnie. He aped his betters, learnt their manners, corrected the unacceptable, and made himself smooth and shiny, like a water-worn pebble. And he gave the approaching William a cold appraising stare. 'You look like a gangster in a movie. I hate to say it, but you're far too hulking for evening dress. You're simply not elegant.'

'Thank you for the beauty tips, Gary Cooper. Are you hungry?' William was.

'I'm rarely hungry.' He ran his fingers through his hair. 'Nevertheless, I intend to make inroads on the wine list.'

William followed as Ronnie marched into the Grand like a prize-fighter, a welterweight, entering the ring, brash and triumphant, and looking to cause a stir. But it was still early, so the restaurant was empty save for an elderly man, a King's Counsel, who William knew had a reputation as a hanging judge. The windows were open a crack, and the smell of yesterday's tobacco and today's floor polish was strong. Waiters' heads turned, but slightly.

William smiled. 'Men come here to eat meat in silence.' It was his sort of place.

'Darling, it's absolutely perfect for you.' Ronnie grinned and rubbed at his nose. 'But I sense these people don't appreciate me.'

'A table for two, sir?' The waiter was well-trained. A superior sort of servant who passes judgement but, unlike the elderly barrister at the corner table, kept his own counsel.

'Yes, and can you bring us two large whiskies.' Ronnie was bent on maintaining his binge.

They were seated in a booth well away from the man of law. William opened the leather-bound menu and pointed. 'Look, this is what you need to go for, Les Grills.'

The waiter brought the drinks.

'Thank you, William. I'm still on the entrées.' Ronnie peered at the close type and sighed. 'I think I may need spectacles. I simply cannot bear the ageing process.' He glanced at the King's Counsel.

'I know what we'll have: Chateaubriand.' William was decided.

'Are you flush?'

William looked him straight in the eye, raised his glass and whispered, 'No, but I just feel the need to celebrate for some reason.'

The waiter returned. William ordered the steak, bloody, and a bottle of good claret. It was quick and soundless service, for the meal and wine arrived just as the Scotch was finished. Then two old men were seated near them, scalps like rice paper, bony and hunched, looking like vultures in their black evening dress. William watched as the blood pooled on his plate. He took a gulp of the red wine. Tannins, like stewed tea, coated his tongue and teeth.

After the meal, William's plate clean, and Ronnie's less so, they ordered coffee and brandy. William patted his belly like a plutocrat in a *Punch* cartoon.

Ronnie lit a cigarette. 'Come away with me. We're not too old.'

'Away with you?' William laughed; for a moment, it did sound as if Ronnie were proposing an elopement.

'Yes, to America. We could go right now. Escape. Pack everything up and get the first train to Liverpool. There's opportunity in America. You could be a real detective, like the ones in the pictures.'

'That's an oxymoron, Ronnie.'

'I can't bear this city, Billy.' Ronnie waved towards the elderly men. He raised his voice. 'You feel it, too. There's nothing for me here. It's a backwater. Look at them all. They disgust me.'

'For God's sake, keep it down.' William glanced about the room, checking that Ronnie could not be heard over the low hum of chatter. Ronnie became silent. The waiter was approaching, laden with a tray of cut glass, china and silver plate. The man placed the coffee pot and brandy on the table with decorous care.

It wasn't until the waiter left that Ronnie turned to William and smiled. 'Darling, you're right. I'm getting hysterical, and that will never do for a man of my obvious virility.' He glanced at his watch. 'Anyway, I'm here to report on this Morton fellow and collect promised expenses.' Ronnie finished his double brandy in two large gulps. 'Never let it be said that I'm not all business.'

'That's the quickest I've ever known you work.' William poured them both a coffee. 'Did you hire a motor by yourself?'

'I'm quite capable of doing so. I know a terribly nice chap on Bristol Street who'll lend you a car by the week. He cares nothing for licences, but he is profoundly fond of cash.' He reached into his breast pocket and handed William a crumpled receipt. 'Here's a chit from the fellow. Do you want to hear my news, or not?'

William accepted the chit. 'You're obviously excited, Dr Watson. Tell me.'

'I find Morton quite repellent.'

'His person or his morals?' asked William.

'I rarely make moral judgements. You know that.' The waiter brought Ronnie another brandy. 'Although there are certain types of chap who are absolutely beyond the pale.'

'For example?'

'For starters, he keeps a very young girl all set up in a modern flat out near the university. Too much rouge and silk to be the marrying kind.' Ronnie drank down his double. 'I believe she's paid to service Mr Morton in her fully serviced flat. Regular as clockwork, so the rather disapproving neighbours say.'

'How young is the mistress?'

'Fifteen or so, maybe even younger. Like I said, *trop de maquillage*. But ...' Ronnie paused. 'She's a tiny little thing. She's as thin as a whip, even in a serge skirt and jackboots.'

William drank his brandy and began to sweat. 'Jackboots?'

'Billy, you're perspiring rather.'

'It's the brandy, or the meat, or maybe the heat.' William paused, and wiped his face with a linen napkin as big as a cot sheet. 'Either way, it's bloody killing me. Is the kid a fascist?'

'I thought Girl Guides, at first. But no, the child is a Blackshirt.' Ronnie, red-eyed, waved to the waiter and asked for more brandy. He paused for a moment, and then said, 'There's much more, too. The things I know about that man ... Well, Morton's laundry is quite filthy. He's the sort of man Queenie would pull apart with her bare hands.' Ronnie laughed at the joyous thought of it.

And William joined him. 'Oh Christ, yes,' he laughed. 'Give Queenie Mr Morton's particulars and she will solve all our problems.'

There was a pause.

'Morton's a problem?' asked Ronnie.

William told his friend everything. From the accidental meeting with Clara Morton in the tea rooms to their secret rendezvous at the folly.

'So the lady sought your services, eh? Now that is terribly interesting.' Ronnie mused for a moment. 'Although one can't blame her. If he were mine, I would divorce him. He's a horrible sweating thing.' Ronnie, cool and assessing, now sipped at his coffee. 'He's even worse than you, old dear. Billy, you really must stop this high living –' Ronnie motioned to the mess on the dining table – 'or you will ruin your looks.' William sucked in his nascent gut. 'Morton will be speaking at a rally with the equally vile Mosley this Sunday. I should think the jackbooted courtesan will be there too. Why not go and report back to the lady?'

'Whereabouts?'

'The Bull Ring. Four o'clock. After Evensong but home in time for late tea. Christ, I'm beginning to hate this fucking city. This whole fucking country.' Ronnie laughed to himself, huskily humourless. Sometimes William would see the old Ronnie flare; for just a moment, the vowels would broaden, and the muscles would tense. 'Why are we all so provincial and so horribly vulgar?'

William rose and opened the nearest window wide, but he sensed that he was only letting in the heat of the evening and that the air would get no fresher. The cathedral clock rang eight o'clock. He returned to his seat, lit a cigarette and thought for a moment. Then the weather broke. Those heavy, purple clouds, which had sagged stormy all day, burst like a salvo. Finally, he said, 'He doesn't beat her, Ronnie.'

'You're talking about the wife.'

'Yes.'

'Then the lady is stuck. She can have no divorce, despite her husband's dalliances with slender little *fascistas*.'

'Not necessarily.' Above the rain, William could hear a band begin to play in a far-off room, an old-fashioned tune, something easy to dance to, romantic, a waltz. 'I want to keep Morton on the books for a week or two. Send him the reports on Clara's movements that he wants. Keep him sweet and happy. I want you to keep an eye on him, too. You seem to have a knack for it, and the more we know about him, the better. Then, eventually, we can provide him with the evidence that his wife is unfaithful. She says he'll never divorce her, but I think he will if his hand is forced. He told me he didn't want to look like a cuckold in front of Mosley and his cronies. Morton will want the divorce to be over and done with before he runs for Parliament.' Now he had spoken his plans out loud, they felt more solid. And the more he talked, the more confidence he had that the whole scheme could work. His brandy headache suddenly shifted as if by miracle.

'Oh, I see. And what does the lady think to your proposal?' Ronnie asked.

'I haven't told her yet.' Behind him, the legs of a chair scraped against the parquet flooring. William turned. The King's Counsel was leaving the premises. 'It would be a redemption for all the Winnie Woodcocks we've set up. Think of it like that.'

'Shifty will have your guts, Billy. He would hate to have you mucking about with one of his rich chums like that.' Ronnie emptied the sugar bowl out on the table, lining the lumps in perfect formation, like soldiers during drill. William sensed his friend's boredom. 'Anyway, I thought you were a businessman,' Ronnie continued. 'Why jeopardise your main source of income and –' Ronnie looked up from his regiment and grinned – 'more importantly, mine?'

'Shifty will be alright as long as Morton never finds out it was a set-up.' William leant across the table, gathering the sugar-lump soldiers and placing them back in barracks. 'We should meet with Clara together. Suggest it – you know, documenting a fake affair. Let her know we know what we're doing. That we've done it before. That we're professionals.' William spoke the last word without the associated confidence. 'It would be a comfort to her.'

79

'Oh my goodness.' Ronnie swung back on the legs of his chair like a child. 'Oh, dearie me.'

'You don't like the idea?'

'I think you're terribly smitten. Oh, my dear.'

'No. I just want to help.' William felt himself blush. 'I want to save her from him.'

'You read too many novels, and it's given you a romantic view of life.' Ronnie gestured to the waiter for the bill. He wouldn't be paying of course, but the click of the fingers was impressive. 'I shan't have time for these dramatic rendezvous you seem to go in for nowadays. Although I can do the job, nice and easy, I should think. Arrange everything, like you usually do, darling. I'm far too busy to comfort the disenchanted wives of tinpot dictators.'

'Busy?'

'I have many irons in the fire, my dear. I've never been busier.'

IO

Sunday, 2 July

The Blackshirt rally was as English as a works picnic. The Bull Ring crowd, all silly with sunshine and making the best of the weather, gathered outside a locked St Martin's. Women in print frocks handed sandwiches and boiled eggs to their menfolk. These men, wages clerks and grammar school teachers in well-brushed suits, slapped each other's backs and made hearty jokes. Someone had a flask of tea. William worried that soon there might be a sack race. He looked about the political mob for Morton and his jackbooted mistress, but he saw only Clara.

He had haunted her all week and regularly reported her innocence to her husband. The visit to the haberdashery at Lewis's for mending thread, taking tea at a café, a trip to the cinema for a matinee, William was a ghost in her small life. It shocked him to see Clara Morton in the Bull Ring, as for the first time since Wednesday, William hadn't been shadowing her.

She stood apart from the jolly middle classes, near another type of men, neither respectable like the mob, nor rich like Edward Morton, but sweating in their flat caps and bagged-out woollen jackets. They were short and squat; shoulders broad and hard, they rolled fags and avoided chatter. William felt a shiver of unease.

Then he noticed her approach. He was no longer a ghost. 'Does my husband know you're here?' she asked.

He smiled and shook his head. 'No. Does my client know his wife is here?'

Clara Morton's mouth was heart-shaped. 'No. He would be terribly surprised to find me at one of his jamborees. I'd hate for him to spot me.'

'Then why come?' William pointed towards the hard-cased working-men. 'Why stand with the Commies?'

'To assess his capabilities.' She squinted against the sun. 'To gauge his sincerity, to see his followers, to get a feel for the future.'

'Bleak.' William lit a cigarette. 'That's my prediction.'

Suddenly, the crowd parted as two flag-bearers marched towards the large wooden platform in the centre of St Martin's Square. William watched as the Union Flag fluttered in the gentle English breeze. And, amidst the usual red, white and blue, was the thick dead spider of a swastika.

Clara nodded to a flag-bearer. 'Those flagpoles must be terribly heavy.'

'Too heavy for a girl,' he said. The women were neat and stony-faced, their uniforms pressed and starched; young muscles and self-importance would see them through. William wondered if one of them was Morton's mistress, but neither girl looked the type.

'They're managing, though. And their gloves are spotless. Quite admirable really,' she said.

'You think?'

'No, honestly . . .' She faltered, and then looked him square in the eye. 'I'm simply being facetious. I'm facetious about fascists. Really, I suppose I don't know whether it makes me want to laugh or cry. And you, what do you think?'

William thought conversation with Clara Morton was an easy pleasure. He glanced towards her and suddenly felt as though God had ripped a rib from his chest. William inhaled at his cigarette – a comfort, a distraction. 'Me, I think it's just human nature. We get tribal when we sense danger, and we think tribalism protects us. It doesn't.' William took another long drag. 'I didn't offer you one. That was rude.' He passed the packet to Clara. She shook her head. William saw frustration or anger burgeoning in her wide eyes.

'But they *are* the danger, don't you see?' She motioned towards the crowd, squinting in the summer sun. 'People like this, who are so very terrified of . . . what? Change, I suppose. Degradation, poverty? They believe so much bile and tell so many lies. And they look so innocent and talk so reasonably. Terrible things are happening in Italy, in Germany, and now here.' She paused. 'It's a sort of international disease of the mind.'

William shrugged his shoulders. He knew what she was trying to say, but he couldn't bear to help her say it. They were everywhere. Little men with big slogans, calling for scapegoats, making the trains run on time. No, not here. William liked his trains running late. 'It's because of the war. They need order. They need to believe in something. Need to follow something. I don't know. God is dead, so they need demigods. Jesus, what about the Kindred of the Kibbo Kift?'

She smiled at him, wide and beautiful. 'Aren't they those types who float about in homespun and make tree houses in Cannon Hill Park? You know, vegetarians, fresh-air fiends. Harmless, surely?'

83

William nodded. 'Calling themselves Greenshirts now. They march in green and talk about social credit. It's a fashion, all this marching.'

Clara guffawed.

'This lot ...' William pointed to a group of young men, engineers or draughtsmen probably, or perhaps junior civil servants busy Monday to Friday doling out the dole. 'They're just in it for the charabancs to Weston and the clubhouse. Like the Scouts but with cheap beer and fighting. It's not like abroad. We haven't got it in us, not revolution. We could have done it in 1917 like the Russians. Look at the General Strike, just a damp squib.'

'I like the flags, though. Sort of pantomime, sort of old English. You know, like the mummers and the morris.' She was right. There was a May Day feel to the Bull Ring, something febrile and giddy, men in fancy dress, all set up for fighting and fucking.

'Very colourful, apart from the shirts,' he said.

'And we're off.' She nodded towards a man a head taller than most of the mob, travelling through his people. Mosley was handsome with moustaches and good nutrition, self-assured and glad-handing his followers, smiling and waving, smiling and waving. 'Good Lord, he's nothing but a fourth-rate Il Duce, yet they all love him so,' she whispered.

Mosley was accompanied by a tall man, a military type, another local politician perhaps, slender and stiff with a long face, hard muscles beneath his conservative suit; his moustache was a mimic of Mosley's. And with them both, wallowing in scraps of their reflected glory, was Edward Morton, fat, sweating and beautifully tailored. William felt Clara stiffen by his side. 'He can't see us because we're too far back,' he said, 'and importantly, he's not looking for us.'

'You sound very sure of that.'

'It's part of my job.' He nodded towards her and said, 'Keep your hat on. Your red hair catches the eye. No sharp or agitated moves. Stand with the crowd but not in the centre. Keep far right or far left of the mob, depending on your politics.' He watched her smile. 'I mean just keep at the periphery of his vision.'

'Now I *am* nervous.' Clara pulled her hat over her eyes and turned to him. 'Do I look like one of your best operatives?'

'Yes. Absolutely.'

Four girls, stark in black in the summer sun, processed towards the platform and stood sentry either side of the make-shift stage, and beside the girls, a group of men, scrubbed and shorn, clicked their polished boots to attention. Mosley stepped up and motioned to the crowd for silence.

'Is my husband still your client?' she asked. 'It's what you said earlier, I mean.'

'He thinks he is,' William said. 'I thought it best not to arouse his suspicions.' Mosley's audience was quiet now, very polite, achingly expectant. William could hear the leaves of the hornbeams rustle with a gust of summer wind. 'It could work in our favour.'

'What do you mean by that?' She turned and smiled. 'I like the way you used the word "our", by the way.'

'Our organisation began as a men's movement: because we had too much regard for women to expose them to the geni-alities of the broken bottles and razor blades with which our Communist opponents conducted the argument.' Mosley's voice was high and nasal, but he needed no notes.

'We shouldn't talk about it here,' William said, 'but I've been thinking over your case. I believe I've got a solution. I know I can help you.'

'Why are men so self-confident? I'm always baffled by it.'

It was still hot, but the sky had darkened. 'It may rain,' he said.

'It may,' she replied.

'A senior appointment in each district is that of Women's District Leader.' Mosley motioned to his fellow fascists. A small woman, a girl William had not yet noticed, moved away from the entourage of Blackshirts which flanked Mosley's stage. She mounted the platform, and stood between the men, rouged mouth smiling tight-lipped, and waved to the crowd with a closed hand. Edward Morton's grin was as rigid as his politics. The fat man placed his hand on the girl's shoulder and stroked it, as if she were a fractious cat. Morton's mistress, William thought, for she fitted Ronnie's description very well indeed.

'We should go for a drink,' said Clara. 'Talk things through. Tell me your news.'

William glanced at his watch. 'Are they still open?' He had seen enough, and so, perhaps, had Clara.

'Come to the museum. Buy me something from the tea rooms. Then we can have fun looking at all the Victoriana if that's to your taste?' Clara Morton spoke like a child desperate to skip school.

'A national movement built in a country where there is a majority of women does not deserve its title unless the women have within it opportunities and responsibilities commensurate with their numerical importance.' There was a smattering of applause from the women in the crowd. The men nodded, tuppenny patriarchs one and all.

'God, he loves women.' William lit another cigarette, offered one to Clara, but again she refused.

'Hadn't you heard? The man's an absolute wolf.'

'What are your tastes, Clara?'

'There's a Canaletto here. It's beautiful and we have the canals in common.'

'We appeal to all Britons, men and women, who love their country and who are proud of the great heritage of British Empire, to do their part to save Britain from sinking to the level of a third-rate power. Britain First.' It was what the mob was waiting for. They roared, approving, and stamped their feet.

'Venice, the Doges, ancient Roman ruins, that kind of thing,' William said.

'I remember now that you're not a complete beginner. I had you pegged for something of an autodidact.'

'I have some experience, and a lot of interest.' And then he added, 'In art.'

'Guard that sacred flame, my brother Blackshirts, until it illumines Britain and lights the path of mankind. Britain First.'

'Did he just use the word *illumines*? God, look at them all, just lapping him up,' said William.

'We should leave before they start their song.' Clara looked about the crowd, worried.

'They sing?' Marching songs, he thought, in synchronism and as one voice, all in tune but none particularly outstanding.

'Yes, it's horrible.'

William placed his hand on the small of Clara's back and made to motion her through the crowd. They were too late to avoid the singing, which was sung heartily like a school hymn.

'Blackshirt scum.' It was a working-man, calling from the edge of the crowd, shouting against the music of the mob. A few glanced at him, but they were only vaguely irritated, as though he had coughed during a play. 'Birmingham workers fight against fascism. Fight against the Jew-hater Mosley.' His fellow workers spoke out, galvanised now. But they had always been galvanised, for they were union men. And so, they too burst into song, the workmen and a few others dotted amongst the fascist pack.

William turned to Clara. 'They're singing the Internationale.' But she looked him in the eye and then sang out too. He tried to lead her by the arm, but she resisted. 'No, please. We must leave,' he whispered. 'This will turn nasty.'

She paused and shook her head. 'I know what song it is. My father and my brother, they sang it. Before Edward. When I was young, I mean. Please wait. Or sing it with me in solidarity.' But William could sense them, these men. There was a storminess to them and soon they would thunder. 'I feel guilty. Responsible. If I don't stand with them,' she said, 'if I run away, what kind of person does that make me?'

And then it came. Someone pushed through the crowd and made his way towards a flag-bearer. He was a big man, much bigger than the girl, and he tugged at her flagpole. The big man wrestled with it and she defended, holding fast. For a moment, it was nothing but a comic tussle. Until he hoisted the pole with such force that the little fascist was lifted too, her feet dangling comically as the man bounced her and smiled, grinning to the crowd. A few people laughed when her spectacles flew off in the fray. And then she fell, hitting her head against the speaker's platform with a sickening thud. Those with jackboots used them, and the big man was beaten to the ground. They clustered around him until he was nothing more than a jolting, quivering heap. The more respectable couples now fled, the middle-aged and the women mostly gone, it was only the young men who were left, and they fought hard. William thought a few of them to be students from the university or the art school. A boy in Oxford bags leapt onto the back of a Blackshirt, kicking hard at the man's flanks, punching at his ears until he fell. The older men aimed their blows with more economy, brutal to bellies and jaws. Some had razors in their caps, like the old days, and threw potatoes studded with glass. William had seen it before, street against street, English against Irish, the union against the blackleg, Villa against City. This is what men did, and it meant nothing. A few Blackshirts bustled their leader, the tall politician, the little lady *fascista* and Morton away. Mosley looked about him, confused, childlike, at the carnage he had created. And the pamphlets, which pretty girls had been handing around Birmingham with smiles and sincerity just a few minutes before, fluttered about him like blossom.

Clara was distant from William now. The mob had moved her towards the heart of the fighting. Shoving her forward with them, jostling her with their shoulders. They were oblivious of her, and she faced away from them, swam against the tide of them. Was it her husband or William she looked for? No matter, for when he called to her, she waved like a woman drowning. He barged through, using every pound of his bulk, elbows sharp into the ribs of others, some gut punches. 'Leave her be, leave her fuckin' be.' He grabbed her by the waist, held her firm to his chest, against the shifting press of men, which was a moving thing, alive and always moving, until suddenly they were alone.

'Thank you,' she said. 'Thank you.' Clara's glance drifted back towards the brawl. 'I couldn't seem to move. I tried, but they wouldn't let me move.' She was flushed, and her hat was askew. He saw a thin trickle of sweat fall and puddle into the cleft of her collarbone. 'All of a sudden, I feel very tired.'

'It's the shock. We should leave now before someone calls the coppers.'

'Don't you know?' she said. 'They're already here.'

William looked around; as yet he could see no uniforms other than the black and red of Mosley's men. 'Did you come by train?' Clara nodded. 'Then let me drive you home. My car is close by.'

'No, I shouldn't really.'

The Communists were fighting hard, beating off boys from the suburbs, Lord Rothermere's boys, who feared foreigners and trades unions and the masses. Class war was not real war. They knew nothing of real war, not yet. William turned his back on them all. 'This is no place for either of us.' He brushed her hair, sticky now, away from her eyes. It was a proprietorial act. 'We need to go.'

Clara glanced towards the empty platform, and then she nodded and said, 'Alright, yes. Take me to the folly, William. Edward won't be home until late.'

II

Clara began to doze beside him before they were out of Birmingham. The city had thinned out, becoming first the suburbs and then just a few straggling villas. Then the road narrowed into a country lane, a drovers' lane of ancient, twisted boundaries, flanked by hedgerows heavy with hawthorn and cow parsley, their petals rotting brown. William stopped the car. The sudden jolt woke Clara, who fell forward and braced herself against the dashboard of the Austin. They said nothing, for they were trespassers, and their accuser stood on his hind legs. He was the colour of late summer, and his body quivered, not in fear, but in readiness. A lean and muscled creature in the centre of the road, glorious and powerful, the hare stood his ground.

'Have you ever seen one before?' Clara's voice was muddy with sleep.

'They say they box in spring.'

'Have you ever seen it?' she asked.

'No, I'm a city boy.' The only farmland William knew was foreign. And they had killed it. War had killed it.

'Oh, I'd like to see that. I'd like to paint that,' she said.

'Should I use my horn?' he asked.

'No. Wait.'

But the hare had given his warning. He would let them pass, for they were humble enough, and so he bounded away in three magic leaps towards the wheat field and the scattered clumps of the Arden beyond.

'Not far now,' she said. The road was soon bordered with oaks so full and wide that their canopy became a tunnel of dark leaves. 'Turn right here.' Clara spoke as if she could sense home.

William obeyed and turned the car onto the now familiar gravel drive. Sheep and small red cattle grazed the flanking pasture, and the manor shone low and soft in the afternoon light.

'Drive to the rear of the house,' she said. 'You can park near the stables. Then we can satisfy your sweet tooth with more tea and cake.'

William laughed. 'You already know me too well. It's my chief failing.'

'One I share.' She was hatless now and ran her fingers through her hair. 'All we seem to do together is dodge fascists and eat cake.'

'It's the difficult times we live in,' he said.

William pulled the car up to a halt outside a bolted and padlocked stable block as instructed. Clara sat quite still in the passenger seat and glanced about at the pointless splendour of the carriage house and tack room. 'There's no staff here,' she said. 'I love this place. It's so beautiful and so old, and we're quite safe.' She turned to him. 'To talk about your plan, I mean.'

'Like I said earlier, I think I've found a way to help you.'

'While you're still in my husband's employment?' William didn't reply. 'I shouldn't trust you,' she said, 'you know that. And yet I do.'

'I believe his mistress was the girl we saw him with on Mosley's platform.' The heat in the Austin became stifling, so William opened his door wide to the cool, shaded air of the courtyard. 'She's the new Women's District Leader, whatever the hell that means.'

'Yes, I saw him touch her, and I thought her Edward's type.' Clara moved to leave the motor. 'He's dressed her up to suit his needs, poor child.' William got out before her and opened the door, a gentleman once more. 'But his adultery does not help me,' she said. 'You made it rather clear last time we met.'

'It does if he intends to remarry.' For a moment, William thought he smelt hay and leather, as if the courtyard were haunted by long-dead thoroughbreds.

'A political alliance with the fascist girl, is that what you're thinking?' Together, William and Clara walked towards the bridge which led to the folly. 'Somehow, I can't see Edward thinking that way. It doesn't square right with what I know of his personality.'

'And what is his personality, Clara?' he asked.

'One of pathological acquisition.'

They were in the ruined rose garden. To William, it now seemed oppressive. The flowers neglected and rangy, their heavy heads drooping, nodding against the thorns. William halted at the banks of the river. 'Christ, what do you mean?'

'That I am his possession, bought and paid for, like a colliery or a factory premises. That I am beholden to him because he rescued me from my class.'

'Good God, woman.' William looked across the river and saw ancient ground, pitted and ridged with the remains of stew pond and culvert, dotted with tufted grass, fleece, and sheep shit. 'Rescued from your class? Wherever did you get that notion from? I've never heard such tripe.'

Clara Morton laughed, hearty and full-throated. 'I may have read that in a book. Does it sound like D. H. Lawrence to you?'

'Easily. He writes a lot of words about how women feel. When they ring true, I reckon it's just because he's played the odds right.'

'You're a reader?'

'I read a lot. I smoke a lot. I eat a lot.' William gave her a knowing look. 'I think too much. Yes, I think far too much. I reckon that just about sums me up.'

Crows spied at them from the tops of the knots of elm trees which bordered the distant marshy field. They let out a collective squawk and flew from their perches. William and Clara, as if startled into action by the birds, moved to cross the bridge.

'Edward doesn't read, and he doesn't think; he simply plots,' she said. 'He has no intelligence, but he does have cunning.' Clara laughed once more, but this time it was brittle. 'I don't know why I'm laughing. I'm stuck with him, and I feel so ashamed of him, and myself. He's stupid, William. I think that's what I can't forgive, ultimately. I can accept his mistresses; in fact, I feel sorry for them, poor dears. I . . . I empathise. At a push, I could accept his venality, if he had other qualities. God, I'm so ashamed. If he had charm, I could accept so much more, but he's so very charmless.' Her voice rose slightly, sounding out into the empty country air. 'It's his stupidity that I can't accept. It's a special sort of stupidity, and one that makes him oblivious to his own deficiencies. Sometimes, when he talks, I feel ashamed to be associated with him. It's a terrible way to feel about one's husband.' She paused at the middle of the bridge. The river below ran dark and quick, and the pondweed splayed and drifted like a woman's hair. 'I've known for a long time that I care little for his money. I'm no clothes horse. I look ridiculous in the jewels he gives me.' William listened, watching the fish, small and swift, dart in the water's shadows. 'I'd rather work in a shop and live in a bed-sitting room. At least then I would be a person. I'm not a person to Edward. I'm a sort of doll, to be owned, and to be used when needed.'

'Then we use this against him. You say he doesn't see you as a person. At the moment, he sees you as a sort of perfect doll-like figure. Then we change his conception of you. We make you valueless, a possession not worth having,' he said.

'You mean that I become the harlot described in the poison-pen letters.' The body of a sheep, its bloated belly acting as a grotesque float, drifted downstream. They viewed its progress in respectful silence, until the corpse bobbed beneath the bridge and on to – where? The River Severn and the sea? Clara turned to him once more and said, 'Do you think it's a bad omen?'

'No, I think it's a dead sheep,' he replied, doubtful of his own self-confidence. They crossed the bridge and were soon on the meandering path amidst the dark canopy of redwoods. 'We don't have to recreate the pornographic ramblings of a fantasist, you know. That would be ridiculous. We must simply fake evidence of an affair. Your husband has employed me to follow you. I'll simply send him reports of a dalliance. Nothing too outrageous. Just you with a handsome man and a nice hotel room. I would need to take photographs of you with the man. Half-naked should just do it. Force his hand and make him divorce you, so that he might marry his fascist bride and live happily ever after in black-shirted bliss.'

'It all seems rather complicated and ridiculous.'

'It's not complicated. I've done it before. I have a friend, an actor I trust, we can call on him. But it is shoddy, I know.'

'And of course, you still collect Edward's fee. Very clever, Mr Garrett.'

William stopped walking and looked upwards. Above the black-green canopy was a touch of warmth, sunlight. And beyond the treetops was a circling buzzard. 'It's not about the money, not this time. You can have my fee as a gift. You can use it to set yourself up in a bed-sitting room. I doubt you'll get much of a settlement from him. His solicitor will be far too good. No, it's not about the money. I think I just want to do right by you. I just want to be a decent man.'

She touched his arm. 'Forgive me. That was low of me. But know this, I don't want anything more from Edward. I'm not sure I can bear any more of his gifts.' Her face was flushed and dark. 'Give his fee to a home for wayward girls or something.'

They followed the path until they reached the small clearing and the folly. Clara, once more, unlocked the door. The room smelt of Ashes of Roses and turpentine. 'Let me open the window. It's so stuffy.' Clara threw her hat, pin and all, onto a low gramophone tucked into an alcove by the fireplace, and then unfastened both windows, wide.

'May I take my jacket off?' William attempted good manners.

'You may as well relax. Pop it over a chair or something,' she said.

William placed his jacket over the arm of the chaise longue, and then he rolled up his shirtsleeves.

'Do you want a bacon sandwich?' She paused. 'I'm very hungry. I always eat when I'm fagged out or anxious.' She clattered about at her electric stove with kettle and frying pan. William walked over to the open door and surveyed the woodland. The stillness unsettled him. A faint breeze shook the treetops, but the crows, squatting high in the canopy, remained silent, watchfully guarding their tall nests. Something made the forest air fizz. Clara came towards him, her face thoughtful. 'I think your work makes you paranoid. There's no one here.' William knew that they could not take that for granted. She stood close to him, side by side in the door jamb. He smelt roses again. 'Edward rarely visits Hindford. It was a place his father loved, and Edward did not love his father. What I've done to the folly is a sort of secret from him.' She may have blushed. 'He lets the manor go to rack and ruin despite the villagers' protests, but places like this should be maintained if only to give country people work.' The kettle whistled, commanding Clara's attention. 'He has no sense of history or responsibility.'

He turned to her and smiled. 'I like your folly, Clara. It's all very nice.'

And then she said: 'I think you're the most attractive man I've ever met.' Clara moved away from him and took the kettle off the stove, but she did not look at him. William, for a moment, held his breath. 'I've never said that to anyone before, you know. But I think you're very attractive and very good. I think you have many good qualities, William.'

She had a fearlessness to her. To say it, to just come out and say it; he admired her bravery and wanted to tell her how he felt, and that he reciprocated. That he appreciated her confidence and friendship and beauty. Instead, he asked, 'Do you need any help with the tea?'

Clara shook her head, but William followed her to the small kitchen area. She handed him a tray of sandwiches, one bitten, the imprint of her small strong teeth on the white bread. She smiled at him. 'I couldn't help it. I was so hungry.' Clara spooned tea into a waiting teapot then filled it with boiling water. They walked towards the table silently, shoulder to shoulder, arms, wrists, knuckles touching briefly. William set down the food.

She surveyed the meal, turned to him and said: 'A scratch tea, but it's nice. Small pleasures, we must take them where we can.'

'Yes, I agree.' William moved forward, cupped her cheek gently with his hand and rubbed a few sticky breadcrumbs from the side of her mouth. 'I'm sorry, Clara. For your circumstances. What happened to you. I think you deserve better. Kindness, friendship, love, I don't know.'

Clara nodded, closed her eyes for a scant moment and then kissed his palm.

Then she came in close. Running the nail of her index finger along his jawline, scratching at his five o'clock shadow, she outlined the muscles of William's neck until her fingers reached the base of his hairline. Clara stroked the soft bristle of the nape of his neck and trailed her other hand along his chest. And moved in, took his bottom lip in her mouth, ran her tongue so gently over it.

He could smell the bacon in her hair, the perfume of fresh sweat and roses on her damp skin; he saw her nails thick with oil paint. She kissed him again, traced the muscle of his shoulders, felt them hard underneath the cotton of his shirt, and played, tentatively, as though amazed, with the rough hair on his arms. She touched the scar. 'Bullet wound?'

'No, shrapnel.'

'I'm so very sorry.' *She meant it. She meant it.* Clara kissed the scar.

Slowly, she undid the buttons of his shirt, and then nuzzled into his neck. Kissing the lobes of his ears this time, she whispered, 'At the art school they taught us how to look. It's the difference, you see – between men and women. It's the difference that matters.' Clara wore no powder on her skin, but a red slash of lipstick stained her mouth. It was smudged a little now.

'I . . . I don't know what you mean.' Clara manoeuvred herself so that he could feel the roundness of her thigh between his legs, her breasts against his chest. He felt suddenly foolish with his shirt tails out, half-undressed like a boy, with this woman.

'I am soft,' she said. 'Can you feel that? The softness, I mean. And men –' the curve of her pressed against him – 'and men are not. When you're taught to look, to observe what a man is, it's good. I like it, this difference.' She explored the waistband of his trousers, lingered as she unbuttoned his fly. She touched his flesh, felt him harden further and ran her hand along the length of him.

He fumbled with her frock, the zipper was at her waist; tugged at the summer fabric until it fell beyond her shoulders, and buried his head in her breasts, heavy in their brassiere, and thought he heard her heart pound. By then his hands were at her arse, all rounded and easy.

'Yes, it's alright,' she whispered. 'I do want to.'

William grabbed her – picked her up and placed her on the tea table amongst the china cups. He shifted her slip and the skirt of her dress up to her waist, felt the soft inch or two of skin between her stocking tops and thighs. They paused. She unhooked her girdle, flipped the fasteners off her stockings, laughed as she let her knickers drop and ran her leg against the inside of his thigh. He moved forward, glanced his lips against her skin from the mouth down to her nipple, which stood lovely under silk, brushed his hand between her legs, felt her quiver.

'Yes,' she said.

William placed his head between her thighs, rested his cheek against the tenderness of her. Then he kissed her. Clara was right about the difference.

12

The windows were wide open to the Sunday evening air, and the afternoon light had shone golden on them both. This was new for William. Until then, sex had always been a quiet act, done with gratitude in the dark. Soft as feathers she had been, and when they were finished, the tea things were a mess on the floorboards. They tidied away the china, giggling like naughty children. When twilight came, Clara whispered, 'I think we're in trouble.'

William kissed her with all the tenderness he could muster. 'You know I have a plan. We can force him to divorce you.' William remembered Morton's use of the word *rectitude*. 'We can stage an affair just as I've said. I know it will work.'

Clara shook her head and smiled. 'But why can't we tell my husband the truth? Surely we don't have to perjure ourselves now?'

William felt himself blush; he didn't speak. She was right, of course. There was no need to commit perjury, as he could testify in court as her co-respondent. 'It's my job, and, honestly, if I'm to be completely honest with you, I'm happier, more content, when I have some control. So much of my life has been driven by chaos; my upbringing, the war. It was all so chaotic. I need to have predictability to feel calm.' William was tentative in his touch now, gently enfolding her in his arms. 'God, I know this makes me sound weak, and selfish, but I want to keep what we have private. I've seen them do it, you see, the solicitors. Rake over all the personal details and make everything so grubby and terrible. I don't want them to do it to us. What we have is so good. It has the potential to be good. I don't want us to start off with a public humiliation. I suppose it's just that I'm a private person, and I like order. It's pure selfishness.' William didn't have the emotional strength of the likes of Winnie Woodcock. Women, he thought, were made of India rubber, but William fretted that he was made of glass.

Clara stroked his face and neck with careful affection and smiled. 'I don't think you're selfish. I think you're very kind.'

'I can fix it so that there was nothing sordid read out in court,' he continued, 'and I would be feeding them the information they have, so all you would have to endure is a tepid fabrication.' He turned and kissed her once more. 'But you will have to endure it, Clara. I'll be testifying against you. Let them rake but let us provide the muck they use. We can do it on our own terms. I could concoct an affair so banal, it would hardly count as adultery; it would be too boring to even make the newspapers.'

Clara buried her head in his chest. 'And your friend has done this kind of work before?' Her voice was muffled.

'Yes, he's very good at it. I trust him. We grew up together. It's carefully done, constructed. Although it's something we do very rarely because we have to be cautious. I never take pictures of his face. He uses false names with the women, the hotel staff and so on. We never use the same hotel twice, and they tend to be out of town.'

William felt her body tense in his arms. 'The women,' she said.

'You will have to say you were lonely and seduced, that's all,' he continued. 'That you met him while you were painting, or something. You chatted. He invited you for dinner, dancing and so forth. One thing led to another. It was a temptation because your marriage was so lonely as your much older husband is often away from home. I can coach you.'

Clara disentangled herself, rising from the couch still naked; then fumbled in her handbag for cigarettes. She walked over to the window and lit one. Clara took a long, deep drag, and gazed out onto the dark evergreens of the copse. Then she shivered. 'He has legal rights over me. I'm his wife.' She threw the cigarette out of the window and began to dress. 'There's a possibility that we could provide such evidence and he refuse to divorce me. Edward could make my life a misery, William. He could keep me prisoner in my own home, or worse. He could send me away to some ... some godforsaken place.'

'Yes, I know that too.' William thought of the wayward wives and daughters languishing in the nation's more select rest homes. *Hysterical.* 'I want to help you.'

Clara's fingers trembled as she buttoned her brassiere. 'No,' she said, 'I simply have to wait for him to die.' They looked into each other's eyes for a moment, then Clara whispered, her voice husky and deep, 'William, I didn't mean that.' She turned away from him, and sat on the chaise, pulling on her stockings. 'Perhaps we could meet here, say once a month. We could be discreet. Could you live with that?' Then Clara began to answer her own question. 'But it seems so shoddy and piecemeal, and I do want a real love affair. A real love affair with you. I don't want to be afraid or ashamed.' She was suddenly hunched on the chaise with her head in her hands. 'Oh God, I'm in such trouble.'

'I think he will divorce you, Clara. Let me help you,' he said.

Clara shook her head. 'I think you're very lonely, and I think you're very good, but I don't want you to rescue me.' She waved her arm about the folly as if encompassing the entire Morton estate. 'I've had enough of fairy tales.'

'I'm not good.'

She looked up at him. 'I think you are.' Her wide eyes appeared bluer with the tears. 'I think you can't help being good like some people can't help being bad.' Clara turned away, refusing now to look at him. 'He would ruin us both.'

'He would try, no doubt, if he knew. But we can fix it that he'll never know we're lovers. I can advise him to cut all contact with you to avoid a scandal. Remarry quickly and imagine you never existed.'

'Edward is ruthless, William.' Clara rose from the couch and slipped her dress over her head. 'He has a stupid sort of cunning.' She glanced at her watch. 'Oh God, look at the time. Will you drive me to Warwick station? I need to catch the train to Coventry. He's never home before midnight on his fascist Sundays, but I want to be there when he returns.'

'I can drive you home.'

'No, you can't. If we're seen, then that would be the end of your plan.' She began to gather her things, tidy the folly. She handed him his trousers. 'Please get dressed, William. I must catch the ten-thirty.' She bent down once more and picked up William's shirt. 'What will you tell him in your report?'

'What do you want me to tell him?' William began to dress. Clara was correct. They were adulterous; they had no right to linger over their love.

'That I visited the castle, had tea, walked by the river, went to the double bill at the picture house, that sort of thing.' She looked up at him and said, '*Cavalcade*'s on at the Odeon. Look what an accomplished liar I am. Tell him I took the train to Coventry and arrived home by eleven o'clock. He knows I don't like the Armstrong. It's too big and ostentatious, so I say it's too powerful for me. Again, I lie to Edward. I lie to him all the time.'

William sensed her surging guilt but ignored it. 'We can spend the day together tomorrow, Clara. I'm meant to be following you anyway.'

She shook her head. 'I don't want to make the servants suspicious.'

'An hour in the afternoon. Just to talk.'

'To talk?' She laughed. 'Is that what you want?'

'Yes,' he said. 'I want us to be together. I want us to be a normal couple and have a normal afternoon.'

'A normal afternoon,' she repeated. Then she smiled up at him as they came together again; Clara resting her head on his still naked shoulder, William gazing up at the faux firmament of golden stars on the painted ceiling, and feeling, somehow, that he was in heaven. 'You're so good and brave.' Her kisses were light and gentle. 'And I think you're very admirable and so kind.' She looked up towards him and said, 'If we do your plan, I'd want to do it quickly before I get the wind up. Get it over and done with, like tearing off a plaster.'

William inhaled deeply – roses, bacon, cigarette smoke, sweat – and whispered into Clara's hair, 'I think I'm falling in love with you.'

Then they left the folly and he drove her the few miles into town, parting for the final time, quietly and solemnly, with chaste kisses at Warwick station.

'I feel you're sending me to Coventry,' Clara joked, tenderly brushing the hair away from his forehead.

'Not forever,' he promised. 'Meet me at midday tomorrow. Somewhere nice and for tourists. How about the new theatre in Stratford? I could take you to a play.'

She nodded. 'Yes, alright. I can do that.'

And he held her close in that moment, only letting her go as her train pulled in, and the guards busied themselves with carriage doors and whistles. She waved from the window as it left the station, and William watched through the clouds of steam and dust until she disappeared from his sight.

13

Monday, 3 July

It was not yet eight o'clock when William watched the Daimler, as black and ostentatious as a gangster's funeral, pull into Needless Alley. But Morton's unexpected arrival didn't bother William. He was intoxicated with the prospect of blossoming love, and the feeling smoothed his tattered nerves as if it were opium. He glanced at the hand that held his cup of tea. It didn't shake. Fuck Morton, he thought. Fuck Morton and whatever he's up to. He could handle him. The front doorbell rang out peremptorily. William ran down the two flights of steps from his flat, and opened the door to the building, still in his shirtsleeves. 'This is an unexpected pleasure, Mr Morton.' He smiled, and Clara's husband entered the foyer. 'Shall we go up to the office?' The entrance way was narrow and dark, so that he stood chest to chest with Morton, forced into a disconcerting physical intimacy with his lover's legitimate bedfellow. Drops of sweat formed on Morton's forehead, and there was coffee on the man's breath. The air became muggy with cologne and expensive hair oil.

'Your fees suggest that you are able to afford better business premises than your current building.' Morton's scolding was hearty and avuncular. 'Needless Alley has a poor reputation and –' the fat man glanced up at the vertiginous climb – 'there are too many stairs.'

'Flashy offices are redundant in my line of work.' William gestured for Morton to go first. 'My clients tend to prefer anonymity.'

Morton ascended the one flight of steps to William's office door. 'I have another letter, Mr Garrett.' He paused as if catching his breath. 'You said that I shouldn't throw them away.'

So, this was the reason for the early visit, a vulgar and upsetting arrival in the morning post. 'Yes, I did say that,' said William. He unlocked the door, and Morton entered first, filling the chair opposite William's desk, squinting at the morning sun. William propped open a window and pulled the blind. 'May I read it?'

Morton handed over an envelope. The stationery was the kind you could buy in any corner shop in the city – not quite the cheapest brand. The letter was posted in Birmingham, first class, on Saturday afternoon. The fat man noticed William's noticing and said, 'It arrived this morning, with your report.' Morton, sweating with the gravitas of his wool business suit, patted at his forehead with a white handkerchief in what was now becoming a familiar gesture. 'I read both over breakfast. But the letter and your report are at odds. Why is that so, Mr Garrett?'

William removed the envelope's contents and read:

My Darling Edward,

Why are you not answering my letters? Surely you know who I am by now. I'm tiring of your games, dearest. Don't you know it is only ladies who play hard to get? Answer me, Edward. I am eager for your response. I'm still taking care of you. I'm still watching over you. I don't like to see you

humiliated. Your wife continues to demean you, Edward. She
is an embarrassment to you. For example, on Sunday, 25th
June, whilst you were having fun with your little mistress, Mrs
Morton was similarly engaged. I saw him. So very tall and
dark and handsome. Quite the type women go for.

William's stomach lurched. On 25 June, he and Clara Morton
were sharing walnut cake in the tea rooms of the Birmingham
Museum. And William could be described as tall, dark and, at
a push, even handsome, by the two fascist girls whose arrival
that day so spooked Clara.

He fucked her up against the wall of a well-known hotel in
Stratford-upon-Avon. A stand-up fuck by the tradesman's
entrance like a whore. She didn't have the good manners to be
bedded in a hotel room like a lady. Just a little tart in a back
alley, knickers round her ankles and cock up to the eyeballs.
But it's the way they all behave, in the end, if not properly
managed. I hate to be the bearer of bad news, my love. But I
cannot remain quiet in the face of her contempt.
Your devoted
'O'

And although it was feasible that Clara left William early that
day to meet a lover in Stratford, he knew the letter to be a
fiction. But what was the letter writer's motivation? She had
asked for no money. She wanted Morton's recognition and his
attention – his acknowledgement of her. She had used endear-
ments, but William felt there was true malice behind the letter,
and it was directed towards both Morton and his wife.

'The letter writer thinks she knows you,' William said. 'It's
grammatical, mostly, if a tad fruity. She's very happy to use

expletives. I know very few women who do, unless they were out deliberately to shock, and it's obvious that she is.' William glanced at the layout of the letter. It was poorly indented, as if the writer overused the space bar, and poorly justified, too. Some of the typeface was darkly inked and some was barely legible. 'She's not a typist. Or she's doing a good impression of someone who doesn't type. I think we can rule out your secretary. I think this is written by a woman of some education but no office experience. Could this be a woman from your own social circle?' William paused for a minute. 'Is this your mistress, or even an ex-mistress? Do you know any women whose names begin with O? It's unusual. Olivia? Ophelia?'

'I have no mistress. I am faithful to my wife,' Morton lied. 'And I didn't come here to listen to some shoddy Sherlock Holmes claptrap.'

William lit a cigarette. 'I wasn't in your employ on the twenty-fifth of June. Our formal business relationship began on the twenty-sixth, the Monday. Your wife's movements up until now have been innocent, rest assured in that. However, this may change. We are early on in the process.' The letter writer had forced Morton's hand, and this was a gift to Clara. William could now make the imaginary handsome man a reality. 'What course of action will you take if she does have a lover? Will you require photographic evidence for future divorce proceedings?'

'I require all the evidence you can give me. Photographic evidence, most definitely.'

William lit a cigarette. He didn't want one, but he hoped the mundanity of the action masked the importance of the coming question. 'Do you want to divorce your wife, Mr Morton?'

'No, I don't. However, to remain in a marriage with a woman who is so sexually incontinent, unstable, is unconscionable. I would be determined to act if that were true. I would be forced to act.' Morton shifted in his chair and crossed his pudgy legs at the ankles – a strangely feminine action. 'My concern is that I'm away on political business this weekend. A rally with Mosley in Manchester. This gives Clara opportunity, freedoms to … Well, this weekend you must pay particular attention to my wife.'

William nodded, a serious, professional man. 'Rest assured, Mr Morton, I shall. Mrs Morton is my top priority. If this lover exists, I shall find him. If your wife is unfaithful this weekend, I shall get your proof.' William stubbed out his half-smoked cigarette and smiled at his client.

Both men rose and Morton moved to shake William's hand. It was clammy and soft, like graveyard moss. 'Reports, Mr Garrett. I want reports and facts.' Morton performed his ridiculous Masonic knuckle fiddling, and then screwed his face as if in thought, William still tight in his grip. 'I want photographs now, I think. Yes, take regular photographs of her daily movements. Photographs don't lie.' Morton looked at his watch in a pointed gesture. 'Shouldn't you be on your way to Coventry now, Mr Garrett? You're hardly dressed.' Morton, finally, dropped William's hand.

'Just as soon as I find my camera, Mr Morton. Then I shall have the pleasure of your wife's company.'

Morton paused as if he needed a second to process William's weak joke. Then he laughed. A genuine, roaring bellow. He slapped William on the back. 'Good fellow, yes, most amusing.' Another hearty slap on the bony ridge of William's shoulder blade. 'Good fellow. Don't let me down, now. Don't let me down.'

And then he left. William heard his weighty tread on the stairs, the lifting of the Yale latch, and the slow swing of the front door open, and then close. Seconds later, elated at his luck, camera in hand and jacket on, William too left Needless Alley. He wanted to make his date with Clara Morton and let her know about their stroke of good fortune. Ripping off a plaster, she had said. Well, Miss Poison Pen and a fascist shindig in Manchester had provided the incentive for fast action; now all they had to do was form a detailed plan and make their move. It meant freedom for Clara, and, for William, the chance of something better than lusting after money, fags, food. It meant he had a chance at giving, and receiving, love.

14

William spent a happy afternoon with Clara, discussing their plan of action but briefly, walking by the river, looking at the newly built theatre, talking about the future. So by the time William returned to Birmingham, the pubs were open. He parked the Austin outside the Needless Alley office and went on foot to the White Swan, in search of Ronnie.

The door to the main bar was wedged open to let out the heat of the day. William made his way through the crowd of black-clad customers. He recognised a few sullen faces from the canal basin, but not one of them said hullo. The men wore their dark wool suits too tight, and black flat caps pulled low over their brows, as was the fashion amongst their kind, and the few women amongst them were plainly dressed and clutched their port and lemons with gloved hands. William noticed Arthur Stokes and his big bastard brothers, grudge-holding boatmen from the old days, huddled in a corner. They stopped their chatter as he passed, making eye contact but saying nothing. When he got to the bar, the landlord nodded but didn't greet him. 'I'm after Ronnie,' said William. The landlord was a dandy, and very particular over handkerchief squares and boot polish. Notoriously monosyllabic, he let his sartorial flair do all his talking and simply motioned with his thumb towards the ladies' lounge, Ronnie's de facto office.

The ladies' lounge was scoured spotless: linoleum gleaming with floor polish, bar rails glittering with Brasso, the smell of Jeyes Fluid filtering in through the open windows, for Ronnie's office backed onto the lavatories in the yard. A cloth-covered trestle table, scattered with the remnants of a buffet lunch, was butted against the far wall. The room had been cleared of furniture; only a few tables and the bench seating remained. This is where he found Ronnie, prone as if asleep, a large gin at his side. 'Are you sleeping or are you dead?' William asked.

Ronnie opened his eyes and sat up straight. 'What ho, Billy!' William heard a sing-song begin in the background, the tinny clink-clink of a bad piano; a chorus of rough tenor voices rose and then fell. *You made me love you. I didn't want to do it. I didn't want to do it.* 'Welcome to the Royal Albert Hall.'

'It's on, Ronnie,' he said.

'The Mrs Morton job?' Ronnie blinked and reached for his gin. His eyes were dark hollows in the cold dim light of the small back room. 'When?'

'This Saturday. Morton's away with the fascists,' said William, attempting to mask the excitement in his voice.

'You seem terribly eager.'

'I like her, Ronnie. I like her very much.'

Ronnie's face hardened; he took a gulp of his gin. 'You're a big man, Billy. So, when you fall, you fall fast and hard.' He leant back against the wall and closed his eyes once more.

'What is that meant to mean?'

'It means you hardly know the lady, that's all.'

William walked to the serving hatch and peered through. The landlord had a sweat on. The boatmen kept him busy with their orders, for the evening was muggy, and they were thirsty customers. William caught the landlord's eye and ordered a pint of shandy and a double gin.

'It's a free bar tonight, Billy,' Ronnie called out. The landlord looked over his shoulder briefly before handing over the drinks.

'Why is it a free bar?' William gave Ronnie his gin and took several thirsty gulps of his shandy.

'Some detective you are.' Ronnie lit a cigarette. 'It's old Mr Stokes's funeral today. I do hope you paid your respects to Arthur and Bob.'

'Oh, fuck it. I didn't know he was dead.' William sat down heavily next to Ronnie. 'Is Queenie here?' William asked.

'You just missed her. She was asking after you. She always does.' Ronnie yawned and stretched out his long limbs like a cat. 'I take it you have my Saturday evening all planned for me.'

William nodded. 'Yes, I've been thinking it over all day, on and off. I think it'll work. It'll be easy, I reckon.' He finished his beer and wanted more but dared not be seen to trespass too much on the Stokes brothers' hospitality.

'Spill it. Show me your genius, your treasons, stratagems and spoils.' Ronnie finished his gin.

There was a ruckus in the main bar – more singing – someone with a sweet high tenor, a gift of a voice, was putting on a show. William and Ronnie rose in unison and peered through the serving hatch, shoulders touching. It was a *tableau vivant* in a Birmingham pub – big, black-clad men with silent, reverent faces upturned towards Bob Stokes; who, copper-topped table for a stage, was belting out 'Nellie Dean'.

Then the audience broke the quiet, joining in with a loud, enthusiastic chorus. They clasped pint pots to their chests, as though the beer were a lover, and swayed as one to the heavy rhythm of the ballad.

'How terribly sentimental they all are.' Ronnie turned to William. 'I know them, and I understand them, but I'll never be one of them. You and I were born outsiders. Queenie wasn't. But you and I were.' The landlord handed Ronnie a gin. There was no need for Ronnie to ask for one when he was in the White Swan. 'They'll go home tonight rather the worse for drink and give their women another baby or another belting.' Ronnie shot him a pointed glance, full of shared knowledge, shared trauma. 'Either way it's tough luck for her.'

'Is she dead?' William asked.

'Who?' Ronnie's voice rose. 'Christ, Billy, what on earth are you talking about? Do you think I'm a mind reader?'

'Nellie Dean. I never understood this song. I reckon she's in heaven. Or perhaps she left him.'

'How on earth would I know, darling?' They moved back towards the bench seating. 'Personally, I hope she ran away with an elderly millionaire.' Ronnie ran his hands through his hair. His eyes were rheumy, and he looked greasily pale.

William frowned. 'You don't seem yourself today.'

'Don't worry, Mother. I'm simply rather fatigued, that's all. Funerals make me lethargic.' He shook his gin at William. 'I shall soon brighten up, never fear.' Ronnie looked out of the window towards the yard; William followed his gaze. A few mourners were queued outside the lavatories, smoking, chatting, orderly. Then Ronnie stood up, patting his pockets as if searching for his cigarettes. 'Excuse me, Billy. Call of nature.'

William watched through the window as Ronnie joined the queueing men. He didn't appear to be an outsider, for the boatmen turned to greet him, smiling, laughing, sharing fags. It was William who didn't fit in. He felt suddenly maudlin, and so drank the rest of Ronnie's gin, and thought about eating the leftover sausage rolls, languishing grey on the buffet table.

'Tell me your plan.' Ronnie was back sooner than he expected. 'All of a sudden, I feel like a man of action.'

'That was quick, but your flies are undone.'

Ronnie buttoned up, his fingers twitchy and fumbling. Then stood straight, wiped his nose on his shirtsleeve – with vigour – and waved his hand airily about the room. 'I am the world's fastest pisser.'

'Do they know you at the Grand? The hotel, I mean, not the chop house.'

'It's like a retirement home for King Edward VII's mistresses. But despite its aura of positively antique sordidness, no, it's one of the few places in Birmingham where I am not well known.' William suspected as much, but this was good news. The Grand was an old-fashioned hotel perfect for the staging of an old-fashioned seduction, and famed for its wealthy, if somewhat aged, clientele who would not like to see their favourite watering place featured as a palace of lust in the daily press. Yes, the hotel management would attempt to play down any scandal that occurred at the Grand. 'Is this where Mrs Morton and I will rendezvous?'

'Yes, I want you to book a table for two for eight o'clock. And a room under the name of . . .'

'Novello? Coward?'

'Don't be ridiculous,' said William. 'Are you taking in what I'm saying? I want you to—'

'Waltz with the lady whilst you peep behind a potted palm?' Ronnie pantomimed a 'what the butler saw' peek between his own half-closed hands. 'Feed her oysters and champagne, and kiss her fingertips in public like the roué I am?' He chuckled, low and humorous. 'I know, what about Valentino? Shall I book it under the name of Valentino?'

'Johnson will do,' said William. It was a common name but not ridiculously so.

'That's the American euphemism for one's cock.'

'Appropriate, then.' Both men laughed. 'Check in quite early and say that your wife will be arriving later and take both of the room keys.' William offered Ronnie a cigarette, lit it for him and passed it over. 'But then leave the hotel and post the extra key through the door of the Needless Alley office.' If William were asked in court how he had a key, he would say that he had bribed a maid, but the girl had left town and couldn't be found.

'Righto,' Ronnie said, but he was distracted, twitchy and – God – bored.

'Are you listening to me, Ronnie?' The boatmen began to sing once more. *Pack up your troubles in your old kit-bag and smile, smile, smile.* Fuck, they were on the war songs already. 'We have to get this straight. Christ, what a racket. Why don't they just shut up about the bloody war?'

'Sentimentality is the opium of the masses, I told you.' Ronnie flicked ash onto the floor.

'That's religion.' William leant forward and clicked his fingers in front of Ronnie's face. 'Buck up. I've told Clara to meet you in the lobby of the hotel at half-past seven. Dance, and then eat a romantic meal for two—'

'But how will the lady know me? Shall I wear a red rose in my lapel?'

'Tip the waiter well. I want him to remember you.'

Ronnie raised his perfect brows. 'I am always memorable.'

'At ten o'clock, use the main lift to the upper floors and go to bed.'

'Ooh la la.' Ronnie picked up his empty gin glass and frowned at William. 'Do you trust me?'

'Remember to lock the door. I need everything to play out just as if I was a detective on a case and no more. Any accidental witness must think I don't know you or Clara. We can't afford to raise any suspicions. I want it to be perfect. For Clara.'

Ronnie hesitated; turned to William, his eyes distant and glassy, took a long sniff and an intake of breath, then said, 'Billy?'

'Yes?'

'I love you, and I want you to be happy. Everything I do, I do with your best interests at heart. You must know that.' Ronnie shouted over the roar of the singing men. 'Therefore, I shall book the hotel room and act the seducer, for I am an inveterate . . .' He paused for a moment.

'Drunkard? Gambler? Libertine?' offered William.

'Well, I was going to say *professional*, darling,' Ronnie laughed. 'But your assessment of my character may be more accurate.'

15

Saturday, 8 July

The moon, wondrous and huge, hung like the backdrop to a pantomime in a sky the colour of split damsons. An angry summer storm, which had raged all evening, now stuttered to a stop, clearing the air as it went. William looked out onto the courtyard of the Grand Hotel: red brick walls, now purple with the night, glittered in the last of the rain, and puddles reflected the light from the service corridors. Two men in mucky aprons stood on the stone kitchen step, smoking. And the men must have been talking about the moon, for they squinted up at the sky, pointing and waving their hands.

William had been lingering on the dogleg of the back stairs for over fifteen minutes, perfecting the plan in his imagination so that its constant repetition had become a compulsion. It was watertight, he thought. But it had been pricking at his nerves all day, making him long for darkness, and his bed, and for Clara and, importantly, for it all to be over. He stubbed out the last of his cigarettes on the windowsill and took one final look at the moon. Then he opened the door, which separated the back stairs from the main hallway, and went to work.

In the corridor, his footsteps were silenced by thick carpet. The lighting was low but good enough to see by. There was a faint smell of lavender polish, and a large vase of scarlet dahlias stood on a console table under a picture window positioned to frame the view of St Philip's, its cupola sprouting verdigris, and atop, not a cross, but a wild boar weathercock, its teeth bared at Birmingham's faithful.

The odd numbers were on the left-hand side of the corridor. Room eighty-one – the bedroom booked under the name of Johnson – was close to the window, so close to the cathedral and the eyes of God, and the beady eye of the wild boar. William knocked softly and then unlocked the door with Ronnie's room key as arranged. The heavy fob swung like a pendulum. He watched it spin until it steadied, and then entered the room.

It was the stillness that shook him, and not the dark. The eerie stillness and the smell. A half-forgotten smell of blood and cordite. William stood, for a moment, on the threshold of things, swallowing back the hot bile which had risen to his throat, waiting for his eyes to adjust to the murk of the room. Finally, he flicked the light switch.

The electric lamp made Clara's once beautiful skin look sallow. Her knickers, pink and silky, were around her ankles. The stockings, on her bent legs, were still straight and unwrinkled, the seams – like arrows – leading to a bare arse, for she lay on her side and the soft white chiffon of her frock was rucked up over her waist.

William crossed over to the other side of the bed. A bottle of champagne on the bedside table clinked in its bucket in response to his tread. Clara's arms were raised; her wrists bound to the bedpost. Her head, graceless, slumped to the right, nestled into a pillow. A pale ligature was buried deep into Clara Morton's slim neck. William touched her gently, caressed her cheeks, shut the lids of those wide and now protuberant eyes, brushed his hand against her mouth, which was just a little open. Clara's lipstick was still perfect; no one had smudged it. William sat with her. Her skin was warm and scented. She wore Ashes of Roses.

Time did not exist for William, only feeling, and yet he did not know if he was numb or hypersensitive, for he did not cry out, shout, sob, shriek, but gazed at each vivid cruelty in the room.

The man, whoever had done this, had sliced at the bodice of her dress, for Clara's breasts were exposed. Deep red on the frills and flounces, bright scarlet runnels on the ruffles of her skirts, the pink and paleness of her now cut up. The bedlinen, crisp like snow, held a flood of blood, sullying the sheets, starkly flagrant and outrageous.

The air in the room was clammy and ferrous, hot, like his mother's wash-house in October after the pig slitting. The windows, behind heavy curtains, were closed, and William dared not open them, despite his need for air. Someone had overturned a tray of champagne flutes, and a crystal bowl of lilies had been upturned and crushed into the bedroom floor. Their fat petals, glossy and bridal, bruised; their thin, potent stamens soiling the cream of the carpet. It was only then that William thought of Ronnie. The champagne and the flowers and the cordite. Ronnie.

William moved to the bathroom. Harsh white light on harsh white tile made the room severe. He was sitting on the lavatory. Dressed for dancing, the pleats in his shirtfront as sharp as razors, he was slumped towards the corner, shoulders forwards, and arms drooping like a doll or a drunk. In between his feet, just a few inches away from dangling fingertips was a pistol. Thick swathes of blood and brains had doused the cistern. Ronnie's mouth gaped open as if he were about to burst out singing – no, not a mouth, but a bloody cavern of a wound. Film-star chops gone, the left side of his skull was blown, like a bird's egg. His thick dark hair, once so carefully pomaded, was comically unruly around the gaping hole. William gawked idiot-like at his dead friend. What he saw was unbelievable, for Ronnie was no suicide. Ronnie who clung to life, hard – resolute. Ronnie who gleaned joy from all fate doled – and was relentless. Ronnie who skirted trouble – always. Yes, Ronnie would run if in bother. Oh God, yes, he would run. The cordite stink was now overwhelming. A familiar soft thud pulsed above William's left eyebrow. Soon he would vomit. Christ, not here.

Morton's words – words which William may have previously misinterpreted – echoed through William's mind. 'To remain in a marriage with a woman who is sexually incontinent is unconscionable. I would be determined to act if that were true. I would be forced to act.'

And so William took photographs with shaking hands. The mechanical soft click-whirr of the camera sounded unnatural in the bloody silence of the hotel room. But William recorded every detail, not stopping until the film was spent. Proofs were needed of this outrage, his instinct told him. Proofs were needed so that justice could be brought to bear. And photographs did not lie.

When he was done, William scrubbed at the door handles and the light switches with his handkerchief – first the bathroom and then the bedroom – his left arm over his nose and mouth, blocking out the smell, stoppering his sick; scrubbed the key to the room too, dropped it – and paused only to pick up his spent flashbulbs, which had rolled underneath the bed, and lay next to a discarded trench knife, violently bloodied and obvious with what William believed to be Ronnie's fingerprints.

William closed the door behind him cautiously, quietly, as though he were protecting a sleeping child. The corridor was still lavender-scented; still silent, still softly lit, and the dark, red dahlias by the picture window had lost none of their petals. Nothing had changed during the time William had been in the room. William took the back stairs and left, unseen, through the tradesman's entrance.

He walked away from the Grand like a drunk. His skull was full of the thud of his own heartbeat, loud and fast and dizzy making. It was kicking-out time, and the Saturday night crowd passed by, glassy-eyed and raucous. They weren't real, they were ghosts. If he reached out, tried to touch them, his hand would cut through them as if they were mist. Neither could they see him, for William existed only in his own thumping head. His sweat was cold. William felt it creep down towards his jaw. He swatted it as though it were something live, a spider or a fly. But it was the wind up, that's all. That commonplace, sad feeling which meant his nerves were shot. William pressed both palms flat against the nearest wall and leant forward, breathed deeply. Then, he cried. He was in Needless Alley. William had returned there by instinct, like an abandoned dog.

Part Two

16

Saturday, 8 July, nearing midnight

William paused at the water's edge. The towpath was narrow, as were the warehouses – all gawky, thin and mean. And the canal itself, a thick black slick, shiny and potent, reflected the chimneys, the buildings, the boats, and the wobbling picture of grief that was his own face. William looked up. In the far distance, a small group of men were working in the night-time chill. Lit only by braziers, they were unloading coal from four narrowboats up at Oozells Loop. Barefoot children darted in between them, jumping from boat to path, picking up stray lumps of coal and throwing them onto a high bank where a heap lay ready for the morning.

William approached, and the children stopped. Dark eyes stared out of smutty faces. One of the workers called out to his friend. This man paused, climbed off his boat and onto the towpath. It was Arthur Stokes. He leant against his shovel, waiting. The sound of the men scraping their spades against the mounds of coal was thunderous, keeping to the same pounding rhythm as William's grieving heart.

William stepped forward and called out, 'Yowright there?'

Stokes nodded and lit a fag.

'I'm after Queenie. Do you know where she is?' William's voice sounded desperate, shrill even, in the dark of night.

'You've got big old bollocks, Billy, coming around here at this time of night.'

Cold sweat soaked through William's shirt. He pressed his left palm against his chest to see if it was hollow, but there was no gaping Clara-shaped hole. Losing Ronnie was like losing a limb, so William glanced at his right hand, clenched, and then unclenched, and then clenched his fist once more. He was not a man intact. 'I've gotta see her now. Where is she?'

Arthur Stokes looked down at William's bunched fists. 'I ain't privy to Miss Maggs's comings and goings.' Gas Street Basin was Queenie Maggs's domain, for Ronnie's baby sister owned a fleet of boats and half the men who ran them. And now, William knew, even the Stokes brothers showed her due deference.

'Miss Maggs? Fuck me, Arthur. Is that what you call her now?' It had been months since he had last seen Queenie – Christmas, he was sure of it – and much had changed. William's nausea rose. He wanted to vomit in the cut. Clear out the bile in his guts. 'Where's the boss lady? She needs to hear what I've got to say. It's bad news. Bad business. Otherwise, believe me, Arthur, I wouldn't be here.'

Stokes performed a slow appraising nod. 'The *Little Marvel*'s further on –' he pointed north – 'up as far as Soho Loop.' The canal basin quietened. The other men paused mid-job to listen in, unabashed. They filled pipes, rolled fags. The children still ran from boat to bank, like water rats.

'Shit.' It was nearly a mile away. William shuddered hard. Delayed shock ran through him like a jolt of electricity.

'You cold?' Stokes looked him over. 'You're shivering.'

'A bit.' He moved towards the brazier and warmed his hands.

'Well, fuck off back home to bed. Get yourself all safe and warm.' Stokes rubbed at his chin, took a long drag of his cigarette. William didn't shift. A show of weakness wouldn't do. Let them keep their grudges and their bad blood; William had bigger things on his mind. The man laughed. 'You're a brazen bastard, Billy Garrett, and you ain't welcome here.' He nodded a dismissal, but William stayed put, warming his hands. A girl, no more than six or seven years old, ran by him and then dipped swiftly to pick up slag. Stokes called to her, whispered in the child's ear, gave her a penny, and then sent her on her way. She flew towards Oozells Street intent on her mission. The workers were silent.

William ignored the advice and walked north towards Soho. It was a decision made from bloody-mindedness, a refusal to be bullied, but also made from a deep need to find her – Queenie. He was thirty feet or so along the towpath when he finally heard that steady, heavy heave of coal continue.

Away from the basin, and the waterside became wild. The towpaths were overgrown, just a narrow strip of tamped-down red clay and pockets of gravel to walk on, rutted with ponies' hoof prints and rat-holes. The banks were a riot of blackthorn. Their branches of dark sloes and slender briers swayed over the path, whipped at his face in the dark, tangled themselves in the weft of his jacket. And above the blackthorn, Birmingham: the factories and the shops, the roads and the houses, all looming and all last century. Not a light could be seen away from the neon of New Street. It was quiet, too. No boats passed, no lovers, no thieves on the run, just the odd whisper of movement on the bankside, the scurry of city vermin.

The *Little Marvel* was moored alone. But a soft, warm light shone from the cabin windows. Someone was up. William climbed on deck and called out, 'Put the kettle on, Queenie.'

There she was with her head and shoulders out of the door, a night creature with her thick black curls and her pale round face like the moon. Beautiful Queenie, the former belle of Gas Street Basin, once all soft tits and soft hair, but hardening now. A couple of kiddies and a decade of graft will do that to a woman. She beckoned him inside.

'You got my note then?' A child, an infant, swaddled, was clamped to her chest. Three kiddies. He followed her into the cabin. Spotless, as always, it was lit by a single oil lamp. Her babies were behind closed doors at the far end, top-and-tailed in a bunk. William could hear that husky, deep breathing which only sleeping children made. Inside, the air was milky and perfumed.

'No,' he lied. He had received the letter, addressed to him in her rounded child-like hand, in June. He had binned it, unopened.

'I haven't seen you since Christmas.' She was matter-of-fact, not unwelcoming, but not herself.

'Queenie, I'm sorry.' William steeled himself.

'It don't matter. I'm just glad you're here. I want to talk to you.' The child had finished feeding and was asleep but still clamped to her nipple. She ran her little finger around the baby's gums – a swift, deft action – and off the child came with a smack. Queenie slipped her breast back in her night-dress and put the infant in the crib. Then she fussed about with teacups and plates.

'Sit down,' he said.

She turned to him and smiled. 'I've got biscuits.' Ronnie's little sister, with all her brother's dark good looks and physicality but none of his charm. Queenie was the sibling blessed at birth with brains, apart from when it came to men. *I'm cock happy, Billy. That's my trouble.* She offered the biscuits to William. William refused. Queenie took a few grateful gulps of tea and sighed. 'I needed that. I reckon this is my last kiddie. I ain't got the energy for many more.'

'Queenie, I've got bad news.'

'Hospital or nicked?'

'He's dead, Queenie.'

'Oh, I see.' She was looking over his shoulder, not meeting his gaze, but staring at her own dark reflection in the window.

'Someone shot him.'

'Shot him? My brother. My Ronnie?' Her lip trembled. She controlled it, formed her face into a grimace, then fired out questions in a fast barrage. 'Whereabouts? In the city? Who's responsible?'

'In a hotel bedroom in the Grand. He was on a job for me. Someone killed the woman he was with –' William took a sharp intake of breath – 'and then shot Ronnie. Made it look like a suicide.' It was an assumption, William knew. And one made in a state of shock, but his friend was no rapist, no woman-hater, and neither was he a suicide. Ronnie fought for life, eked out his independence, scrabbled for autonomy in a society that demanded conformity. 'But I don't reckon it was suicide. I reckon someone must've murdered them both.'

'No fuckin' fear was he a suicide.' For a moment, William became puzzled by the look of relief which passed across Queenie's face. She was still a Catholic, William thought. Not practising, but hardly lapsed. 'You better tell me what you and him were up to, and don't treat me like some bloody fool woman.'

William told his story. From Shifty setting up the meeting with Morton, and the coincidence of seeing Clara in the Lyons' Corner House that same day, to his final conversation with Morton about the poison-pen letters. He confessed his plan to fake an affair, and Ronnie's willingness to act gigolo. He told Queenie of the two dead bodies – those most precious to him – violated, bloodied and languishing above the ball-room of the Grand Hotel. One, his oldest friend, his crutch and his burden – a brother. The other, a lightning bolt of hope; a woman who had briefly promised him a more complete life. William gasped. He had lost both his past and his future.

'Ronnie was skittish all month,' he said finally. 'I felt like he was living on his nerves again. And booze. A lot of booze. Not eating, not sleeping, you know. He was too jittery to do the job. When he's like that, he's vulnerable. He don't make proper decisions. I should never have involved him.' He paused. 'And Clara, she ...' William could not articulate his love for Clara. Grief lodged the words in his gullet.

'Did you go to the coppers yet?' She could look at him now, but her eyes had none of their usual come-hither compli-ance; they were hard black pebbles. Spots of colour rose to those pale cheeks.

'No bloody way,' he said. 'Christ, no.'

'Well then, you're a fool cos they'll find you soon enough, and you'll have to lie about being in the hotel, and that makes you look shady when really you've just ...' William sensed that she was choosing her words with care. 'Just had an attack of nerves.'

'I've still got time. I wanted to speak to you first. I felt that you should know. I ... I suppose I needed to talk to you, for my own sake. And I wanted you to hear it from me.'

132

'Thank you,' she said. 'You're a good man. You've always been a good man, if a little soft.' She rose from her chair and gathered up the teacups, swilled them through at the sink, and then filled them again from her huge black teapot. In went sugar and fresh milk and a slug of Glenfiddich from a half-pint bottle she pulled from her shopping basket. Queenie wasn't a drinker. Whisky was medicine used for shock, teething gums and poorly tummies. 'So, you say the girl was cut, your Clara.' She handed the fresh cup to William and, as she did so, touched his arm very gently. 'And raped,' she said.

'Yes, bad. It was bad. He sliced at her body, torso, breasts . . .' His voice faltered. 'And her knickers were down. Her dress was all rucked up.'

'There are simpler ways to do a murder.' Queenie was sharp. Something inside had hardened further. 'It just seems wrong, somehow. All complicated and emotional.'

'Jesus, Queenie. You're cold.'

'Never cold, Billy. Never that.' Her eyes were green, like bottle glass. She drummed her fingers hard on the arm of her chair and surveyed him. 'Drink your tea, bab. Something about this ain't right. You just can't see it yet.'

William did as he was told. He had been shivering, but he hadn't realised it until he began to drink. The tea was stewed, potent and hot, generous with whisky; it worked its magic. William felt bone tired and fought the impulse to sleep, but he was warm now and quietened. It would be good to curl up, top and tail it with Queenie, just like when they were kids. 'Murderers ain't right, though, are they?' he said. 'To kill someone. Well, it's not right. It ain't moral.'

Queenie wrapped her shawl close around her body and handed William a counterpane, pink and artificial silk. 'I reckon most murders are done for reasons you and me can understand.

Money, love, revenge, I can understand all of that. I'd kill anyone who'd hurt one of my babbies.' She glanced towards her sleeping children. 'What about the husband?' Queenie leant back in her chair, closed her eyes and rubbed at her temples. 'But there are better ways to get rid of a woman. Cleaner, easier, unless he's wrong in the head. Is he wrong in the head?'

William shrugged. 'I honestly thought he had no idea of what we were doing. I thought he was a fool.' William had been too cocky in his dismissal of Morton. 'He's meant to be in Manchester tonight at a political rally. He's one of these fascists.' But William hadn't checked if there was a rally in the north, or if Morton was advertised as a speaker. 'Christ, Queenie, I can't think straight. Morton told me that if he caught his wife cheating, he would be forced to act. I thought he meant divorce, but now I'm not sure.' That heavy sorrow, lodged deep in William's chest, welled, and then burst. He sobbed hard, guilt-ridden, shoulder-shaking sobs.

'It's alright, Billy. You don't have to think straight right now . . .' Her voice faltered a little. 'But you will have to, soon. You'll have to get it straight very soon.' She stood up suddenly and refilled her teacup, sipped it still standing, and then rubbed the small of her back.

Fear, sorrow, hate, even love, strong feeling muffled reason. He shook his head, as if shaking water from his ears, and said, 'Ronnie told me he had stuff on Morton. I ignored him, but he said that Morton's laundry was filthy. I didn't press him. I just wanted to get on with the job in hand.'

Queenie walked over to the sleeping baby and lifted it out of the crib. She handed the child to William. He was shocked by the smallness of it, how light and fragile it was. The child opened its eyes wide once, closed them and slept. 'He likes you,' she said. Queenie lifted the mattress and bedclothes out of the cot with one hand, pulling out a small bundle wrapped in brown paper with the other, brandishing it like a magician does a rabbit. 'Billy, you're a detective, ain't you?' She took the new-born from William and handed him the parcel. He opened it. 'Count it out,' she said.

William counted one hundred pounds all in crisp, new notes. Christ, she was paying him to do the whole gumshoe routine. But wasn't that what he was planning to do anyway? He shook his head. 'I don't want your money, Queenie.'

'That's just your fee. I ain't asking for no discount. I'm paying you straight. I'll pay you a good amount to do a proper job.' Then her voice carried thick and strong in the darkness, and she spoke with a clarity that startled him. 'Billy, this business with Ronnie, it ain't your fault. God knows I don't blame you. But mark me, I want these bastards dealt with proper. Do you understand? I want to employ you to find whoever did for Ronnie. Once you find 'em, you bring 'em to me. I must have my dues.'

Queenie's voice held a sob. She was spent now. William realised that her baby was only a few days old. He rose, placed the pink counterpane over her knees and returned the money to beneath the sleeping baby. 'Pay me after the job's done.' He turned towards her and asked, suddenly curious, 'What was in that letter you sent me, bab?'

Queenie glanced towards the children's cabin. 'It ain't important. Not now it ain't.'

William looked at his watch. It was only half-past twelve. There was still time to go to the police. 'I'm off to Steelhouse Lane, love. You're right about telling them before they find out for themselves.'

She moved over to the oil lamp, snuffed it out. All was dark. He could hear her pad about, the creak of her bunk, the snuffle of her sleeping children and the rustle of bedclothes. 'He didn't do it, you know. Whatever the coppers say, I know he didn't do it.'

'I know.' It was time to leave. 'I'm so sorry, Queenie.'

'Be careful about the canal, Billy,' she said. 'They're all bastards round 'ere and they like nothin' better than to hold a grudge.'

'They won't harm me. They haven't yet. Anyway, it's ancient history, love.'

'No, it's bad blood. You know the way we are. Justice, vengeance – Christ, us lot, we ain't right. We feel things too strong. I'm like it. It's in my bones.'

'I understand, Queenie. I do.'

Eye for eye, tooth for tooth, hand for hand, foot for foot, wound for wound, stripe for stripe. Here endeth the lesson.

17

Sunday, 9 July, in the early hours

William had decided to tell the police the truth, everything. He still had faith in the rule of law, and Queenie was right, it was better to speak to them before the bodies were found. But the thought of further confession made his heart pound against his chest in a painful bursting tattoo, and the events of the past week – and his part in them – ran through his mind like a newsreel on a loop, and his guilt weighed as heavy and black as a sack of coal. William turned left as soon as the canal branched off towards Digbeth, and his sweat ran cold. The water was so close that he could smell its oily dankness. This was not the route he came, for he took a lonely narrow path, darkly dangerous, ill-kept and ill-lit, but it was also the quickest way to the police station in Digbeth, and the safety of the city's neon.

William stopped suddenly. He heard the panicked flutter of wings, the swoop and whirr of house martins or swallows, disturbed. William was groggy with shock, he knew, but the black of the canal and the slag-strewn track of the towpath seemed the same, merged into one vast and shadowy trap. That great summertime moon was now covered in cloud. He breathed, hard and steady; lit a match with a quivering hand.

Neurasthenia. The Curzon Street bridge was ahead. He saw its brick arch, its enamelled number, and the black arrows of darting birds flicker then die with the flame of the match.

Under that bridge, he knew, the towpath was a narrow ridge of brick. And it had been years since William had shuffled along the ledge, as a boy, back to the wall, overwhelmed by the darkness and the water. William felt for his fags and struck another match, and in the faint glow glimpsed a shift in the murk of the tunnel. Not a boat, for there was no engine sound. But there was a movement, brisk and sharp, perhaps human, and it had disturbed the birds.

And it was then that he heard them, footsteps behind him rasping on the gravel and slag, clear in the night air. The clouds shifted. William turned and saw two men, at least, and travelling along the path, twenty or thirty yards away – tall shapes shrouded in overcoats, but walking fast, and bunched up close, a young man's gait. They were lithe under heavy tweed, William could see that, even from a distance, even in the dark. Not drunks taking the short cut home, for drunken men were rarely quiet or fast, but lads with a purpose and as such best avoided.

Those coming from the tunnel now came into view. There were another two men, caps over their eyes, dark jackets buttoned up tight. William could fight. He was a big man and he'd been taught well. But he had only his bulk and his fists – no knife, no razor, poor odds – and he'd be properly fucked if these men meant business and their business was with him.

William chose to run. But the steps to the bridge were on the opposite bank. This side was nothing but an incline; a steep slope, feral with brambles, their blackberries still green, and snarled-up crab-apple trees, and shoots of silver willow, and broken brick and bits of slag. He hauled himself up by grabbing on to a spindling tree trunk. It snapped, and he fell. The soft mud crumbled under his feet. He didn't look, but he could hear the footsteps of the two men quicken into a sprint. William took another run at the bank – leapt and landed near the brick rim of the bridge wall, his fingertips grazing the edge. But then felt a strong grip on the waistband of his trousers, pulling him down as he clawed at any bit of scrub, trying to get a handhold. The brambles and the blackthorn scraped his face, got tangled up in his suit and, as he slid down, the men drove heavy kicks into his kidneys. He tried to push himself up, twist his body so he could fight them off, but by now they had him on the towpath and could aim their blows with greater force. William felt two more land on his ribs and one to his head. They were silent, competent in their work. Boatmen, criminals, fascists, who knew? Then, one last painful kick levelled right at his groin. William felt himself reel, then a moment of dark nothingness. Hot, sharp vomit rose to his throat. He opened his eyes and sicked up on the men's well-polished shoes. Then, their hands were on him, and he felt a firm pushing against his painful chest, and one big shove, another booting, and finally, the agonising cold of the canal soaking into his clothes, making him sink heavy with the black water. He closed his eyes against its sting, and floundered, his arms flailing in panic. The canal entered his ears, went up his nose and into his lungs – he was guttering now, drowning.

Ronnie said, 'Come with me, your dad's a bastard and your mom's always pissed. Come and see my dad.'

The canal, a dark moving strip of fear – a blemish on his boyhood. Oh, the stories he could tell.

And his mom said, 'My babby, it's the Ten of Swords. Don't go near the water. There's danger there.' She had a wicked pack of cards.

Murder. Murder and rape and death by drowning. Death by misadventure and infanticide and suicide.

Uncle Johnny said, 'Don't worry, Billy lad. Most boatmen can't swim. We're Midlands people, after all. It don't make no difference, anyway. Canals aren't as deep as you think.'

18

Sunday, 9 July

'Of course, canals aren't as deep as you think.' It was a woman's voice, clear and authoritative.

'Gosh, I didn't know that.' This one was softer, girlish. She had a Scottish accent.

The sky was painted Prussian blue; the stars were cadmium yellow. She floated, splayed – a dead starfish. Skin like grey jelly.

'Yes, you can bottom them. Most of them.' There was a muffled sound of activity, hushed conversations, the scraping of chairs, perhaps the drone of machinery.

A pike, slick and quick, swam towards her through the black, baring its needle-sharp teeth. It could bite off a baby's arm.

A floor-polishing machine, that's what he could hear, and something else, he wasn't sure – the hum of traffic.

'But babies have drowned in puddles. Grown people too, drunks mostly.' It was the girl talking.

All the bastard babbies lay swaddled in the bottom of the canal. Food for fish.

'I'm not saying he wasn't lucky. He was very lucky. If those girls hadn't heard the splash. Well, who's to say? It's diving in that'll kill you. Jump in, but don't dive. Head injuries, you see.'

141

There was a very light breeze, he could feel it, and behind his eyes, he could sense the morning.

'Good Lord! Who would want to dive into a canal in Birmingham? Ghastly, dirty water.' The innocent Scot was probably young and well brought up.

English authority laughed. 'Oh, my dear, they do it all the time. Particularly in the summer. It's so hot for them, and they have no real idea of hygiene. You'll see.'

Boys and girls in nothing but their drawers, hold your nose and in you go. Splash about in the run-off from the foundries, the boatman's shit and scrapings. More canals than Venice.

But William could not swim. He had never learnt. It didn't matter. Canals weren't as deep as you think.

'I think he's awake. Sister, look.' The Scottish girl was excited. He heard the rustling of skirts, a few footsteps on a hard floor.

William blinked. The room was shrouded in pale wisps of smoke. It hung like tattered lace curtains, blurring figures, softening objects.

'Mr Garrett, stay nice and still, there's a good chap. You've had a nasty bump on the head.' She smelt of carbolic soap and lavender. He could feel her near him, hear her breathing. The light in the room was becoming bright and painful.

'Where am I?' It took him a moment to focus on her, to see her properly.

'You're at the Midland and Birmingham, on Easy Row.' She smiled at him. 'I'm afraid those roughs gave you quite a going-over.' She was dressed in the navy blue of a nursing sister. Her blonde hair had been tucked away under a starched, white cap. And behind her, the windows on the ward had been opened wide. He could smell cut grass, flowers perhaps. Sun flooded the room, making the linoleum shine. She was a fragrant saint.

'The police?' His mouth was sore, his lips swollen, claggy with scabbing blood.

'An ambulance brought you in. You were rescued by two girls. Brave of them, really. Didn't leave their names, of course. That time of night, that part of town. Well, you know.' When she spoke, she kept her voice soft. 'You still have your wallet and your house keys. No need to worry about that. We can contact the police for you.'

'No, no.' William moved to sit up, but flinched – yelped, like a booted dog. He was stiff with bandages; his ribs had been heavily strapped.

The sister looked concerned. 'A doctor may give you more morphine if the pain is very bad.' She took a step towards him, laid a cool palm on his forehead. 'Keep calm, Mr Garrett, and do try to rest.'

'More morphine, please, Nurse,' he murmured. 'I do want more morphine.' William lay back. He kept his breathing shallow, quick, his lungs seemed to burn. The canal was still in them, he knew it, puddling thick, slapping against the fissures of his ribs.

'I'll call for the doctor. But first you must take some liquid. Perhaps a little breakfast.' She nodded to the younger woman and then moved away.

Young and fresh, green-eyed, swamped in white linen and cinched at the waist in the old-fashioned style by belt and silver buckle, she held a glass to his lips and told him not to move but to take sips. The water was tepid; it had been standing around in the warmth of the morning for too long. After a few moments, William took the glass from her and drank in short, untidy gulps.

Then there was a doctor, tall, stooping; he walked towards the bottom of the bed, stopped and read William's chart. 'Two cracked ribs, contusions, a concussion.' The green-eyed nurse moved to roll up the sleeve of William's hospital gown and then stepped back. William watched as clear liquid was drawn from an ampoule into a syringe. In went the morphine. 'Sleep's the best thing for you. Rest is a great healer, Mr Garrett.' The wisps of smoke returned. William slept.

The light in the ward was different when he woke, rich and gold and beautiful. The windows were still open, and the half-drawn blinds fluttered like the wings of a bird. He shut his eyes again. Someone, quite close, was turning the pages of a book.

He needed a piss. He had been dreaming of pissing. William roused himself, sharp. The room had changed. It was busy now. And hot; the air was moist. A few men sat up in bed, outside of the covers, reading newspapers or novels. There was a faint smell of cabbage. He could hear the clinking of a trolley in the corridor, the low professional chatter of the nurses. William's bare toes touched the floor. He stood, but then wobbled and had to steady himself against the wall. The back of his gown gaped open. His clothes, still damp, reeking of filth and wet wool, were in the drawers of the bedside cupboard. William put clean, stiff legs into dirty trousers and buttoned his fly with numb fingers. Those two nurses must have washed him while he slept. He placed his shoes on the floor.

'What on earth are you doing?' Precise, efficient tones called from just across the ward.

'I need to use the lavatory.' He slipped his feet into his shoes – didn't lace them up.

'You must wait for a bedpan.' She was worrying over paper-work and seemed unwilling to leave her desk.

'No. I can walk.' He kept his voice steady, deep. Softened his accent, muddied his class, summoned a vestige of mascu-line authority.

'You can't wear those trousers. Night shift should've put them in the furnace. They're unsanitary. Take them off and wait for a bedpan.'

'No.' He felt his pockets. The nurse was right about the wallet and keys.

'Wait. A staff nurse will help you.' She moved to get up, looked around the ward for the junior, and frowned.

'I don't need help.' He mustered his strength and walked towards her, as if walking were something he could do easily. 'Bowels,' he whispered. 'I don't want a nurse.'

She sighed but was appeased. 'That's the morphine. You may need a suppository. The facilities are opposite. I'll check on you in five minutes.' She called after him, 'We must arrange for some nice, clean pyjamas, Mr Garrett, if you are to stay with us.'

William took a piss. He looked at himself in the mirror as he washed his hands. Both eyes had blackened now, and his mouth was a tender, bloody gash. The left side of his face was striped with grazes. They had beaten him stupid. And the morphine had made him stupider still – slowed his racing thoughts down to a gentle meander – dulled him very nicely. William splashed cold water on his tender face. 'I am still alive.' He had said it out loud.

There was a sharp tap on the door. 'Mr Garrett. Are you alright?' The nurse; she said she'd knock. 'There are some gentlemen to see you. From the police.'

'Give me a moment, please.' There was no escape now. He could try charming the nurse, tell her that he wasn't up to answering their questions, but he would only be postponing the inevitable. Get it over and done with, Billy. Be weak, be stupid, but tell them the basics, he thought.

He unlocked the door to the lavatory and stepped out. She was there, waiting. And she took William by the elbow and guided him back to his bed. William noticed two men in dark suits sitting on the hard chairs by the double doors to the ward. One of them was Jim Prior. In London no one knew each other, they said. But Birmingham was not like London. Prior was a bastard from long ago become police detective. The nurse drew the curtains against the police officers and undressed William with a surprising deftness. She was silent in her work and tender. Then, she tucked him in tight, motherly.

'I'd like you to keep your voices low, gentlemen. Please consider my patients. Also, Mr Garrett is ill. Do not tire him.' They were at his bedside already, standing over him.

'She's quite the dragon.' Prior watched the nurse as she walked away.

'She's an angel.' William had warmed to the woman.

'Been in the wars, Billy?' Prior pulled up a chair, scraping the legs over the linoleum until it squealed. The angelic nurse glanced up from her desk and frowned.

'Set upon. Last night.' William kept his eyes closed for a moment and when he opened them, he fixed them on the window. The sun was low in the sky; the curtain still fluttering.

'Who?' Prior, again. The other man stood silent.

'Dunno. Just a gang of lads. After my wallet.' No, it was a competent and deliberate fuck-off of a going-over, William thought. Someone wanted him out of the way.

'Where?' Prior asked.

'Out near Digbeth. On the canal.'

'Not a place for respectable types. Not after dark. You ought to be more careful.' Prior pulled a notepad out of his pocket and licked the tip of his pencil. 'No street lighting on the canal, sir. Quite a nasty place to find yourself alone.'

Prior nodded to his boss. 'This is Chief Inspector Wade, Billy.'

There was something about the Chief Inspector which worried William's dope-soothed nerves. He screwed his face up, attempting to remember why he felt fear, but the morphine told him to stop.

William acknowledged the senior officer but spoke directly to Prior. 'Do you want me to make a complaint? Take my statement?' William surveyed him steadily. 'It was kind of you to come, Jim. Detective and all, and to bring your boss.'

'Detective Sergeant.' Prior tried, but failed, to keep a note of pride from his voice.

'Well done.' William was deadpan.

'Personally, I find it very interesting that you're in here with the shit kicked out of you.' Prior pulled his chair in closer, kept his voice low. 'Interesting but not surprising. It's nice to see you here. A comeuppance and a long time due. If I find those lads, I'll shake them by the hand, but I doubt if I'll ever find them. A shame, that.'

'Police cuts, Jim?' William watched Prior's face twitch. 'We need more bobbies on the beat. These are troubled times, indeed.' Below his left eye, and pronounced since childhood, Prior's tic meant he could never play poker.

'Mr Garrett, do you know a Mrs Clara Morton?' The commanding officer spoke with a measured calm, but the question generated a flurry of anxiety in William's chest; shame and sorrow pounded like a trapped animal against the cage of his broken ribs. He closed his eyes and waited for the dope to do its job. The dope refused to comply. He opened his eyes and looked at Wade. He was the third man on the platform that day of the fascist rally: Mosley, Morton, Wade. 'Don't you know? The police are already here,' Clara had said.

And she had been right. William wanted to howl. Instead, he was silent. In the background, in a recreation room, music, indistinct at first; a gramophone record played low, Dick Powell crooning about shadows and dancing in the dew. William would tell the coppers nothing they didn't already know. 'Yes, she's the wife of a client. What about it?' William worked his voice hard, attempting as much measured calm as Chief Inspector Wade.

'The late wife of a client, Billy. Quite a nasty business. Turn a man's stomach, it would.' Prior grimaced and mimicked retching in a comedy grotesque.

Wade frowned. 'I would like to know your whereabouts, Mr Garrett.' His tone towards William was matter-of-fact, professional. And William, doped up, grieving and in a flurry of panic, was unable to read him. 'Where were you last night between ten and twelve o'clock?'

'I was working late in the office and then went to see Miss Queenie Maggs,' he replied. 'I was on my way back from Queenie's when I was robbed.'

Prior whistled through his teeth. 'She still your bit of stuff? Bloody hell.' He gave William a filthy grin. 'Although I reckon it's more the other way around. Queenie is the trouser-wearing kind, no doubt about it.'

'And why did you visit Miss Maggs at that time of night?' Chief Inspector Wade was expressionless.

'She's a close friend. I often see her late at night.' Prior whistled and let out a smutty chuckle, but Wade shot him a sharp, warning look – so Prior couldn't command the man's respect, William thought. 'She's a night owl. I was coming back from Soho, and I got set upon, and I got a dunking. Someone dragged me out of the canal and called an ambulance. The nurses will tell you all of this. I've been here all day.'

'Do you know a Mr Ronald Edgerton?' William concentrated on his interrogator. Early forties, tall, and still muscled, as if he maintained a physical training regime, he was military straight. William knew that posture well, the composure too. Wade was the self-disciplined type, and perhaps also the unimaginative type, and more of the obvious fascist type than Morton. William kept his answers short and clear, something he too learnt from his army days. Yes, he was beginning to have the measure of the man.

'Ronald Edgerton works for me on a part-time basis as a research operative.' William refrained from saying 'sir'.

'Am I correct in thinking that the name Edgerton is an alias?' asked Wade.

'Not an alias. His name was changed legally by deed poll over ten years ago,' answered William.

'And his original name?'

'His original name was Francis Maggs.'

Wade frowned once more at Prior, who had the sense to blush an apology before he began to talk. 'He was Queenie Maggs's big brother and old Johnny Maggs's son. The whole ruck of 'em is as rough as boots. They're water gypsies, sir. Billy here ran with 'em when he were a lad, didn't you, Billy? Old Johnny was a small-time crook and a proper fuckin' Fagin.' Prior knew the history alright, but he was too lazy or too stupid to have informed Wade before the interview. And Wade was a man who liked to be informed, William guessed. 'Frankie Maggs had ideas above his station and changed his name so that he could tread the boards. The sister is our Billy's bit of skirt. She runs what she calls a haulage firm from a warehouse up at Gas Street Basin.' Prior, the eager dog, wagged his tail in the hope that his boss might still throw him a bone. 'She's a bad 'un, but nothing sticks to her. She's one of these clever women, sir. Got her painted fingernails in a lot of rotten pies does our Queenie.'

'It's not looking good, Mr Garrett, is it?' Unlike Prior, his boss was deadpan.

'I don't know what you're going on about. You just seem to be talking in circles,' William muttered. 'Confusing me, that's what you're doing. I have a concussion. It's all so vague. Just a lot of unconnected questions. I don't understand what you're doing here.'

Prior glanced over to the nurse who sat bent over her paperwork, and then tapped William hard three times on his swollen cheek. 'Don't have a fit of the vapours, William. It just wouldn't do.' William's painful mouth throbbed.

'Mr Ronald Edgerton is dead. His body was found with that of Mrs Clara Morton,' said Wade. 'And Mr Garrett, you don't look terribly shocked.' Again, Wade was deadpan.

William saw the sky, as pink and silver as a cooked salmon. Soon, it would be teatime. He closed his eyes – the sunlight seemed a smear of blood – then opened them again, quickly. 'I've had a lot of morphine.' William would have liked some more.

'Had Mr Edgerton been acting unusually recently?' Wade had changed tack, and William now saw which way the wind was blowing.

Prior snorted.

'No,' William replied.

'Not drinking to excess?' Chief Inspector Wade's questions were rapid fire and designed to throw a doped-up man off his guard.

'Not that I know of.' Again, William didn't say 'sir'.

'Can you tell me something of Mr Edgerton's state of mind?' asked Wade.

'I wouldn't know.'

'Had Mr Edgerton been under an unusual amount of pressure lately?' Wade's questions were becoming predictable. William knew the line of enquiry the police were following – obvious murder suicide after an illicit hotel room encounter. Morton's name would not be mentioned, for Morton was Wade's fellow traveller.

'Not that I know of,' replied William.

'Was Mr Edgerton a habitual user of cocaine?'

The question came like a punch in the gut. William hesitated, aware that his bloodied mouth gaped, like a fool, or something more horrific, a painting by Goya. 'No,' he replied. He shook his head until it hurt. 'Christ, cocaine, never. No. Nothing stronger than whisky. He was a drinker, that was all. A heavy drinker.' William had given them too much.

'Sergeant Prior informs me that you and Mr Edgerton served together during the last war?' Wade paused for effect like a detective in a bad play. 'Was Mr Edgerton ever treated for shell-shock? Hospitalised? Was he a mental case?'

'No, I don't know. It was a long time ago. I'll have to think about it.' *We both were. We all are. Only the dregs survived. My lungs are shot, I know they are. More morphine please, Nurse.* And now William was sure that Ronnie was cast in the part of battle-mad ex-soldier, and Clara was just another female casualty of that lingering, pervasive war.

Prior laughed. 'Billy lad, lying comes natural as breathing to bastards like you.'

Finally, Wade sat down; he was heavy on the edge of William's bed, creasing its apple-pie order. 'Well, Mr Garrett, Sergeant Prior also informs me that the nature of your business is somewhat suspect. The sergeant is of the opinion that you are a professional Peeping Tom. Well, I don't know about that, but I don't like it. Adultery, divorce, poking about in a man's private life, making money from it. It's squalid, Mr Garrett, squalid.' Wade was so close now that William could feel the man's breath on his cheek, smell the sourness of it. 'But what I am sure of is that your little friend Edgerton was a nancy-boy, a woman-hater type. We found cocaine and a certain kind of foreign magazine in those digs of his.'

William frowned. 'I don't know what you mean.'

'He means musclemen magazines. Big lads in the alto-gether, Billy, all doing unspeakable things.' Prior snorted again and then gave out a low chuckle. 'Billy was once a solicitor's clerk, sir. He knows what's legal and what ain't.'

But Prior's boss continued, his voice intense, quiet. 'This is what I think happened last night, Garrett. I think you and Edgerton were setting Mrs Morton up in a blackmail scam, because we've spoken to her husband, and he has no clue who you are or what your business is. Edgerton's job was to wine and dine the girl, take her dancing and sweet-talk her into going to bed. Your job was to photograph them together and extort Mrs Morton. But when you went to take your pictures, you found them both dead. A chap like that, well, he couldn't get it up. Too much pressure.' Wade tapped his temple. 'Edgerton must have had a funny turn and cut her, cut her bad. He strangled her and then topped himself through shame. But you know all this. You knew it before we did. And I'd like to prove it. I'd very much like to prove it.' There were signs of a sleepless night about the man: a mustiness to his clothing, stale sweat and something chemical; and his eyes red-veined, their bags as purple as William's bruises. 'You're just as respon-sible for her death as the little poofter.' Wade's knuckles screwed hard into William's strapped ribs. 'You stink of degen-eracy.' The man leant close into him; the pressure of his entire body weight amassed in Wade's bunched fist, which twisted further into William's chest. William remained silent, biting his lip, taking his punishment. Wade whispered, 'You let a dipsomaniac and a nerve case muck about with a pretty little lady like that. You deserve everything you get.'

Both men stood.

Prior, now a happy dog, called out, 'He's all yours now, Nurse. Look after him for us. He's looking a bit peaky.'

19

William waited for another dose of dope before he discharged himself from the Birmingham and Midland. The hospital had been a place where drug-ridden dreams and memory fused, stopping time. And although William yearned for drawn-out days of drifting in and out of sleep, secure in the comfort of women and morphine, a gouging stab of terror jolted him from further stupefied convalescence. It was Sunday, half-past six; a nurse had told him. And less than twenty-four hours since the deaths of Ronnie and Clara. The repercussions of their murders were forming like a great wave, and William knew that if he did not act, the violent swell would soon crest, surge and drown him. And now he was in a telephone box, just outside the hospital, popping pennies in the slot, asking the exchange to connect him to Q. Maggs Transport Ltd, and praying that the police had not yet paid Queenie a visit.

'Billy, is that you?' Her voice was pregnant with relief. 'I've been waiting by the telephone all day. No one's come from the coppers yet, Billy. Did you tell 'em what happened? I've been worried sick—'

'They're on their way, love. That's why I'm calling.' William's breathing was shallow and painful. He couldn't gather his thoughts. 'I got beaten up last night and it put me in hospital—'

'What?'

'Queenie love, listen to me.' William's mind was full of morphine and black water. He rested his forehead against the cold hard glass of the call box. 'The coppers already know about Ronnie and Clara. I don't know how, the hotel staff, perhaps. They just interviewed me, but I said nothing.' He took a deep, excruciating breath. 'It'll be Jim Prior who comes to see you, love, and another senior officer. That man, the tall man, Wade, I know he's a friend of Morton. They're in the BUF together, Queenie.' William heard her children playing in the background. 'Keep mum, love. Act shocked when they give you the bad news. Tell them that you were with me all night, and that I left about half-past twelve. Tell them that you haven't spoken to me since.'

'Who beat you?'

'I dunno. The murderer or someone sent by him, but it don't matter right now, love. Christ, I had a run-in with Arthur Stokes before I met you.'

'It wouldn't be Arthur. He knows better.'

'Queenie, it don't matter right now. You gotta listen to me.' William closed his eyes. Thinking was swimming, somewhere dark, somewhere deep. He dived down, touched Clara's silk stockings and Ronnie's faceless head, saw Morton suck on his humbugs, and watched typewritten poison-pen letters float on the current, pale and flimsy, like dead cuttlefish. 'They think that Ronnie and I were setting Clara up in a blackmail scam. They reckon that Ronnie did her in and then topped himself. They talked a lot about him being a mental case and a dope addict. They found cocaine in his flat. Christ, Queenie, I'm out of my depth.'

'They found cocaine in his flat?' Her voice was as hard as steel. 'What did you say to that?'

'I told them I hadn't got a clue. It was the only honest fuckin' thing I said.' He sniffed at his canal-soaked suit but decided to forgo a bath and change of clothes. He needed to go straight to Ronnie's digs in the hope that he might unearth something – anything – to illuminate the last few days of Ronnie's life and shed light on his death. 'Morton is denying he even knows me. The coppers are gonna try and make this all go away. Clara and Ronnie'll never see justice. I can feel it in my gut.'

'What's your plan?'

'I'm off to Ronnie's digs now. I wanna see if the coppers missed anything. I think it's worth looking.'

'You mean they may have missed the stuff Ronnie said he had on Morton.'

'Yes, they didn't know Ronnie, but I did. I knew the way his mind worked. There may be something. I know it's a long shot.' Shock and grief had terrorised him, making his heart pound and his brain fog. 'I'll ring you, Queenie. Once I've got the measure of everything.' He breathed deeply. He was in pain. He was exhausted. 'Christ, my chest. I've got a couple of cracked ribs and that fuckin' copper made sure he did a bit more damage as he left.'

'Never trust a copper, bab.' Those were Uncle Johnny's words. He hated to hear her repeat them. In the background, William heard a sharp rap on the door. The children became silent. 'I think that's them now.' The sharp rap became a pounding rattle. 'I'm gonna send a lad around with something to help with the pain. If you're out of the hospital, you'll need it. Summat to help you sleep too. The lad'll post it through your door. It'll be waiting for you when you get home. Take 'em, Billy. You're gonna need all the help you can get.' William heard the sudden, decisive click of the terminated call. He waited for a moment, listening to the mechanical buzz of the receiver – inhuman, emotionless and somehow comforting – until he too, finally, rang off.

A few cabbies lingered outside the entrance to the hospital. They leant against their spotless cars, chatted, smoked fags, waited hopefully for fares to appear once visiting time was over. William walked to the first cab in the queue. The driver clocked him, stubbed out his cigarette and moved towards him, asking, 'Where to, pal?' William gave the man Ronnie's address, and sat in grateful silence as they drove the few minutes to the jewellery quarter. The cab slowed down, and William looked out onto Vyse Street.

'Is this the place?' the driver asked.

William nodded and paid up, exiting the cab and not asking for his change.

Few people were ever allowed entry into Ronnie's flat, but William had a key. It was to be used for emergencies: for times when Ronnie forgot to eat, forgot to work, forgot to sleep, and it remained on William's fob. William fiddled at his key chain and opened the door to the house with swollen, bruised hands. The communal hall smelt of cooked greens and gravy, sour now with soap suds, a Sunday afternoon smell, unappetising. A neighbour, big-boned and in late middle age, poked her head out of the door of the ground-floor flat. 'The police have been, you know.' She was not accusatory, only curious. 'Mrs Wilkins says they were searching Mr Edgerton's room. But I said to her, that he's a respectable gentleman and won't be in no trouble.' She surveyed William keenly. 'You're his friend, ain't you? I've seen you here before. You don't look well.'

'There's been an accident, Mrs …?' William attempted friendly professionalism.

'Grayson, dear. And I'm still a Miss.' Miss Grayson stepped into the hallway, fastening the top two buttons of her floral housecoat and patting her netted curls. 'They weren't here for long, you know. No more than five minutes. So I said to Mrs Wilkins, if the police weren't that bothered, it can't be very much, can it?'

'Well, Miss Grayson. I'm just picking up a few of Mr Edgerton's things.' It was as William thought. The coppers' search had been merely cursory, for they had Ronnie in the frame for murder suicide. This was a closed case for Prior and his governor. Prior, whom William knew to be on the take, and his boss, a man who stank of Masonic ritual, military two-steps and golf club backhanders, were public servants who knew their place, and their place was to serve men of power first and the public second.

'Oh, poor dear. Poor you, too. You do look done in. Which hospital is he in?' She eyed him with a clear-cut intelligence. 'I should like to go and see him, come visiting hours.'

'Miss Grayson, if anyone comes here, apart from me or Miss Maggs, will you telephone me? Even if it's the police, or men who say they're the police.'

'Miss Maggs? Is she that dark piece – all red silk frocks and musquash furs?'

William thought Miss Grayson's appraisal of Queenie to be terse but accurate. 'Yes, Mr Edgerton's sister.'

Miss Grayson moved forward and tilted her head to one side. 'I ain't got a telephone here.'

William was reminded of a pub he knew in Fradley Junction that kept a clever parrot at the bar. It remembered the regulars' names and recited dirty limericks for peanuts. Miss Grayson, too, was a crafty old bird. 'Here's my card and a twelve-bob note. Use it for the telephone box over the way.

Anyone at all you don't like the look of, call me. You're a friend of Ronnie's. I can tell.' William felt his bloodied lips crack as he spoke.

'That's too much for just a telephone call,' she said. 'I wouldn't want you to think I'm not a good neighbour.'

'I'm paying you for your trouble. I can pay you more if what you tell me is useful.'

The woman accepted William's damp card and damp cash, and then turned slightly, undoing the buttons of her dressing gown, slipping the money snug in what William thought to be her brassiere. Then someone began to play the violin. William shook his swimming head. Arpeggios drifted down the stairs in muffled salvos. Miss Grayson pointed towards the staircase. 'That's Miss Sweet in flat four. She's an artiste, too, like Mr Edgerton. On the halls. She plays a fiddle and rides a unicycle. Must be quite the spectacle, eh?' The hibiscus print on Miss Grayson's housecoat became ghastly vivid: medicinal pink, fat green leaves, bulbous nodding stamens. Miss Sweet started a tune William once knew well. His thoughts meandered until he could place it: *Your baby has gone down the plughole, let's hope he don't stop up the drain.* William's temple twitched in rapid, painful spasms. The morphine was wearing off. He managed to nod his good-byes to Miss Grayson.

Scales bowed allegretto, over and over, as William climbed the stairs.

'Are you alright up there? You don't half look peaky,' she called after him.

William was close to fainting by the time he got to Ronnie's digs.

He expected to see some evidence of a police search, but the flat appeared untouched. In the kitchen, tea things lay draining near the sink and half a bottle of milk had soured. He sniffed at the bottle. A thin layer of yellow liquid formed, and it stank. William poured it away, gave the bottle a rinse and opened the window. A pile of newspapers was stacked on the kitchen table; the headlines bleated of dead blondes, dirty vicars and dire warnings from the Continent. They were weeks, months out of date. Empty bottles of Glenfiddich, lined beneath the table, clinked with William's weight as he passed. There were fifteen, maybe twenty, bottles – Christ, Ronnie.

Next to the tabloids was a brand-new typewriter with a sheet of foolscap askew in the roller, no carbon. William glanced at the page. It was the beginnings of a play Ronnie must have been writing, incoherent but meant to be a mystery, perhaps. He smiled at Ronnie's aplomb; his friend's unshake-able belief that one or another of his artistic endeavours would soon come good. William took the sheet of paper from the roller and placed it in his jacket pocket. It would be nice to read it, once this was all over. He would toast Ronnie with a large Glenfiddich and read his ridiculous play.

William's examination of the kitchen was thorough but took no more than minutes to complete, for the room was small and Ronnie's possessions few. He moved carefully through the rest of the flat. There was a gramophone in the corner of Ronnie's parlour. It was an expensive machine, and a present from Queenie, but the lid was still up so the disc and stylus gathered dust. William wound the handle, blew lint off the needle and placed it on the record. He let the music play out, loud. It was some show tune, some Noël Coward thing: 'Mad About the Boy'. Jessie Matthews warbled and seemed shrill. *I know that quite sincerely Housman really wrote* The Shropshire Lad *about the boy.*

On the mantel, below a fly-blown mirror, were invitations to parties; a stiff formal collar and cufflinks; a bill, in red ink, from the gas board; a framed picture of them as children, all thick with dust. William felt punch-drunk. He caressed the photograph. The *Little Marvel* was newly painted, and a ten-year-old Queenie, fierce-eyed and dark-haired, stood at the tiller in Ronnie's hand-me-down coat; Ronnie crouched beside her, eating bread and jam; William, the biggest, the eldest, was standing away from the water's edge, his face smutty with coal. Uncle Johnny, worms' meat now, praise Jesus, was not in the picture. But he had been there, that day. Supping whisky at the stern, quick with his fists at perceived insubordinations, quick with his orders to thieve or fight. William sat on Ronnie's sofa and cried. *Last week I strained me back and got the sack, and 'ad a row with Dad about the boy.*

The record stopped and scratched a loop. William wiped away snotty tears with the back of his hand, child again, pocketed the photograph, and then rose and went into the bedroom. It was cheaply fitted out with a matching suite of modern furniture – Queenie's doing, no doubt. Ronnie's single bed had been hastily made up: the counterpane askew, the pillows dented, the sheets untucked. William searched through drawers and found nothing but Ronnie's clothing and the anonymous detritus of a dead man's life: aspirin; a few seaside postcards sent by fair-weather friends; a copy of *True Detective* magazine; a bottle of expensive cologne.

Then, underneath a bundle of neatly paired socks, he found Ronnie's bank book. His account was still in the black, but a hefty withdrawal of fifty pounds had been made on Thursday. William once believed that the detective work that he gave Ronnie was his friend's sole source of income. He now knew that this was not the case, for a quick scan of the cash credit column showed that Ronnie had deposited, but also spent, over three hundred pounds in the previous six months. There was nothing else in the chest of drawers: no letters, no paperwork, no diary, no photograph album.

After the war, Frankie Maggs disappeared into the Malvern Hills with a fellow who had once been valet to the Duke of Rutland. Frankie returned to Birmingham six months later, having broken the gentleman's heart, but with a new name, a new accent, and a meticulous attitude towards personal grooming. Ronnie Edgerton's wardrobe therefore was, unlike the rest of his flat, pristine. William searched the pockets of Ronnie's discarded suit, and then, finding nothing, hung it next to a Harris tweed overcoat with due reverence. Examining the remainder of Ronnie's clothes proved fruitless, and his good quality leather suitcase was both clean and empty. William began to believe that the police had been more thorough in their search than he had first thought, until, behind a pair of tall riding boots, of exquisite handmade craftsmanship – riding boots, Christ – was a canvas haversack, ex-army issue. It was the only item in Ronnie's wardrobe which was not smart. And it was heavy.

William sat on the bed and fumbled with the tough straps and buckles of the bag. He emptied the contents out, seeing first an old-fashioned family album that had belonged to Ronnie and Queenie's mother. William flicked through it: wedding portraits of brides he did not know, the Maggs children as babies, the usual stuff. But, as William turned the final cardboard page of the album, carefully snipped newspaper cuttings parachuted out onto Ronnie's white sheets, all detailing his early acting career: musicals, whodunnits, Prince Charming in panto, 1929. There was a bundle of photographs tied in red ribbon; mostly the typical headshots all actors have done. But one also of Ronnie and William, tender comrades with arms about each other's shoulders, boyish in army uniform. How old were they? Seventeen? Finally, a photograph of a blonde, demure in pre-war frock and hat. And on the back, in careful, rounded script:

To my Dearie and beloved Boy Frankie with true and best honest love from his Forever intended Alice and I shall Always remain the same my lovly one this is all I have to say on hear Frankie in Gods name I'm dead true, let me know what you think of the cards Frankie will you bless you. All on hear is Meant. Xxxxxx

William barely remembered the hapless, despairing Alice. She had been a ghost to him even before her death: pale, insubstantial and fluttering on the periphery of William's life. And Ronnie never mentioned an engagement, even in the depths of his many drunken reminiscences. Alice had committed suicide after she gave birth to Ronnie's child; this had been a constant source of shame and guilt for Ronnie. But it was Queenie who accompanied Ronnie to the Waifs and Strays Society in Handsworth to give the kiddie away, for that was women's work. William's job was to provide liquid solace to the relinquishing father in the White Swan after the business was over and done with.

He flicked through Ronnie's paperwork, glancing at birth certificate, army discharge papers and the lease on his digs. Ronnie had nothing on Morton – or if he ever did, the police had discovered it on their cursory search. William patted down the bag. There was something hard inside the zipped compartment. He opened it to find a small manilla file and a tin of Pepsodent. He laughed, puzzled for a moment at the absurdity of his discovery, and then undid the file. There were more headshots of Ronnie, a few shirtless. No, not just head-shots, arty stuff: Ronnie naked posing like some antique god, a laurel garland on his head, loincloth over his crotch – thank Christ. More of the same: Ronnie with a spear; Ronnie with a bow and arrow; Ronnie wrestling with two other men. In the next one, Ronnie wore a top hat set at a jaunty angle – and nothing else – tackle on show. Another one: Ronnie, still in top hat and made-up to look like Ivor Novello, had a blond boy perched on his knee. The boy was fully clad in evening dress, petulant and round-eyed like the Prince of Wales, his arm casually draped about Ronnie's shoulder. And Ronnie's legs were wide apart; his cock was flaccid – just.

There were more photographs to see, but William was bone weary and ashamed. Dead men had few secrets, William knew, but continued gawping would be a kind of betrayal, so he replaced the pornography in the manilla file, and then stuffed it, the paperwork, the bank book, the photograph of them all as children on the *Little Marvel*, Ronnie's ridiculous play, and Alice's sad postcard – all he had of his friend – back in the haversack.

But the tin of Pepsodent lay garish mint green on Ronnie's bedclothes. William closed his eyes and saw Ronnie's film-star smile. He shook the tin. It was full and looked brand new. William opened the can and sniffed at its contents – no peppermint. William dipped his finger in the white powder and rubbed it on his gums. It wasn't toothpaste.

20

The outside world was off kilter with William's own night-
marish reality. He lumbered along Vyse Street, bloodied
and monstrous, with a haversack brimming with pornography and cocaine – both rich man's poison – slung over his
shoulder. The evening was warm, and a small group of children was still out, playing those final frantic games of Sunday,
before the call to bath-time and a bread-and-butter supper.
Those households which had a wireless played them low, and
the windows were open to let the air into the stale, one-day-
a-week parlours. Along the street, net curtains fluttered, and
pots of geraniums dripped with watering. And William knew
that the contents of the canvas bag, slapping heavy against his
strapped ribs, were enough to do murder for. But he also
knew that none of the terrifying weight he carried could
be proved to be Edward Morton's dirty linen. The bulk of
William's work was not yet done.

It was near nine o'clock by the time he got home, and an
eerie urban dusk, blood red above the always lingering haze
of factory smoke, had settled on Needless Alley. William
unlocked his door. It was jammed, stiffened with the damp
heat of the day. He glanced down at his feet. A large envelope
rested on his doormat. It took him moments to process that it
was Queenie's package – her pills to help him sleep. Practical

Queenie, mother to them all, had raided her medicine box and sent the boy around as promised. William bent down to pick them up, aware that each movement had become increasingly painful, and then walked the flight of steps up to his office.

He opened the window, propping the sash with his grubby, rolled-up newspaper, and spread the contents of the haversack out on his desk. The family album, paperwork, bank book, letters, pornography, cocaine: he kept each aspect of Ronnie's life discrete, tidy, disconnected. The evening light was dim, but he couldn't face the glare of the electric lamp, so he flicked once more through the pornographic pictures in near darkness. The shock of the initial viewing had subsided; exhaustion, or growing familiarity, had made him immune to their power, for each one now seemed tame. Most were of Ronnie in various poses with other men: the small blond boy featured heavily, as did another man of Ronnie's height, naked except for the armour and helmet of a Roman centurion. The final photograph was of a woman. A nude, reclining on a chaise longue, with her back to the camera. She held a mirror before her face, as if in contemplation of her own beauty, but that beauty was tantalisingly obscured. William had seen the image before, and felt, disconcertingly, that he had seen the woman before, too. The photograph was a reference to a famous painting, he knew, but for the moment, he didn't have the intellect to place its significance.

William reached for the Glenfiddich in his desk drawer, toasted Ronnie with a gulp of whisky, and then emptied the contents of Queenie's envelope. Inside, was a pink packet of Veronal, with dosage instructions in German, and a tin of aspirin from Boots the Chemists. He opened both, and the hard white pills tumbled into the palm of his hand like hail-stones. William took three of each with another swig of whisky and thought of Clara. Too exhausted to go to bed, he placed his head on the desk and cried himself to sleep like a child.

'What the hell are you doing with his things? Stealing his private things.'

At first, William thought he'd dreamt him.

He raised his head and squinted against the harsh electric light. Slight frame in a Windsor-check suit, schoolboy parting sharp and neat, he was shorter than William remembered – five foot three, perhaps five foot four. It was Ronnie's chippy sixth-former from the White Swan; it was the pouting, perching Burlington Bertie from Ronnie's erotic photographs. And he was brandishing a knife like an actor in some worthy play about Borstal boys. William blinked once more. 'Why have you turned on the light?' It was all he could muster, that ridiculous question, and he was embarrassed by his own voice, so slurred and heavy with dope and booze. The boy glanced at the pink packet and the near-empty Glenfiddich, and then began to pack up Ronnie's haversack with his free arm.

William kept silent, gathered himself with silence. The boy's right arm, the knife-wielding arm, became limp in the conviction of William's incapacity. William took advantage of the boy's self-confidence and leapt forward, grabbing his arm, twisting it with ease behind his body until he yelped, and both the knife and Ronnie's haversack fell to the floor. The boy cowered and cradled his arm; William kicked the blade away from them both.

'I think you've broken it.' The boy panted. 'You've broken my arm.' He seemed more irritated than injured.

William moved in quick and close, slapping the boy hard across his downy cheek. 'Whoever sent you is a fool, lad.' William glanced at the Pepsodent tin and gave the child another fat slap. 'Tell me who you work for before I do break your arm. I'm all out of patience.' His voice was punchy and thick like a henchman in a Hollywood movie.

'Work for?' The boy shook his head. 'You left your door wide open, you drunken fool.' The left side of the boy's face began to redden and swell. His wide eyes watered, but he had lost none of his fierceness. 'I know who you are,' he wailed, pointing shakily with his good arm, his long, slender fingers accusatory, like a queer, offended god. 'I know you got him killed, you brute.'

William couldn't answer. He went to hit the boy again, desperate now to quieten him. But the accusation had slowed his already sluggish body, and the boy darted away. William stumbled against the open drawer of his desk, dislodging it, so that at first the photographs fell and slid across the floor, and then his old service revolver tumbled down, hitting the linoleum with a thud. They both looked at it, sitting hard and flagrant on top of the black and white exposure of Ronnie and the boy in a tender embrace. Then they looked at each other. The boy spoke first.

'My God, you have a gun. A gun. And he was shot. They told me that Ronnie was shot.' His voice was high-pitched now, quaking and breaking in fear.

In one swift move, William swept the boy up from behind, held him tight and covered his mouth, whispered, 'Be quiet. Before someone fetches the coppers. I didn't kill him. I couldn't kill him.' The boy thrashed about; his legs danced wildly, and one kick landed sharp on William's shin. But he wasn't used to fighting, and was a panicked bird in William's arms, fragile and light, flailing about in terror, all his blows pathetic. How much did he weigh? No more than eight stone; he was vulnerable, no muscle. William tightened his right arm about the boy's slim body, brought his mouth close against his ear. 'I said be quiet. You know what I could fuckin' do to you. You're no match for me. Behave yourself.' The boy whimpered a soft, terrified whimper. It was then that William understood. He closed his eyes, prayed or something, held on tight. 'I'm so sorry,' he said, gently now. 'I didn't mean to hurt you. I thought you were a lad.' The kicking stopped. 'Are you going to be calm? Promise me, and I'll let you go.' The woman nodded. Her deep, heavy sobs were like convulsions, and William could feel the thump of them against his own strapped and painful chest. He let her go. 'I didn't kill him,' he said softly. 'He was better than a brother to me.'

'He was a wonderful man, magical.' She turned to face him. Her lips were thin and obstinate. She let tears fall and then dry on her cheeks. 'He was the most wonderful man I ever met. He spoke of you often. He loved you.'

William flinched at her words, and then nodded. 'Can you move your arm?'

'Yes, I think so.'

'I'll make some tea.'

'Tea?' She spat out the word in a half-furious laugh. 'Are you mad?'

'I've got tinned milk. Why, don't you want one?'

The woman shrugged.

'You've had a shock. I've hurt you. Anyway, it's easier to talk over tea.' William pointed to the whisky bottle still intact on the desk. 'Look, Ronnie's already watching us from heaven,' he said. 'We didn't smash the Glenfiddich.' The woman smiled at the name. 'Bring it with you. We'll go upstairs.'

With Ronnie's packed haversack slung over his shoulder, William locked the door to his office and then the door to the street. The woman followed close at his heels. They climbed the two flights of stairs to his flat in silence. William turned as they entered and nodded towards the whisky. 'We'll have some in our tea. It'll be a tribute to Ronnie.' In the kitchen, a room meant for one, she was close at his elbows, and intrusively domestic, rinsing the teapot, inspecting the state of his china. William filled the kettle and placed it on the gas burner.

'Have you killed before?' she asked.

'Yes. No. During the war. I know how,' he said. 'Does war count? What kind of question is that anyway?'

'I could feel it. Feel that you were a killer.'

'Don't say that. Jesus, it's really fuckin' rude.' Steam filled the room. William let the tea brew. 'I was a good soldier, that's all.'

'I think you got him into something awful.' Her voice was gruff with snot and tears. She took a deep sobbing breath. 'I'm so angry with you. The police came to the White Swan. They told me that he had killed a girl and topped himself. Asked a lot of questions about you and your business. I told them nothing because I knew nothing.' She wiped her cheeks with the sleeve of her jacket. 'I was rather hungover, and I threw up on the linoleum. I cried and made a fool of myself. I've been horribly nervy ever since.'

'I cried and vomited, too. It'll do that to you, shock, grief. Hand me the whisky.' William thought it odd that Prior and Wade had been so forthcoming with the facts of the case in front of the regulars of a rough city pub. 'We've got a lot to talk about,' he said.

'You're a funny sort of tough guy, all tea and sympathy.'

The girl passed him the booze, and William poured a slug into the teapot.

'I'm not a tough guy.' It was becoming dreamlike, this conversation with Ronnie's boy-girl. William blinked and then opened his eyes, but the pale face was still intent, earnest in her appraisal of him. He was overwhelmed by the urge to pinch her, or himself, and test the materiality of her. The Veronal, William thought. It had taken the edge off reality. 'Sometimes I act tough, just for survival,' he said. 'But that's all it is, an act. What kind of man would I be if I couldn't be decent to a friend of a friend?'

'I think you got Ronnie mixed up in something rotten,' she repeated, like a catechism. 'I got myself all fired up because whatever you and he were up to, I think it killed him.'

William's strapped chest tightened. The haversack hung heavy against his thigh. 'Like I said, we've got a lot to talk about.'

They took the tea and whisky to the living room. William lit a side lamp and glanced at the clock. It was a quarter to three in the morning. He placed the haversack on the table and sat down on the sofa. The woman pulled up a dining chair and put the whisky on the floor between her legs. She could use the bruised arm.

'The police were vile. They said vile, frightful things about Ronnie.' She spat out the words, steadfast in her loyalty. Then she softened. 'Who was the girl they said he killed?

'Have you ever met a man called Edward Morton?' he asked.

'No.'

'Or Clara Morton?' William glanced at Clara's painting of the sleeping woman, hung with pride over his dingy mantel, and was overwhelmed by a tremendous loss. 'She was an artist.'

'No.' The woman shook her head. 'Is that her name? The dead girl, I mean.'

'She was a client of mine.' William felt a pang of pain and shame, but he couldn't face talking intimately about Clara with this stranger, not yet. 'She employed Ronnie and me to help her divorce her husband. Ronnie was tailing the husband. He told me he had dirt on the man but didn't go into details.' He let the words linger for a moment, giving the woman time to understand their importance.

'I've honestly never heard the name. I didn't know much about Ronnie's other work. I'd tell you if I knew.' She was honest in her delivery, as fresh and innocent as a Boy Scout.

'Tell me about the pornography,' William said.

The woman sank back into her chair but kept her legs open, like a lad. 'What pornography?' She paused for a moment, sipped at her tea. 'I have no idea what you're talking about.'

'Those pictures of Ronnie stark bollock naked with you perched on his knee. Don't fuck me about.'

'Oh, those pictures. They're art.' She grinned. 'I'm an artist's model, amongst other things.'

William rolled his eyes.

'It's rude to pull faces.' The woman paused to light a cigarette. William was reminded of a German actress in some film he saw at the Electric Theatre. It was about a girl called Lola who was imperious and bohemian. Such unruliness got her, and her lovers, into strife. 'What do you know about art, anyway?' she asked.

'Not much.' He paused for a moment. 'But I once knew a woman who was willing to teach me.' William's voice cracked. He gulped at the booze-spiked tea. 'I think I need more whisky in this.'

The woman topped up his cup. 'Are you in a lot of pain?'

'Yes, plenty. More than you can imagine.' He closed his eyes and counted. If this were a dream, he thought, the doctors in the infirmary would be operating on my broken heart. They would fix the shattered pieces, and I would arise like Lazarus back from the death of grief. One, two, three. William opened his eyes once more, but nothing was changed.

'You look appalling and not quite compos mentis.' She wrinkled her nose. 'And your suit is rather musty.'

'I stink of the canal.' Yes, he did. He really did. And yes, he may be going mad. 'How did you know Ronnie?'

'Parties, nightclubs and such. We knew the same people.' She took an elegant drag on her cigarette. 'Don't you meet new friends at parties?' William shrugged at her evasion. The woman sighed, slumped in her chair, and then closed her legs, suddenly prim. 'I adored him. And I'm furious that he's dead. I feel mad, crazed. It's a peculiar, ancient sort of feeling. I can't explain it. But it brought me here, the feeling. It made me come to you.' Her low voice cracked in speaking the truth. 'I don't go to bed with men, but I loved Ronnie. I loved him with all my heart. He was so terribly kind and brave and alive. I suppose that's what is so upsetting. He was the most alive man I ever knew.' The woman paused to flick ash in her saucer. 'When we first met, I had sunk rather low, you see. But he helped me out with money, introduced me to all the right people, offered me work.' Her voice trailed off. 'But mostly he made me feel alright. He liked me as I was.' She grinned her boyish grin, as if in remembrance of Ronnie. 'He thought the very core of me to be absolutely splendid. Wouldn't change a hair on my head. It's something to be treasured, isn't it? That kind of love.'

'Yes, it is. There's nothing more important.' Clara had taught him that. William thanked her silently for the lesson. 'What's your name, by the way?' he asked.

'My name is Hall, Phyllis Hall.'

Phyllis Hall rose with grace and held out her hand as if she were a true lady. In a dream, William thought, I would kneel and kiss the tips of her white fingers. Instead, William stood, and the grip of his handshake was firmer than his grip on reality. 'Pleased to meet you, Miss Hall,' he said.

'It's just Phyll. Everyone calls me Phyll.'

'Tell me about the photographs, Phyll.'

'Ronnie always said that you were alright. Are you alright?' Her voice held a doubtful note of caution.

'I hope so. I don't know. I honestly don't know if I'm alright or not.'

'Well, you really don't know much then, do you? It's refreshing. Most men know everything, or think they do.' Phyll smiled over her teacup and was gentle with him. 'I think you have to decide that, by the way. Whether you're alright or not, I mean. You have to make peace with yourself, William.' She knew his Christian name and used it like a mother would, and like his lover had.

William rose, his head gone giddy, and emptied the contents of the haversack onto the dining table. He beckoned Phyll to join him, and then spread out the pornography, arranging it as carefully and reverently as his mother did her tarot. 'This is you.' He gestured to photographs of Phyll and Ronnie both dressed as toffs. 'Many of them are with you.' Phyll nodded. 'Who is the tall man in the Roman get-up?'

'Oh God. I don't know. You can't see his face, and besides, the only person I ever posed with was Ronnie.'

'And this one? Do you recognise it? This one of the fair-haired girl on the chaise.'

Phyll peered at the photograph. 'It's a pastiche of the Rokeby Venus,' she said, 'and hardly pornographic unless you're the militant suffragette type.'

'Yes, I thought I recognised it. I just couldn't place it in my current, temporary state of madness.'

Phyll smiled at his self-deprecation. 'It's very famous. It inspired Manet's *Olympia*.'

William remembered the painting hitting the headlines before the war. It was in the National Gallery. A posh woman did a six-month stretch for vandalism. 'But do you recognise the model? The girl on the chaise longue?' he asked.

Phyll shook her head. 'Her face is too obscured.' She touched the Greco-Roman photographs of Ronnie acting all playful with the dark centurion, paused as if in thought, and then said, 'You should ask Mr Quince.'

'Mr Quince?' he asked.

'Quince pays well, and Ronnie was very thick with him.'

William remembered the large, and therefore incongruous, deposits of cash in Ronnie's bank book. 'Who is Mr Quince, Phyll?'

'Quince is a photographer. He has some talent. The composition and lighting of his work can be beautiful, if not particularly innovative. He specialises in pastiche.' She gestured to the Rokeby Venus. 'These pictures of Ronnie with the other man, even they're copies of the kind of things you see on ancient Greek vases. Although, I grant you, the Roman get-up is all wrong and very silly. Derivative but competent, that's where I'd place Quince.' Phyll paused for a moment. 'William, I've never done anything for Quince of which I'm ashamed.'

'My friends call me Billy.' William to Clara and Clara alone, he was too tender for Ronnie's girl to call him by his full name. 'And I know nothing about art,' he lied. He talked of art with Clara, and no one else.

'Billy, there are men, wealthy people, friends of Quince, who will pay for photographs, bespoke photographs, artistic, or perhaps inspired by art.' Phyll now seemed more reluctant to talk, as though she were passing on a secret that she had no right to tell. 'Quince is adept at reproducing his clients' vision. They may have a particular type of girl or boy in mind, or perhaps a scenario. Mostly, when we worked, men would be there watching. They paid to see the photographs being taken. For the performance.' Phyll slumped back in her seat. William thought her fagged out and close to sleep. 'Quince's work, well, it treads that fine line between the vulgar and the beautiful. I'm not naive. Throughout time, art has been created to be seductive or even erotic. It is chicanery to deny it. A nonsense we indulge in en masse. Who is to say which nude is art and which nude is pornography? Who makes those decisions? This is what interests me.' She talked like a woman formulating a manifesto. 'Billy, you're suddenly rather quiet. Have I shocked you?'

'Not in the way you think, but we need to talk to this Quince.' William's drifting thoughts drifted further. Morton, wealthy influential husband of a female artist: how much would he pay for bespoke pornography?

They had been talking in the half-dark, for William could not bear the glare of too many electric lamps. But a shaft of yellow streamed through the window; the coming dawn, it shone golden on Phyll, illuminating her profile, so that – to William – she was akin to a Renaissance Madonna; her serious, smooth face appraising and righteous. 'One can't just talk to Quince,' she said.

'Why not?' he asked. 'Why have you changed your mind? Have you got the wind up?'

'It takes an introduction.'

'Then introduce me.'

'I don't think that I can,' she said.

'You may be right about it being my fault.' William watched as Phyll turned her face away from his gaze. 'But what's really gnawing at me, worrying away at me, is that I don't know Ronnie as well as I thought I did. I worry that if I had been a better friend to him, this never would have happened.' The clock on the mantel struck four o'clock, reminding William of his bone-deep weariness. He closed his eyes once more. If this were a dream, he thought, I would be in a labyrinth. No, not a labyrinth, but amidst a giant, tangled ball of string. I would be trying to find the start of the thread, so that I might begin the unravelling. My mind is a tangled ball of string. This is the madness of grief. William opened his eyes. 'The police have their own pat version of events, but you and I know that they're wrong, and this bothers me. They're sweeping dust under the rug, but for whom? Morton?' William paused. 'Or for one of Ronnie's rich clients? Was Morton one of Ronnie's clients? He said he had real dirt, but all I've found is this.' William motioned to the pornography on the table, and he watched as Phyll's mouth hardened into a thin, pale line. 'This is why we must speak to Mr Quince. We must find out exactly what Ronnie was doing for him and on whose behalf.' William, at the point of sleep, was self-aware enough to realise that he could no longer articulate his thoughts. 'We need to untangle it, this mess.'

'We?'

'Yes, we.' William reached in his wallet for a business card. Still filthy damp, he handed one to Phyll. 'Once you've sorted things out with Quince, telephone me.'

'Aren't you taking rather a lot for granted?' She scrubbed at the dark circles under her eyes with her fists.

'No, I don't think so,' he said, confident in her somehow. 'I need a pal in this, Phyll, and I've decided you're it. You're my pal.'

'Billy, you are alright, aren't you?' she asked, softly.

'Yes, Phyll. I'm alright.' William smiled and felt his bloodied lips crack.

21

The baby was a boy and they called it Ronnie. It was Christmas time, and he had bought the child a train set. Built in Birmingham, good but not the best quality, they set it up together in Needless Alley, for there was little purpose in having such a toy on a narrowboat. Miles of winding track snaked its way through the office. A world in miniature under his desk, of tiny stations and bridges, trees and cows and sheep gathered near the points, a mansion in the shadows, a folly in the distance. Coiling onward and into the hallway, it met the sea. The line hugged a cliff edge. The waves were angry and red; they lapped against a galleon in full sail. And the child, Ronnie, ran. Keeping up with the train, his small, bare legs padded heavy alongside, making the waves swell, and the ship dip and spiral as if it had hit a great maelstrom.

Queenie was there. She was young again. As she was during the war, everything about her tender and welcoming. Lily of the Valley – fine white skin and green eyes – he had bought it from Boots, and she had worn it. Worn his brooch too. *Mizpah*. They sat on his desk and the little boy played. Queenie cut a hunk of Christmas cake, and then ate whilst he placed his head on her lap. 'Oh, Billy. Don't you worry, my Billy. It'll all be over soon. I love you. I love you.' She stroked his hair and bent to kiss him. There was booze and dried fruit on her breath, cinnamon and nutmeg, bitter almonds. And little Ronnie darted in and out of the office following the train, his feet scudding heavy on the linoleum, his breath sucking hot like steam. The child was going too fast; he would tumble and cry. William should warn him.

Then there was a wail and an almighty crash. William was at the top of the stairs looking down. Ronnie had fallen and smashed through the glass of the front door to the building. He was out on the street. His little body slumped against the kerb like a broken doll, pale face nestled into his chin, and his thick, brown cowlick bloodying now from the fissures in his skull, cracked like an egg. A bruise, fresh red, like a rose, formed on his eye. And the women of New Street passed by, and the men of Temple Row did not care. Queenie opened the door and looked at her son. 'Our boy is dead,' she wailed. 'My boy is bloodied and dead. Do something, Billy. Do something for our boy.' And her sobs rang out along Needless Alley like funeral bells.

The sheets were damp when he woke, damp and twisted about his lower legs. The early morning light was pearly grey. It would be another hot day. William rose, bathed, dressed, and then finally walked into the living room, pulling the curtains, opening the window. Not quite dawn, the blackbirds sang out full force and wondrous. He made tea, sat at his dining table, and listened to the birdsong. The power of Queenie's drugs had soothed him into a twenty-four-hour sleep. This sleep had cleared his head, but the Veronal numbed the edges of his grief, and his muscles were still sore from Sunday's beating.

His dining table was set out as it was the night of Phyll's visit: the canvas bag; the pornography; the cocaine; the family album; the paperwork. William picked up the haversack. He shook it, felt the seams, turned it inside out but found nothing. All he had of Ronnie was spread out on the table in front of him. And it represented the two sides of his friend's character. William knew the Ronnie of the childhood snapshots, the Ronnie of the army discharge papers, Ronnie the absent father, and Ronnie of the small acting parts and less than average reviews. But cocaine and pornography were not of William's world, and any attempt at navigation would require outside help. He hoped Phyll would keep her promise and call soon.

William had seen French postcards, of course. A soldier in his platoon kept a stash. He would lend them to a fellow for a shilling each. They were produced by Parisian brothel owners as souvenirs of a chap's stay – or as proxy for a tart: can't afford a real girl, then this'll do you, son, *fils*. William lit a cigarette and became contemplative, mulling over Phyll's revelations and the type of man who desired, needed, such an experience. Quince was a smut-merchant in spats, William knew it. The man had cornered the market in high-class pornography and mollified the qualms of his customers with a window dressing of voguish gestures and artistic sentiments. William was hardened to the sexual sensibilities of his own clientele. Rich men paid good money to have their fantasies enacted, of that he was certain. What shocked William was the arrogance of their risk – their hubris. Dark desires enacted, but kept well-hid, because money and power alone were thought to be a sufficient safeguard against ruin. The whole enterprise was a blackmailer's playground, and Ronnie may have been up to his neck in it.

And in his own drug-numbed state, he hadn't asked Phyll about the cocaine. The contents of the tin were worth a fortune, and surely not for Ronnie's personal use. Was Ronnie peddling dope to his punters? Had he fallen foul of his supplier? Oh Christ, what had Ronnie got himself into? There came a sudden faint but constant clangour – no, not from inside his head. It was the telephone, ringing out from his office, unrelenting. He glanced at the clock above his mantel. Phyll was telephoning early. William ran downstairs and answered the call.

'William Garrett, private enquiry agent.'

'Billy boy, I hoped against hope that you'd already left the city.' It was Shifty on the line. So news of the murders had already reached the solicitor's dainty ear.

'I'm not going anywhere, Mr Shirley,' said William. He was surprised by his own voice. No longer slurred and punchy, it held a note of firm resolution.

'They say you've been in hospital. Very poorly, they said. Quite done in. Done over, rather.' Shifty was a solicitous solicitor, no doubt.

'Who are *they*?' William asked.

'What you need is a nice holiday. A rest cure. Leave the city for a couple of weeks, perhaps a month.' Shifty was stalwart in his proposal. 'I can recommend Weston-super-Mare. Very good if you've been poorly or had a nasty shock.'

'Are you telling me to lay low in Weston-super-Mare, Shifty?'

'No, I would never dictate. Live and let live, that's always been my motto.' The bells of the cathedral rang out six o'clock. William wondered if this was the first call Shifty had made that morning. Or, perhaps more worryingly, that it was his last call of the night. 'You don't have to go to Weston. You could try Blackpool or even Morecambe if you prefer. You can take the sea air, bracing.' Shifty's voice was bright, as if he were placating an errant, but favourite, nephew. 'I somehow can't imagine you in Devon. You'd stick out like a sore thumb amongst all the old dears in Torquay.'

'Fuck me, Shifty. Who's got to you?'

There was a pause. The din of church bells now over, the blackbirds sang out once more. 'I'm very fond of you, Billy boy. Very fond. That's why I'm calling. But this business has angered people I don't much like. You've wound the wrong blokes up, old son. Played it all wrong with the coppers. Yes, Blackpool is always a bit of fun, listen to your Uncle Shifty. Let the stink blow over.'

'I haven't played anything, Shifty. I've been set up. Ronnie was set up—'

Shifty interrupted. 'No, tell me nothing. When I plead ignorance, I want to be ignorant.'

'Shifty, what do you know about cocaine in the city, and pornography?'

'Is this what this is all about?' Shifty let out a great sigh. 'Well, I tell you what I know about the dope and smut business. I know enough to keep well clear. The sum total of bugger all. I recommend that particular phrase to you, old son.' There was a pause. 'Was it the woman? You're generally very intelligent. I can only think that you got silly over the woman.'

For a moment, William could not speak. No, he had not got silly over the woman. His burgeoning love for Clara had been sincere, earnest even. He shook his head. No, it was not a fling. What they had was good, true. 'She deserved better than Morton. She was—'

'I don't want to bloody know.' Shifty's natural curiosity had been usurped by his even more natural inclination towards self-protection. 'I shouldn't have asked. I never had you pegged for a romantic.' Shifty sighed once more. 'They're cross with you, Billy boy. But they want it all to go away. It would be a favour to your dear old Uncle Shifty for you to leave town. A great favour.'

So this was why the coppers had blabbed Ronnie's name and alleged crimes about the White Swan but didn't mention Clara. The story of Ronnie's degeneracy had to be fixed in the city's gossip. Then the rest of the facts needed to be buried, and fast. Whoever they were, they wanted William out of town, and they'd ordered Shifty to ask nicely.

'You're not going to take my advice, are you?' asked Shifty.

William placed the telephone receiver back in its cradle.

But the phone rang out once more and immediately. William answered.

'I'm not fuckin' leaving the city, Shifty.'

'Who's Shifty?' asked Phyll.

'My solicitor. He's a good enough chap. He's worried about my health and wants me to take the sea air.' He heard the last vestiges of the dawn chorus over the line. Phyll was in a call box. 'You're an early bird.'

'I was trying to ring you all yesterday.' She was a little breathless, her voice worried. 'I was becoming concerned about you taking too much Veronal.'

'I was asleep.' William wasn't the suicide type, he hoped. 'Is there such a thing as too much? I'm beginning to like the stuff.'

'Billy, it's on with Quince. Tonight. A place in Nechells.' She spoke quickly, as if her pennies were running out. 'You must act the customer. I've told Quince that you're a fan of my pictures and want to see me perform. You must pay Quince twenty pounds. It was the only way I could think to get you in.'

'That's great, Phyll,' he said. 'Give me the address.'

22

The sunset smouldered red over the thick iron lattice of the gasometer. Casting dark shadows along the narrow Victorian streets, making the air rank with sulphur and thick with dust from its vast black bulwark of coke, the gasworks loomed skeletal over the straggling eastern edge of the city. And the mean slum houses, sooty viaducts and disused factories made Nechells an unlikely place to see a sex show.

Phyll was waiting for William as arranged, leaning against the brick wall of the railway bridge. Suited in Harris tweed, booted in soft brown leather, capped oversized in the newsboy style, she had the appearance of a well-tailored ruffian, a sensitive hooligan – now without a knife. As William arrived, she offered him a cigarette.

'You look much improved,' she said.

'I slept for a whole day. Then I slept some more.' William accepted the cigarette and glanced at his watch. 'I hope I don't become nocturnal. It'll ruin my complexion.'

'Didn't Shakespeare say something about sleep unknitting the something something of care?'

'Sleep that knits up the ravell'd sleeve of care.'

'I knew you'd know the full quotation. I clocked all the books in your flat. You need to return them to the library or else you'll get a whacking fine. I imagine you read Shakespeare to while away long and lonely winter evenings. I've forgotten most of it. I wasn't too bright in English and composition at school.' She waved her cigarette airily. 'I was good at games.'

'You were born to wear an Aertex shirt.' William flicked his fag into the gutter.

She scrutinised him. 'Is that your best suit?'

'Burton's finest.' William was neat, clean and sober, and he wanted her to know it. 'This is as good as I get.'

Phyll sighed. 'You'll have to do, I suppose.' She motioned to a sign above the door of a factory on the opposite side of the street. 'Workpeople and Goods Entrance. That's us. Quince is waiting, and he wants his money.'

Phyll unlocked the door into a corridor with walls tiled thick in municipal green. It was one of those companies gone bust just after the war, when the demand for metal goods fell. She moved him to the main works via a series of offices, the fittings all intact and eerie: files of mildewed correspondence, glass partitions flimsy-dusty, pine drawers, stained dark oak, bitumen-painted floor soft-sticky under foot: all as if a slatternly bookkeeper had, at that moment, left for lunch.

Then they were on the factory floor. A Gothic cathedral of a factory floor and built to last. Massive, now stripped of machinery, its high round windows let in shafts of pink light. An intricate filigree of cast iron beams, rusted to the colour of Clara Morton's hair, hugged the edges of the building, and girders, heavy and hummocky with rivet, bolt and shank, supported a high-pitched ceiling. Dirt-free and degreased, the honest filth now gone, the factory had been swept and garnished as if for Mass. Church candles in brass sconces illuminated the walls; vast vases of roses, velvet petals the colour of old blood, stood beside a large vat. Meant for silver-plating, it made a makeshift stage when draped in white linen, and a few pine chairs, the kind used for Sunday school, were lined in neat rows as if before an altar. Here a man flitted and fussed with what William knew to be precision-made, German photography equipment, lighting and camera all shining pristine chrome, and top of the range. This was Mr Quince. A head shorter than William, running to fat and trying, but failing, to disguise his paunch with a Fair Isle sweater. His fashionable moustache was a trimmed strip above his lips, and his eyes were rimmed red – a drinker or a crier, or prone to head colds, perhaps, or maybe one of Ronnie's customers: dope-fiend.

The photographer turned as they approached, assessing William's bruised face and cheap suit. 'Hullo, Phyll.' He nodded. 'Good evening, good evening.' Mr Quince liked to be double sure. 'Mr Garrett, is it?'

'Yes.' Phyll smiled in introduction. 'This is Mr Garrett.'

'I am Quince.' Quince went by a single name, like Michelangelo. The great artist offered his hand and William shook it. Quince was a clammy bastard; the kind who eschewed green vegetables and fresh air.

'I don't usually allow gentlemen into an event at such short notice,' Quince simpered, 'but Phyll is such a favourite and a true professional. You will pay cash as agreed, yes?' Quince smiled briefly, showing small white teeth, and then scrubbed at his nose, using his large, tartan handkerchief with some vigour.

'I have the twenty pounds.' William pulled a wad of notes from his wallet.

Mr Quince looked sharp about him, as if footpads might pounce unawares, and counted the cash, twice. William felt a sudden urge to belt the man, and belt him hard, twice. 'Ooh, yes, yes.' He made double-sure, Quince. 'That all seems to be in order.' His pointed pink tongue darted from his wet lips, twice. 'I will have to ask you to wait outside with the rest of the gentlemen, Mr Garrett, until Phyll and I have set up the tableaux, yes, tableaux.'

Quince motioned to the wide carriage doors at the far end of the building. This was not the way William had entered the factory floor, and he turned towards Phyll for reassurance. She nodded and grinned. And William realised then, that for all her studied masculinity, Phyll knew the danger of anxious men, for she had placated him with comforting smiles. William laughed and did as he was told, walking across her performance space and into what he felt to be an improvised lobby.

Cigarette smoke hung in a thick miasma about the heads of the men. They were huddled in groups of three or five, their voices a low rumble in talk which ceased, for a moment, when William entered the room. The atmosphere was acrid enough to make his eyes water, and it took some minutes before they could adjust to the environment. Phyll's audience was rich in sweat and good cologne. Men of William's age and older, red-faced in evening dress or stiff office collars and sober silk ties, they were gathered in what would have been the staff canteen. A few men sat on bench seating at the still intact trestle tables. Shaded electric lights glowed above them like the glass moons on a Victorian orrery. A long heavy counter, complete with massive tea urn, ran along the length of the room. It all seemed suddenly benign, convivial, like a regimental reunion. And William was chilled by his own instinct to scan the room, not only for Morton, but for Sergeant Prior and Chief Inspector Wade. All three belonged in this fug, this club-like atmosphere, this tense bastion of masculinity and privilege. But William recognised no one, only types. He breathed in hard, attempting to shake the dread of paranoia.

William distracted himself by examining a series of framed photographs, left hanging on the limewashed brick walls, unwanted by the bankrupted former owners of the foundry. He moved in closer. Girls in white cap and apron, munitions maids, stood two abreast beside huge field artillery, factory-fresh brass gleaming.

'Small women with big guns. They must've made the eighteen-pounders here. It makes one shiver to remember.'

William nodded. 'All over now.'

'Is it?'

He turned towards the speaker. The remnants of a great shrapnel wound flared concave across the man's cheek. William had seen worse cases when visiting Ronnie in Highbury Military Hospital after the war. And William had seen Ronnie slumped in the hotel bathroom. 'I mean that girls no longer make guns here.'

'They simply make them elsewhere. Germany is re-arming,' said the scarred man.

'I know.'

Then the carriage doors opened full. Two big lads, in suits like his own, stood sentry on each side of the entryway. The rat-like Quince had hired muscle. Not professionals, William knew by instinct, but locals in it for the beer money and the tits, and eyeing the clientele with hard contempt as they wandered onto the factory floor.

And here, Phyll was illuminated. The focus of the room. A radiant object, motionless and elevated, the rich men already at her feet. She was a mockery of them, or perhaps of herself, for she wore trousers, and they were about her ankles. She had changed clothes, for pooling around her bare feet was the dark, woollen stuff of male evening dress. The open waistband was visible, lined and stiffened with white linen, hook and eye and button fly. And above them, her slim calves and her fuller thighs and then her mons pubis – a shocking, feminine triangle of thick, black curls flanked by boyish hips. Surprisingly, she was not flat-chested but had high round breasts above a ribcage so prominent William could count each bone. Did women only have twenty-two? Were they really so deficient? Her hair was white in the light, but her eyes were made-up so that they were almost blackened. A prize-fighter of a girl, for her nose was wide. She looked up and away from the men, saint-like, and each wrist was cuffed to an iron girder, and her arms splayed out so that her whole torso was exposed, allowing no modesty of slumped posture or folded arms. Gagged too, by a necktie – motifs William did not recognise: a regiment, a club, a school. Phyll had acquiesced. It was what these men paid for – her unspeaking acquiescence. And William knew, felt sure to his bones, that their cocks were hard at her capitulation.

Even the twitchy Quince was hushed in Phyll's presence, his only movements a fixation on camera and light meter, flashbulb and spotlight. He scurried about in a strip of brightness between the men in the shadows and the brilliancy of the girl on the altar. And he was wound tight. William fancied that he could see Quince's veins pulse hard on his temples. Fussing over his production, perfecting and controlling, peering down into the viewfinder at Phyll's inverted image – it was all a masquerade. Quince had stage fright, and he was acting out his part poorly. The men whose scrutiny so terrified Quince paid him little regard. They streamed in, anonymous in dinner jackets or business suit, and lounged on the pine chairs or hunkered down on the factory floor, some smoking, some drinking from hipflasks, watched for a while and then left. A few were stalwart. Had they requested the pose; asked for the new, steel handcuffs specifically? These were the men who examined, whose gaze was not casual but exacting, proprietorial, and votaries to the image. And then Quince broke the magic: 'That is all from Miss Hall for the time being, gentlemen. There are other exhibitions throughout the evening which you may enjoy. A copy of each production will be posted in due course.' *Ite, missa est.* The last of the supplicants withdrew and William, who could bear Quince no longer, left alongside them and waited for Phyll at the entrance for workpeople and goods.

He smoked under city gaslight and became contemplative, mulling over Phyll's performance. This was Savile Row smut, nicely tailored, and nothing vulgar. Smut for gentlemen rather than players. Smut for the officer class, no doubt of that, poor bastards. If Quince were raided tonight, any decent lawyer could prove his photographs were art. There was precedent for Phyll's performance in every gallery in the country. But this caper was no artists' cooperative. He remembered Quince's little pink tongue darting lasciviously from his lips as the man counted out William's twenty quid. Quince was motivated by money. But his was a tricky business and would need a firm hand on the tiller. Sex and money were a potent combination. It made strong men lose their otherwise sound judgement. And from what William had witnessed, Mr Quince was no firm hand.

A half-hour passed before Phyll, now proper in her tweed suit, exited the metalworks. William pointed to the sign over the factory doors. 'Are you a workperson or are you goods?'

'Both. I am artist, and I am art.' Phyll motioned for a cigarette.

'Oh Christ. You're delusional.' But William was delighted she understood his remark, for it had taken him the full thirty minutes to come up with it. 'I've only got gaspers.' He moved forward to light Phyll's fag, bashful of his trembling hand.

Phyll took a long first drag. 'Do you want to speak to Quince, or not?'

'Oh, indeed I do.' It would be a pleasure to bully Quince – and bully him hard.

'You're not going to get heavy with him, are you?' Phyll frowned.

'Not yet. And not with his muscle around. My parts are still tender.' Now was not the time to cause a ruck, for William's ribs ached. He made a pantomime of doubling up in pain. *Clowning about for the girls – not now, Billy.* A ball of anguish formed in the centre of William's chest, as though Clara, and the guilt and agony he associated with her, was curled in his thorax. Grief had burrowed deep in him, nested and made herself at home. He shook his head like a dog batting away a fly.

Phyll ignored, or did not notice, William's behaviour. 'He won't be finished just yet. There are three more performances this evening.'

'You have more work to do?' William asked.

'Not me. There are other models and other scenarios. You've paid for the whole evening. You can go back inside.'

William and Phyll were the only people to have exited the factory. The remainder of Quince's clients wanted their money's worth.

'I don't think waiting will be wise. Besides –' William thought of Quince's two hard men – 'I promised that we'd meet Queenie. She should be around.'

'Ronnie's sister?' Phyll stubbed out her cigarette, scrubbed at it with her small foot and then kicked it into the gutter.

'Don't be scared.' He laughed. 'I telephoned her after we arranged to meet. I had to speak to her. I had to tell her all I know. It was necessary to keep her informed, I mean.' William wondered why he stumbled over this description of his relationship with Queenie. 'She wanted to see Quince for herself. She's that kind of person.'

'I'm not scared, and you're being ridiculous tonight.' Phyll's bullish response did not tally with her guarded, pinched face. 'That's Quince's car.' She nodded towards a Bedford van, spanking new and as green as Christmas, parked across the street in the lee of a scrapyard wall.

'Oh Christ, he's a baby photographer.' Quince had splashed out on good livery. The hand-painted face of a fat-cheeked child, golden curls tied in pink ribbon to match her complexion, beamed above lettering which blazoned: *Mr F. Quince, Professional Family Portrait Photographer, Mafeking Road, Chad Valley.* And below that in too elaborate script: *All Babies are Bonny in Quince's Careful Hands.* William turned to Phyll, pointing to Quince's Bedford van, disbelieving. 'Why is he so careless? I know his address. I can pay him a visit.'

She shrugged. 'Please be subtle.'

'It's my middle name.'

And then Queenie emerged from the gaping mouth of road beneath the railway bridge. William watched her. She was a moll, a bad girl trussed up in expensive clothes. Fox fur draped over her shoulder, its animal face dangling with its dead, glassy stare, its claws scratching her best wool suit. Her skin like cream, and green eyes and red lips, were all part hidden in the shadows of the filmy black veil which covered her face. Queenie, like her brother, knew how to make an entrance, and William felt suddenly at home, relieved.

'Where is he then?' she asked.

William motioned behind him. 'Still in there, doing his dirty business.' He then nodded towards the Bedford van. 'That's his van. He's got a legitimate studio in Chad Valley.'

'I clocked that. Brazen, ain't he? To leave it out here like that. It's like he feels safe, or something. You'd think he'd take better care. It ain't a good neighbourhood. Anything could happen to a fella with a nice van like that out here.' Queenie turned her attention to Phyll. She was quiet for a moment and sniffed, animal-like and assessing. 'This our Ronnie's new friend?'

William nodded.

'Miss Edgerton—'

'Maggs.' William and Queenie spoke in unison.

'Miss Maggs, I was just saying to William that it would be best to go gently with Mr Quince. That aggression may not be the best strategy.'

William laughed.

Queenie lifted her veil and peered at him, surveying him steadily, wincing at the scabs and bruises on his face. 'You seem to be putting a lot of trust in this girl. What is it with you and women?'

'I like women.'

'Don't you bloody just. Come with me.' She nodded at Phyll. 'You too.'

'Where are we going, Queenie?' asked William.

She pointed to beyond the railway bridge. 'To the *Little Marvel*, of course.' And then she beckoned them both towards Quince's van, fiddled with the clasp of her handbag, peered inside, and finally – with a showman's flourish – she brandished a large, steel nail file and ran it along the length of Quince's spotless paintwork. The vandalism squealed out into the night.

'Oh, Miss Maggs, do you think that wise?' Phyll was unsure of her allegiances, William knew. Quince held sway as her employer. Benign, a little pretentious, ineffectual to her, he was no threat. 'Should we draw attention to ourselves?'

'That's the whole point. He is a shameless, filthy bastard. There ain't no doubt about that,' said Queenie. 'You need to learn to care less about the likes of Mr Quince, bab. I hope to give him a bit of a funny turn, you know, when he comes back to his van. Shit him up. Make him realise that he ain't got no friends about here.' Queenie gave Phyll a beautiful wide Ronnie grin and winked. 'And you better call me Queenie.' She had used the ubiquitous Brummie term of endearment; had invited Phyll to call her by her Christian name; had forced her to witness – be complicit in – an act of petty criminality. This was Queenie's way of inducting Phyll into the tribe.

'Yes, alright. Yes, Queenie,' she smiled in return with acceptance. And, in the shadow of the scrapyard wall, beside Quince's ravaged paintwork, William thought he saw Phyll fall a little in love.

23

Queenie was moored near the Lawley Street viaduct. An old city place where road, canal, railway and river nudged and jostled for place and purpose amidst the great industrial boundaries of Birmingham. Away from the dense back streets, the evening breeze was constant and cool, and the stars were bright against a night sky like a swathe of blue velvet.

And the *Little Marvel* was changed, slightly; quiet. It was the birdsong – a robin – the distant hum of traffic, the flaps and scuffles of canal-side creatures. William could hear it all. 'Where are the kiddies, Queenie?' he asked.

'They're on their holidays. I sent 'em off to Weston with old Mrs Stokes? She's very good with 'em.' Queenie neither shifted from the deck nor invited them on board. 'They did a proper number on you, whoever did you over. They meant business, no doubt.' She was sombre in the moonlight, like a goddess. 'At least you look better in the dark.'

William reached to touch his swollen face. 'Even the babby?'

'He's off the tit and on the bottle. I had to do it. Couldn't have the kiddies here. I feel something bad brewing. Something violent and nasty, something ain't right.' Queenie and Shifty shared the same crystal ball; both foretold dangers, and both believed the vulnerable were to seek sanctuary in Weston-super-Mare. 'Let's talk inside.' She beckoned them to join her, at last. 'I'll make some tea.'

Inside, the *Little Marvel* was darker than the city night. And it was a woman's place, smelling of beeswax and talcum powder. Queenie lit an oil lamp, but it was a moment before William's eyes adjusted to the warm gloom. The copper kettle shimmered with Brasso, and the gilded teacups glistened, but the dim, golden lamplight could not properly penetrate the shadowy corners of the cabin, as its walls were painted part peacock blue and part deep red.

'I've never been in a barge before.' Phyll looked around her, appreciative of the *Little Marvel*'s gypsy romance. 'It's very mysterious and beautiful. It must be a lovely place to live.'

'She's a narrowboat, not a barge. Barges are mostly London things.' Queenie placed the kettle on the stove. 'There ain't nothing modern on her. She's old and a bitch to work, but she's home, was home, for me and Ronnie and Billy.' Queenie turned to Phyll and smiled at the younger woman's admiration, and then removed her hat and furs. 'You're right about her being a beauty, though. She's all my own, and I feel sort of comforted here. It's the only place where I get a good night's sleep.' William remembered the warmth of their childhood bed, the lapping of the dark water against the hull of the boat, the coal-black nights of country moorings, and he understood how the *Little Marvel* had become a refuge to the grieving Queenie. 'I had to identify the body today. His face was all gone, destroyed.' She turned to them both, a rare note of fragility, and anxiety, in her voice. 'I know I ain't got much in the way of morality. I know my faults. But I just can't fathom the evil of the thing.'

For a moment, they stood silent in their collective sorrow and disbelief. And then William was suddenly isolated. Severed from the women at the realisation that their mourning, both expressed and unexpressed, was for Ronnie alone and not Clara. They did not love her, had not known her. Now, William understood the way the night would go. The spotlight would be on Ronnie, for he was the leading man. Clara remained in the shadowy wings of the women's attention. Yet, for William, thoughts of Clara dominated. William touched his bandaged chest in a brief, involuntary gesture. Dope-numbed anger, fear and desperation crouched monstrous within him: here, beneath William's broken ribs, grief lay coiled, biding its time. And grief's name was Clara.

'Take a seat.' Queenie motioned to the upholstered bench which ran along the length of the boat. At her words, William returned from isolation to the comfort of collective mourning. Queenie turned her black back to him, rattled teacups at the sink, and said, 'I was at the foundry earlier before you pair arrived. I like to see things for myself, you know. There were one or two pretty folks milling about. The sort of people our Ronnie was always drawn to. Unusual, artistic, even the lads.' Then she faced them for a moment, catching William's eye. 'A little fella was fussin' about 'em. Never stopped talking, moving his camera equipment from that van, smiling at a pair of good-looking girls. Chat, chat, chat. Sociable little bastard. Was that Quince?'

'Sounds like it,' said William.

'Hard-working type, ain't he?' She turned and placed the tea tray on the table. 'He's the sweating type. The type who should only wear cotton next to his skin. I can't say I took to him.' Queenie poured, like mother.

'He's quite harmless. I don't think he'd hurt a fly, honestly I don't.' Phyll sipped at the proffered tea. 'The good-looking people you saw were the models scheduled for other performances, I should think. There were several tableaux to be performed tonight. He pays us well and is very kind.' Phyll looked first at William and then at Queenie. 'Do you think we should go back?'

'There's no point in seeing any more,' he said. 'I know the set-up. I'll go to Chad Valley tomorrow. Cause a stink at his studio if I have to.'

Phyll put down her teacup. 'Really, Billy. What was the point of me going to all that trouble of arranging a meeting if you're going to jib out at the last minute?'

'I agree with Phyll. Go back tonight. Wait by his van; put the frighteners on him.' Queenie spoke in staccato imperatives. Her tactics were offensive and full-on. 'Let him know we're on to his game. That he's visible now.'

'I've had the shit kicked out of me. I was nearly drowned. I can't take on Quince's muscle tonight, not unless you want me back in the infirmary. Is that what you want, Queenie?' William lit a cigarette. 'And besides, you don't have your lads with you. Not that I'd ever want them.' William shifted the fag to the left side of his mouth, for the right side couldn't bear the puckering drag of smoking. It had been tenderised by a boot in the early hours of Sunday morning. 'I'm on my own, and I ain't up to another brawl.'

'Yes, love.' Queenie smiled. 'I can see that.' She rose and offered the biscuit tin to her guests as though she were hosting a Mothers' Union meeting, and then paused for a moment, as if in thought. Suddenly, she said, steady and quiet, 'Tell you what, if you're too poorly to do it, drive me back to the basin, and I'll get a few lads to help. We can get the little bastard and take him north out near the Dunlop. Then, we'll hold him by the ankles over the canal bridge. It generally works. Keep him dangling until he squeals. Spills everything he knows about Morton and our Ronnie. Hands over his client list, the lot.'

'For fuck's sake, Queenie. Your tactics are a last resort, love. Quince has a lot to lose. A nice little legitimate business, for one. And besides, he won't have proof that Morton was involved with the pornography on him right now. Let me go there tomorrow and persuade him to be free with his knowledge or take a financial hit. A little light blackmail if you will. I'll tell him I could make life very awkward for him. Then, if he doesn't come up with the goods, we get heavy. Pull his fuckin' fingernails out, for all I care. I can't stand the bloke.' William had appeased Queenie with a politic vow of violence. He flicked his cigarette into his tea, half-smoked, hating himself. And then he lost his temper. 'Why do you always have to go in, guns blazing? You'll get us fuckin' nicked or murdered, girl. I thought you had brains.'

The biscuit tin plummeted to the table, landing with a thud. Queenie squared her shoulders.

'But there are other tableaux tonight, don't you see?' Phyll's raised voice held a note of panic. 'Just because I didn't recognise the people in Ronnie's photographs doesn't mean the other models won't.'

'What photographs?' asked Queenie.

Phyll turned towards William. 'You haven't told her?'

'Only about the ones taken with you.'

'I am here, you know,' said Queenie. 'It's my bloody boat you're on.'

William reached into his breast pocket and placed the photographs of the dark centurion and the Rokeby Venus on Queenie's table. Queenie reached for the oil lamp and scrutinised the pornography under its golden light. She touched the pictures of her brother with tender care. 'Silly bloody fool,' she said. 'Silly bloody fool.'

'Do you recognise him, Queenie?' asked William. 'The dark lad, I mean. Is he one of Ronnie's fellas?'

'I can't see his face. I can only see his helmet,' she said.

Phyll let out a childish guffaw.

Queenie caught her eye and gave her a stage wink. 'You gotta admit, it's very impressive.' And, for a moment, Ronnie was back in the room. 'Oh, Christ. What was he playing at?'

'It's very beautifully done.' William couldn't tell if Phyll was being comforting or defensive. 'I don't think he's done anything to be ashamed of.'

'It ain't the morality of the thing I'm worried about, bab. It's the danger.' Queenie took her seat and eyed Phyll shrewdly. 'But you're right. This is tame. It's just that they're both fellas. If it were naked girls –' she pointed to the picture of the Rokeby Venus – 'it'd be called artistic. But I reckon that the average fella ain't really into art.'

'I believe Billy secretly is,' said Phyll, 'even though he says he isn't.'

William's chest tightened as he remembered the hours spent with Clara in the art gallery.

'He ain't average,' said Queenie. 'None of us are. Not me, not Billy, not Ronnie. It's our curse.'

There was a silence. Phyll fiddled with her cigarette case. William leant forward and lit her fag, and then lit one for himself. He watched Phyll take a long drag. Finally, he asked, 'Has Quince persuaded you to do stuff that crosses the line? That fine line you told me about.'

'Quince can be terribly persuasive. One often feels obliged to do tableaux without merit. I was once asked to wear a gas mask,' she said. 'The kind you chaps had on the front. I didn't mind, as the premise sounded interesting, but the first time I did it, it was rather suffocating. I couldn't breathe. The hood was attached too tightly, and I panicked and struggled. The handcuffs bit into my wrists and it hurt rather. They even bled a little.' She paused once more, drawing heavily on her cigarette. The ash fluttered into her teacup like dirty snow and melted into the dregs. 'But when it was all over, Quince was so very pleased. He gave me extra money and said how delighted the man who requested the picture was. I was asked to repeat the performance a few weeks later. This time, they put me in khaki and puttees as well. Quince hinted that the more distressed I acted, the better.'

'Why on earth did Quince retake the photographs on a different date?' asked William.

'No, no, you don't understand.' The edge in Phyll's voice was painful. 'Quince filmed the whole thing, Billy. The second time around, he had a motion picture camera.'

There was a silence. The air in the boat was thick with a fug of smoke. Queenie rose to open a window. When she returned to her seat, spots of colour had risen to her pale cheeks. Finally, she said, 'They took a moving picture of you all trussed up and half-naked and struggling?' Phyll nodded. Queenie's eyes narrowed further, shining in the gloom of the cabin like those of a nocturnal creature. 'A man would pay a good deal of money to get the exact girl he wanted to do the exact thing he wanted, and it all to be filmed as a moving picture.' Queenie became all poised muscle. She turned towards William. 'Billy, has this ever been done before?'

'Probably,' he said, 'but I've never seen one. I've never heard of it, even, you know, in my job. And I've seen all sorts. It must be a new thing.'

'There's money in it. More money than I first thought. If Quince owns the image, he can sell as many copies of the photographs and the movies as he likes, abroad, whatever. Was our Ronnie making these films?' asked Queenie.

'Ronnie only pretended to be candid, you know. He was a very private person. He only told me things when he was squiffy. He was often – always, really – tipsy or high as a kite. It became difficult to know what he was getting at. Eventually, one tuned out of the conversation. But I did love him. I did love him so.' Phyll's strained voice sounded out into the hushed half-dark of the cabin. 'Ronnie was with Quince from the very beginning. It was he who introduced me to Quince. I would be surprised if Quince did not make several films with Ronnie. And Billy, Ronnie did sell Quince rather a lot of cocaine. The poor man is self-conscious of his looks, and Ronnie told him it would keep his weight down. Although I think Quince mostly used it for his nerves. He is a timid man –' she glanced at Queenie – 'weak, and I believe the dope gave him confidence when he was around his clientele.'

William stared into his tea. He thought of the man who had requested Phyll's performance: his need for the gas mask, and his need for Phyll's fear, and his need for Phyll's pain. And then he thought of the man who tortured and strangled Clara Morton. The hard ball of angry grief in William's chest grew so large, he feared it would choke him. 'And the men watch the films as a live show just like they do with the photographs?' he asked.

'Yes, they watched me. They always watch. Once, Quince asked if a client could participate.'

'Participate?' Queenie, perceptive as ever, pounced on the word. 'Quince has probably photographed, filmed, rich men, powerful men ...' She paused for a moment. 'Fucking my brother. No wonder our Ronnie's dead. No wonder he's murdered.' Queenie turned to him and said, 'This Mr Morton, he's a rich man of influence, ain't he?'

'Yes, love.'

And Quince, William thought, a man motivated by a love of money, how far would he go to protect his business, protect a rich man of influence?

'And what you gonna do?' she asked.

'I think it's about time we tried to speak to another of Quince's models.' William gathered up the pornography and placed it back in his breast pocket.

24

When they returned to the foundry, William knew they were in luck. The girl was alone, half-cut perhaps, and danced, in precise formal steps, around the courtyard with her arms about an invisible partner. Her long hair was let down, wild and dark about her shoulders, and she wore nothing but a slip and a robe, both silk and both expensive, and stained with sweat and rouge. As they approached, she turned and saw them. Her face was stony, but she did not cry out. 'Do you waltz?' she asked William.

'No.' William glanced towards the entrance way. Quince's muscle was nowhere to be seen. 'I don't dance,' he said. William edged closer to the girl, but the women kept near Quince's van, now emblazoned with Queenie's violent signature, as if sensing the girl might get skittish, and bolt. William suddenly felt the need for a sugar lump.

'That's a shame. I adore it.' The girl raised her dancing arms a little higher. 'You're very tall, aren't you?' Her tone was accusatory. 'Short men are better dancers.'

'I didn't do it on purpose. I just grew that way.'

William beckoned to Phyll, but both women moved forward. The girl did not acknowledge them but continued with her waltz. 'Do you know her?' he asked Phyll.

'No,' she said. Phyll took the girl's hand, partnering her in a few skilful steps, and brought the dance to a natural halt beneath the dirty yellow glow of a street lamp. 'I'm a friend of Quince,' she told the dancing girl. 'Are you a friend of Quince?'

William joined them. Underneath the light, he saw the girl's shiner, made by a good-sized fist, and purpling fresh. She had a swollen mouth, too, her lip cut. Remnants of heavy eye make-up ran down her pale cheeks and made rivulets in old pancake and powder.

'Quince –' she stared at them both with bloodshot eyes, her slate-grey pupils large – 'is everybody's friend unless you've been a bit naughty. And then –' she paused in theatrical emphasis – 'he releases the hounds. I hate those big brutes, they're so very common.' She touched her face as if testing the reality of her bruises, and then crooked her finger, inviting William closer, considering him as a collector does a dead moth under glass. 'Have you been naughty?' she asked.

'Very.' William reached into his jacket pocket, and then fanned out the pornography, like a magician asking to choose a card. 'I have some of Quince's photographs,' he said.

The girl smiled. She liked the game. 'That's Ronnie –' she pointed, and waved at Phyll – 'with the pretty blonde boy. Ronnie is fun. Are you fun? Ronnie brings the sugar.' She began to dance the shimmy and sing, '*I need a little sugar in my bowl, I need a little hot dog on my roll.*' The girl halted as if expecting applause. 'I'm trained, you know.' She eyed them all carefully. 'I'm professionally trained for the theatre. I'm too good for this muck.' The girl gestured with her thumb towards the factory.

'And the other man?' William asked.

'Lordy, I haven't a clue.' She began to sway as if about to faint, but then became suddenly aggressive. 'I don't know everyone, you know.'

'What about this girl?' William handed her the photograph of the Rokeby Venus.

'Oh, that's just Fay,' she said. 'I haven't seen her for a few weeks. She's fun. She's fun just like Ronnie. Are you fun?' The girl frowned and mimicked pushing William away. 'No, you don't look like fun. You don't look like fun at all. You look like a bad headache.'

'Fay what?'

William handed the girl ten bob; she scrutinised the bank note as a child does a picture book, reading the printed declaration from the Bank of England with moving lips. 'How on earth am I meant to know that?' The girl shook her head and slumped to the floor, as if thinking and talking had become too exhausting. She was hunched now in part-shadow, and William saw more bruises as the silk robe slipped from her shoulders. She leant back against the foundry wall, legs curled beneath her like a cat, and smiled, eyes closed. 'Quince doesn't like us to use our real names, silly. He doesn't like us to make friends. "No chatting, girls," he says. He's like a prim schoolmistress. Horrid old Quince.' The girl put her hand on her mouth, as if she'd told a secret. Then she removed her hand and turned to William, wide-eyed, and said, 'Fay is kind. When she was flush, she lent me money for my rent. She is a kind friend, and she's fun.'

Queenie approached the girl for the first time. 'She's off her head,' she said, 'and I don't think it's cocaine.' Queenie hunkered down, lifted the lid of the girl's good eye and felt her forehead with the back of her hand. 'What are you on? Is it heroin?' she asked. Then she prised the picture of Fay from the girl's fingers and passed it over to William; the girl let out a chuckle like a low hiss. Queenie looked at William and said, 'We're not gonna get much sense from her. She's about to pass out.'

'Why was Fay flush?' asked William. 'Did she sell you sugar, like Ronnie?'

She opened her eyes quick and wide. 'Fay had a gentleman. Oh my, oh my. He bought her a fur. She showed me. Not some horrible vulgar old fox —' she fingered at Queenie's get-up — 'but a mink. She had that fat old man wrapped around her little finger.'

'Fat old man?' William asked. 'Tell me about him.'

'He is old, and he is fat.'

'What was his name?'

'I told you. Fat. Old. Man.' Another low hiss of a giggle. 'She would wrap her legs around him and squeeze, squeeze, squeeze him tight for all he was worth. I haven't seen her in weeks, you know. I miss her. I miss Ronnie. They're fun. Are you fun?'

'I'm like a bank holiday weekend. What did the fat man look like? Was he one of Quince's clients?' William wished he'd had the presence of mind to clip Morton's photograph from the copy of the Blackshirt newspaper. 'How was Fay getting money from the fat man?'

She blinked at William as if uncomprehending. 'No, you liar. You're no fun at all. You're tiresome. You're just another big, cross man.' The girl turned her attention to Phyll. 'You're not cross. You're cute. I'd like a cigarette, cutey.' Phyll squatted next to the girl, placed a cigarette between her lips and lit it. The girl took a few soft puffs and considered Phyll through lowered, fluttering lashes. 'I was right, you are cute. I like my boys pretty and short. They make better dancers.'

'Where does Fay live?' asked Phyll.

The girl shrugged and squeezed Phyll's knee. 'Fay is such a lot of fun.'

'What else do you know about the fat old man?' she asked. 'Can you tell me?' The girl considered Phyll with a groggy absorption, grinned, pulled her shoulders back military straight, and then gave Phyll a fascist salute. William was silent. The steady splutter of a narrowboat crossing the viaduct sounded out into the night like a lunger's cough, but the slum streets were empty. They were quite alone under the sickly grey-yellow light of the street lamps. 'Did Ronnie know Fay? Were Ronnie and Fay friends?' asked Phyll. But the girl did not answer, for she had not heard the question, and had drifted into a dope-fiend's sleep, her trembling eyelids like the wings of a dying butterfly.

William glanced at Queenie, heart and head pounding. They had found the connection between Morton and Ronnie; it was the girl, Fay. A young woman who, quite probably, was now in very real danger. Had she provided Ronnie with the dirt he had on Morton? And Quince, a man capable – judging by the little dancer's bruises – of doing violence by proxy, did he know of Fay's financial relationship with his client?

Queenie nodded towards him, and then squatted next to the sleeping dancer. She took the ten-bob note from the girl's lap, placed it inside the pocket of her own fox stole, and felt the girl's pulse. 'We need to find this Fay before it's too late,' she said. Then she wrapped her furs about the sleeping dancer's shoulders and said, 'Get everything you can from Quince first thing tomorrow. You're a big lad, Billy, bloody well belt him if you have to. And if you fail, let me know, because I ain't one bit squeamish. And I cannot bear a ponce.'

25

Wednesday, 12 July

It was lunchtime already, and William, head still fogged with Veronal-induced sleep, drove through Chad Valley in search of Quince. The terraces ran uphill towards Edgbaston – Sunnyside, Thornhill, The Willows, The Nook: the house names were like a poem, but the streets were named after battles. The forgotten kind from the last century; won with gallantry and Gatling guns and public-schoolboy tactics. And there was something of the old Queen Empress about Mafeking Road, for the villas were fat and dark and hard and respectable. He parked the Austin several doors down from Quince's shop and reached in the glovebox for his service revolver. The Webley was insurance against the fist-happy fuckers in Quince's pay. The same men who, on the pornographer's orders, and William was sure of this, beat the dancing girl as punishment for some perceived infraction, or, in her own words, naughtiness.

It was a garden-variety, suburban afternoon; a lawnmower buzzed, a radio hummed out Elgar, saucepans clattered, and William walked the hundred feet or so to Quince's premises. Plate-glass windows bowed either side of the door, with its paintwork as brown and sticky as chocolate. And above the front door was Quince's name in sepia italics: *Mr Frederick Quince, Portraitist.* William entered, and a bell rang out.

'I shan't be a moment, do take a seat.' Quince's voice called, obsequious, from another room, his studio.

William sat in a sturdy cushioned chair and waited. It was a nice little set-up, indeed. A modern mirror advertised Kodak film; a smart, hand-painted sign bragged of same day development; a stout mahogany counter, uncluttered but for a brass till, held gilded photograph albums – 'Our Wedding', 'Baby's First Steps', 'Family Memories' – in its glass belly. The light dimmed. Outside, the clouds shifted across the sun. And, for a moment, William saw the small, spidery etching of a child's handprint on the near spotless windows of the shopfront.

'I do beg your pardon. My assistant's half-day. How can I help you?' Quince was wearing a white coat, like a scientist. The buttons pulled tight over his paunch. His face hardened as William rose and came towards him.

'Oh, it's Mr Garrett, isn't it?' He rubbed his hands against the side of his body. 'I'm afraid I'm terribly busy with a customer. A portrait of a little one.' He pulled a stuffed animal from his pocket and waved it at William. 'I've got the knack with them, but it doesn't do to keep them waiting. They can get fractious at this time of day. Nap-time for baby, don't you know, don't you know.' He made to move back into the studio. 'Do telephone before you come again. An appointment is best. Then, we can talk business. Or better still, most of our business can be conducted via the telephone. A marvellous machine, is it not?' Quince smiled and then lowered his voice. 'I do try to keep the more *artistic* side of my work apart from the day-to-day stuff. Yes, yes, *quite* apart.' He stood by the red velvet curtain which separated the shop from the studio and laughed just a little. 'Well, goodbye.' William did not move. Quince nodded towards the door, his smile a panicked grimace. William waited. Tears formed in Quince's eyes. He blinked but kept his grin. 'Well, I really must ask you to leave. You see, I'm most terribly busy.' A child behind the curtain let out a frustrated cry. A woman's voice called for Quince. Finally, William spoke:

'Ronnie Edgerton.'

'Oh, but he's dead. Don't you know he's *quite* dead?' Quince hissed.

'I want everything you have on Ronnie Edgerton, and I want everything you have on Edward Morton and the girl Fay.' Quince's face blanched to the colour of boiled bones. 'Every print, every film, all the negatives. Times, dates, names of those involved. Then, I'll leave.'

'I really don't think you quite understand. I'm with a customer. A young mother with a baby. This is –' Quince's voice was quick and nasal – 'my business. I've a respectable business.'

'No doubt. It looks a nice little earner.'

The young mother called again for Quince.

'You *must* leave,' Quince pleaded.

William realised the man had no idea of who he was or what his motives were. Quince's ignorance would work to William's advantage, and so he acted. Moving towards Quince and shoving him aside with force enough to make the pornographer stagger, William pulled back the velvet curtain. The brass rings clattered sharply on their brass pole.

Quince had turned the back room of the shop into a large photographic studio. The space was well lit with good quality photographic lamps, and a painted linen backdrop – a fantasy galleon in full sail – filled the far wall. In front of the story-book ship, a toddler steadied himself against the seat of a highchair. A woman, back turned, on her knees, sang out, '*Two little dicky-birds sitting on a wall, one named Peter, one named Paul.*' She was the good-wife type, round-faced, plump and homely. She turned and looked up at William with placid confusion. 'Where is Mr Quince?'

'Well, he's a fine-looking little fellow. What's his name?' asked William.

'Christopher,' she said. 'I do think that Mr Quince should finish his business soon. I did pay for the full hour.' She crawled towards the child and gathered him up, then stood and stared, wide-eyed and cow-like.

William had frightened her. He had meant to, but he felt shoddy about it.

'Mr Quince will give you your money back. Find another photographer for Christopher. Someone in the city.'

Quince appeared before William could say more. 'Yes, do, Mrs Irving. I'm afraid I've had some rather bad news and shan't be doing business for the rest of the day.' He glanced quickly at William. 'I shall fetch your hat.'

'You do look rather pale, Mr Quince. Are you quite alright?' Quince nodded to her, his grin a strange contortion. The woman fussed about with her straw cloche for a moment and then hurried Christopher out of the shop. The child, bonny and sweet-natured, waved its pudgy hand to Mr Quince as he left. William followed them to the door, flipped the Yale mechanism to the lock, and then turned the sign so that it read *Closed for Business*. He pulled the blinds, throwing the shop into sudden shadow.

'That was very bad of you,' said Quince. 'Very bad. I really should telephone the police.'

'And tell them what?' William asked.

'I have friends. Friends who'll be most upset at your behaviour.'

'Ah, yes. I've seen them. Those fellows in dinner jackets. They like you. You're chummy with them. They'll do anything for you, I'm sure.' William lit a cigarette and reached for the pornography in his breast pocket. He held out the picture of Fay for Quince to see. 'Did you take this picture?' Quince winced and turned his face away from the photograph. 'Is this Fay? Has she made films for Edward Morton?'

'There are so many considerations. You must understand that my business relies on my discretion.' Quince faced William once more, puffed out his cheeks and straightened his sloping shoulders. 'There is a relationship of trust between myself and my clients and to sever it would be a terrible betrayal. The kind a gentleman of status and fine sensibility would consider quite bad form. Yes, terribly bad form.' William was unable to fathom whether Quince saw himself as a priest or as an old family retainer. Either way, he derived pleasure from keeping rich men's secrets.

'Just give me what I want, quickly and quietly.' William took a drag of his fag and placed Fay's photograph back in his pocket. 'The way I see it is this. Tell me what you know about Fay and Edward Morton.' Quince shook his head. 'Be sensible, man. You either take a hit on the pornography, or you take a hit on both the legitimate business and the smut. I'm more than happy to fuck up both. Very content to do it. Those Nechells lads you employ don't look too loyal. I think they'd like me, though. I reckon I talk their language.' William inched closer to the photographer. 'I'm a man of leisure, Mr Quince. I've got a lot of time on my hands. Give me the girl's address, or I could come here every day and hang about like a bad smell. Me being here is worse than having problems with your drains. That nice Mrs Irving didn't take to me. She looks like a talker, though. That type always is.'

'I have important friends, you know.' This was becoming the pornographer's prayer, and it worried William, Quince's stubborn assertion of power by proxy. The man might not be that easy to break. 'They won't take kindly to this intrusion.'

'Who? What muscle do you really have? Your lads are big but they're just for show. There to keep the talent in their place, and the rich punters feeling safe and cosy, no doubt. Nothing more. Nothing organised. Christ, man, you're just a bunch of fucking amateurs.'

'I run a bespoke service, for men of importance, discernment,' said Quince. 'If I give you what you want, they could ruin me.'

William stubbed his cigarette out on the polished shop floor next to Quince's brown brogues. Leaning in close, William smelt his own sour breath as he spoke. 'You're ruined already. You're out of your depth. You think I'm the nastiest bastard you could come across? Once the gangs know what you're up to ...Those lads, they like their monopolies on girls and dope. You're fucked. Dead in a ditch.'

'Oh God. I knew it, I knew it. Do they know? Did they send you?' he asked. 'It's played on my nerves terribly, but Ronnie always said I wouldn't be troubled by them if I kept it discreet.'

'You're a fool.' William paused. 'Tell me about Edward Morton's relationship with the girl Fay.'

'Please stop mentioning those names. You're confusing me. Frightening me.' Quince blanched once more, deathly pale. He took a deep intake of breath. 'And I really don't know who you're talking about.' He looked about to cry. And he was lying, of course, for Quince had no poker face.

'You are a lying little fucker.'

Quince flinched. 'No, no, I'm not.'

Queenie was right after all. William would have to belt him. So he did.

Quince dropped hard against the shop-counter, cracking the glass with his back as he fell. He was curled on the floor, his body twitching like fresh fish on a slab, and he held his nose and mouth with both hands. William saw blood well up and spread between Quince's fingers. 'Get up.' Quince shook his head. 'Get up.' Quince didn't shift, so William moved down towards him, sat on his haunches and talked quietly, became mild. 'Give me what I need, and I will go away. I want everything you have on Ronnie Edgerton, Morton, the girl called Fay. And this man.' He reached once more in his pocket and forced Quince to look at the picture of the naked centurion. 'Who is he? I want everything you have on these people. Everything, including the motion pictures you made.' The pornographer's body became taut. 'And don't tell me you don't know Edward Morton because you'd be lying to me. I don't like liars.'

Quince edged his way up slowly and sat slumped against the counter. He still held his nose, and fat drops of blood fell like tears onto his white coat. 'I think you've broken my nose.'

'Perhaps.' William gave Quince his clean handkerchief.

'Oh, why don't you just leave me alone?' It was a lamentation, wailed desperate between sobs.

William kicked gently two or three times at Quince's side. 'That's not going to happen, now, is it? Be sensible.' William was play-acting tough guy. It took a lot of hard work to be so violent. If Quince didn't spill it soon, it would be William who cracked.

'No, I do know that. But there's so much at stake. Such a lot of money. I've made such a lot of money.' Quince began to cry. 'I do like money, very much.'

'Now is the time to call it quits. Go back to brides and babies. You haven't got the stomach for this business. You've got the wrong sort of nerves. I saw men like you at the front. They crumbled, then they died quick. Got the wind up and did stupid things. Are you going to do stupid things, Mr Quince?'

'No, I shall tell you. I don't like pain. I am a coward.' Quince seemed neither proud nor ashamed of his confession. 'I shall tell you what I know. Please do help get me up.' William bent, wincing at the pain in his ribs, took Quince by the under-arms, and then hauled him to his feet. Despite his paunch, Quince was light, like a woman. 'Come into the studio.' William followed Quince through the velvet curtain and watched as he rolled the painted backdrop up like a blind, revealing a heavy door, double-bolted. Quince unlocked the door and switched on the light – a red light, for this was Quince's darkroom. It was well set up with expensive modern equipment, including a film projector and screen. Quince walked over to a double porcelain sink which stood on the far wall, and ran the tap. He dampened William's blooded hand-kerchief with cold water, and dabbed at his nose, wincing and tentative. 'Is it broken, do you think? It's terribly sore.'

'I don't know. It bled enough.'

Quince slumped down into a wooden chair and held his head back to stop the bleeding, pinching the bridge of his nose. The red light made Quince's blood look black. William shut the door.

'I don't know everything, you know. I want to make it absolutely clear that I know nothing of poor Ronnie's death.

Nothing. I learnt about it last night from young Phyll. I was terribly shocked and unnerved when she told me. You are quite a perceptive man, Mr Garrett. My nerves have never been good. I didn't serve in the last war. I was unfit.' Quince got up from his chair and opened a cabinet at the far end of the room. He pulled out a large manilla file and gave it to William, then took his seat, pinched his nose again. 'This is all I have on dear Ronnie, prints and negatives, and that is the truth. The young man dressed as a centurion –' Quince paused – 'is a friend of Ronnie's. One of those soldier boys who hangs around Station Street. A mousy-haired, buck-toothed boy with a fine figure. Of course, he could've been a sailor on leave, a man in uniform. Everyone loves a man in uniform. I don't know his name. Tommy, perhaps. He was just a pick-up of Ronnie's.' Quince frowned in thought. 'Those pictures are in the manilla file I gave you and, well, a few, shall we say, are somewhat Greco-Roman in inspiration. Have you seen the wall paintings in Pompeii? The constabulary would take exception to those types of photographs. Yes, yes, quite. Please be very discreet, Mr Garrett. They were commissioned by the son of a wealthy manufacturer, himself an Adonis.' Quince was warming to his subject. He was a gossip, at once libidinous and prim. And he was talking too much, far too much, but saying nothing of value. 'In jam and with a knighthood, the father.'

'In jam?' William checked the filing cabinet. He found a drawer full of folders of semi-pornographic stills, hardly smut. He flicked through each file, examining the photographs in search of Fay, but found nothing. And there were no film reels.

'Yes, marmalade, also. A jam magnate, and a very broad-minded young gentleman, if I do say so.' Quince nodded towards the file. 'You'll see.' Quince's voice was breathy and pervert-low.

'And the films?'

Quince slipped beside William and slammed the cabinet shut. 'I don't keep that kind of material here. They are kept at the Midland Bank in the city centre. But I truly cannot go there now. It's far too late in the day, and I think I must see the doctor about my nose.' The pornographer returned to his seat, tilted his head back, tended once more to his bloodied face.

William laughed. There was a doggedness to Quince which he was beginning to admire. 'Mr Quince, the good people of the infirmary will see to your nose at any time. Banks close at three o'clock.'

'Nevertheless, Mr Garrett, I doubt we can get into the city centre in time. Tomorrow, if you please. You've given me quite a shock. My nerves won't take a drive into the city.' Quince rose as if to leave, but William pushed him back into his chair, then blocked the doorway with his bulk.

'Tut, tut, tut, Mr Quince. Have you been telling me lies?' William pulled his old service revolver from his pocket and watched Quince shrink.

'Oh my goodness, is it loaded?' It was a pitiful question, yet William acted without pity and moved forward. Quince flinched and curled into foetal position, his hands crossed over his head, protecting the bloodied nose, his feet on the chair, knees hunched up to his chest, as if his very smallness could save him. William did not shoot but instead hit Quince hard on the skull with the butt of the pistol. Quince, so compulsive in his pleas for mercy, uncovered his face and looked up at his attacker, doe-eyed. 'I heard a crack as if from the inside. It's probably my skull. I have a terrible headache. Do please have compassion, do, please.'

William was tired. Tired of Quince's pathetic self-interest, his perverse, steadfast endurance of William's bullying, and he was tired, moreover, of being the tyrant, the big man with the hard fists only good for his muscle. William wanted information, and he wanted to leave, and he wanted things to go easy, and he didn't want to hit Quince again. 'Be sensible, man. I know the motion pictures aren't in the bank. You must have a safe here. There's nothing in your filing cabinet. Open the safe. Give me the films. Tell me what I need to know, and I'll be gone.' Quince drew further into himself, unable to capitulate despite his admitted cowardice. William knew the man feared something worse than his own measured violence. 'Whoever you're afraid of is already circling, man. The gangs, the rich men you serve, they're after you. Ronnie's death is just the start. Give me what I want and close up shop. Leave the city. Do you like Weston-super-Mare?'

Quince shook his head. 'No, I like Devon.'

'Then have a little holiday. Think of me as a good friend who gives sound advice.' William smiled. 'I have no interest in your business other than the work you did with Ronnie Edgerton and –' William paused – 'with Edward Morton and his blonde girl Fay, yes?' Quince nodded again, but this time tears formed. 'Give me what you have and leave Birmingham to avoid the inevitable war, yes?' Quince nodded. 'Pop to the safe, like a good chap. As soon as I've gone, head for the south coast. Soothe those nerves of yours. I don't think I cracked your skull, by the way. Well, not yet.' William spoke casually.

Quince nodded and unfurled himself like a waking dormouse. 'Oh, please don't be like that, Mr Garrett. One knows about men such as Edward Morton through the work. But I have no personal dealings with him. None whatsoever. And neither did Ronnie, as far as I know. It frightened me when I learnt that he had been found dead with Morton's wife. I've been a nervous wreck since Phyll gave me the news.' His voice was comically adenoidal. William could hear the blood and mucus bubble in the back of Quince's throat. 'Edward Morton is a Blackshirt. Quite high up, too. It's the way the world is going, Mr Garrett. Your way, perhaps. The way of diplomacy through muscle. I had a very strict father. Fascists scare me.'

'I know you're lying. I know that Fay was squeezing Edward Morton for all he was worth. I want the girl's full name, her address, the films she made for Morton. Talk to me, Quince. Talk to me, so I can talk to the girl.'

'I shan't.' Quince shrugged and then laughed – an irritating, girlish giggle – his shoulders juddering in mirth. 'I really shan't.'

'Is Fay blackmailing Morton? Is she sending him poison-pen letters?'

'Oh, I see.' Quince removed William's handkerchief from his nose, sat up, and faced him. 'You know nothing, Mr Garrett. And I have absolutely no intention of educating you any further.' Quince's laughter had now become a bloody gurgle. 'Don't you understand? You're far too reasonable for this line of work. I rather think you're quite decent,' he said. 'And you told me yourself, there are much nastier bastards than you in the world. And my dear chap, you're really not the type to shoot that gun of yours, are you?'

William dropped the manilla file. The photographs hit the floor and slid under the filing cabinet with a hiss. Quince looked down at the sound, and William stepped forward, throwing a hard right hook across Quince's jaw which toppled the little pornographer from his chair. William crouched beside Quince's crumpled body. 'Tell me now,

Quince. What do you know about Edward Morton?' But the man was silent. Blood welled in Quince's ear and then fell in a thin rivulet along his pale neck. William checked his pulse; Quince was out cold but still alive. He had played it all wrong, for the pornographer was right; William had no stomach for the kind of work needed to break the man. That was a job for Queenie.

William gave the studio and filing cabinet one last-ditch search and came up with nothing but well-ordered paperwork for the administration of the legitimate business. Quince may not have been lying about keeping the illegal stuff in the Midland Bank. The whole day had been a bust. He had no information on Fay, or her relationship with Edward Morton; he had no further knowledge of Ronnie's associations with Quince, business or otherwise; Christ, he had even forgotten to ask the man about the cocaine. All he had were a few scraps of information about a part-time tart called Tommy.

William bent to retrieve the dossier of photographs which had scudded beneath Quince's filing cabinet, but could not reach them, and so shifted the heavy Victorian affair out of the way. It took some heaving for a man with cracked ribs. William paused to catch his breath, straightened for a moment. It was then he realised that his luck had changed, for behind the filing cabinet was a cast-iron safe, recessed into the wall and about as old as Quince's shop. Victorian, like the filing cabinet, it was the kind which opened not with a combination but with a key. William searched Quince's clammy, still unconscious body and found a heavy fob hooked to the man's belt loop. William tried each key. The third one worked like a charm. The safe opened with a heavy groan. Inside, much to William's pleasure and relief, were three tin canisters each containing a reel of celluloid film.

William left Quince's shop and locked the canisters of film, the dossier of pornography – including his own photographs of Fay and the centurion Tommy – safe in his boot. And after some consideration, he returned and stole the still unconscious pornographer's film projector and screen. It was William's way of further salvaging the almost fruitless day.

26

William drove back to the city centre through minimal traffic and under a perfect cloudless sky. He arrived in Needless Alley unsure of the day, for in his grief they had become shapeless, but certain of the time, as the town hall clock had just chimed three o'clock. William parked the car and walked towards his office door, glimpsing his reflection in the windows of the hat shop. He stood and watched himself light a fag with his own shaking hand. William was punchy with pain and barbiturates, but still sharp enough to notice, mirrored in the glass, a Wolseley – police issue – pull into the alley. Quince had called the coppers. No, that wasn't possible. The man was knocked out cold; William was sure of it.

And Chief Inspector Wade, black suit, black hat, army straight, a hulking shadow against the hot white of the afternoon, moved towards him with confident strides. He was soon upon William. 'Come with me, Mr Garrett.'

It was an order from a fascist copper, and William was not inclined to comply. He drew hard on his cigarette and shook his throbbing head. 'No,' he said.

'Don't be stupid, Mr Garrett.' Wade stepped in close so that William felt his breath as he spoke.

'It's my permanent state of being. Now, unless you're going to arrest me, fuck off.' The words were sounded before rational thought had a chance to form in William's addled mind. Adrenaline surged, and William chose retreat, escape. He fumbled with his keys, attempting to unlock the door to his office with stiff, bruised fingers. His fob dropped to the floor, and he too quickly bent to pick it up, forgetting in his exhaustion the broken ribs, and let out a yelp of pain – the cigarette falling from his lips. William heard Wade laugh, and then he felt the copper's firm hand grip his shoulder. William stood, shrugged him off and turned, bracing himself. He anticipated a few seconds' pretence of negotiation, time to think and talk, time to act with sense. But William was wrong.

He had boxed as a boy but not well. Once, in the ring, some fellow from Coventry fought favouring his right. Then, just as William thought he had him licked, the man led hard from the left. It was a sucker punch from a southpaw to his jaw that knocked him flat out. William just hadn't seen it coming. This past humiliation spun through William's head as he took a blow so powerful to his gut, he believed, in that moment, that death was not only inevitable but would be a sweet release. He fell to the floor, on the ropes. Wade grabbed William under the arms, hauled him a few feet along the pavement and then bundled him into the back seat of the car. The last sound William heard was the door to the Wolseley close with an efficient click.

He just hadn't seen it coming.

William woke from a black and dreamless sleep to the rhythmic thud of his own heartbeat – or footsteps, heavy and marching quick time in formation. A man's voice – Wade – quite close – close to his ear – said: 'He's stirring.'

Torchlight shone into William's sleep-sore eyes. The iron-fisted copper took a few steps back, and the hard, bright light receded with him. It shook, and then disappeared. Wade had placed his heavy torch on the floor. The room was rank with the stench of all-day drinking – expensive brandy. And above the stink of stale spirits was the sweet ghastly scent of lilies; sickly, deathly lilies, their bruised petals crushed into the carpet, their funereal scent merging with the ferrous tang of Clara's blood. He rubbed his tongue against the roof of his mouth. Oh God, he could taste death. *More morphine, please, Nurse.* William pressed his face into something soft – soft as feathers, she had been. And then he shuddered. Clara was dead, and William knew it. He was just a poor, grieving fool, prone on a velvet couch, like some poet junkie, his body heavy with Veronal withdrawal, exhaustion and heartbreak. William blinked, teared up, and then heaved himself into a sitting position. The inevitable nausea rose.

He was in a long, low rectangle of a room, modern and affluent. Chinese vases, converted into electric lamps, stood on side tables and threw glittering circles onto the parquet floor. Two sets of French windows, heavily draped in yellow velvet, provided him with possible means of escape. William's eyes adjusted further to the room's now softened light. At the far end, tucked in a corner, was a grand piano. Vast arrangements of flowers, funeral fat, ivory petals fresh and firm, stood on its cloth-covered top.

'I don't want him touched. Not yet.' The other man's voice was rounded, avuncular in tone. 'Mr Garrett once told me that he'd never been in love.' It was a well-fed voice, breathless and husky. It seemed far away. 'I have been in love. I loved my wife. I even built this house for her, although I don't think she much cared for it.'

William was in Morton's Coventry mansion. And Morton was right; Clara had hated it.

'Sir, I think he's going to be sick again. He's in a bad way.'
Wade then turned to William and spoke with authority. 'You
need to learn to follow orders, Garrett. I don't like using
violence, but I will if I must.'

'You vomited in the police car, Mr Garrett. It gave Wade
much inconvenience. He thought you might choke on your
own ejecta. Although, for you, it would've made a fitting end.'

It took William a few seconds to see Morton. Several feet
away, slumped in a high-backed armchair, shrunken in a silk
smoking jacket, he nodded to Wade. At this brief gesture,
Wade returned to his boss, flanking Morton's chair as a knight
to a king. A gramophone played opera on low, William realised. He watched as Morton self-consciously flicked through
the libretto of *Tristan und Isolde*. 'Join us, Mr Garrett.'

William rose and found an occasional chair. Scraping the legs
along the parquet floor, he complied with the Blackshirt's
request and sat square before Morton but said nothing. In
moving, William had become aware of the damage inflicted on
his tender gut. He was in no fit shape to fight. He patted the
pockets of his coat, and then realised his Webley was missing.

Wade, watching this performance, asked, 'Why does a man
like you have such a weapon?'

'They gave it to me during the last war. I just didn't give it
back.'

'It's a service revolver for officers.' Wade glanced at the
piano. William's pistol sat hard and threatening under the lilies.

'Or trench raiders,' he replied.

Wade nodded and then looked sharply at Morton.

'You look bad.' Morton's drunken glance was cursory. 'And
you smell terrible.'

'I was just gut-punched by your pal there,' William
answered. 'It was unsporting of him to use a knuckleduster. It

228

made me sick on my shirt.' But he wasn't the only one who stank: strong drink, cigar smoke, the flowers, Morton reeked of corruption. William longed to pull down the heavy curtains, throw the French windows open onto the garden, sterilise the room with honest fresh air.

'The beating you received at the canal side, Mr Garrett, was not my doing.' William remained stony-faced. 'I want to make that clear. However, I can sympathise with your attackers. You are the kind of man who must collect enemies.' Morton reached for the large glass of brandy on the side table with his doughy hand, and he downed it in three thirsty gulps. His voice faltered as he spoke once more. 'Wade cannot tell me if Clara had been violated, Mr Garrett. Isn't that a terrible thing?' A drinks cabinet, like something from Versailles, stood massive in the far corner. Morton rose and stumbled towards it, and when opened, it was a house of mirrors, distorting the reflections of the room. 'The letters, such filthy accusations. I never dreamt that they were true. It's come as a shock. I'm so very tired. My beautiful Clara, murdered and raped.'

William became lost in a stupor of bewilderment. Morton was in a genuine state of drunken consternation over Clara's death. The man was grotesque, putrid with depravity, but he had not murdered Clara. Indeed, in his own way, Edward Morton mourned her. Suddenly, William became less alone in his grief, intimately connected to Morton through the kinship of shared sorrow. William flushed in anger and shame at the thought, but then shook it off as a dog does a bluebottle. Now, more than ever, he was confused by Morton's motivations. 'Why the hell am I here?' William spoke the words aloud.

'Mr Garrett isn't much of a talker, Wade. Did I tell you?' Morton returned to his seat with a fresh bottle in his hand. 'Neither is Wade. Wade is a man of order. Wade hates chaos, and language is chaos.' Morton gestured towards the silent, upright police officer. The fat man fumbled in opening the bottle. Wade stepped forward, broke the wax seal and poured Morton his liquor.

'What the fuck are you talking about? I can't be doing with your pointless fucking fascist philosophising. I'm in a cantankerous mood, and your copper has pissed me off. Get to your point, Morton.' William acted tough guy to Morton's devoted widower.

Wade stepped forward. 'We want your silence, Garrett. We gave you fair warning.' He acted the man of reason, for Wade hated chaos. 'We don't like you playing at detective. Keep your nose out of Mr Morton's business. The woman died. Your friend killed her. That's the truth. Leave the city. Take the sea air. It'll settle your nerves.' Wade's clipped orders were a direct echo of Shifty's avuncular pleas.

'You are in danger of making me a public cuckold when my express orders were to the contrary.' Morton motioned towards him, spilling a little of the drink onto his smoking jacket. He perched on the edge of the seat as if poised to leap. 'There will be very little of the matter in the newspapers. I've stopped 'em; I'm not without influence.' Morton's raised voice was a pitiful whine. 'But I don't trust 'em. They must make their profit from a man's private tragedy.' He paused and licked brandy from his full pink lips. 'I can't afford a scandal, I tell you. My plans. My long-term plans. A deal with the Americans so crucial to the economic well-being of the country. My political plans. The plans of the party—'

A brief twitch passed across Wade's face. He placed a restraining hand on Morton's shoulder.

William turned to Wade and laughed. 'Christ, you've got your work cut out.' He nodded towards Morton. 'This one's got enough dirty linen to keep you scrubbing for years.' He leant forward and clicked his fingers in front of Morton's booze-rheumy eyes. 'Who's Fay?'

The fat man's pupils widened and then hardened to a cold blank black. He chewed his pudgy pink lips, demented with good brandy. 'I can't recall a Fay, but there was definitely a Fanny.' Morton chuckled. 'I know any number of amenable girls.' He slumped back in his chair. His chins sagged and folded into his chest; round shoulders hunched forward. William saw grey scalp between stripes of oiled hair, and was reminded of a great, obscene toad. 'But Clara was always my favourite.' Morton hauled himself from his armchair and moved towards the lily-strewn piano in short careful steps. Wade followed close behind, as if Morton were an elderly aunt prone to taking a tumble. The fat man pointed to a series of silver-framed photographs turned face down in the shadow of the flowers. 'Show him, Wade,' he ordered. 'Show him how beautiful she was.'

Red-faced and refusing eye contact, Wade beckoned William over and then lifted each portrait back into position, one by one. Clara on tiptoe, her young face formed into a coquettish pout, wearing nothing but a silk slip and silk stock-ings. The next portrait was more modest, and the silk of the wedding dress was real. She held, poised against her stomach and her groin, a huge bouquet of roses like a dark stain. The final photograph was of Clara, her torso half-turned, in a backless evening dress, sophisticated in soft black velvet.

Morton caressed the picture of Clara in her underwear with fat, manicured fingers. 'I've had a terrible nightmare about her, Mr Garrett. These girls, with their youth and pret-tiness, they wield such power.' He hobbled back to his armchair. Wade, once more, kept up the rear.

William became suddenly unable to bear the weight of his grief. He steadied himself for a moment against the table, realising that none of Morton's portraits were of Clara. They were simply manufactured fantasies created by Morton for his own pleasure – Quince's stock-in-trade. No, William did not mourn with this man, for Morton never knew Clara. She was never real to him, never quite human. At least William had given her that – true, sincere human connection. William returned to his hard-back chair and spoke with as much formal clarity as he could muster. 'Morton, you prefer girls, don't you?'

Morton shrugged. 'All men like younger women. Girls have good tempers, and better figures.' His jowls quivered; brandy and spittle fell from his mouth. The man was sloppy, incautious in drink. 'Clara was thirteen when I first saw her. So fresh and pure. Like fresh air, good for you. I had known women. I had spent some time in Paris before the war on business. Women can be jaded, cynical and tiring.' Morton placed the framed photograph on the side table, toppling the empty brandy glass which fell, but, strangely, did not shatter, onto the polished floor. Morton gaped as it rolled towards William's feet.

'Does Mr Quince provide you with the kind of girl you like?' William leant forward in his chair, expecting either a revelation from Morton or a beating from Wade, but the police officer appeared momentarily perplexed. So Quince had not telephoned Wade. And if he had contacted Morton, the fat man had not told Wade about his connections to Quince before sending him to find William. 'Quince is a part-time pornographer and Morton's good friend, Wade. Didn't you know?'

'Quince is a fine chap, terribly understanding and accommodating.' Morton brooded for a second and then raised his voice. 'Why did you set Clara up with such a man? This man, Edgerton? I never asked you to do this thing. You overstepped the mark. Bad form.' He turned to Wade. 'Bring me the brandy.' Wade followed orders but stank of discontent. Morton's dissipation, or perhaps his loquaciousness, had offended the copper's puritanical sensibilities. And drunkenness had blinded Morton to Wade's growing distaste, for when the fat man received his bottle, he winked at Wade, jovial and over-hearty, saying: 'We shall need much more of this, Wade old chap, before the night is through.'

'What proof do you have that I set Mrs Morton up?'

'I have no proof. I only know what the police have told me. But you small men, you pettifogging types, you can't seem to understand basic instructions. Even the police are the same.' Wade's face was stony. 'I ask a simple question and all I get is obfuscations, lies, damned arse-covering cowardice.' Morton fell to his knees, scrambling for his glass. Wade bent, heaved the fat man to his feet and thrust him into the armchair. Morton poured more brandy and became pensive, his face red and his breathing heavy. Finally, he said, 'Do you think Edgerton fucked her before he killed her? The police doctor could not tell.'

William winced at the man's depravity but said, 'Is Fay demanding money from you?' Morton gaped, uncomprehending. 'Is Quince blackmailing you, Morton?'

'I'm asking the questions, Garrett.' It was a great croaking bellow, and in its discharge Morton's remaining power was spent.

'Not from here you're not.' William glanced at Wade. The man stood by the French windows as if ready to leave a particularly unpleasant dinner party. Tomorrow his allegiances would be fixed to a stronger, purer man than Morton. William wondered if all fascists were such fair-weather friends. 'You're not capable. You're pissed up. You're slurring your speech, man. You're in a bad way and it will only get worse for you. Whoever did these murders means business. They mean to hurt you, Morton, they mean to make you suffer before they kill you.' William thought at first that he had said those words to frighten the fat man but realised soon after that he meant them. He truly believed that Morton did not kill Clara and Ronnie, and this revelation shook him to the core.

'I find your manner offensive. Extremely offensive. You're no gentleman.' The words were mumbled, for the fat man was drinking himself into a slumber, sucking brandy from the bottle like a giant baby. 'Why can't you tell me what I want to know? Who was fucking my wife? Who was fucking my girl?'

William became giddy with outrage and fury. A brawl would do him quite nicely right now, clear his head and free him up from the chaos of the day. 'My manner? Gentleman? What are you raving about, man?' William stood; the chair fell with a fat thud as he rose. 'You're trying my patience with these theatrics. Having some half-arsed lackey come at me with a fist full of brass, dragging me to Coventry, all to have you blarting brandy and fussing over what the papers might say. I hold you responsible for their deaths, you pathetic old soak. I'll find out who killed them even if it kills me, and if you have any sense, you'll tell me about Fay.' William saw Wade glance at the fat man with contempt, and although he was now unlikely to follow Morton's orders, William risked offering one last show of strength, and turned to the police-man, saying: 'Wade, it's not my silence you should be worried about.' He pointed towards Morton. 'You and your party have hitched your wagon to a liability. You better tell your pal Mosley.' Wade stepped forward, and William shook his head.

'If you're going to fuckin' belt me then fuckin' belt me. But mark me, I'll take you down while you're trying. Are you willing to take a beating for this fat pervert?'

'You, sir, are a disgrace. I could have you shot.' Morton attempted to stand – and failed, remaining half-raised, the whole quivering weight of his body steadied against the arms of the armchair.

'Not tonight you won't. Go fuck yourself, Mussolini.' William made for his Webley, but Morton took a few wavering steps, moving to grab him as he passed. William dodged from his grasp and grabbed the pistol. Morton fell, tumbled like an unsteady toddler, lying prone on his belly at William's feet.

And Wade, his angular face a raging red, stepped aside without a word as William left through the French windows.

27

Thursday, 13 July

She was a blonde. A blonde in the cut, her long white dress billowing in black water. Late spring floods – blossom, cow parsley, wild garlic, the smell of it. Her hair like fronds of pondweed; her head bashed against the boat and the lock gates. She sank to the silt. Eels old as Adam's ale – thick as tarred cordage, scavengers in the dregs – fed. Deep down, at the bottom of the canal lay Alice, at rest.

And now the powerful weight of water rested on his chest. His breathing was shallow, painful. A heart not up to the task, it was too troubled; it would buckle under. Cold, hard pinpricks of ice fell on his face. They smacked against his skin, cheeks, shoulders, and were ceaseless. William flailed, furious, he cried out. But the hailstorm would not be fought.

'Who's Alice?' Phyll stood over his bed with a basin of water in her hands. 'You were calling for Alice.' She was dressed smart: lightweight Windsor-check suit; pale green tie; silver tie pin; a tiny posy of violets in her buttonhole. She wore a slate-grey hat, a woman's trilby. It covered her blondness and hardened her face with shadows. She smelt of cedarwood and cinnamon. 'I've been trying to wake you for fifteen minutes. Flicking cold water on you, but even that wouldn't do the job. I was beginning to get worried.'

'Why are you here?' William sat up, groggy, legs tangled in damp sheets. 'How did you get in my flat?'

'Queenie gave me a key. She sent me.' She placed the bowl down on his bedside table and moved to pull the curtains. 'We've been worried sick about you.'

The afternoon light was brutal. William rose to open a window; the air in the room was still thick with sleep. He staggered, his legs buckling, but then steadied himself on the sill until he had strength enough to heave the rotten sash upwards. Fresh air smacked the stink from the room. William stood for a moment and breathed it in. Too late in the day for birdsong, only the rattle of traffic on New Street and the distant hoot of the factory sirens could be heard. That terror, which was always with him and hung heavy and permanent in his gut, was now gone. It had been usurped by hollowness. William shook his head, violently.

'I need coffee. A black coffee. That Veronal Queenie sent is good, strong.'

They walked to the kitchen. William had an electric coffee percolator, bought on a whim, and so filled it, his fingers fumbling, with ground beans and water. He rested his eyes and waited for the bubble, the drip.

'Christ, you're the last person I thought would have a coffee maker,' said Phyll.

'I bought it in Lewis's.'

'You're slurring your speech. How many did you take?' she asked.

'Enough. I'll be alright after a coffee. Do you want one?'

'For God's sake, put on some clothes.' Phyll's face was pinched and dark. For all her smartness, exhaustion had taken her boyish good looks.

'I never had you pegged for a prude.' William opened his eyes and looked down at his gut. He couldn't see his cock. Christ, he was getting fat. Phyll was right, he should cover himself up. William wandered back into the bedroom. It took a studied concentration to put on his underwear and trousers: geometric calculations; a bearing; trigonometric algebra.

Back in the kitchen, William poured Phyll a coffee, and heaped in three spoons of sugar to sweeten her. 'Are you in a mardy with me?' he asked.

'I have no idea what that word means.'

'Don't lie,' he said. 'You've lived up here long enough.'

'Did you speak to Quince?' she asked. 'We were trying to find you. What were you up to last night?'

William focused on a memory that seemed distant, dream-like. 'I spoke to him. He handed over a dossier of photographs of Ronnie with a tart called Tommy. He's the lad in the centurion garb. But he was just playing for time and fobbing me off with scraps. I reckon most of the stuff we need is in Quince's bank. Christ, Phyll, I left him knocked out cold. I used my pistol and my fists. It ain't like me. I raided his safe and stole some film, his projector and screen, too.' William drank his coffee and poured some more; his numbed mind struggled to process and recount his meeting with Morton. 'Then I got beaten up again – by a copper called Wade. He's a Blackshirt bastard and Morton's minder. He took me to Coventry. Morton denied knowing Fay, but he happily admitted to knowing Quince. I don't think he killed Ronnie and Clara unless he's an actor. Unless he's a very good actor.' The coffee had cleared his head, but the fear had returned in a

238

tempest of sudden gusts and squalls of thought. It was Quince who was at the eye of the storm, at the centre of it all. 'I can't fathom what's going on. But Quince is a clever, venal bastard. He was genuinely frightened when I mentioned Fay and Morton, but less so Ronnie. I need to go back there and pay him a visit, and next time I'll take Queenie and her lads. I reckon the reels of film I have were just in that safe temporarily until he could take them to wherever he stashes the stuff for the pornography business. He said he kept the films at the Midland Bank. It seems so comic to keep them there.' He turned to look at Phyll's now softened face. 'Christ, Phyll, I just couldn't break him.' William held out his arms straight, parallel to the floor like a monster in a movie. His knuckles, bloodied and bruised, were beginning to swell. Both hands shuddered in a terrible trembling beyond his control. 'They call this neurasthenia,' he said.

Phyll placed her palm on William's right forearm and gently moved his hand to his knee. She repeated the action, his left arm this time, with a tender calm, and then said, 'Quince is dead. Burnt to death in the flat above his shop in the early hours of this morning. They say the celluloid in his film set alight. Poor Quince had no chance.'

'Fuck.' William had no idea that Quince lived above his shop. Had he stashed his less legitimate photographs and films in his flat? It seemed unlikely, although Phyll talked of burning celluloid. William attempted to light his first fag of the day, but his heavy, nervous fingers wouldn't allow it. 'How do you know about the fire? Have the coppers been calling?'

'No, Queenie found out. I think she decided to take things into her own hands when you didn't call yesterday. But when she arrived at Quince's studio, the fire engine was there. She didn't have the opportunity to dangle him from any canal bridge.' Phyll leant forward and lit William's cigarette. 'Things are getting nasty, aren't they?'

'I've been a bloody fool.' William took a drag on his fag. He was no copper. He was just a solicitor's clerk with fallen arches. Besides, inside, he was shot. Brain, heart, nerves all riddled with sorrow. 'I played it all wrong with Quince. I'm really not much of a detective.' He paused once more. 'I've not been thinking straight.'

'Billy, will the police have you in the frame?' Phyll talked in a scratchy whisper. 'Were there witnesses? To your visit, I mean?'

'One woman saw me act the heavy.' He took another gulp of coffee. Thank God, he'd made it strong. 'But the coppers are busy cleaning up after Morton. They may leave us alone for a bit. I dunno. I told Wade last night that Morton and Quince knew each other, but I don't think Wade had heard of Quince's name before I mentioned it.' William wiped a cold creeping sweat from his forehead. 'I suppose if Quince's death can be seen as accidental, the police might let it go. Quince had a lot of rich friends with a lot of dirty secrets. Fuck me, Phyll. I feel awful. I've got the wind up good and proper.' She pulled her chair quite close to his, and the heat of her slim, soft body comforted his nerves. 'And do you know what else? We're back to square one. We know nothing.'

'I have a big brother, you know.' She glanced at William's juddering hands. 'He went through the war, suffered. In the end, it was all too much for him to bear. The burden of all that carnage, I mean. It's a lot for a chap to deal with.' Phyll paused for a moment. 'He's in, well, a sort of sanatorium now. Quite near Birmingham. It's why I moved here, to be close to him. The thing is, Billy, and I know we're hardly good friends, but my instinct is you have strength. You're stronger than my brother, and you're stronger than Ronnie. And I don't mean physically. I simply think you have the gift of resilience. The instinct to withstand the monstrous rattling of the guns and keep yourself, the core of yourself, intact.' She placed her head tenderly on his shoulder and then sniffed. 'Bathe, for God's sake, you're quite foul.' Her voice became muffled in the warp and weft of his suit. 'And then have something to eat. Your nerves are shot because you've been living on booze and barbiturates. And what's happened to you, what's happening to us all, well, it isn't quite normal. You need to take care of yourself, then you'll be more able to think straight.'

He was grateful for her simple kindness, the sharing of herself with him, but shook his head. 'No, Phyll, I've got to get the film reels and projector in from the Austin. Those moving pictures are the only lead we have. It was stupid to leave it out there all night where anyone can get at it.' He could hear the thrum of the city rush hour. Outside, the sky had mellowed to a less perfect blue. It was late. It was very late. 'We have to act fast and watch Quince's smut before the coppers come calling. I may not have an alibi for Quince's murder. I took the train back from Coventry after meeting with Morton, but that was around two o'clock this morning. After that, I just took the dope and slept. What time was the fire?'

'Queenie was at his shop first thing sharp. I think it'd been blazing for a while. Perhaps a few hours? It's just a guess, but I would think it started around four or five o'clock this morning. And Billy, you have no alibi but perhaps neither does Morton or Wade.' Phyll reached once more for his hand. She held it tight. William realised it was to stop the constant drumming rhythm his fingers made against the arm of his chair. 'Do you think whoever killed Quince also killed Ronnie and Clara?'

William shrugged his shoulders. 'Quince's death could've been an accident.'

'You don't believe that.'

'No, I don't. I think we've rattled our killer.' William felt no comfort in the realisation that his questions may have led to Quince's death. 'Phyll, I want you to leave town. I can give you money. Go anywhere you please but far away from Birmingham. I should never have got you into this mess.' Phyll shook her head and frowned in protest. 'I had a terrible dream last night,' he said. 'It felt prophetic. I don't think I can protect you. You know too much, Phyll. You knew both Ronnie and Quince.'

'No, I shan't go away. It's not your job to protect me.' She lit them both a cigarette. 'You said you needed a pal. You said I was it. Well, we are pals, and we'll look out for each other. But I'm not your responsibility. We'll work together to sort out this mess. And we are getting somewhere, Billy. We are moving forward with this thing.' She paused, turned to him and smiled. 'Do you want some tea?'

William laughed. 'Tea? Are you quite mad?'

'I'm sure you have a tin of milk somewhere.' Phyll's wide grin was like a panacea. 'I want you to make some sandwiches and tea. But first, give me your keys. I'll get Quince's films and projector in from your car. And then I'll telephone Queenie. Once you've made the food, bring it down to the office, and then we'll have a film showing.'

William found comfort in doing as he was told and made a plate of sandwiches. He ate two. Then he carried the remainder and a pot of tea down the flight of steps to the office. The door was unlocked, but the room was dark, for although Phyll had placed the projector on his desk, she had not yet opened the blind. He put the food next to the machinery and moved to open the window. He heard steps behind him, started and turned. It was only Phyll. She had returned with her arms full of film reels and manilla files. His leather fob in her mouth, she shook her head at him like a dog, and he retrieved his keys. 'It's horribly musty in here, Billy.' She dropped the canisters of film and the files on an office chair. 'Let some fresh air in, do.'

William attempted to prop the window open with his battered and rolled copy of the *News of the World*, but he fumbled it, his fingers too stiff and sore to manage this once daily balancing act without difficulty. He heard the faulty sash rattle shut, closed his eyes and stilled himself as a recollection, an image, swam to the forefront of his memory. A pale face haunted him. A murdered blonde floated in the canal, and she crowded his dreams. 'Why do the woman-haters, the maniacs, like a blonde, Phyll?'

'I don't think maniacs have a preference. It's just that the scandal sheets mention hair colour like it's a scarlet letter. You know, being a blonde is sort of code for being a fallen woman. I think they report on dead blondes because it increases their circulation, or whatever they call it.' She spoke distractedly, for she was now pouring tea. 'It gives the story sex appeal, I suppose.'

'Ronnie loved the scandal sheets,' said William. 'It's how he spent his Sundays, nursing his hangover, smoking Lucky Strikes and clicking his tongue at the dirty vicars. He used to say that women had it rough. He was right.' William remembered Ronnie's pronouncement quite clearly. It had been made on the day of the Winnie Woodcock case. In June, that was, early June. Ronnie had been reading out loud from the Sunday papers.

William saw himself as if from a distance, or as the star of a film, retrieving the fumbled newspaper from the office floor, scanning through the headlines, folding down the page, flattening it with his hand, glancing meaningfully at the curious Phyll. His disassociated movements were acted out, at once portentous and false. 'I've been dreaming of nothing but dead blondes, Phyll.' She looked at him and frowned. 'I must've recognised her all along. I think I've found Fay.'

Her blurred photograph was a mess of grey dots, hard bobbed curls a bright white blonde, her face a hazy blur. The story was told frugally in just three columns of newsprint. '*Fay Francis, of no fixed abode, sixteen years of age, was discovered in the canal near Fazeley Street,*' William read. '*She had been strangled. A silk stocking, found wound about her neck, was used as a ligature. The coroner estimated that she had been in the water for no more than three days.*'

'Oh, God. Is that her?' Phyll peered at the newspaper. 'It must be her.'

William reached for the picture of Fay as the Rokeby Venus. He had placed it in the manilla file after his visit to Quince's studio. He passed it to Phyll and watched as she scrutinised it, along with the photograph from the newspaper, under the harsh glare of the office's single electric bulb. 'They have the same-shaped face, and the same eyes. This is our Fay, Billy. This is our girl.'

William winced in pain as he took a deep breath. At first, his mind would not allow him to recall it. He screwed his face in concentration. Hands bound to the bedpost; a ligature embedded deep into her pale neck. 'Fay Francis was killed in the same way as Clara,' he said. 'And I've got photographic proof.' He turned and unlocked the filing cabinet and touched the cold, hard metal of his camera with a tentative hand. He drew it back quickly, as if it would bite. And then he braved it, grabbed it, and laid it on the desk before Phyll, saying: 'I took photographs of the murder scene.' Phyll, hatless now, gazed up at him with round, dark-circled eyes. 'I don't know why, but I did,' he said. 'I photographed it all.'

A few seconds lapsed before Phyll spoke. 'Billy,' she said, 'I believe we have a maniac on our hands.'

28

William cast dark shapes. He watched the creeping shadow of his hand, a monstrous blood-black in red light, lift the exposure from its chemical bath. It was his death portrait of Ronnie. He pegged his friend's blown and broken face out to dry, recalling the scarred man from Phyll's performance in the foundry, and the head wound victims he had seen hospitalised after the war. Handsome Ronnie, so proud of his looks, it had meant something to the murderer to obliterate those fine features. William became skittishly conscious of the blood-sodden tile in the picture, as he listened to the last of the photographic fixative drip musically down onto his own porcelain washbasin.

The bathroom was humid, acrid with the smell of developing fluid. William's ribs ached as he bent over the final exposure, counting the slow sixty seconds until the image materialised. It returned to him like a ghost. Red-drenched in red light, Clara's lifeless face lolled in the foreground, a ligature wrapped taut about her neck. He heard a low, profound groan – primal, animal-like – but it was some time before he realised that it came from deep within his own chest. William dipped the photograph in the last of the chemical trays and then placed it on the line to dry. There came a sudden insistent banging. 'Are you there, Billy? Are you there, Billy love?'

The voice didn't come from his own thumping head, it was Queenie, hammering on the bathroom door.

William let her in. 'Did Phyll tell you what happened?'

Queenie nodded. Dressed in mourning, the veil of her cloche pulled full over her eyes, fine lines of black silken thread covered her pale face. Queenie's lips were darkly reddened. 'Will I ruin the photographs if I come in?'

William shook his head. 'No, that bit of the process is all over.' He removed the now dry pictures of Ronnie from the line and placed them in his pocket.

Queenie stepped into the crowded bathroom. 'Phyll said that the girl Fay is dead. Do you think Morton killed her?' William shrugged. It was best to keep his own counsel. Queenie moved, as if compelled, to examine the pictures of Clara's lifeless body. 'Oh, God. It's awful. This is an awful thing. Poor, poor woman. She was stabbed and strangled. He must've hated her. He came prepared to do the job.'

'What do you mean?' he asked.

'She's wearing both her stockings, Billy.' Queenie's voice was full of pity. 'Hadn't you noticed?'

A great upsurge of panic formed deep within William's chest. A swimming disorientation, it rose and quivered, so that before his eyes Clara's photograph seemed to undulate and flicker. He said nothing but concentrated hard on Queenie's words.

'It's a third stocking around her neck.' She squeezed his arm as an act of comfort and then pointed towards the pale silk biting into Clara's flesh. 'See? She was strangled with a third stocking. And it must be his. It must be the murderer's and brought with him to suit his purpose.'

'I never saw. I never realised at the time.' That night, hadn't William used his camera to distance himself from the horrors of the room? And later, hadn't he wanted to numb his grief with dope and booze? Now, in his darkroom, and with Queenie by his side, it was time to face facts. 'Premeditated,' he said. The word felt fat, far too big for his mouth.

'Yes, of course it was. What do we do now? How do we get this Morton?'

But William wasn't even sure if Morton was the one who needed getting, for the fascist had denied having any relationship with Fay. He was indiscreet in his drunkenness, admitting to a taste for young girls, and Fay Francis was just sixteen when she died. He had also confessed to knowing and liking Quince, but he had been genuinely perplexed about Clara's death, and he was addressing a BUF rally in Manchester on the night of the murders, a fact that would be easy to check. Moreover, their deaths were so very personal, so brutal, William couldn't imagine a hired thug committing them. Queenie had said there were easier ways of killing someone, and she was right. She was also right about the stocking. Clara's murder was premeditated. It was a complex undertaking: timings, understanding of Ronnie's and Clara's whereabouts, three weapons – knife, stocking, pistol – to lug about. The method, the process, of the killing must have been just as important to the murderer as the act itself.

'It's all in the papers,' said Queenie. William felt that she was starting to climb the upward slope towards high dudgeon, and he braced himself. 'They say he murdered an unnamed woman in a lover's tiff and then committed suicide. The bastards brought up his war record, and that time, you know, when he was in the rest home.' Morton's sway over the newspapers wasn't as strong as the fat man believed. His name wasn't mentioned, of course, but the story was out. 'They said he was depressed because his career was on the slide. They called him an alcoholic.' She reached into her handbag and handed him the evening paper.

William glanced at the few inches of newsprint. The story had been half buried on page five, no photographs. 'It was bound to happen, love. We're lucky it's not on the front page.'

'I've written a letter of complaint. Delving into a man's private life like that. I want an apology. What d'ya call it, a retraction. I've been at it all day, trying to sort it out. Clear his name.'

Queenie was whitewashing Ronnie's story, so that there was purity in its remembrance. This was how the Maggs family worked, elevating their dead to a sanctity they could never achieve in life. And what about Clara? Soon there would be a funeral. How would Morton memorialise her? William closed his eyes. The parish church at Hindford lay squat and low against a sky clouded with swallows. Six tall pallbearers, smart in black shirts and jackboots, carried a coffin draped in the flag of the BUF and carpeted with lilies. Morton in full mourning, hunched by the graveside like a fat crow, wept brandy. And the elderly sexton read the eulogy, '*Her job was done, so to speak.*' William opened his eyes and switched off the red light. He and Queenie stood together in the dark. 'Queenie,' he said, 'even you can't bend Lord Rothermere and the rest of them to your will. They're bigger bastards than you could ever hope to be.'

'It ain't right to spread lies. A drinker, yes. But he was no dipsomaniac.'

'Jesus, let it lie, for God's sake. He drank like a fish and was off his head on dope. But he's dead, and it don't matter what they say about him now. Christ, he ain't gonna care.' William's voice rose. 'You've gotta learn that not everything's a fight, girl.'

Queenie was silent; she was stewing on something, of course. A quiet Queenie always gave him the wind up. 'Young Phyll says you fucked it up with that Quince.'

'I'm pretty sure she didn't say that.'

Queenie shrugged.

William closed the bathroom door and made for the office. 'We haven't seen what's on the films yet, and we can't make a proper decision what to do next until we've seen them.' She followed at his heels. William stopped and then turned towards her. 'If you must see 'em, then think about what the next best move is afterwards. Don't just go in all guns blazin' with Morton. We need proper evidence before we speak to him again.'

'You never change, do you, Billy?'

'Jesus Christ, woman. I don't know what you mean.'

He was halfway down the flight and Queenie was a few steps behind. She looked down on him when she spoke. 'You don't talk about nothing. And you don't do nothing. And you don't fight for nothing.' Queenie delivered the line in the manner of a leading lady before curtain-fall on the first act. She was just like her brother, and she was wrong. Queenie was wrong, for William had done nothing but talk and fight since the night of the murders and the whole bloody show had exhausted him. She needed to give her mouth a rest.

'You're rarely wrong, Queenie. But you're wrong tonight.'

They entered the office in silence.

The light in the room was smoky, hazy with the coming night, so it muddied familiar objects. William faltered in the doorway, disorientated. Phyll had pushed his desk against the far wall and cleared it too, so that there was a flat surface for the projector, which had been placed on top of a slab of asbestos but not set up. The screen was opposite, hanging from a single nail; it flapped like a sail when he finally shut the door.

'Can I cadge a fag?' she asked.

'No smoking,' he snapped. 'Celluloid is hell near a naked flame. Ask your mate Quince.'

Phyll blushed, glanced at Queenie and then shrugged. 'Please yourself.'

'He's in a bad mood,' said Queenie.

'We should get started.' William pulled the blinds and turned on the electric light. The projector was a new model, still boxed, and came with a good instruction manual. He set the reel in place well enough, clicking each frame onto nicely engineered pins. It would have given him pleasure, but his fingers felt clumsy and numb.

Phyll became alert, ready for orders.

He turned to her and said, 'Will you turn off the light?'

She trotted to the door and flipped the light switch. The room fell into darkness. William covered his fingers with a handkerchief and removed the electric bulb, then plugged the lead of the projector into the empty socket. The projector fluttered into action, and, on the screen, a picture flickered grainy, then became alive.

It is a cocktail bar. The sort you find in a modern hotel, perhaps a mock-up. A handsome man places glasses on a tray. He shakes his shaker with masculine vigour. In come two girls – all fox furs and tight curls. Fashionable hats, the veils coquettish over one eye. They kiss full-mouthed. The barman wags his finger. A woman extends a leg. She caresses the body of the other girl with an elegant foot still shod in satin shoes. Her friend's fur falls open. The woman is naked under her coat.

'Oh, Christ. Do you know who that is?' Phyll pointed towards the film.

'The naked girl?' asked Queenie.

'No, the other one. She's big in the Women's League of Health and Beauty. She's the wife of a Liberal MP.'

'Very liberal,' said William.

The wife of the Liberal MP drops to her knees. Her fur falls about her in soft waves. She buries her mouth into the mons of her friend who opens her legs a little wider. They fade away like ghosts.

The film flapped against the spool – bird's wings – yes, the sound of a bird trapped in a chimney breast.

William drew the blind a fraction. The city twilight shone into the office as a sickly yellow glow.

'I'll set up the other film. This one may be of Ronnie.' He glanced over to Queenie, but she was a shadow to him; he couldn't read her.

'It's quite a long shot, Billy,' said Phyll.

This film is titled 'Arcadia'. A forest glade. A real spot of woodland augmented with pots of daffodils and large faux ferns, too – the kind you get in a tea room – and a path of flagstones, perhaps made of heavy cardboard or plaster of Paris. The path leads to a pool. It is deep enough to swim in. From behind the tree peeps a youth. A wreath of ivy and spring flowers rests on his dark hair.

Queenie let out a single, deep sob.

'I'll stop the film,' he said.

'No.'

A close-up of a handsome face. Kohl-eyed and Vaseline lips, it is Ronnie, so not a youth. He is too soft around the edges. Ronnie steps out into a spot of artificial sunlight and stretches. The camera lingers, lascivious. His chest, his shoulders, the perfect definition of stomach muscles – a fine specimen – his cock rests against strong thighs. Ronnie skips to the pool in pantomime moves and considers his reflection. He runs his hand through the water, gently rippling his own beautiful face. Ronnie hams it up, wide-eyed and pouting – a working-man's Valentino. He loves himself. There is a sharp and obvious cut to the film, so that the reflection is seen to rise from the pool. Ronnie is astonished (more pantomime) but mesmerised. He caresses this image. The face, the definition of his biceps, the ridge of his pectoral muscles, along the stomach. Both cocks twitch in miraculous synchronism. Ronnie is on his knees, worshipping the phallus. The other man half-closes his eyes. His eyelids flutter.

William waited for Echo to appear. It was a while before he realised this wasn't her show.

'That was the stupidest fuckin' thing I have ever seen in my entire life.' Queenie spoke first. 'What was our Ronnie thinking?'

'Quince paid well,' said Phyll. She hesitated for a moment. 'Herr Freud would have an absolute field day with it, and I didn't know he couldn't act. He was very bad, wasn't he?'

'Yes, love. He was bad,' Queenie agreed.

William knew that the women were referring to Ronnie, and to his acting talent and not his morals. 'Christ, the other lad looked just like him – build, height, colouring. Younger though, and his jawline wasn't so strong. It's all so fuckin' weird.' William was perplexed. He couldn't see the whole picture. He was sitting at the back of the stalls and some big man was deliberately obscuring his view, allowing him glimpses, fragments, of the full story. 'Quince told me that Ronnie worked with a sailor or a soldier. He picked him up. Maybe a prostitute called Tommy. Could this be him?'

'It's the dark lad from Ronnie's photographs, ain't it?' Queenie shook her head and laughed, a note of astonishment in her voice. 'Jesus, are you pair daft? It's the Roman soldier lad. Same cock, same torso.' Her voice now held a note of reticence. 'I suppose I know my way around a fella,' she said.

'We need to speak to him. If he is a tart, then he might be easy to find.' William glanced at the shadowy Queenie. 'And easy to bribe. He wouldn't be like Quince; there would be no need for violence. Quince said he was mousy and buck-toothed. I know it's a long shot, but he might know some-thing, anything. Why else would Ronnie keep the photo-graphs? Christ, I'm getting desperate—'

'The lad in the pictures and the films ain't mousy, and he ain't the one opening his mouth neither, so we can't tell if anything is up with his teeth. But I suppose anyone can dye their hair,' Queenie interrupted. 'Anyway, we should watch the final film before we make any decision, Billy.' It was a pointed reminder of his own advice.

William set up the next moving picture, noticing how little film there was on the reel, no more than a few minutes of viewing. He was overcome by a wave of pessimism. The whole evening – no, the whole day – had been more than a bust. The projector buzzed into motion.

This film is titled 'Olympia'. She faces away from them, half-prone on a Victorian chaise longue, like the Rokeby Venus. Her luscious skin is dotted with a constellation of freckles. She has deep dimples on her arse, and the black silk stocking about her throat dangles in a bow down her small back. A mirror, the kind you find on a dressing table, before her, reflects a fragile, nebulous English fairness. There is a sharp unprofessional cut and a few seconds of scratchy grey.

'Oh, my Christ,' said Queenie.

'Yes, it's Fay. It's Fay Francis.' Her face was much clearer than in the newspapers, or the photograph he found in Ronnie's haversack. What was it about this girl that William recognised?

Fay now faces the camera. She is Manet's Olympia, but she cannot mimic the confident, confrontational gaze of the French original, for her large eyes are bewildered and rather childlike. Alone, with no comfort of a servant woman offering carnations, she trembles for a moment as if there is a sudden chill in the room. There is another cut, but this one is smoothly done and leads to a close-up. The camera lingers over her pale oval face, her pursed rosebud of a mouth, her smooth, young neck. We only see the man's hand and arm. He caresses her cheek, slides his fingers across her mouth, pulling down her bottom lip and exposing her small white lower teeth. He tugs at the stocking, tightening it, and then presses his thumb gently into her larynx.

The film ended and the reel flapped. William's stomach lurched with fear and fury. It was the least explicit of the three films, but it was the most horrific. Was the terrified child at the point of death? Or did the strangulation which killed her happen off camera?

'Oh, God. It's absolutely awful. Absolutely terrible. It's horrendous. So frightening.' Phyll's voice wobbled with outrage. 'But what has it got to do with Ronnie? What did he know?'

'Nothing,' said Queenie. 'Absolutely nothing.'

William glanced at Queenie but could not see her clearly, for she stood in the shadows as stiff and hard as a funerary statue. Her quick response to Phyll's question had made him uneasy. Queenie had recognised something and had come to her own conclusions. And she had decided to keep schtum.

He unplugged the projector from the light socket and then screwed in the electric bulb. 'Turn on the light, Phyll.' She flicked the switch, and they were all blinded and blinking, eyes watering from the sudden artificial glare. 'Spill it, Queenie,' he said. The office was hot with electricity and bodies. William sensed thunder in the air. 'Spill it. You owe me. Don't keep whatever you know all bottled up.'

Queenie nodded in grim silence. It was a moment before she spoke. 'She looks just like Alice, Billy.' Queenie watched him carefully. 'And it said in the newspaper that Fay was only sixteen years old when she died.'

'Oh, fucking hell,' he said.

'I've asked you this once before, Billy,' said Phyll, 'but who's Alice?'

29

The room darkened. William opened the window once more, propping it up with the remains of the rolled newspaper. Outside, the clouds loomed like a great purple bruise over the city's skyline. The thunder, at first, seemed a distant growl. William counted silently – one, two, three, four – as would a child, then came a sudden spark of illumination, not the comic zigzag crack of lightning as seen in the movies, but a yellow flash, a glimmer in the leaden sky. William took a few gulps of tinny fresh air and then asked, 'What did Alice call the baby, Queenie?'

'She called her Frances, after her father.' Queenie's reply was quiet and tentative.

Francis Maggs had become Ronnie Edgerton. His daughter, Frances Maggs, had become Fay Francis. Transformation, a need for the escape of glamour, ran in bloodlines, no doubt. But William wanted confirmation, proof, that Queenie's suspicions were true. He thought about the contents of the canvas bag. There was a picture of Alice and a birth certificate – but for whom: Frances or Francis Maggs? And what exactly were Ronnie's suspicions about Morton? Christ, did Ronnie know his daughter was working for Quince? Had he and Fay met before she died? A cold sweat rose on William's forehead as he considered the terrible implications of such a scenario.

And those letters, those taunting inventive letters detailing Clara's sex life, when did Morton first receive them? Yes, it was just after the story of Fay's murder had broken in the scandal sheets. William glanced about the office, searching for the haversack. 'Where's Ronnie's bag, Phyll?' he asked.

Phyll ignored the request. 'I need to know who Alice is,' she said, turning to Queenie. 'I feel I'm the only one in the dark.'

'She was Ronnie's sweetheart,' said Queenie. 'She was delicate, and she had a babby in 1917.' Queenie removed her black hat and ran her fingers through her dark curls. Her voice became strained. 'Ronnie was too poorly after the war to do right by Alice. He had to spend some time in the sanatorium. Then he ran off with some fella for a few months. He ignored all her letters. He was cruel. When he came back, he weren't Frankie no more, he was Ronnie. But when Frankie died, so did Alice. She topped herself when the kiddie was about eighteen months old.' Her face, now unveiled, was pinched and drawn. 'She put pig iron in her pockets and jumped in the canal out near the Typhoo. I don't reckon our Ronnie has been right since. I gave the kiddie away to the Waifs and Strays. Ronnie weren't cut out to be a father, and I didn't want to take her on. I'm ashamed of myself. I did wrong by Alice that day. Little Frances was a Maggs, and I gave her away.'

'Pig iron in her pockets?' Phyll frowned, confused.

'We use it in the boats as ballast. Alice did similar. She wanted to weigh herself down. She meant to drown,' said William. 'Alice knew the canal. She knew that it took work to die.' Exhaustion rippled through his body like a wave. William slumped into his office chair. 'Where's the haversack, Phyll? It was on my desk. Did you shift it when you set up the projector?'

'No, your desk was empty,' said Phyll. 'Poor Ronnie.' She moved to open the drawers in William's filing cabinet. 'Both his sweetheart and daughter found dead in the canal. How absolutely awful for him. He never told me a thing.'

'Ronnie talked all the time, but he said nothing. He kept his business private by never shutting up about the things that don't matter.' Queenie was motionless for a moment, preoccupied, and this worried William. Then she turned towards him, pronouncing her wisdom like a prophet. 'This is a bad business, Billy. There's much more heartache to come, I can feel it. I'm warning you both. If we're not careful, there'll be more bloodshed.'

It was William's habit since childhood to be heedful of Queenie's premonitions, and so, at her warning, his heart thudded, hammering against his cracked ribs like a foundry press, and a long-brewing hunch irritated him like an itching scab. He turned towards Phyll, but she was distracted by the search for Ronnie's haversack. She looked up from the filing cabinet, and met his eye, frowning once again. 'There's nothing here, Billy,' she said. 'I can't see the bag at all. Is it in the flat?'

'No, I doubt it,' he said. 'The bag must have disappeared last night. The night I spoke to Morton. The night of Quince's death.' His voice trailed off. She had already left the office. He heard her quick, light tread on the steps, and then the creak of the door to his digs. William rubbed his pounding temples, reached for the packet of aspirin in his desk drawer, chewed a couple and took his shot in the dark. 'How much was the cocaine in the Pepsodent tin worth to you, Queenie?'

'Plenty.' Her smile was cat-like and without humour. 'But if I wanted the cocaine, I wouldn't have taken the whole bag.'

'You took the haversack. You're the only other person who has a key to the office.'

'Why would I do that? Ain't I got bigger things on my mind?' She wasn't angry, not yet. 'Besides, I gave Phyll my key this afternoon.' She picked up her cloche, placed it back on her head, adjusted the black spider's web of a veil. Queenie was about to make her exit. 'You're addled. You ain't been thinking right since this thing happened. Really, I don't reckon you been thinking straight since the war. You ain't never been right since you got back.'

'Christ, Queenie, that ain't true.' She could wound him because she knew him. They had been intimately and painfully tied since adolescence. 'I'm thinking straight enough to know that you ain't getting your money from hauling coal no more. You can dish out Veronal quicker than Boots the Chemists. You've got a working-man's yearly wage stashed in your babby's crib. What else you got in your floating fuckin' pharmacy, girl?'

'Why should I go into details with you?' Beneath her veil, Queenie's green eyes were circled slate grey with fatigue. 'It's my business, ain't it? What right have you got to go making judgements?'

'You supplied Ronnie with cocaine.'

'He said it kept him and his friends slim.' Queenie was steely. At that moment, she was not her brother's keeper. 'A lot of people take it if they can afford it. Ronnie just sold what he had spare to his friends.'

'Who's supplying you? London bastards?' For a moment, he couldn't read her face. Then her lips pursed. 'No, Liverpool bastards.' This time, it was William's smile which was cat-like. 'You head up north to the docks with a boat full of coal and come back with a boat full of dope. A few more trips like that and you will find yourself in London. A nice five-year stretch in Holloway, I reckon.'

'No copper looks twice at a woman with a narrowboat full of babbies,' she said.

'You take the babbies?' William couldn't suppress the note of disapproval in his voice. 'You take your children on these dope runs? Stop it. Stop it now. These men you're tangled up with, they're bad bastards. I'm worried for you. Stop it now.'

Then the weather truly broke. Those sagging, purple clouds, which lay threatening in the evening sky, no longer shook and grumbled but burst like a salvo. 'Bad bastards? You don't have to tell a woman like me about bad bastards,' Queenie stormed, each word a hailstone. 'Men – all my life I've fed them, fucked them and feared them. But mostly, I've feared them. That's what I've learnt. And Billy, who the fuck are you to give me lectures on motherhood? What do you really know about responsibility? You can barely look after yourself. And you're a proper selfish fucker to boot. You think of Billy Garrett first, and the rest of us come poor second.' She moved forward, prodded him hard against his painful chest – at the place where the sleeping Clara curled – with her red painted finger-nail. 'You think I don't look after my kids. They don't suffer, not like I fuckin' suffered. I know what it means to protect a babby. It takes keen eyes and a strong will and all your fuckin' energy and a shit ton of money. No fucker'll hurt my kiddies. Not while I have breath in my body.' Her green eyes sparkled wild.

'And what about Ronnie?' he said. 'If he wasn't off his head on your dope these past few months, he wouldn't have got mixed up in the smut business. You call me a selfish fucker, what about you? Christ, he weren't right at the best of times, but you used him to peddle the dope and didn't much care if he became an addict and reckless and dead.' William stopped. He had gone too far with her, and he knew it.

She opened her mouth as if to speak, then hesitated for a moment. He saw the pupils of her hard green eyes shimmer magpie black, and finally she said, 'Fuck you, Billy. You're on your own. You're no use to me. You're dead weight. You're nothin' but fuckin' pig iron.' Then Queenie Maggs left the building. Entrances and exits, they were her family's stock-in-trade.

As the front door slammed, Phyll returned to the office, flushed with either her search or with embarrassment. 'I think your neighbours heard every word of that, Billy. And you were both swearing rather a lot.'

'The whole of Birmingham heard it. Queenie wanted a ruck. It's been brewing for ages, months. When she kicks off, she kicks off hard and loud. Really fuckin' –' William blushed – 'very loud. Did you find the bag?'

'No, I didn't.' The question was a long shot, and they rarely hit the mark. 'I even looked in your car,' said Phyll. 'Will Queenie be back?'

'Not tonight, she won't.' William sat at his desk with his back to the open window. The rain hammered against the panes hard like bullets, and icy splashes flew through the sash, hitting the back of William's head. He didn't move; it cooled him. Then he lit a cigarette, the flame of his match perilously close to the celluloid film. 'She's too fired up.'

30

Phyll placed the reels of film back in their tin canisters. William offered her a cigarette, and then poured them both a brandy from a bottle he had always kept secret from Ronnie. Locked in the bottom drawer of his filing cabinet, it was an expensive brand.

'Are we very stuck without the bag?'

William shrugged but said nothing.

'Do you really think Queenie stole it?'

William shrugged once more.

Phyll took a drag of her fag, and then sipped at the brandy. 'We've still got the lookalike chap in Ronnie's film and photographs to look into, that Tommy boy.' She considered him carefully. 'What are you thinking, Billy? Do say something.'

William closed his eyes and attempted to order his thoughts. 'I think that during the making of a pornographic film, Fay Francis was strangled. We know that she worked for Quince. She could've been strangled by another performer by accident, or it could've been done by one of Quince's clients. We know that Morton was a client. We know that Morton likes adolescent girls. We know that a few days after Fay's body was discovered, Morton began to receive sexually explicit letters about his wife.' William paused and took a deep, painful breath. 'We know that a month after Fay's death, Clara was killed in a similar manner, except she was also mutilated.' William lit another cigarette. He had been smoking hard since the murders, he realised; knocking back the booze, too; dreaming more and sleeping less. 'Do you want another brandy?' Phyll nodded and he poured. 'In the moving picture, do you remember, the man tightened the stocking around Fay's throat and pressed his thumb against her larynx. These were the actions of Quince's client, and I think they are crucial to this man's sense of satisfaction, completion.' He hesitated at his own squeamishness. 'I suppose I'm talking about orgasm. The stocking is significant to the man who ordered the film. Just like the gas mask was significant to the man who ordered the movie you starred in.' Phyll shifted in her seat, stared into her brandy. 'And Clara wasn't killed with her own stocking, like the police said. She was wearing them both. The murderer brought the stocking with him. Because despite having a knife and a gun, the strangulation was important to him. It was significant. Whoever murdered Clara, and whoever commissioned Fay's film, they were both men aroused by the sight of a choking woman. A maniac, like you said. A mental case.'

'Morton is a manufacturer of artificial silk, hosiery.' Phyll let the thought drop, and then land, like a five-nine.

Beads of sweat – hard drink, the heat of the night – formed on his upper lip. William wiped his face with a handkerchief. It was a Morton move, a strange sick mirroring of that obsessed, panicked creature. The nausea rose. Clara had been so gentle with William's wounds – had kissed his shrapnel-scarred body and salved the lonely core of him with fellow feeling, tenderness. She was so good. And she had died, brutal-ised – perhaps just as she had lived. Oh, Christ, what had she suffered at the hands of men? William took another sip of brandy.

'Although it doesn't necessarily follow that the man who commissioned Fay's film and Clara's murderer are one and the same,' Phyll continued, 'and it definitely doesn't prove that it was Morton.'

'You're dead right there, Dr Watson.' Hadn't William left Coventry the previous night convinced that Morton had not murdered Clara? Morton had been genuine in his grief for his most treasured possession. And although he believed that Morton could kill Ronnie out of expediency, he could not believe that Morton was capable of such a complex and bloody act of retribution. He wasn't intelligent enough. The man had no flair. And there were easier ways of getting revenge, as Queenie once rightly pointed out. But had Morton killed Fay? That conjecture was more probable. It fitted. 'We know that Fay's body was dumped in the cut in early June, late May. The newspaper report said that she was found out in Digbeth, and she'd been in the water for no more than three days. I don't think the murderer knew much about the canal, otherwise they would've dumped the body out on a lonely stretch and used a few pounds of pig iron, like Alice. The cut isn't like a river. There's no current, wash some-times, but no current. Dump a body in a city stretch, and it won't shift far, and it will be found. Canals aren't as deep as you think; the average man can bottom them. Dead bodies obstruct the waterway, bang against the hull.' William inhaled and closed his eyes, dredging up a memory from deep within his psyche. 'We once found a body, me and Ronnie and Queenie. A baby wrapped in brown paper like a parcel. Queenie thought it was a little dolly at first. She unwrapped it, you see. It hadn't been in the water long and looked perfect.'

The day they found the baby was the last time he saw Queenie cry, and she had howled. William exhaled. 'Fay was found near where she was dumped, Phyll. I'd put a fiver on it. And I'd put a fiver on Ronnie realising this too. He was more boatman than actor.'

'Do you know what I've been thinking?' Phyll reached forward and helped herself to another brandy. 'I've been thinking that Ronnie hid the haversack because it was a collection of evidence, evidence about Fay's death. He kept it in his own haphazard sort of way with other secret, personal stuff. But nonetheless, it is a collection of evidence, isn't it?'

This was a thought William shared. 'Ronnie read the story in the newspaper on the fourth of June, but I don't think he knew that Fay was his daughter then. He asked me if I recognised the girl. I think when I set Ronnie off to follow Morton for me, he did some sleuthing of his own and began to believe that Morton had murdered a girl. Eventually he must've learnt that the girl was Fay. I don't know what Ronnie would've done then. Did he threaten Quince or Morton? Either way, Ronnie got himself killed. He wasn't forthcoming with me about whatever he found, although he was hopped up on dope and practically begging me to go to America with him.' William glanced at the Veronal in his drawer and thought about Queenie's cocaine, took another slug of brandy, gulping it down as if it were good for him – better for him than the dope, no doubt. 'When I think about all this, it feels like my mind is a tangled ball of string. The ball of string is intact, but it's of no use until I've straightened it out.'

'We've still got the photographs of Tommy. It's an avenue we haven't explored. They might have meaning, more meaning than is strictly personal, more meaning to the case. There are knots we can still untangle, Billy.'

William nodded. He hadn't lost hope, not quite yet. 'We can show the pictures around the tarts on Station Street. I've got enough petty cash left to loosen a few tongues.'

'I think I've got a better idea.' Phyll looked at her watch. 'Bring the photographs and your cash to the Archway Club instead. I have a pal, Jonesy, and I think she might, just might, be willing to talk to us.'

William stubbed out the last of his cigarettes. 'I have no idea who or what you're talking about,' he said.

'That really doesn't matter, Billy.'

31

Outside, the storm was over. The night was cool. The grass of the cathedral close was dewy underfoot, and there was still a tang of rain, perhaps thunder, in the air. William looked over at the Grand Hotel. It had not changed since the murder: the building was not shrouded in black crape to honour William's loss. He was shocked to see the clientele crowd in and hear the music drift out. He closed his eyes and imagined Ronnie and Clara. Ronnie with his kohl-black eyes, and Clara like a bride, smiling in white, and they were dancing a waltz, a merry dance.

He was on the brink of an understanding, he knew that. The murder, and its motive, was not a jigsaw to be put together, a child could do that, but a vast dark pool, cold and treacherous. He would wade about, and – if brave enough – plunge in, dive down to find his answers. Phyll touched his arm. William jumped and took a sharp step backwards.

'It's only me,' she said. 'Didn't you hear what I was saying? I was talking to you.' Phyll offered him a cigarette and William accepted. 'You look absolutely dreadful. Have you got the wind up again?'

William nodded. 'I'm not happy with you sleuthing. You're not Lord Peter fucking Wimsey. People are dead. I don't want you to be next.' He was worried now, more than ever, for her safety; and believed it politic to return to Needless Alley and fetch his Webley, for the stars of Quince's pornographic films had a low life expectancy. 'Just tell me where this club is and then go home. Keep your nose out of this, Phyll.'

Phyll looked away from him, chewing her lip like a sullen child. Finally, she said, 'I'm doing exactly what you asked me to do, help you get to the bottom of all this mess.' She turned once more to face him, blowing smoke rings out into the night air. 'And I shall put your rudeness down to nerves. Do you do this often? Start fights because you're more comfortable alone. Besides, you'll never get into the Archway by yourself.' She looked him up and down and then let out a touchy laugh. 'Jonesy is a good sort, but she keeps things close to her chest. Even if you got in, she'd never talk to you without me. And talking to her could be a good starting point to finding Tommy. Jonesy knows everything about everyone.'

If this were true, then Jonesy was both exceptionally gregarious and exceptionally discreet. And few people, in William's experience, managed such exceptionalism.

'I take it you remembered to bring the photographs?' she asked. William motioned to his breast pocket. 'Then come with me.' Phyll led the way. They veered westwards, past the art school and towards the Jewellery Quarter.

It was a silent walk. He had offended her, he knew. Yet he sensed Phyll's charged, tight-mouthed wordlessness came from something deeper.

Finally, she spoke. 'I don't think Ronnie was the person I thought him to be.'

'What do you mean?'

'I thought he was a true bohemian. He was forceful, vocal, about Quince's work. I thought he believed what we were doing was art. The art of subversion, he called it.' She paused, gathering her breath. 'He talked such a lot about personal freedom, appeared so self-assured and so terribly anti-bourgeois. But now I know he was just rather broken, and rather flawed. It was all just an act.'

William paused for a moment. It was obvious that she hero-worshipped Ronnie, but she was also an innocent. To laugh at her naivety would be cruel. 'Ronnie was human, Phyll,' he said, with as much tenderness as he could muster. 'He was damaged, and a bit useless, just like the rest of us, and changeable, always on the run from something. He was easy to love, and by the time you began to see his failings, it was too late to change your mind. You just loved him.'

'Oh, God. I've never been a fool for a man in my entire life.'

'We're all fools,' he said. 'We're all fools for someone.'

'Do you think Mrs Morton was a fool?' she asked.

William wanted to cry. He glanced at his watch. 'We better get a move on,' he said.

They found Jonesy's place through an archway, built for a carriage, at the far end of a nineteenth-century courtyard. Georgian workshops, with flat fronts and high windows, were lit only by a meagre strip of yellow slithering in from the gas lamps on the main drag. And beyond the courtyard were more red brick warehouses, hoists and jetties, the black artery of the canal. It was quiet now, the workmen gone; the yards were swept, and the shutters bolted.

Phyll tapped on a freshly painted green door. A woman opened it immediately. She was silent as she beckoned them both inside, and remained so, simply nodding to Phyll as she led them down a set of steep, narrow stairs to a reception area softly lit by a single electric bulb. Phyll smiled at the girl behind the desk.

'Hullo, Rita. I'm back,' she said.

Looking down on the seated Rita, William felt the swimming pull of vertigo. Two double brandies on an empty stomach, and he was half-cut, on his way to fully cut, he thought.

Rita smoked French cigarettes with a jade holder. Her mouth was soft and red. 'I don't mind him, Phyll,' she said, 'but he must understand the rules.' She pointed towards William, the bangles on her bare arms glimmering and clattering, but did not meet his eye. 'I don't want him trying it on with any of the girls, even the pros. If they're in here, they're on a break. He keeps his hands to himself, and there'll be no bloody gawping. No fighting and no bad language. Any of that and he's out.' Rita finally turned towards him, eyeing his build like a quartermaster sergeant. 'Try to blend in. Be inconspicuous.' She shook her head at the impossibility of such an action and then said, 'Any complaints from the regulars and you're out, comprenez?' William nodded, suppressing his instinct to salute.

Rita rose from behind her desk to open the door to a bona fide dive bar. Phyll entered like a queen and heads turned. The place was crowded with girls. Girls leaning against the bar, flirting, chatting, kissing. A few off-duty tarts, in for a breather and gathered in groups of two or three, sipped neat gin, and swapped tall tales and small grumbles. One laughed and called to him as he passed, 'No more tonight, kidda. I've had cock up to the eyeballs.'

William turned to her, shrugged his shoulders and smiled. Couples were dancing, a few managing the correct steps, but most shuffling improperly close. There were women dressed like Phyll but not as sharp, their suits unfashionable, their breasts too big, and their hips too wide. Some in smart dresses were plain and old-maidish – librarians and teachers at the board schools. One or two women, thin as reeds, wore the evening gowns and the insouciance of characters from a play by Coward. It was a windowless room and dank with sweat and smoke and perfume.

'Christ, where am I?' Heaven, William thought. I'm in heaven.

'I told you, it's Jonesy's.' Phyll turned to him and grabbed his hand. 'She won it in a card game. You've got your Shakespeare and Trocadero; I've got the Archway Club.' Phyll waved her arm proprietorially, like a master of ceremonies. They muscled their way through the regulars to Jonesy, the big blonde manning the bar. She wore workman's trousers over striped combinations, and her curls were cut close and kept controlled by hair oil.

'Alright, Phyll, what can I get you?' She had class, not looking twice at William.

'Two large brandies, please, Jonesy.'

The woman poured the brandy into tumblers.

William handed over the cash. 'Have one yourself.'

'Not like you to run around with fellas, Phyll.' She nodded towards William, savvy. 'What are you after?' she asked. Jonesy poured herself a double from a good bottle of brandy.

William pulled the photographs from his jacket pocket and placed them on the bar. 'Can you put names to the faces?' Jonesy considered William and then said, 'I'm not the talkative type, Phyll. Drink your brandy.'

Phyll leant over the bar and grabbed the other woman's hand. 'I'm desperate, Jonesy, and so is Billy. It's so important. A friend of ours was mixed up in something bad. We just want a few answers. Billy's not a talker. He hardly utters a word in normal conversation, do you, Billy?' William shrugged and said nothing. 'You know I would never hurt a soul from the Archway. You know you saved my life, know it. Please, just tell me what you know.'

Jonesy ran her fingers through her curls, eyed them both up. William could see his own reflection in the bar mirror. It was impassive. Finally, the woman talked. 'I don't know the bloke –' she placed a stubby finger on Tommy's helmeted face – 'but I know the kid.' Jonesy raised an eyebrow and nodded to the picture of Fay. 'She's a local kid, and I do mean kid. Told me she was twenty-one. Bollocks was she. Came around here looking for work last January. Said she had no mom or dad. She came from the Waifs and Strays. Told me her name was Fanny Maggs, of all the bloody stupid names. Change it, I said.' William glanced at Phyll. Fanny: such an old-fashioned shortening of Frances; she was Ronnie's daughter, and William wished it wasn't so. Jonesy smiled but did not laugh. 'Phyll, she did change it. Next thing I know she's calling herself Fay Francis, and she's found dead in the cut. June, it was. I said to Rita at the time, it was in the *Birmingham Post*, you see, I said, "Was that the little wench who was around here sniffing for work?" And it was. It was her. She was murdered, so the papers said.' Jonesy knocked back her brandy. 'I can't get mixed up in a murder enquiry. The coppers aren't keen on the Archway, although Christ knows I pay 'em enough to keep away. They'd love to shut us down. But she was a sweet kid. If you're after whoever done her in, fair play to you. Give the bastard a kicking from me.'

'Did Fanny ever mention a man called Quince? A photographer?' William asked. 'Did she ever talk about starring in moving pictures?'

Jonesy laughed and shook her head. 'She was no Garbo, love. She was a mousy little kid with the puppy fat still on her. And as for this Quince, never heard of him.'

In January, Frances Maggs was still Fanny and looking for work. In June, she was Fay Francis, found dead from strangulation. The kid had it rough. William knocked back his brandy and asked, 'Ever heard the name Edward Morton?' He offered Jonesy a cigarette and she accepted. 'Or Ronnie Edgerton?'

'Christ, do I look like I've got a ton of gentlemen callers on the go?' Her laugh was sincere. 'I don't know where she went after she left us or who she went with. I told her to try factory work. I don't think she took my advice, poor kid. She said she couldn't bear to work in another factory.'

William felt a flutter of anxiety. He would numb it with drink. 'Let's all have another brandy.' He passed a pound note over to Jonesy. She poured three more large drinks. 'A few of these girls, they're working girls, yes?' William asked.

'We get all kinds in the Archway. Women only. You're in here because I've got a soft spot for Phyll.' Jonesy grinned a gap-toothed grin at Phyll. 'If you're alright with Phyll, you're alright with me and Rita.'

'I'm only after information, and I'll pay them well.' William patted the wallet in his jacket pocket. 'I'll buy them a few gins. I want to ask them who the lad in my photograph is, that's all.'

Jonesy moved to William's right, leant over the bar and tapped a woman on the shoulder. A brass with brassy blonde hair, it was the working girl who had had her fill of cock. Jonesy said nothing but simply pointed to William. The woman squeezed in beside him, grinned a wide, toothless smile and asked, 'What you after, bab?'

The natives were friendly, but not stupid, William thought. He told the woman the truth. 'I'm a private detective.' But the words sounded absurd, grandiose, like something from a film. The woman raised her eyebrows. 'I'm after a lad. Tall, nice-looking, twenty-five or thereabouts.'

The woman interrupted. 'You ain't the only one, kidda.'

Gin-induced camp was the gallows humour of her trade. William ignored it and carried on with his questioning. 'He's probably one of the boys from near the Silver Slipper.' William mentioned the only place he knew in town where men went to pick up men. 'He goes by the name of Tommy. Do you know him?'

'I've got a terrible thirst on me, dearie.'

'Can I get a double gin please, Jonesy. And I'll have another brandy.' Jonesy, the perfect barman, poured out the drinks and moved along, polishing glasses, nodding to the regulars.

'That's the ticket,' said the friendly tart. 'I hate drinking alone.'

William pulled the picture of Tommy and Fay out of his breast pocket. 'He was once mousy-haired, but he's recently dyed it dark,' he said. 'But I'm also interested in the girl. There's a pound note in it for you.'

The woman pressed the gin glass against her heavy rouged lips. 'Bottoms up.' She drank it down and William matched her with his brandy. 'What's your name?' she asked. She was a friendly sort of tart. The easy-going type who liked a good time, a natural in her profession. 'My name is Loretta. And I'm on the game because I need new teeth.' She gave him another gummy grin.

'I'm Billy, and good gnashers are a blessing.' William pointed to the picture of Tommy. 'This lad suffered with his teeth, too.'

'You'd be surprised how many of us do.' Loretta motioned to William's jacket pocket. 'A charitable contribution to the dentistry fund for common whores will be much appreciated.' William gave Loretta another quid and ordered them both more drinks. He liked the woman's company. 'You're a good 'un.' She winked, pocketing the money and knocking back the gin. 'They call themselves Tommy as a way of getting trade. Johns who like a lad have a thing for soldier boys and sailor boys.' Loretta eyed him intelligently. 'They like a man in uniform the way you like French maids, bab. What is it with fellas and dressing up? It's as though fucking has to be a game, all make-believe. I've never been able to fathom it.' She shook her glass at William; he ordered her another gin and a brandy for himself. Loretta nodded towards the photograph. 'I can't really tell from the picture because I've never seen him in the buff –' she gave out a filthy guffaw – 'but I reckon I know the lad you want. If it's who I'm thinking of, his proper name is Sean, or perhaps Seamus. It's summat Irish. Dyed his hair from mouse brown. Looks like Gary Cooper if you squint hard. I don't know him well, but he did have digs on Milk Street. You're right about his teeth. Ain't as bad as mine, though. I had a doctor fella tell me it was from bad nutrition when I were a babby.' William realised that Loretta had a brave face. Her lack of teeth was a preoccupation, and it was making her blue. 'That little girl were a friend of his. I saw 'em together once, springtime it was, because the blossom was out. They were eating their sandwiches in the park.' She glanced at Fay. 'She looks young, don't she? Poor little cow. I started young.' Loretta, now in danger of becoming gin-maudlin, wiped the tears from her eyes. 'Thanks for the two pound, bab.' Loretta drifted away from him. William blinked a slow drunken blink; his brain was fogged with brandy; she receded further into her huddle of fellow tarts. 'It'll go a long way to getting new teeth. False teeth will really sort out my looks.'

William wanted to talk through the implications of this new information in private with Phyll, but she looked at him with a swimming, drunken grin and wandered off towards the dancing women. The music changed, and she began a mad sort of Charleston with a petite girl, a hoofer type. Phyll couldn't keep up; she was too full of brandy to match the steps.

He was alone at the bar with Jonesy, the club emptier now. 'Loretta wasn't lying about her teeth. She's saving up. You were generous. Once she has teeth, she can get work in a shop.' Jonesy waved the bottle of brandy at Billy. 'You are alright. Phyll was right about you.' Jonesy poured more brandy. William and Jonesy, barflies both, were halfway down the bottle. It turned out they had much in common. He liked Jonesy. Her dad trained dogs. She could give him a few tips for the next race up at Perry Barr. They drank more brandy. He told her about the Somme and how he was scared of rats. More brandy. Now they were best mates. She lost two brothers at Gallipoli. The best of the bottle gone and kaylied – fuckin' kaylied. A singsong now – *The old tunes are the best* – with Jonesy and Loretta and another two tarts who had taken a shine to him. Where was Phyll?

You know you've got the brand of kisses that I'd die for.

He bought the girls a few gins. One got a mardy on about something he couldn't fathom. *Leave it out, love, it ain't worth it. Let it lie, let it lie. Have a gin.* Loretta was on the game to save up for false teeth. New choppers would sort out her looks. *Bad nutrition, love.* A few more gins and out of gaspers. A cigar from Jonesy and on the house. *She looks quite antique, my dear. You've got nothing to worry about.* Rita with the soft red mouth gave him a funny fag – got him all giddy. She was a VAD during the war. Drove an ambulance. Lost her fella. *We're all surrounded by death. How do we cope?* William cried. Rita gave him a cuddle. She was damp with sweat. He didn't mind. *There, there, ducky.*

He had lost Phyll and there wasn't a gents. *Piss outside if you can manage the stairs, we can't have a fella in the lavs.* The stairs were steep – Everest unconquered. William climbed them on his hands and knees. Jonesy and Rita followed – keeping up the rear. *Don't have a tumble.* A nice long piss against the wall.

'We should get you home, Billy. You're rather the worse for drink.' Pissed up, ready to sick up, and blarting like a babby, William was rather the worse for drink. He rested his head against the cool of the red brick. His cock was still out. Phyll tugged at the sleeve of his jacket. 'Come on home. The birds are singing. Listen to the morning. And for God's sake, sort out your flies.'

William loved his mum, and he loved Queenie. 'I love you, Phyll.'

'That's because I'm easy to love.'

'Like the song.' He couldn't walk without her. She was propping him up; she was his crutch. 'Clara was perfect, ideal. I could have loved her, married her and talked about books and poetry and good food and drink and art. All of those things I daren't talk about. Not allowed to talk about.' *There, there, ducky.* 'Fay and Tommy sat in the park under the cherry blossoms. They were friends. She was so young, a baby, and she had been murdered like Clara. She had it rough, so rough. Women have it so rough.'

Women. He wasn't a nancy-boy, not like Ronnie. Besides, Ronnie liked the company of men and men liked him. William could never get the hang of men. He much preferred the company of women.

32

Outside, a night-time mizzle – the warm kind, but William was safe from it. Deep underground and secret in Station Street, he was in the Silver Slipper looking for nancy-boys. Victorian tile all pissy, the dirty drip of a cracked cistern, and no lavatory attendant to clean or intervene, William wasn't pissing. He was waiting. There was a glory hole in the wall of the stall at crotch height. You could fit a cricket ball through it if you wanted to – or a clenched fist. He bent down towards it. A big brown eye peered through. Dilated, bloodshot, pulsing – Ronnie's eye. 'Can't you see me, Billy? Why don't you just wake up?'

'I am awake, Ronnie,' he shouted to his friend. 'I am awake.'

William woke fully clothed – suit greasy, shirt crumpled, clammy skin rank with sweat and brandy – to the sound of knocking-off time. He sat up and blinked, gormless with booze and dope, and heard the heavy hum of traffic, the shrill call of factory sirens, the distant clatter of rush-hour trams. William sighed in relief. He was home in Needless Alley. 'I am awake,' he said. Beside him, neat in his own striped pyjamas, slept Phyll. Curled like a dormouse, puffing soft puffing breaths, blonde hair covering her thick, dark brows, she looked more like a boy than ever. William got out of bed and glanced down at her, heart hurting at her frailty, but resisted the urge to tuck her in. Now fully conscious, his anxiety returned in a great, powerful wave. He had promised to protect Clara, and he had failed. Phyll's friendship was no salve to this grief, and this guilt, and yet he felt a similar instinct towards her. He must shield Phyll from the worst of the coming sorrows.

William set up the coffee percolator and then bathed. He dressed in the bathroom, avoiding the sleeping Phyll, and then took his coffee and collection of photographs – a testimonial to the departed – downstairs to the office.

William raised the blind, and propped the window open a crack so that the scant breeze would drift in and cool him. He drank the coffee and sat listening to the comforting thrum of the city. He was struck by the calm of solitude. Without Phyll, without Queenie, he had more room to think. He laid each picture out carefully on the desk, once again like the ordered placement of the tarot. His mother had read the cards. She earned a few pennies from women who could not afford to spend them. Done in by life, her customers sat secretive in the front parlour every Wednesday evening, and the tarot told them one thing: you will endure; you are able to withstand. The cards told a good lie, his mother had said.

And what could William divine from the placement before him? He examined the post-mortem photographs of Ronnie and Clara. It seemed like weeks since he had developed them, but in fact, it had been only twenty-four hours. Then he glanced at Fay as the Rokeby Venus, and the helmeted, face-less centurion Tommy. He rummaged in his desk drawer and pulled out his magnifying glass. He was quite alone, and yet he blushed at the action, for it was the move of a hammy stage detective.

He held the glass steady over Fay. She was prone on a sheet-covered chaise longue. The outline of her pale face was reflected in an elaborate hand mirror she held awkwardly, and at length, so that the muscles in her arms were tensed in maintaining the requisite position. The black stocking tied about her neck dangled down her back, following the curve of her spine, and the rounded sweep of her hips flared seductively, for she had been positioned to accentuate her natural shape. An acquiescent and mouldable form; her waist appeared tiny, and her arse appeared huge, giving her acres of creamy flesh. Fay was not a sixteen-year-old child, naked, cold and afraid; Fay was a body on which to project a fantasy. She was to be looked at, touched, penetrated, and to remain passive. *Shush, Fanny, shush. Remember you are not a real girl.*

He glanced over to his photograph of Clara's dead body, and he saw what he knew to be true in his bones. Prone on the bed, legs bent awkwardly to accentuate the shape of her bare arse, a stocking cut into her pale neck, she was positioned as a deliberate mockery. If Fay was a pastiche of the Rokeby Venus, then Clara was a pastiche of Fay. William closed his eyes in shame, sick to the stomach at the entitlement of his own sex.

Then, in his mind's eye, he saw a pattern, a sudden flash of the familiar. William opened his eyes and returned once more to the photograph of Fay. He moved the magnifying glass closer. The mirror she held was tilted slightly upward, so that the photographer and his camera were not in shot – clever Quince, the double-sure perfectionist. But there was something reflected in that mirror, a pattern, a definite pattern. Stars. Golden stars, painted onto a darkened ceiling by a lesser pre-Raphaelite, a chum of Burne-Jones. Morton had brought Fay to Clara's folly. He had enacted his fantasies out on a child in the sacred, personal space of his now disappointingly adult wife. The picture had been taken in Clara's studio.

And William remembered Morton admitting to knowing – biblically – a Fanny. A girl supplied by that good chap, Quince. But what to do now? He had no hard evidence that Morton murdered Fay, and William had no intention of deliberating the veracity of his hunches with Chief Inspector Wade. To go cap in hand to Queenie with circumstantial evidence of Morton's guilt would mean certain death for the fat man. Peace with Queenie meant an offering of Morton's head on a platter, for Fay was of the tribe Maggs; she was Ronnie's daughter and Queenie's niece. Queenie would not flinch at enacting her own bloody vengeance. There would be no second thought to the rule of law and trial by jury.

William gathered up the photographs and finished his coffee down to the gritty dregs. He wrote a hasty note to Phyll, asking her to telephone around and find Morton. He wanted another appointment with the fat man before he unleashed all hell – if it wasn't too late already. Then, William grabbed his Webley and made for the slums. He needed to dig up his Tommy, that Seamus from Milk Street, for that untidy thread needed straightening out.

33

William drove to Deritend, for he knew the car would cause a stir in the back streets. The kiddies crowded about him, out from under their mothers' feet after tea-time, and they were owning Milk Street. Friday, so not a wash day, but the women had strung out the lines across the road nonetheless, as those with babies needed to get the nappies done, and they all had babies. The children kicked their balls low in the gutter; if they mucked up the washing, they'd be in for a hiding, but they were obviously bored with careful play. A few pennies flung at this lot, and William would find his Tommy.

'This your car, mister? How fast does it go?' The boy looked about eight years old but was probably much older. His mother had made him wash his face, but it was a circle of clean on top of a mucky neck.

'Fast enough. You can sit in it if you give me a bit of information.'

'You a copper?' the kid asked.

'No.'

'You a bailiff?' he asked.

'No, I'm a private detective.' There was a momentary hush.

'Like in the magazines?'

'Yes, just like in the magazines.'

'You gotta gun?' asked the boy.

'Yes,' he said.

'If you let me hold it, I'll tell you everythin'.' This was just the kind of witness William needed.

'You don't even know what I want to know yet,' William laughed.

The child pursed his lips and glanced over at his mates. They were already sitting on the bonnet of the car, their grubby fingers all over the brightwork; one or two of the younger ones were making engine noises, pretending to drive.

William raised his voice. 'Any of you lot know a Sean, or a Seamus? He lives here sometimes.'

'Ain't that your dad's name, Jimmy?' The children became silent, gawping, shameless, at Jimmy.

Jimmy shrugged. 'I reckon.'

'He's young; he's dyed his hair dark; he's good-looking but got buck-teeth. I bet he sometimes dresses up nice.'

The kid laughed, as though William had made a joke straight off the halls, relieved. 'That ain't my dad, mister. No bloody way. No fear.'

A small child, a girl with eyes like saucers, grabbed hold of his hand. 'You mean Tommy, mister,' she said. 'That's who you mean. He ain't Seamus no more.'

'Yes, Tommy. Is he here?'

'No, not today. You wanna speak to my mom?' she asked.

William locked the car. There were five or six children still milling about.

'You kids mind my motor.' He pointed to a big lad, sitting on the bonnet, king of the street. 'Get off the car. No one to touch it. Guard it, and I'll give you a penny each for your trouble.'

The child tugged at his hand and led him around the block to the yard of the tenement. The brick pavement was glistening with oily water running in the gutter. An upturned stiff brush leant against the wall. Late Victorian; a small sash window bottom, a small sash window top; a cast-iron shute for the rubbish running from the balcony to a covered bin on the street; open windows, fancy lace curtains – the poorer the house, the more intricate the nets. The girl stopped halfway down the row and pointed upwards. 'That's where I live. Come on.'

They climbed a narrow concrete stairway up to the top flat. The stairs were dark with water – just scrubbed – smelling of Lysol and rinsed down proper because the pisspot spills on the way to the lavs at the end of the yard. A yard shared with four or five more families, one flushing toilet for every twenty or so people, the slum was cleared late last century, but the corporation hardly put their backs into the job.

Ahead of him, the child opened the door into the main room of the tenement. The windows were flung open, although there wasn't much fresh air coming in from the courtyard, and gaudy china shone on paper-lined shelves below a tinted photograph of the King and Queen. The table was set with a white tablecloth, teapot and milk, salt and pepper, butter dish. At the table, tied with a bit of rope to his highchair, was a toddler. He was two years old or so and, feeding him a meal of mushed bread and milk, was a girl of five, perhaps six years old. Their mother was rinsing through nappies at the sink. On the range, smoking some and too old to work well, was a stewpot full of whites on the boil. The woman turned and dried her hands, red and cracked with lye, on her apron. She looked about forty-five, but she was probably much younger.

'Who's this?' she asked.

William crowded out the small room.

'This fella wants Tommy, Mom.'

'Well, you wouldn't be the first.' She smiled. Unlike Loretta, she had a few good teeth left. 'What d'ya want with him?'

'I just want to ask him a few questions, that's all,' said William.

'Well, he ain't here. Hasn't been here for over a week. Sneaky little sod buggered off, owing me two weeks' rent. If he's not back soon, I'll chuck out his stuff and get me another lodger.'

William's mood shifted. The ever-present nausea surged. The kid was either dead or on the lam. 'His things are here?' William asked.

'Yes.'

'When was the last time you saw him?'

'You a copper?' She frowned and pursed her lips.

'No, Mom, this fella's a detective, like in the pictures.' The child spoke as if proud of a treasure.

'I ain't been to the pictures since Valentino died.' She untied the baby from his chair, held him to her chest and kissed his head. 'You babbies go out an' play. Mom is gonna talk to this fella in peace.'

William gave them each a penny. The woman watched, hungrily, and handed the baby to the eldest girl, William's new friend. Then, she slumped heavily on a kitchen chair, reached for the teapot and shook it. 'Some left. It's a bit stewed. Do you want a cup?' William nodded and sat without being asked. She handed him a cup of tea, already sugared, and said: 'What do you want to know, and what's it worth to me?'

'How much does Tommy owe in rent?' William asked.

'Twelve shillings,' she lied.

William nodded. 'What's his real name?'

'Seamus Rourke. Came to me a year ago. Straight from outta the army. I need lodgers. I need the money. Ain't got no man since the last babby was born.'

'What did he do for work?' asked William.

The woman laughed. 'We do what we have to bloody do, mister. Seamus weren't no different.' Her voice serious, now. 'I know what you're meaning,' she sighed. 'What do you need to know for your twelve shillings?'

'Ever see him with any of his punters?'

She shook her head. 'Look, I knew what Seamus were up to. It were common knowledge about him amongst the women. But he were good enough to keep his business out of my home. I never saw him with a bloke. I wouldn't let him in if he had a fella with him – Christ, not with the kiddies in the next room.' She looked William up and down. 'You know what it's like around here, don't you? You know that you do what you have to do as long as everyone pretends they're right and proper. A lot of blind eyes are turned because each and every one of us is grubbing about just to keep a roof over our heads. Seamus weren't the first to offer his arse. And the women, well more than one will pop down to Station Street when the rent's due or the kiddies are sick. We're all just pretending we ain't whores and thieves. You do what you have to do.' She paused. 'And I'd give the rest of my bloody teeth if it weren't so, but it is. It's just the way it is.'

Seamus Rourke's landlady would get on well with Loretta.

'Let me look at his stuff.'

'I don't like that. Tommy should have a bit of privacy,' said the woman, and she meant it.

'I'll give you a pound note, right now, if I can have half an hour in his room.'

The woman rose and opened the door to the bedroom. 'Knock yourself out, bab.'

William handed her the money.

His landlady had given Tommy the best room. Cramped and dark, the wallpaper stained with smuts and peeling with damp, it was finery for Milk Street. The furniture, all matching and bought in better times as a wedding present perhaps, and well before her husband upped and died, or upped and left, was now given over to the lodger. The bed was made with blankets and sheets – thin, darned, clean – and a Rayon counterpane which brightened the room. Orange and brand new, it was one of Tommy's purchases, no doubt. William lifted the mattress. There was nothing under the bed but a scrubbed-out pisspot, and a neat stack of *Picturegoer* magazines.

William opened the wardrobe. Seamus liked his clothes. Two suits – one navy and one grey – both brushed clean, and both the best a man of his class could afford. The lad was handy with an iron, too, for his shirts were neatly pressed. A pair of brown brogues, polished and re-soled, and black Oxfords, newer and well looked after, were placed neatly below the suits. Underwear on shelves, his socks were not rolled but pinned together in precise piles of black, grey, navy. Next to them was a sewing basket, and in it a frayed handkerchief, half-mended. And under the basket was a Post Office savings book. It contained one hundred and sixty pounds. William whistled at the amount and examined the carefully noted dates of deposit. Twelve shillings saved every week for over a month, and then, last Thursday, two days before the murders, someone had given Tommy thirty pounds. If the boy had left the city in a hurry, then he had done so without his good clothes and without a savings book containing the equivalent, for a lad like Tommy, of a king's ransom.

William sat on the bed. It was a curiously impersonal room, the Tommy in Seamus, perhaps. Army training meant neatness, conformity, order. But a slum childhood and a stint in the barracks proffered lessons in secrecy. Tommy would have a hidey-hole, a place where something more precious than a bank book could be squirrelled away. William raised a corner of lino. Not a speck of dust. The landlady was houseproud. William felt for a loose board; one lifted. In a cavity between the two tenements was a manilla envelope. He emptied the contents on the bed. Photographs of Ronnie tumbled out. Ronnie lounging by a swimming pool, a snapshot, a nymph, a film-star smile. Now a younger Ronnie, twenty-four or twenty-five, a picture William hadn't seen before. He was smart and smiling under the neon sign of the Hippodrome. Next one, Ronnie in the buff but for a sailor's hat worn at a jaunty angle, he and his mirror image leaning back against the bedstead, hands on one another's cocks – frigging in the rigging – frigging senseless.

William flicked back to the previous picture and looked at the reverse. It was dated April 1933, so no, not Ronnie. He looked closer. The jaw was squarer, the nose a little shorter, teeth crooked, but the resemblance was bewildering. Finally, there was a photograph of Ronnie clothed, casual, laughing, and so recently taken that William shuddered at the sight of it. Ronnie had his arm about Tommy, an inch in height between them, but the same hair line – a widow's peak – the same wide brown eyes. They were brothers, twins, if you didn't know any different. Such striking similarity was significant, William felt it in his gut. And there was no doubt in William's mind that Seamus hero-worshipped Ronnie, for the boy in the photograph gazed at the older man with a near painful adoration.

He closed his eyes and saw a once handsome face now a gaping, bloodied hole, a muscular frame slumped forward undignified on the lavatory of a hotel bathroom. William was heartbroken, he knew. He heard his own blood roil, it churned behind his eardrums, counterpoint to the thumping rhythm of his own heartbeat. He stood so suddenly that he had to steady himself on the bedstead. Nausea rose, churned, and then ebbed away. William breathed deeply, shook his head and wished for Veronal. Then he placed the photographs in his breast pocket, folded the lino back on the floor and neatened the bed.

William closed the door behind him. The landlady looked up from her washing.

'When was the last time you saw him?' he asked.

'Over a week ago, now,' she said. 'Like I say, he owes me two weeks' rent. And it's not like Seamus to cut and run. He ain't a bad lad.'

'How's he been these past few weeks?'

'Up and down. In love, I reckon. One minute top of the world, the next down in the dumps. And before you ask, he never told me the name of the fella. Not ever.'

'Ever meet a girl called Fanny Maggs or Fay Francis?' he asked.

She shook her head. William showed her the photograph of Fay.

'She looks the type to run with Seamus,' she laughed. 'But I don't reckon I've seen her around here.'

'Ever hear Seamus talk about a fella called Ronnie? Or a man named Morton? Or a Mr Quince.'

'Nah, never heard of 'em. He kept quiet about that part of his life. He was a young man and on the game. He's gonna have plenty to keep schtum about.' But then the woman hesitated for a moment, as if in thought. 'Quince is an unusual name, ain't it? You know, there was a green van come around here late one night. And I swear to God it said Quinn on the side of it, but it could've been Quince.'

'When was this?'

'Whitsun weekend. I know that for sure because Seamus said he'd be out all bank holiday. I was up with the little 'un teething. I remember that van because there was a picture of a babby on the side. I'd love a few nice pictures of my kiddies. You know, before they get too old for it.' She turned, then tipped hot, dirty water down the sink. 'But the thing is, I reckon whoever drove that van dropped Seamus home because a few minutes later, when I was putting the babby back down, he came in. I was shocked to see him. He said he'd be away for the whole of the weekend. And Seamus, well, he weren't right that night. Cold, shaking like a leaf, and sopping wet. I had to sort out a bath for him. That ain't half a lot of hard work at three o'clock in the morning, but I thought the lad would catch his death if I didn't. He stank of mucky water. And he was sniffing, rubbing at his nose hard, like he'd already got a cold.'

'Did he say where he'd been?'

'Wouldn't say a word. But I reckon he must've fallen in the canal. And whatever happened that night, it hit him hard. He didn't sleep for days afterwards.' She motioned with her thumb to the back streets of Deritend. The cut was two streets behind her. William knew it to be the stretch of the Birmingham and Fazeley where Fay's body was found. Disposing of a murdered girl, badly, was one hell of a way for Quince and Seamus to spend their Whitsun weekend. 'What do you reckon I should do with his stuff?' the woman asked. 'He's left all his good clothes, underwear and everything.' She frowned, worried now. 'If he ain't coming back, I need another lodger, or I won't manage. You reckon he's alright, Seamus?'

'Box up his stuff. Get yourself another fella for the room. He'll write soon, I'm sure.' But William wasn't sure at all. He handed the woman another five bob and watched as she slipped the money into a garish jug on her china shelf. Her face softened in relief. 'That extra five bob is for your silence.' He was giving money away like a charitable foundation. 'Don't tell anyone what I were asking about. No gossip. If the street ask, just say he owed me money. I'm off now, but here's my card. Telephone me, if you remember anything at all –' the woman looked doubtful – 'or come to see me in Needless Alley.'

The landlady nodded, and William left. And, on closing the door behind him, he thought he heard her say a prayer of thanks. It was a prayer William did not share.

34

William locked the door to the Austin. He was alone in Needless Alley but for the sparrows picking at litter. He watched them for a moment. They were town sparrows full of cheek but barely holding their own in the gutter against a few swooping magpies bent on theft. William wondered for a moment at the inherent brutality of the natural world. Survival of the fittest always seemed to him a cruel, hierarchical system.

'How did you get on with finding Tommy?' At Phyll's voice, the sparrows flew off in a flurry, leaving the magpies arrogant and victorious, stalking the pavement like feathered fascists. 'Billy, for God's sake, can you hear me?'

William shook himself and vowed to give up philosophising. 'You surprised me, that's all,' he said, but then he worried he had lost his capacity for ordinary human interaction. 'You always seem to come creeping up on me.'

'I saw you park the car. I've been looking out for you,' said Phyll. 'How did it go with Tommy, or whatever his real name is?'

'His real name is Seamus, and it went terrible,' he said. 'I thought I was going to have a heart attack in Deritend. It ain't the way I want to go.' A commotion of cawing and flapping made him start once more. A single magpie flew away. He watched its flight. 'Phyll, I feel like I'm playing a game, and I'm not sure of the rules. Like chess – Ronnie and I played it in the trenches. I was shit at it. I always lost because I couldn't anticipate the other man's move.'

'What on earth are you talking about?' Phyll ran her hand through her hair. Hair thick, white blonde and rare. 'You go off on tangents,' she said, 'and it really must stop.' She appraised him further. 'You are done in, aren't you?'

'Yes, I am. I'm at the end of my rope.' The evening air became suddenly close; damp droplets of moisture, tasting of petrol fumes, hit the back of his mouth. 'We should talk indoors.'

They walked the few paces to his office in silence. He heaved open the front door and inhaled. The building had that sordid smell of bachelorhood: of lick-and-a-prayer cleanliness, of strong drink and strong sweat, of fried food and dirty ashtrays. William waited for the door to swing shut – letting in the fresh, disinfecting air – and the Yale mechanism to click, before he turned to Phyll, tight at his shoulder in the cramped stairwell, and said, 'His landlady hasn't seen Seamus for over a week. The boy's not been home since the murders. He left his good clothes and a bank book full of cash deposits behind him, just like Ronnie.'

'You're assuming he's dead.'

'You assume correct. He could have done a runner, but I don't think so.' William began to climb the stairs. He became aware of his heavy legs, his breathing tight and shallow, his laboured, confused thinking. Living seemed a chore. It felt like a prescience into his old age. He stopped midway up the flight, alarmed at the need to catch his breath. 'The lad knew Ronnie well,' he said. 'I think the boy hero-worshipped him.' William glanced at Phyll. 'Christ, Ronnie seemed to inspire it in people.' He stretched his shoulders and patted his jacket pocket. 'I've found another collection of dirty pictures. I'm getting really tired of looking at blokes with their tackle out.'

'They were lovers?'

'Yes.' William mustered himself into climbing the last few steps to his office. 'Christ, I could do with a pint of coffee.'

'Billy, he's not the only one who's missing.' Phyll's raised voice held a note of panic. 'Morton's gone too, since yesterday. His housekeeper told me his bed's not been slept in. She seemed very concerned because, well, the funeral is today. Mrs Morton's funeral, I mean.'

That Clara-shaped grief, curled tight in his thorax since the murders, unfurled and gave his cracked ribs a sharp kick. 'I'm only shocked that he hasn't vanished sooner,' he said. 'I've been a bit blind. Blinded by dope and grief. A bit dim.'

Phyll's slow nod was another silent appraisal of his well-being. 'I'm going to try and use that fancy coffee-maker of yours,' she said. 'Then, we need to talk all this through.'

William watched her sprint up the final flight of stairs to his digs, and then he opened the door to the office. The air, always cloying, was thick with booze and fags. He moved to unfasten the window, propping the sash once more with the rolled newspaper, now ratted and flimsy without Fay's story.

He removed Seamus's cache of pictures from his jacket pocket and placed them with the stills of Fay, Clara, Ronnie. Lined on his desk, he was aware only of body parts. Eyes, thighs, cock, they became a strange, dehumanised, hardly erotic jigsaw.

Phyll soon returned with a tray of coffee and biscuits. 'Oh my God, what's all this?' She put the tray on the desk and scrutinised the snapshot of Ronnie with Seamus, clothed and looking like brothers. 'They look so happy.' She touched the photograph gently. 'I had no idea. Oh God, I didn't know him well at all. The boy seems rather guileless and innocent, rather smitten. Are you sure they're not related?'

'Christ, I hope not,' he said. William poured coffee and sweetened his own drink with two – no, three – lumps of sugar. 'I couldn't cope with that.' He chose a pink wafer and took a bite. 'From what the landlady said, Seamus and Quince dumped Fay's body in the canal. I reckon they were hopped up on dope, too.'

'But Quince was no killer, Billy.'

'Morton killed Fay.' William hesitated for a moment, and then told Phyll all he had learnt from examining Fay and Clara's pictures that afternoon. 'Quince would do anything for a client,' he continued. 'He accommodated the kind of fantasy others may find repugnant. If during filming, a punter, Morton, killed Fay by pulling too tight on the ligature, then Quince may have seen it as part of his service to get rid of Fay's body. It paid for him to be so obliging. Think of the power Quince could exert over such a man.'

'And Seamus?'

'He was probably involved in the filming. There on the ground, as it were. Quince paid him to help shift the body and to keep quiet. Twelve shillings a week. Fay came from the Waifs and Strays, both men probably thought she had no family to speak of. She'd be just another anonymous dead blonde.' But Quince and Seamus were very wrong. Fay had family. William poured more coffee, drank it down. 'Seamus must've got the wind up and told Ronnie. He wasn't a wrong 'un, according to his landlady. I reckon he told Ronnie the big secret because –' William nodded towards the photographs – 'he was in love with him, hero-worshipped him. This was the dirt Ronnie had on Morton. He got his information from Seamus. And I don't think Seamus ever knew that Ronnie was Fay's father. The poor buck-toothed bastard was ignorant of that right to the end. By the time I sent Ronnie off to shadow Morton, Ronnie knew the murdered girl was Fay. And, more importantly, that Fay was his daughter. And last Friday, perhaps even earlier, Ronnie knew that Morton was the killer. I can feel it. I know it in my bones.'

Phyll looked at him and shrugged. 'Oh, Billy. Your bones aren't magic. You're speaking like a tuppenny psychic. We have no proof that Morton killed Fay, or even that Seamus and Quince moved her body. Before we go to the police, we need facts, rather than supposition.'

Phyll was correct about the coppers. Wade would say that the evidence they had was circumstantial. And the Chief Inspector worked for Morton, however grudgingly. Besides, it was too late for the law. Things had already gone biblical. 'You're right about the coppers having no truck with the circumstantial evidence.' William lit a cigarette, inhaled deeply and offered one to Phyll. 'But you know that my bones are right, Phyll. You know it.'

'Yes, Billy. I do think you're right.' She began to sort the photographs. Her tidy mind automatically organising the erotic from the sentimental, and snapshots of Ronnie from snapshots of Seamus, and staring in confusion, swapping pictures from one pile to the next. 'Everything is so confused and macabre and dramatic.' She paused over the word. 'It's like some horrible revenge tragedy. Do you think Morton killed Seamus to keep him quiet, and then ran?'

'Nope.' William's coffee was as strong and sweet as treacle. He gulped it down; the caffeine cleared his head. Then he reached into the bottom desk drawer for the Webley. 'Brothers and sisters, fathers and daughters, husbands and wives. You were right about this being a revenge tragedy.'

'Where are you going with that?'

'I'm going to see if I can find Morton before it's too late.' He stood, gathered up his Webley and put it in the waistband of his trousers, turned to her and smiled. 'I've lost weight since meeting you. Soon, I'll be dapper.'

'You've been living off dope and coffee, like a true man of fashion. I simply cannot wait to get you to a decent tailor,' she said. 'Billy, I'm coming with you.' She was wide-eyed; she may have shuddered. 'If you know where Morton is, you must tell me.'

William shook his head. 'No, you keep safe. You stay put.' ·

'Stop saying that,' she said. Her feelings were hurt, he could tell. He had shunned her. It was true. 'You don't have to protect me because I'm a woman. It's insulting to me. Why must you constantly put my brakes on?'

'Phyll, I hardly knew Clara, I know that now. But I also know that the terrible thing that happened to her was a theft, the worst kind of betrayal and theft. She was human, and she was good, and she deserved a better life. She may have had that better life with me, or on her own. But either way, that opportunity was thieved away from her.' He inhaled deeply, pressing his right hand against his chest at that sorrowful Clara-shaped space. 'I thought that loving her would be a redemption for the way I'd lived my life, the way I'd made my money. But that never was my problem. My problem is that I'm wounded. I carry my wounds about like a bloke with shrapnel in his leg, you just can't see them. And Christ, they're festering. They're green with rot. I need to cauterise them, and it'll be painful. They're old wounds, Phyll. They go back to childhood, and I have to see to them if I'm ever to be a whole man.' He watched Phyll's pale face fall briefly into shock and grief. 'I need to face facts, Phyll. I don't want to hide from the truth anymore, and I've got to make reparation for dragging Clara into this mess.' He paused for a moment, for he did not want to lie to Phyll during this testimony. 'And also, in truth –' he patted his Webley – 'I need my fuckin' dues.'

'I think it's going to be horrible for you,' she said.

'I reckon it probably will.' William looked out of his office window onto a blood-red summer twilight. The jagged Birmingham skyline, now in shadow, stood against the horizon like a set of rotten teeth. 'I never was a proper detective,' he said. 'That fascist copper once called me a professional Peeping Tom, and he got it about right, but if I come out of this –' he paused, struggling for the right word – 'unscathed, do you fancy going into business with me? We could partner up in something worthwhile?'

'I reckon,' she said. 'I reckon I'd like that very much.' Phyll stood, looked into his eyes and held out her hand. He didn't kneel like a knight and kiss her white fingertips but shook on their deal. William's handshake was firm. And for the first time in a week, so was his grip on reality.

35

The *Little Marvel* was moored at the Soho Loop, just as William expected. Near enough to the city to be convenient for business, but far enough away for that business to remain your own. She was moored in Soho on the night of the murders; she was moored in Soho whenever Uncle Johnny had a lucrative job in play.

Black on black water, it hunkered low and wet against the brick towpath, and a soft gleam of lamplight radiated from the cabin like the opening eye of a snake. A breeze blew in from the east; it penetrated William's suit, pricked at his skin. And, from the same direction as the wind, came two swans flying low. Nearing him now, scudding across the skin of the canal, they created a perfect wake, and then landed, gathering in their great beautiful wings. At their sound, the light on the boat shifted, and William heard what he thought to be a deep muffled cry.

There was no way to enter the cabin with any degree of stealth. William was exposed: water before him, factory walls behind, and nothing but the rutted gravel of the towpath to his left and right. He removed the Webley from his waistband and waited for the gun metal to warm in the heat of his hand before climbing on board, trench-raider once more. 'Everyone be calm,' William shouted. 'No one move.' William brandished his pistol and felt suddenly ineffectual and foolish.

He could not yet see who was in the cabin. He blinked against the light. This was no electric glare, but the mellow glow of an oil lamp, and it took his eyes only a few seconds to adjust. Morton was hog-tied like a prize pig prepared for slaughter, his fat carcass filling the floor of the cabin. Gagged with his regimental tie, it dangled from his mouth, and was moist with spittle. He had been beaten about the face, and blinded by the swelling of his eye sockets, so at William's entrance, he wriggled and squeaked like a trapped mole. A stocking was tied around his neck, and a pencil, used as a tightening pivot, was knotted below his chin. Striations, welts from previous constrictions, were beginning to show. William's first instinct was to bend down and undo the ligature, but as he did so, the door to the far room opened and a strong shaft of light, as if from a torch, fell onto the prone Morton.

It was Ronnie who waved the electric torch about the room.

The *Little Marvel* was named after Ronnie. As Uncle Johnny's favourite child, Frankie Maggs, he said, could do just about anything he wanted. Ronnie's resurrection, therefore, was no surprise to William.

And he spotlit William and the fat man as if they were both on stage. 'Pop your pistol on the table, Billy, there's a dear. They make me rather nervous,' he said. William blinked, shielded his eyes, noticed the heavy Colt in Ronnie's right hand and complied. Ronnie grinned a genuine, friendly grin, flicked the switch of the torch and pocketed William's Webley. They fell into the gloom of the lamplight. 'It's terribly nice to see you and all that,' he said, 'but I don't want you interfering with mine and Mr Morton's business.' Ronnie nursed his left arm. He was thinner now, unhealthy. Unwashed, too, and there was an animal smell about him that William didn't like

– an old trauma, bad blood. 'Queenie said you'd turn up; didn't you, old girl?' Behind him now, standing in the doorway to the rear bunk, stood Queenie. Her round face, lit softly by the oil lamp, was solemn; her green eyes were no longer like bottle glass; they were pond water. 'She said you were bound to piece it all together eventually.'

'How long have you had him?' William nodded at the prone Morton.

'Since Thursday.' Ronnie came towards him, and as he did so, he gave Morton a casual kick to the gut. A trapped animal will always bite, William thought. Wounded, cornered, apparently cheerful, Ronnie was terrifying, and he still held tight to his pistol. 'We grabbed him just as soon as his fascist copper friend left. I think there's been a schism in the party. I've been keeping my beady eye on him all this time.' Ronnie pulled down the lower lid of his handsome, made-up eye with his free hand and grinned.

'You kept your hired motor?' Of course he did, William thought. He's been hurtling around the city like the angel of death.

'Now's not the time to be churlish about garage bills, darling.' Ronnie took off his jacket and slumped onto the floor beside Morton. He leant against the bench, stretched out his slim legs and placed both pistols on his lap. 'Take a gander at my arm, will you. It's bleeding rather, throbbing, too. Queenie's being quite squeamish over it.' William moved to roll up Ronnie's shirtsleeve. He unwound a makeshift bandage, made from a man's silk handkerchief, still purple paisley in parts, and replaced it with his own. A gunshot wound, the bullet had lodged in the flesh. Ronnie had lost blood. 'I've been tending to it, but I'm hardly a professional. Is it alright? I do feel a bit sick.'

William nodded, and then moved to the open window and leant out. He gulped at the night air as a man drowning, then threw the bloodied silk dressing into the cut. It floated like strewn petals and sank. William turned back to Ronnie. 'It's alright. You'll live.'

'I'll make some tea,' said Queenie. And they each ignored the brutalised Morton, sweating and squirming at their feet, as though they were actors in some blackly comic farce.

Ronnie smiled up at his sister, his charm obvious, horrifying. 'Yes, how nice. And be a good girl, do, and pop a spot of Glenfiddich in mine. I need it.' And then he turned to William. 'May I cadge a fag? I'm all out of Lucky Strikes.'

William reached for his cigarettes and matches. 'Who shot you?' He kept his voice casual, but his hands shook, and it took a few attempts before William could light up. He passed one to Ronnie.

'Bob Stokes,' said Queenie. 'He's been hiding out with Arthur and Bob since last Saturday.'

Ronnie turned to her, as would a petulant child, and said, 'Billy asked *me*, Queenie. *I'm* telling the story.' He leant over and fiddled with the pencil controlling the noose about Morton's neck. The fat man's groan was pitiful. 'Arthur and Bob were very accommodating at first. I gave them rather a lot of money, and they and their friends were terribly helpful and kind enough to keep visitors away. Even you, Billy.' Ronnie took his fag, blew a few smoke rings and scrutinised William's still bruised face. 'You look terrible, by the way. They really did give you quite a going-over, but I'm afraid they don't much like you. Things turned iffy once we got Morton on board the Stokeses' boat. I worry my fat friend is something of a Jonah. He stirred the pot rather by offering Bob and Arthur countless fortunes to let him go. By that time, we were all getting on each other's nerves and were quite silly on cocaine. Three virile men all cooped up on a narrowboat – well, it was bound to happen.' Ronnie's laugh was mirthless. 'Queenie came looking for me after I retrieved my haversack from your office. I still have a key and you were quite dead to the world, snoring and sweating. That was a mistake.' Ronnie paused. 'I know that now, but I did so need my things. No, I cannot lie, I did so want my dope.' Ronnie grinned. 'She found Bob and Arthur accusing me of all sorts. Oh, I really can't remember. They got the wind up after we grabbed Morton. Reneging on the deal we had. Waving their pistols about. And Bob shot me with this thing.' Ronnie patted his Colt. 'Queenie got me out of there intact. Used her womanly charms on dear old Arthur, and her cash with Bob. Helped me to bundle this one onto the *Little Marvel*.' He stubbed his cigarette out on Morton's pudgy thigh. The tortured man was eerily silent. 'God bless her, one can only truly rely on blood relations, Billy.'

Queenie moved forward and placed a restraining hand on her brother's shoulder. 'Have your tea,' she said. Lavish with the whisky, she poured a decent slug into her brother's cup and gave it to him. Then she turned to William and said, 'He hasn't confessed yet.'

Morton squealed. It sounded like a plea.

Ronnie pointed down at his captive and grinned. 'Look, the Kraken no longer sleepeth.' He tightened the ligature with a hard turn of the pencil and spat in Morton's ear, 'Repeat after me: one must not rape and murder little girls.' Soon, Morton would be dead. And, if he had to, William would allow it, for the fat man was now a pawn to be sacrificed in his own search for the truth. 'Queenie wants you to confess, but it doesn't matter one bit to me. I know what you've done.' Ronnie whispered in Morton's ear as if telling a secret. 'You raped my baby, you pervert.' He picked up his pistol and placed it against Morton's temple. 'Raped and murdered my child.' Ronnie sighed. His head swayed, like a drunken man focusing on the road ahead. 'A man must stand up and be counted at some point, Billy. A father must . . . must take care, protect his children. Actually, I'm not sure what a father must do. Johnny was such a vile bastard, I truly wouldn't know.' His voice trailed off for a moment. 'But the day Seamus told me what Morton had done was a day of wrath –' his voice rose like an old-time preacher – 'of desolation and destruction. Morton, do you hear me? It was a day of darkness and gloom, a day of clouds and blackness.' The fire and brimstone timbre ceased suddenly, and Ronnie became his charming, humorous self. 'Fatty hates it when I talk like that. It makes him terribly nervy.' He glanced about the cabin, looking first at William and then at Queenie, grinning, glittery-eyed, waiting for his audience to be appreciative. He looked confused and then angry, then pursed his lips. 'Oh, please yourselves.'

'Oh, Christ. He did it. Ronnie killed them all.' And although William felt every scrap of Queenie's exhaustion and shame, he was surprised to hear her express such shock and sorrow. 'Every single one of them.' She turned to William. 'Even your Clara.' And at the mention of his wife's name, Morton let out a muted, angry bellow.

Ronnie tapped his Colt once more against Morton's temple. 'An eye for an eye, Queenie. I know you remember the Bible verse because you were such a tedious, pious sort of child. Stripe for stripe, wound for wound, and so on and so forth.' He waved the pistol airily about the cabin. 'I want to go to Liverpool, and I need some money. You pair will take me because Bob and Arthur turned out to be so very unreliable, and I'm ...' He glanced down at his injured arm. 'Weakened. I need a spot of convalescence. I want to catch the boat for America. Queenie, you must organise a passport for me. You have the connections, I know that. You can call me Seamus Rourke on the papers. Ronnie Edgerton is dead. You quite obligingly identified that body in the mortuary as mine.' Ronnie reached up to the table and helped himself to more Glenfiddich. 'They adore the Irish in America. I shall practise my brogue.' He prodded Morton with the Colt. 'We can dispose of this one on the way.'

'Go fuck yourself.' She paused for a moment and glanced towards William. 'Me and Billy are going to the coppers.'

'Nice language for a lady.' Ronnie once more waved his pistol playfully. 'And Queenie, do play nice. No one is going to the coppers because each and every one of us will end up inside – particularly you, old girl. You're quite the career criminal nowadays, and poor Billy here has been obstructing justice all over the place, I'm sure.'

'Go fuck yourself.' Queenie bent down and pinched her brother's cheek, hard. Ronnie smiled, bared his perfect white teeth and tightened Morton's ligature.

The cabin was rich with the smell of blood and hard drink and unwashed bodies. William got out quick, thinking he might vomit. He jumped onto the towpath and untied the *Little Marvel* from her moorings. And William let her float away – one, two, three feet – Queenie and Ronnie and Morton on board. Let the fuckers go; let the past go, he thought. But he couldn't escape them. He needed a resolution. He needed justice in order to be a whole man. William chanced the leap. Back on board, he started the engine and took the tiller.

Ronnie called out from the cabin. 'That's the idea, Billy. The sooner we get to Liverpool, the sooner you will be rid of me. I understand that I'm rather a nuisance. All I want is a nice new passport and my fuck-off money.' If Ronnie needed them, he would not kill them. He couldn't manage the boat alone, injured as he was. And without Queenie's cash and contacts, there would be no America, and therefore no escape, for Ronnie.

Queenie joined William and perched herself on the edge of the boat. Ronnie rocked out – pistol in his good hand – and sat on deck, leaning against the cabin wall, grinning. 'Don't leave me lonely. Mr Morton is such poor company.' He wedged the Colt between his knees. 'Throw us your gaspers.'

William chucked the last of his cigarettes over and Ronnie lit up. Queenie shone the oil lamp straight at her brother. She moved towards him, sat on her haunches. He smiled. Then she clouted him, hard. Ronnie's head hit the open cabin door and then flopped forward, his fag falling from his mouth. He shook himself like a dog and made a slow move to belt her back. But Queenie stood upright and screwed her foot heavily into the hand of his bad arm, as though stubbing out a Lucky Strike. Ronnie reached for the pistol but did not shoot. Instead, he cried and nursed his injured fingers. 'Ow, Queenie. You've hurt me, hurt me terribly. I think they're broken, Queenie, look.' He held his bruised hand out like a schoolboy, just caned. 'Why be so rough?' Ronnie began to weep.

Queenie was motionless for a few seconds but dropped to her knees and cradled her sobbing brother. 'I'm sorry, bab, so sorry. But you've done a terrible thing.' She kissed his fingers better, motherly. 'There's no excusing it. You do know that, don't you? That what you've done is bad. Not Morton, I understand that, but . . .' She trailed off. 'But his wife and the lad, Tommy. You've done an awful thing.' Queenie kissed him and wiped the sweat-sodden hair away from Ronnie's face. 'I'll get you a flannel and some more whisky. It'll take away the pain.'

Ronnie turned his reddened face towards William and said, 'Queenie is a good sort. She can't help her temper.'

And William could bear it no longer. 'You killed Clara because Morton killed Frances.' William could hear the catch in his own voice. Clara was collateral damage in Ronnie's mission to torture Morton. William knew it to be true, and yet he found it all so hard to reconcile. 'Why do that, Ronnie? She was such a good person.'

'Plenty of good people die, Billy. It was for a good cause.' Ronnie shrugged. 'She was a casualty of war. And I'm terribly sorry you became fond of her, old son, terribly sorry, but it never would've worked. You're Queenie's boy, you always were.' Against the black velvet backdrop of night, and lit golden by the oil lamp, Ronnie became a movie star. His eyelids lowered, fluttered. 'Seamus told me how Frances died, despite poor Quince paying for his silence. He confessed like a good Catholic, saying that a girl he knew died during filming. Choking her, that's what Morton was doing. Choking her with a stocking made in his own factory. Masturbating himself silly and got carried away, so Seamus said. He pulled the ligature too hard. Seamus fucked her before Morton choked her. That tuppenny whore laid his hands on my girl. He said it made a change from old men and the girl was a nice sort, although a bit dim.' Ronnie pulled the Webley from his jacket pocket, eyed it for size against his own Colt, and then said, 'To his credit, he never knew Frances was my daughter. I killed him quite early in the evening. Told him to dress up for dancing and a night of romance. We had champagne in the room, a little Veronal in his glass, then I killed him in the bath-room when the band downstairs started playing. He knew who Frances was at the end though, pissed himself with fright in that bathroom before I pulled the trigger. Ruined a perfectly nice suit.' He chuckled, mirthlessly. 'Seamus was actually a very sweet boy, but he had to go.' Ronnie drummed his fingers on the Colt. 'It was what God would have wanted. Seamus died so I could live. It was God's will.'

Queenie returned with a flannel and a freshly opened bottle of Glenfiddich.

'He's not normal, Queenie,' said William.

'I know, love. We're none of us normal.' Queenie mopped Ronnie's brow with tender affection. 'Let's get you cleaned up.' She spoke lovingly to her brother. 'Another drop of Scotch and a rest. You're as weak as a kitten. You've lost a lot of blood.'

'I learnt about her death in the newspapers, as if she was just some dead blonde. Some silly dead blonde who got herself into trouble. But she was my little girl.' Hunched in the corner of the deck, bony and dark, Ronnie was a wounded bird, a jackdaw, and he looked like his father. He sucked at the whisky bottle, and William saw his mood darken sharply to black. 'Do you know what a sin-eater is, Billy?' William shook his head, and Ronnie pointed westwards. 'When a fellow dies out in the border country, they pay a poor man, a rascally sort of chap, to eat bread and beer over the coffin. It isn't much of a meal, but here's the thing, it contains all the dead man's sins. Think of that, Billy. Every little shame and secret all baked into a scrap of bread. This was the sin-eater's job. Eat a meal full of sin. Risk his immortal soul for a shilling and a bit of bread. Take on sins that aren't his own because he's poor and at least in hell he'll be warm. And the rich man, he'll rest easy in heaven, like his sinful carcass rested easy on earth.'

Exhaustion rippled through William's body like a wave. 'I don't know what you're getting at,' he said.

Ronnie spoke carefully as if addressing a child. 'Frances was a sin-eater. My baby took on the rich man's perversions, took them on like they were her own. She didn't want to be fucked by some old bloke, and strangled, and filmed. She did it because she was poor and motherless, and she wasn't worth anything to anyone.' Ronnie's voice cracked. 'But she was worth something to me. When I first held Frances in my arms, she was like a bud. Swaddled tight, all pink and white, so new, and I blessed her.' Ronnie lowered his eyes and made the sign of the cross. 'I blessed her with averageness. Not beauty or intelligence, but normality. Why wasn't she adopted by some nice suburban couple? Why didn't she become a secretary, or a teacher in an infant school? I never wanted her to fuck men for money.' Ronnie's eyes, now doe-like, gathered in the attention of his audience – a true trouper. He reached between his knees for the Colt, placed its muzzle against his moistened lips, took the width of the barrel in his mouth for a few moments, and rolled it on his tongue with a lascivious delight. His eyes gleamed wide with self-conscious obscenity. Suddenly, Ronnie dropped the act, and with it, the pistol. It thudded hard and masculine onto the deck of the boat. 'God failed me. I never wanted Frances to fuck men for money. Somebody's got to start eating their own sins, Billy.'

William remembered the piles of scandal sheets in Ronnie's flat, pored over and squalid. Frances's face, so like her mother's, appeared as a murdered blonde in a newspaper, and then Ronnie's world, and his mind, fell apart. 'But you only realised the girl Morton killed was Frances when you saw the report in the newspapers that Sunday in June.'

'You are a clever boy, Billy. It took me a day or so to put two and two together. It was her face. She was the image of Alice.' Ronnie lit another cigarette, waved it in the air. The smoke drifted, floated, dissipated. 'Seamus said he and Quince disposed of her in the canal, thinking she would float away on the water. Fools. It was all part of Quince's bespoke service, to clean up after unfortunate accidents. Why should a man of Morton's standing sully himself with corpses?' Ronnie sighed and rose, as if he were an exhausted housewife suffering one more endless chore, stubbed his fag out on the deck in one violent action, bent and then picked up both pistols. He paused at the door and said, 'Of course, I did for Quince in the end. Set him aflame amidst his own celluloid filth. He was such a vile syco-phant to these rich fellows.' Ronnie prodded hard at his own chest with the Colt. 'Me, I'm cut from a different cloth.'

William remained at the tiller, and Queenie followed her brother into the cabin to the dying Morton. There was a moment's silence, a squeal and then a gentle, puffing groan. As the Maggs siblings returned to the deck, the canal – a black mirror – reflected their pale, beautiful faces. Queenie settled her brother down beneath his counterpane. 'I rather lost my temper,' Ronnie said. 'We do have terrible tempers, don't we, old girl?' He patted Queenie's hand and lit another of William's cigarettes, chain-smoking.

'Is Morton dead?' William asked.

Queenie said nothing. She didn't, couldn't, meet William's eye.

'Why be so brutal with Clara?' William's voice was calm, and yet understanding the truth had become a fixation, a cruel need to know. He was reminded of Morton swigging brandy, surrounded by lilies and sweating possessive obsession. 'You still haven't told me.'

311

Ronnie smiled. 'Queenie, where's the cocaine? I wouldn't mind some. I have an inkling that the night will be long and fractious.'

William shook his head. Queenie did not move. Ronnie smiled once more.

'I see.' Ronnie took a deep drag on his fag and batted his mascaraed lashes. 'This is rather like a play, isn't it? Will a copper be waiting in Liverpool to haul me off once I've confessed to the great detective? Know your fucking place, Billy. Dad's not here. This is my boat now.'

William let go of the tiller. The *Little Marvel* veered into the right bank of the canal, the engine still on full. He stood, and the boat rocked, the bow butting against brick. There was a sickening scrape; a trio of ducks, once nested in the reeds, fluttered out and flew low over the black water. 'Take the tiller off me, Ronnie. Come and take it, you fucker. Shoot me with one of your guns.' Queenie remained impassive by her brother's side.

'I never thought of killing her, you know, before you showed me her photograph that day in the White Swan.' Ronnie shouted over the rasping thrum of the snarled-up engine. 'I had no idea my letters would have such an effect on Morton. I was never quite in my right mind when I wrote them. Giddy on cocaine, writing gruesome, rather sadistic erotica about his wife all through the night. It was facile, really. It was just to taunt him. I wanted to let him know I knew what kind of man he was. But he was simply too stupid to take the hint. For all his breeding, Morton had no subtlety.' He peered at William with his dark crow's eyes. Ronnie was tiring, his head tilted into his good shoulder. 'It was fate that he came to you, wasn't it? I had no idea how much he loved her until you told me. Obsessed with her, you said. And when I knew how precious she really was to him, I realised I could have my dues. I was ineffectual until you came along. You started it all, Billy. You were an instrument of fate. Of God's will.'

Ronnie and Queenie believed in God and appreciated Him as a nasty bastard. William preferred the comfort of atheism.

He stopped the engine, and then pushed the boat out of the tangled weed and undergrowth. The *Little Marvel* drifted back into the centre of the canal.

'Start the engine, Billy. Do it now.' Queenie spoke up. 'We need to get moving.'

36

William let the boat drift through a tunnel of green. Trees on either bank arched over the canal, and chinks of moonlight shone through the canopy. He heard nothing but Ronnie's phlegmy breath, and then a shuffling on the water, and the rustle of the willows at the margins of the cut. Uncle Johnny once said that in their murmuring leaves lay the ghosts of murdered women. William started the engine and took hold of the tiller.

'You are very adept at handling him, Queenie. It's nice how he listens to you. You must thank me later for getting rid of the inconvenient Clara. She was a drip compared to you.' Ronnie nestled his head on his sister's shoulder. 'Do go and fetch me some cocaine, there's a good girl.'

'No, not yet, Ronnie. Later.' She tucked the pink counterpane about him, held his hand, kissed his cheek and placed the bottle of Glenfiddich to her brother's lips with her free hand. Ronnie drank the whisky in sloppy gulps. 'And you mustn't be cross with Billy,' she said. 'He just wants to know the truth, that's all.'

'But the truth hurts, Queenie.' Ronnie looked at William with rheumy eyes. 'It's often best avoided, in my experience.'

'The final letter you wrote,' said William. 'The one Morton showed me, the one signed "O", was that for Olympia? You

wrote that one on purpose. That one was manipulative.'
Queenie was right. His need for the truth about Clara's
murder had become monstrous and overwhelming; it nour-
ished his sense of betrayal, fed his touchy grief, nurtured the
coming chaos. 'You knew exactly how I felt about Clara, and
you used it. The letter was to push me into setting up the
honeytrap. It was a Judas kiss.'

'A detective with the soul of a poet. I adore this side of you.
It's terribly attractive. I signed all the letters "O". Morton's pet
name for Frances was Olympia. He named my child after a
famous French whore.' Ronnie sighed. 'You had such a lovely
plan in place, darling. All you needed was a little direction to
act at the most convenient moment. And you took the bait
easily because you were so smitten. I do believe you rather
saw yourself as her rescuer. How ironic?' He waved his hand,
a deliberate, theatrical act. 'I am schooled in tragedy, hamartia.
I learnt from the best.' And then his grin became a poor echo
of his usual charisma, for loss of blood and hard booze made
Ronnie dribble. 'I don't want you to think that I didn't like
her, Billy. She was a very nice sort. And she wasn't a bit frightened of me. We danced and drank champagne and had a
terribly nice time, all while poor Seamus lay quite undignified
upstairs in that bathroom. But you know me, Billy, if they're
nice, I do like to give women a good time.' Ronnie's hunched
shoulders shuddered in mirth.

'Fuck you, Ronnie. You are a lying cunt. You tortured her,
you fucker.'

'Billy, darling, you're becoming terribly tiresome and sentimental in middle age.' Ronnie attempted to stand, but failed;
instead, he half-leant against the cabin wall, his long legs in a
painful crouch. The counterpane slid from his knees. Ronnie
fumbled in his pocket for the Colt but found William's Webley.

He waved it like a toy, dropped it and watched it tumble to the deck. Queenie picked it up like a tidy mother and placed it on the roof of the boat. Ronnie gazed at her and it, slack-jawed and uncomprehending, and then he grinned at William and said, 'Alright, old son, here's your truth. I belted her until she was quiet, and then I gave her a quick fuck. She didn't make a noise when I put the noose about her neck afterwards. She was as silent as a little mouse. Morton taught the woman well.'

Eye for eye, tooth for tooth, burning for burning, stripe for stripe.

And there it was. Spoken stark in the dark – the truth. And yet the Clara-shaped grief nestled deep in William's chest did not shift at this telling, but swelled and roiled until it engulfed him. Chaos had come, and William was grateful.

Queenie, eyes like pond water, gazed up at William, and nodded as she held the whisky bottle up to the oil lamp. There was a mouthful left. She shook it and placed it on her brother's lips. Ronnie sucked at it like a baby.

'It's so nice being with you all again, telling stories. Queenie, can you remember when we would hide under the tarpaulin and read *The Halfpenny Marvel*, and I would do the voices? Can you remember when Billy cried? When we read about the gypsy gang and we said the gang would get him because he was a half-breed gypsy, and they wanted their blood-kin back. Can you remember?'

Billy remembered.

At Fradley Junction, the canal basin became a black mirror, reflecting the Fighting Cock, all lit up, for it was not yet closing time. And the gibbet-like cranes and hoists were poised ready for the morning, and the few silent coal-laden narrow-boats rocked, only slightly, as they passed. William turned the tiller to the left – north-west – towards the Trent and Mersey.

'There are five or so locks comin' up, Billy. You wanna get off? I can take the tiller,' said Queenie.

It had been twenty years since William had handled a flight of locks. He closed his eyes and imagined each gate; the water flooding in; he and Ronnie stuck in the depths, sheathed in clammy brick, and the sheer, terrible, force of the canal shifting them skyward.

But Ronnie had sensed Queenie's concern and so pounced on William's weakness. 'What yow sayin', Queenie bab? Yow think our Billy's a fraidy cat? Y'owv not still frit of the watter, are yow, Billy?'

'I'm alright, Queenie, honestly.' William slowed the boat down. Queenie jumped off. It was only then that William noticed she wasn't wearing shoes. Queenie ran ahead. He heard the regular clink of the lock gates open. The *Little Marvel* began to sink.

'I've lost a lot of blood, I think.'

'Yes, you have,' said William.

Ronnie shuffled forward and came so close that William smelt his sour breath. 'I don't want to lose my temper with Queenie, but she keeps cocaine hidden on the boat, and I'm worried she won't share. I left mine on Arthur's boat, and I'm rather desperate.' Ronnie's voice was little more than a whisper, barely heard over the slow slurping drain of the cut water. 'Billy, if you find Queenie's cocaine for me now, I will share it with you. You're my very best friend. You could do whatever you want with it. Or come with me to America. You have a head for business. We could take the dope to America. Make our fortunes. You're my best mate, Billy. You know I love you. Come with me.' Ronnie reached out a pale hand; touched Billy's knee. 'Can you remember when we would run off together? We were proper pals. We would muck about, and Dad would lose his rag, and he would give you a proper belting, but never me. I was his favourite.'

William was in a deep, black hole.

'Y'alright down there, Billy?' William looked up, craned his neck, and saw first her pale, bare feet, then the dark of her dress and hair, her face – a Madonna's face – Lacrimosa. Above her, the moon was a shard of glass, the North Star a lantern, lambent.

'He's gone to sleep now, love,' William replied.

She nodded and closed the gate.

The water sluiced in. The *Little Marvel* began to pitch and rise.

But let judgement run down as waters, and righteousness as a mighty stream.

Queenie, a queen, had been lacing whisky with Veronal all night, so that William, the knight, could do his duty by the dead.

Queenie gazed down on it all, bearing witness, as William screwed his jacket into a tight ball and placed it hard over Ronnie's nose and mouth. He ignored the pistols, for William needed silence. Instead, he crouched over Ronnie, rocking the *Little Marvel* with his body weight – snot and spittle on the good woollen cloth, a little blood, too – it took minutes before Ronnie's pulse faded to a stop and all dues were paid.

37

They weighed the bodies down with pig iron. Queenie sewed ballast from the boat into the pockets of both men's finely tailored suits whilst Billy managed the boat. They travelled miles to a quiet – near abandoned – stretch of cut they knew well as children. Overgrown with hogweed and dock, bordered on both sides with woodland: rangy buddleia, crab apple, thickets of elder, branches drooping heavy with bitter berries: it was somewhere in Warwickshire. On the towpath, William saw a rat creep through a nettle patch. Then, as black night became grey, and a strip of dirty yellow formed on the horizon, William, rolling each body over the side of the boat, laid Morton and Ronnie to rest.

Morton sank first, for Queenie weighed him down well, but Ronnie sank slowly.

William watched Ronnie's face drift pale in the oily water; it flickered beneath the skin of the canal; hair like waterweed, it spilled and drifted with the wash of the cut; his suit ballooned, his white fingers splayed and elegant. Then, Ronnie was gone. Asleep on crumbling brick.

William started the engine. The willow branches bowed; their silver leaves caressed the cut. The early morning light was like a fine gauze, a shrouded glimmering haze. A blackbird trilled. He sat on the edge of the boat and smoked his last cigarette. Queenie fried bacon.

She came out with a plate of sandwiches and sweet tea, her dark hair unpinned; her stays loosed. 'We'll soon be home,' she said. 'My kiddies will be waiting for me. I miss them. I've been desperate to see them this past week. Life goes on, Billy love. Life goes on.'

'Did we do the right thing, Queenie?'

'We played the cards we were dealt, that's all. We just did what we must.'

'You haven't made me bacon sandwiches since last November.' Queenie reached over and squeezed his knee. They ate in silence as they crossed an aqueduct. The Tame ran sinuous and shallow below. The north Warwickshire country-side, or Staffordshire, William could never tell where the winding ancient border ended or began. But there was dense copse on the off-side, and the towpath was bordered by thick sedge and meadowsweet. Beyond, the stubble plains and hedgerows glowed golden in the dawn, and the air was fresh with pig shit and turned clay. Each day, William thought, was a rebirth. 'Have you got a name for your last babby, yet?' he asked.

'I do,' she said. 'I named him William.'

Epilogue

Water is powerful, if you know how to use it. Water is patient and strong. Ronnie's abdomen bloats, but he remains anchored to the canal. *Birmingham slag.* The narrowboats clip at the corpse. A pinkie finger detaches and rises. Narrowboats, heavy with coal, lying low in the canal, brush Ronnie's nose. It is blunted; the tip floats and is food for fish. Narrowboats, their bellies full of brick, heading for building sites in Coventry – *new garden suburbs* – dislodge a shoe and expose a foot. It is a tramp's shoe now, and good for nothing. *Put it down, our Charlie. You don't know where it's been.*

Crayfish nibble at Ronnie's toes. In the dark, eels inky and supple bite at Ronnie's eyes, made-up eyes like Ivor Novello. Pike, the great slime predator, with needle teeth and scales like razors, keep company with Ronnie.

The leaves of the willow and the hawthorn and the blackthorn fall and make a rotting counterpane for the body. The crab apples drop and sink. Bad apple. Poison apple. *Snow-white, Rose-red, don't beat your lover dead!*

The cut is a stew of life. Ronnie turns to waxy, coarse soap. *Lux: Preserves Your Natural Beauty.* The water softens and rots his clothes, and the bullet dislodges from the wound. *Birmingham brass.* The buttons of his jacket fall to the canal bed like pennies in a wishing well. *Birmingham brass.*

At Christmas the water freezes. The narrowboats cannot pass. Ronnie, as black as the canal – without a face, cut up by the cut – lies in an icy coffin.

In the spring, the canal thaws and floods. The cut gushes like a septic wound. It stinks of wild garlic and elderflower, cow muck and coal smuts. The foreign body surfaces, in parts. The phalanges of the hand, the zygomatic and lacrimal bones are spotted by kiddies playing with sticks and an old tin bath. They play pirates. They become bored and throw them at nesting ducks. They bury the bones in loose soil, cover them with dock leaves, in a solemn ceremony for the pirate king. Then the children are called home to bread and jam and Uncle Mac on the wireless. Ronnie is forgotten. *Them were just the bones of an animal, them were.*

Author's Note

Needless Alley is something of a love letter to my grandmother. A working-class woman and an obsessive reader of genre fiction – particularly hard-boiled detective stories of the interwar period – she inspired my own lifelong love of reading, and indeed my obsession with the music, film, art and literature of that era. If any fellow film or music fan notices inaccuracies of date in the song and film references in *Needless Alley*, then please forgive me. They were included out of a sentimental need to pay homage to her, a woman of fierce intelligence, cultural savvy and remarkable resilience.

Acknowledgements

First, I would like to thank Dr Laura Joyce, formerly of the University of East Anglia, my tutor and my friend, without whom *Needless Alley* would not have been written. Thank you to everyone at The Good Literary Agency for their faith in my writing, particularly my agent Abi Fellows, who is a wonderful champion to all underrepresented writers.

To Jade Chandler, thank you for telling me how much you liked *Needless Alley* during that lunch break telephone call. It was a life-changing moment. Thanks also for your, and Zulekhá Afzal's, continued support, advice and kindness. Thank you to Micaela Alcaino for bringing Queenie, in all her art deco glamour, to life on the beautiful book cover.

I would also like to thank Denise Beardon, Roe Lane and Mark Wightman for all the friendship and patience given so selflessly to me over the past few years. Let us continue to waffle on.

To my family, particularly my parents and my girls, thank you for understanding my need to write. We'll continue with our regular coffee dates soon, Mum.

Most of all, to my husband Andy, thank you for being the best man I know. I couldn't have done this without you.